BLACKWING

BLACKWING

The Raven's Mark
BOOK ONE

ED MCDONALD

GOLLANCZ
LONDON

First published in Great Britain in 2017 by Gollancz
an imprint of the Orion Publishing Group Ltd
Carmelite House, 50 Victoria Embankment
London EC4Y 0DZ

An Hachette UK Company

1 3 5 7 9 10 8 6 4 2

A CIP catalogue record for this book is
available from the British Library.

ISBN (Hardcover) 978 1 473 22201 4
ISBN (Export Trade Paperback) 978 1 473 22202 1

Typeset by Deltatype Ltd, Birkenhead, Merseyside

Printed and bound by CPI Group (UK) Ltd, Croydon, CR0 4YY

MIX
Paper from
responsible sources
FSC® C104740

www.edmcdonaldwriting.com
www.orionbooks.co.uk
www.gollancz.co.uk

1

Somebody warned them that we were coming. The sympathisers left nothing behind but an empty apartment and a
few volumes of illegal verse. A half-eaten meal, ransacked
drawers. They'd scrambled together what little they could
carry and fled east into the Misery. Back when I wore a
uniform the marshal told me only three kinds of people
willingly enter the Misery: the desperate, the stupid and the
greedy. The sympathisers were desperate enough. I gathered
a dozen stupid, greedy men and set out to kill them.

We left Valengrad on an afternoon that stank of drains,
regret and the end of another bad summer. The money
didn't justify the risk, but hunting men was what I did,
and I didn't intend to allow our quarry to get far. Half the
rabble I'd raised hadn't been out in the Misery before; they
were practically shitting themselves when we headed out
through the city's narrow gate. Within a mile they were
asking about gillings and dulchers. Two miles out and one
of them began to cry. My old timers laughed, reminded
him we'd be back before dark.

Three days later the arseholes were somehow still ahead
of us. Nobody was laughing any more.

'They made for Dust Gorge,' Tnota said. He fiddled with
the dials on his astrolabe, held it up to eye the distance
between the moons. 'Told you they would. Didn't I tell you
that, captain?'

'Like balls you did.' He had. The footprints in the grit were proving him right.

'I sure did.' Tnota grinned at me, mustard-yellow teeth stark in his treacle-dark face. 'I remember. You came into the bar with the papers and I said, "I bet they make for the gorge." Figure that earns me an extra share.'

'Even if this job paid well enough for extra shares, you still wouldn't get one. And it doesn't,' I said.

'Not my fault. I don't pick the jobs,' Tnota said.

'That's the first time you've been right today. Now keep quiet and plot us a course.'

Tnota raised the glass eye piece towards skies the colour of a week-old bruise. Dirty golds, hints of green, torn purples and ugly blood-browns merged together, an easel of ruptured fluids and broken capillaries. He counted on his fingers, traced an invisible line from one moon to the next. The cracks in the sky were quiet, barely a whisper passing through the banks of restless cloud.

Everything in the Misery is broken. Everything is wrong. The sooner we shot the bastards and were heading back west, the happier I would be.

We rode through banks of grit and sand, the rock black and red and drier than salt. Something rises up from the Misery. You can feel it all the while, like air, but it's your enemy rather than your friend. It soaks into you, gets in your gums until you can taste the poison. I just hoped it'd be over soon.

Three days into the Misery, cutting south and east over black sands, we found the remains of their stolen horse. Whatever had torn its legs off, the sympathisers we were hunting had done the smart thing. They'd left the horse to its fate and run. A temporary respite, since they couldn't outrun us now. I could read relief in the way the men sat in their saddles. We'd have a pair of heads bagged and slung by sundown, be heading back towards what passes for civil-isation along the border.

I took my flask from my coat and shook it. Not the first time I'd done that. It remained as empty as it had been on the last three occasions. Since I was out of brandy that meant we only had small beer to drink, and not a great deal of that. The Misery is dangerous for groups of heavily armed soldiers. That a pair of untrained, unprepared and unarmed civilians had stayed alive and ahead of us for three days was enough to give me nerves. Another reason to get this over with as quickly as possible.

The sand wrote a trail clear to see. Ahead of us lay Dust Gorge, a narrow fissure in the earth. The gash cut through the landscape of shifting dunes, caustic sand and brittle stones. The lightning-bolt corridor mirrored one of the rents in the sky, the split in the earth a reflection of the damage in the heavens. One of the sky's cracks began its high, sonorous wailing, causing my troop of not-soldiers to reach for spirit-stones and amulets. Free company men might have grit but they also have more superstitions than a priest on festival day. They wanted out of the Misery as much as I did. It was making them jumpy, and jumpy soldiers make a mess of even simple work. A generous man might call my troop of cut-throats soldiers. Generous men are generally idiots.

'Nenn, get up here,' I called as we approached a slope that led down into the gloom. She was chewing blacksap, jaws working, teeth dark as tar. There is no more irritating sound this side of the hells. 'You have to chew that stuff?'

'All the ladies chew it.' She shrugged.

'Just because some duchess has a mouth full of rotten teeth, it doesn't mean you have to imitate her sycophant friends.'

'Can't blame me for fashion, captain. Got to keep up appearances.'

Why Nenn thought anyone would be looking at her teeth when she was one nose short of a face was as baffling as the trend. Chew, chew, chew. I knew from experience that telling her to stop would be as pointless as telling Tnota to keep it in his trousers.

I glared at her anyway.

'You got work for me, captain?' Nenn said. She paused, spat half a lump of blacksap into the sand.

'We're going down. Just me and you.'

'Just the two of us?' The wooden nose strapped to her face didn't wrinkle, but the skin between her eyes creased.

'There's only two of them, and they aren't even armed. You don't think we can handle it?'

'It's not them I'm afraid of,' Nenn said. She spat the rest of the blacksap the other way. 'Might be anything in there. Might be skweams. Dulchers.'

'Might be a big pot of gold too. But we're too far south for dulchers anyway.'

'And for skweams?'

'Just get your shit sorted. We're going down. We need both heads intact if we're going to get paid, and you know how the lads can get. Can't trust them not to get carried away; courts don't pay out if there's any way they can avoid it. Remember what happened at Snosk?'

It was Nenn's turn to scowl.

'Yeah. I remember.' Snosk was a bad memory for all of us. Missing out on a full job's pay over a technicality doesn't sit right with anyone. To this day I'd still have argued that you could just about make out a face if you arranged the pieces right.

'Good. So get bright and ready up.'

I dismounted. My legs were sore from the saddle, the ache in my lower back crackling in a way it wouldn't have ten years ago. Didn't spend enough time in the saddle any more. Getting soft. Soft, not old, that's what I told myself. Tnota got down to help me ready up. He was even older than I was, and though I could trust him not to put a sword through anybody's face, that was only because he's about as useful in a fight as a wax helmet. More likely to injure himself than anyone else, and it was Nenn's brand of nasty I needed down there. Tnota checked over the straps on my half-armour, primed my matchlock as I selected weapons from the arsenal on my saddle and belted them on. I strapped on a short-bladed cutlass and a long-bladed dagger. No room to swing anything longer than an arm down in the gorge. I'd been down there before, a few years back. It didn't get very wide. More alley than valley.

Nenn looked suitably fierce in blackened steel. Tnota sparked up a flame and got our match cords smoking, the firearms primed and ready to spit lead. Didn't plan to use them. A matchlock ball will make an awfully big mess of something, but like Nenn said, there might be skweams. Might be anything down in the dark guts of the soured earth.

The sooner we cut the sympathisers' heads off and started back towards the city, the better.

'There's only three places you can climb out of the gorge,' I said. 'You remember where the others are?'

Tnota nodded. He pointed the other two out to me, one about a mile off, the other half a mile east of that.

'Good. If we flush them out, ride them down and wait for us.'

'Easy work.'

'Tnota's in charge,' I hollered at my boys, and they almost looked like they were paying attention. How I'd managed to pick up such worthless gutter rats I couldn't recall. Out of brandy, twenty miles into the Misery and a troop of vermin at my heels. Somewhere in my life, things had gone very, very wrong.

A slope of loose rock and ancient, fossilised tree roots led down into the crevice. Not easy to navigate when you have a weapon to carry and the walls are only seven feet apart.

There wasn't a great deal of light, just enough to pick out some poor footing. It was hard to avoid kicking showers of grit down into the dark, but we kept quiet as we could. Dust Gorge was deep. Probably one of the reasons that the enemy liked to use it as a meeting point for their spies and sympathisers. Our patrols didn't often sweep this deep into the Misery, nearly out of the Range altogether, but if they did they wouldn't go poking around down in the dark. Even the officers had more sense than that.

The air possessed a dry cold, no moisture at all. Tree roots protruded from the rock around us. A thousand-year-old forest had stood here once, back before the Misery had come into being. Only the roots remained now, as dry and grey as old bones. There was no water in the Misery, and the occasional oily black pool helped nothing to grow.

'I have a confession to make,' I said.

'You got religion all of a sudden?' Nenn grunted.

'Hardly.'

'You wanted to get me alone in the dark?'

'Unlikely.' I picked my way around a boulder. I put too much weight against it and it crumbled away like chalk. Nothing in the Misery lasts. 'The court are paying more than I said. Not a lot more, but enough that it got me thinking.'

'You lied about the fee?'

'Of course. I always lie about the fee.'

'Arsehole.'

'Yes. But anyway. Got me thinking maybe these targets are more than just sympathisers.'

'Spies?'

'No. What if she's a Bride?'

'There are no Brides in Valengrad,' Nenn said, too quick for conviction. As we descended, the lattice of roots above blotted out both light and wind. Nenn blew on her match cord, kept the tip red and smoking. The glow lit her face red

6

as a devil's. The smell of burning slow match was comforting in the dark, like wood smoke but bitter, acrid.

'They'd love us to believe that,' I said. 'The citadel found one last year. A big one, near wide as a house. Burned the building down around her, claimed it was just a fire.'

Nenn tried to snort. She'd never lost the habit. Sounded odd without a real nose to hawk it back through.

'Bullshit. It was just some fat old whore who pissed off the wrong officer. Squawks get funny when some lowborn doxy turns them down. He burned the brothel out of spite and made excuses.'

Nenn would believe what she wanted to believe and not an ounce of truth more.

'Regardless. If there's a Bride down here, I don't want any of the men near her. You know what can happen.'

'What makes you think you can resist a Bride better than they can?' Nenn said. I lowered my voice. Sounds didn't carry far along the tangled walls of the gorge, but no harm in being careful.

'Nothing. I just trust you to ignore me and blow her head off.'

'Thought you said not to spoil her face?'

I gave her a serious look, entirely lost in the gloom.

'If she's a Bride, blow her fucking head off. Got it?'

'Got it, Captain Galharrow, sir, blow her fucking head off, sir. Be a bloody shame, though, all this work for nothing.'

'Would be. Better than the alternative. If they're marked we'll get paid anyway.'

I slipped on loose gravel and Nenn reached out to steady me. The stones rattled away down the narrow incline. We both froze. If they were still down here, we'd need to be more careful. Talk was distracting. Time to shut up and get bright. There was a curl in the rock ahead, and I brought the butt of my matchlock up against my shoulder as I slipped around the corner. Just more gully. We crept on.

Slow match smoke trailed lazily behind me in the dead air. I hoped that the lack of breeze meant it wouldn't carry on ahead of us and warn her. The smell is unmistakable. If she was a Bride, our best chance lay in taking her by surprise.

'Look,' Nenn whispered. 'Light.'

The pale, artificial glow of phos light around the next bend. I crept forward, placing my feet against solid rock as daintily as a man of my size can manage. Should have paid more attention in my dancing lessons. Nenn moved more nimbly, something about her reminding me of the stray cats in the city, all lean tautness and hiss. She rounded the rock wall with her weapon raised.

I half expected her to give fire, but she paused and I swept around close behind. The gorge widened, not a lot, but fifteen feet feels like a good lot of space when you're cramped down in the earth. The sympathisers had made a little camp for themselves. They had a pile of worn old blankets next to some sticks they'd failed to light into a fire. An empty bottle lay on its side. The light was coming from a small lantern, the phos globe within it guttering. The battery coil was nearly spent.

Our quarry sat with their backs against the rock wall. They were both dead. No doubt about that. Eyes bulged wide in their sockets, jaws hung open. Side by side, propped up like a pair of grisly puppets ready to launch into action. Alive, she would have been ordinary. A woman in her middle years with brown curls caught beneath a white cap, blue eyes flanked by crow's feet. In death, her face and dress were stained with flakes of dried blood. It had leaked from her nose, her ears, her mouth. He'd gone the same way. His uniform was stained with worse than Misery dust and sweat.

In life I wouldn't have looked twice at either one. In death I couldn't take my eyes away.

My unease intensified, rising from my guts to my chest.

No visible wounds, just a lot of blood. Hadn't seen anything like this for a long time. The things in the Misery are vicious but they kill like animals. This was bloody, but it was neat. Almost like they'd sat there, waiting to be killed.

'Something got them,' Nenn said. Has a real talent for pointing out the obvious, my Nenn.

'No shit. It might still be here.' I didn't know what in the hells it was, but it had done our job for us. I sucked in match smoke, took comfort in the acrid tang.

'It's long gone. Blood's been dry for hours.'

Nenn lowered her firearm. She sat down on a large stone, looked across at the corpses with an expression that didn't usually register on what was left of her features. I couldn't tell what she was thinking. Didn't want to ask. I found a small pannier and rifled through its contents. Part of me hoped I'd find something that I could sell to the marshal or the courts, make all this worth a little more of our while. They had little enough. A few jars of salt fish, not enough coins to make a decent wager. No secret missives, no maps to enemy tunnels, no list of sympathisers and spies in Valengrad. She'd been a Talent, a phos-mill worker. He'd been a lieutenant serving in an artillery company. Whatever their reason to abandon humanity and run out into the Misery, they'd taken it to their grave. Which, I guess, we were standing in.

What a waste. Waste of my time, waste of the court's money to pay me, waste of their stupid lives. They hadn't even brought enough water to make it halfway into the Misery, let alone across it to the empire beyond. Waste upon waste upon waste.

Time to get some heads and get out of there.

I froze as I saw something down in the grit and sand of the floor. I stared at it a few moments, unable to bring myself to move. Listened.

'We need to get out of here.'

'What is it?' Nenn was going through their pockets.

'We have to go.'

Nenn caught the fear in my voice. She glanced over, caught sight of the footprint. Such a small thing. It shouldn't have terrified us the way it did. She looked at me wide-eyed.

'Get the heads,' I whispered. 'Fast. Fast as you fucking can.'

There are a lot of bad things in the world. Some of them are people, and some of them happen to live in the Misery. The worst of them come from beyond the Misery, far to the east. I knew chance could have formed that childlike footprint, maybe just a scuff in the sand. But it could have been made by a Darling.

My breath came too shallow. Perspiration pricked a course down my neck. I listened for the slightest sound and kept my matchlock raised. I gripped it hard, tried to stop my fingers from trembling.

'Come on, come on,' I hissed.

Nenn is very efficient and she wasn't about to abandon our prize, not after three days of breathing Misery dust. She took out her sword and went to work like a butcher. I fingered the barrel of my weapon, checked the match was rigged to hit the flash pan. In the quiet of the gorge, everything seemed still. Nenn began to slice and saw, arms working hard and fast. I scanned the ground again, but it was just the one footprint. Half the size of an adult's. Both of the sympathisers had larger feet than that.

'Not fast enough,' I hissed.

'Got it,' Nenn said. She yanked her prize free of clinging threads of gristle. She was going to need a bath. 'They're always heavier than I expect.' She held up the heads for me to inspect. All in one piece.

'Don't wave them around like that. Have some respect.'

'I don't have two shits of respect for sympathisers,' Nenn said. She spat on the dead man's decapitated body.

'They want to go join the drudge so much, they think being human is such a problem? I'll treat them inhuman if that's what they want.'

'Enough. Let's move.'

We wrapped the heads in one of the old blankets. The blood might have had time to dry, but that didn't mean that whatever had gracked them had gone far. Beneath my armour my shirt was wet through with sweat.

We retraced our steps back to the mouth of the gorge, scrambling across the loose rock. The need for stealth ground against the desire to get clear, the heads bouncing along in the makeshift sack looped through my belt. Nenn was right, they were heavy, but we still scrambled fast through the scree and the desiccated grey roots. I kept an eye behind us the whole way, skittering backwards as often as forwards. My pulse was up, my guts starting to turn sour. Part of me expected that when we climbed out we'd find the company nothing but dismembered bodies. I reminded myself that the blood had dried. The killer had done his work and gone.

My fears were unfounded. My arsehole soldiers gave a cheer when we climbed out, red-stained sack in tow.

'All smooth?' Tnota asked. I ignored the question.

'We're going,' I called. 'Saddle up, move your sorry fucking arses. Move! Anyone not saddled in half a minute gets left behind.'

The good humour evaporated. They were a sorry-looking bunch, but they heard the urgency. Nenn practically vaulted into her saddle. My men didn't know what had us spooked, and they didn't need to.

'Think we can get to a Range station tonight?' I asked Tnota.

'Unlikely. Hard to chart a course, and we're at least sixteen standard miles in. Red moon's starting to rise and she's throwing off the normal lines. I need an hour to plot a good course if you want due west.'

'It'll have to wait.'

I kept to my word, put my feet in the stirrups and kicked my horse to a gallop. I lashed the reins, kept my eyes westward and didn't let up until Dust Gorge had vanished from sight. I drove a hard pace until the horses were near blown.

'Captain, we have to stop or I'm going to lose all reference for positioning,' Tnota insisted. 'We get lost out here and you know what happens next. We have to stop.'

Reluctantly, I allowed the horses to slow to a walk, and then a half-mile on from that, drew to a halt.

'Be quick,' I said. 'Fastest course home.'

Finding your way in the Misery is never easy. Without a good navigator you can travel in the same direction for three days and find yourself back where you started. Another reason I hadn't wanted to risk Tnota down in the gorge. The only constants in the Misery are the three moons: red, gold and blue. Too far away to get twisted around by all the poisoned magic leaking out of the earth, I guess.

I went to make some water against a rock. As I laced up, the inner side of my left forearm started to sting. I fastened my belt and told myself I was imagining it. No. Definitely getting warmer. Hot, even. Damn. It was neither the time nor the place for this.

It had been five years since I'd heard from Crowfoot. Part of me had wondered if the old bastard had forgotten all about me. As he sought to contact me now, I realised what a foolish notion that had been. I was one of his playing pieces. He'd just been waiting for the right time to move me.

I stepped around behind a dune, drew back my sleeve. My arms carry a lot of ink, memories in green and black and blue. A small skull for every friend I'd lost on the Range. Too many fucking skulls. Couldn't remember who a lot of them were for, now, and it wasn't the skulls that were starting to heat anyway. On the inside of my forearm, an intricately detailed raven stood out amongst the crude soldiers' tattoos surrounding it. The ink sizzled and began spitting black as it grew unpleasantly hot. I yanked off my belt, wrapped it around my upper arm like a tourniquet. Past experience told me I'd need it.

'Come on then,' I growled through my teeth. 'Let's get it over with.'

The flesh strained upwards as something sought to escape my skin. My whole arm began to shake, and the second thrust hurt more than the heat. Steam sizzled from the flesh as it turned red, burned. I winced, gritted my teeth, squeezed my eyes shut as my skin stretched to its limit, and then I felt the ripping as the raven forced itself up and out of me. Big fucking bird, a raven. It came out through the torn flesh, sticky and red like a newborn, hopped down onto a rock and looked up at me with black eyes.

I clenched my jaws shut against the pain. No use showing weakness. Crowfoot would have no sympathy anyway.

I bowed my head to the bird. The Nameless aren't gods, but they're far enough from mortal that the distinction matters little, and gods and Nameless both like us on our knees. No point in speaking. Crowfoot never listened to what I had to say. I had no idea whether he could hear through the bird or whether it just came to say its piece. The raven's beak opened and I heard his voice, a growl of gravel and phlegm. Sounded like he'd smoked a bowl of white-leaf every day since the war began.

'GALHARROW,' it shrieked at me. Furious. 'GET TO STATION TWELVE. ENSURE SHE SURVIVES. DO NOT FUCK THIS UP.'

The sticky red raven cocked its head at me, then looked down at the ground as if it were just an ordinary bird looking for worms. Maybe after it gave its message that's all it was. A few moments later it jerked rigid, its eyes burned with flames, a puff of smoke boiled from its beak and it collapsed dead to the ground. I wiped blood from my forearm. The wound was gone but the pain remained. The raven tattoo was back in place again, faint against the skin like an old man's ink. The bird would come back to full definition in time.

'Change of plan,' I said as I rejoined my troop. 'We're going to Station Twelve.'

I received a few puzzled looks, but nobody argued. Good thing too. Pulling rank is that much harder when you have absolutely no idea why you're doing it.

Tnota looked up at the moons. Cool blue Clada had sunk down against the horizon. The bright bronze cracks carved the sky into discoloured pieces. Tnota licked a finger, checked the wind, then knelt and brushed fingers through the grit.

'Twelve ain't the nearest station, captain. Won't make it before dark,' he said. 'Can get us out of the Misery and then take south along the supply road.'

'That the fastest way?'

'Fastest is direct. But like I say, won't be out the Misery come dark.'

'Fastest course, Tnota. There's an extra share in it for you if there's ale in my hand before we lose the light.'

Tnota grinned. We'd be there.

2

The horses were spent, but I didn't think any were damaged. They wanted out of the unnatural tundra as much as their riders. Smart animals, horses.

Two moons had dipped down beyond different horizons, leaving only Clada's slender sapphire crescent to gloss the night sky as we approached Station Twelve. Tnota had cut some strange, risky route through dunes with long snapping grass, but we'd made it with all our limbs intact. He might not have a shred of violence in him, but the old boy could have navigated for the marshal if he hadn't been such a degenerate. We left the growling of the stained sky behind us, forsook the bright white-bronze gashes running through it and fell into the more natural night west of the Miscry.

The station was aglow with hollow light, a pair of phos-powered search beams conducting lazy sweeps of the approach. One of them caught us, followed us as we drew near. A lone, half-interested face peered down over the battlements. The fortress was standard design, same as its four dozen sisters spread along the length of the Range. High stone walls, big guns, flags, narrow windows, the smell of manure. Standard fortress stuff.

'A jester's hat,' Nenn said as we approached. I arched an eyebrow at her. She pointed upwards. 'That's what they always remind me of. The arms of the projectors. They look like the four fronds sticking out of a jester's hat.' I followed the line of her finger, high. Four vast metallic arms rose from the top of the central keep, arching spider legs of black iron, illuminated from below by weak yellow phos light. They even had black iron globes at their points, hollow bells silhouetted against the red of the sky.

'I don't think the projectors tell any good jokes,' I said.

'Can't say I agree.' Nenn grinned. Her eyes had the same gleeful intensity as a cat's when it gets its claws into a mouse. 'There's something funny about all those drudge walking into the Range, getting turned to ash. That count as a joke?'

'No,' I said. 'Just means you got a twisted sense of humour. Now shut up, I need to work out what I'm going to say to the station commander. And for fuck's sake, stop chewing that shit.'

Nenn ignored me and carried on talking through a wad of blacksap. When you've ridden around together as long as we had, got stinking drunk together more days than you've been sober, you end up having to tolerate a degree of insubordination. Some people wrongly assumed we were lovers, as though scars sought out scars. She claimed to be a hellcat in the sack, but I could never have dealt with either her spitting or her complete lack of regard for manners. With that wooden nose on her face she'd never be asked to sit for an artist, but my own portrait wouldn't exactly moisten the ladies at court. I'd breathed the grit of a dozen sandstorms, drunk more liquor than most men drink water and if anyone tried to compliment me on having a jaw like an anvil, can only say it's certainly taken enough of a pounding. I guess I could see why people thought we made a neat pair.

We had to ride all the way around to the western side of the fortress. No gate faces the Misery. The Range stations exist to keep the east to the east, wardens against the things

16

that used to be men. Spirits alone know what they are now.

The gate sergeant looked us over, peering through a head-sized window in the gate. He yawned, wine on his breath, but the seal I showed him dashed the insolence from his face. The embossed iron disc told him I was Blackwing. Not a lot of love for the Blackwing amongst the state troops. Some of them saw us as little more than head-takers, bounty hunters, heard stories of innocent men accused and put to the question. They resented that we had no regulation buttons to polish, no drills to conduct and they spat and called us rats when they thought we couldn't hear them. But mostly they feared that one day the Blackwing would turn accusing, soulless eyes in their direction. Everybody has something to hide.

'You know if there's any high-ranking women here? Officers? Nobility?' I asked.

'Sorry, sir, so sorry. Only just started my shift. There's some fancy-looking carriages parked up in the yard, though. Have to belong to the cream I guess.'

I scowled at him. His uniform was crumpled, like he'd just thrown it on. His belt wasn't even done up. Standards seemed to have fallen a long way since the last time I'd been down this way. The old officer in me rose past the years of contempt to snap at him.

'Since you're manning the gates of a Range station, shouldn't you know who's here, sergeant?'

He gave me a bitter look. My seal told him that he had to let us inside, but he didn't take his orders from me and he didn't have to put up with my shit. Not unless I had dirt on him, which I didn't. The guilty are so much more malleable.

'Listen, feller. My little one's been up all night with the wet cough. Probably won't last much past the week, and that's got my wife wallowing in her own self-misery. You want to add to my worries? Go make a complaint to the duty captain.' He spoke past me to my men. 'Get in. Mess hall's through the gatehouse. Avoid the ruby ale. Gave some of us the shits.'

I hung back, but decided not to point out that it was forbidden for children to enter a Range station. Probably wouldn't have been helpful.

'Show me the recent arrivals.'

The duty sergeant shrugged, hugged himself as if to say I was letting cold air into the fortress and he needed to get on with closing up the gate. I took the ledger and leafed through it.

Whoever had arrived with the carriages hadn't been written into it. The record was sketchy at best. I scanned the signatures of recent entries. It wasn't just Crowfoot's lady I was looking for. I figured I'd know Maldon's signature by his dreadful handwriting if I saw it, but there was nothing listed but supply caravans, changes of guard units and the occasional doxy signing in and out over the last couple of months.

Gleck Maldon had been a good friend and a powerful ally before the magic had got into his brain. A good man, far as any man that kills for a living can be called good. He'd ridden as artillery for me a score of times over the years. Then he started barking moonwards so they'd locked him in the asylum, but Spinners of Maldon's ability don't find walls a significant impediment. He got loose. Loose, and dangerous. Finding him in the ledger had been a long shot. I asked the sergeant anyway.

'You see a man come through here, tall, about fifty? Brown hair gone grey at the wings?'

'Can't say I remember anyone like that specifically. He got a name?'

'Gleck Maldon. A Spinner, out of Valengrad. Would likely have sounded a little crazy.'

The sergeant shook his head and took the ledger back like I was intruding by reading it.

'No sorcerer types here. Not for a long while.'

I thanked him, though I didn't feel like it. There wasn't any reason Maldon might have come this way save that it was south, and south was a direction, and any direction was better than being where he was meant to be: locked in the asylum back in Valengrad. I put Maldon out of my mind. He'd gone to ground. I missed him.

The doors clunked shut behind me and the gate sergeant began to crank a heavy handle, a portcullis beginning its slow descent. I never like feeling locked into a place.

'Want to buy me a fancy ride like that one, captain?' Nenn grinned, drawing my attention to the stable block. She'd spotted the spring-mounted carriage, the kind usually occupied by the same courtly ladies that wouldn't frig themselves off to my portrait. The wheels were meant for the well-paved avenues of city boulevards and looked to be in need of attention after clattering along the poorly tended border roads. Painted blue, chased with golden embellishments, its owner had to be cream. Probably the lady Crowfoot had sent me after.

'When you start listening to my orders, I'll start buying you pretty things,' I told the swordswoman at my side.

'Wonder what brings the cream out to Station Twelve,' Nenn said. 'Nothing here for nobility.' Nenn didn't like the higher-ups any better than I did.

'There's nothing out here for anyone,' I said. 'The food's shit, the beds are worse and soon as you look east, reality starts getting jumpy. Problem is, the higher up you're born, the less sense you arrive with. Probably some fool looking to raise a commission, wants to see life on the frontier. One good look out over the Range, a taste of the Misery, should be enough to send her back the way she came.'

Nenn always enjoyed hearing me bad-mouth the elite. I didn't have many kind things to say about them. My experiences with the ruling class hadn't been much better than hers.

I dismissed the company for the night. They'd find some open barrel to dip and waste the evening singing badly and losing money to each other. As long as they didn't get into fights or steal anything, I didn't give a shit. They headed off to drink away the Misery shakes. Getting the shakes was normal, when you got out from under the sundered sky. I figured whatever magic we'd soaked up out there had to leave the body and the shaking got it out, but that was just a guess. It wasn't as though the Nameless ever chose to let us know why their magic affected us the way it did, and it wasn't as though we had the guts to ask.

Crowfoot was to blame for the Misery, if attributing blame to something like him counts for anything. He and the other Nameless are beyond the reproach of us whimpering mortals. Some people formed cults around them as if they were gods, but if Crowfoot is a god then creation isn't worth spit. For two centuries the Nameless warred with the Deep Kings and their empire, Old Dhojara, and what had been accomplished in that time? A lot of weeping, a lot of bones turning yellow beneath the Misery's sands. We'd managed stalemate, not even peace – and in the central states they don't even understand that only the Engine and the Range Stations provide any protection against the Deep Kings at all. They don't know how close we stand to the gallows, how tight the noose is cinched around our neck. But my master would not stand to be defeated, not if he had to sacrifice every last man, woman and child in Dortmark to do it. Which he would. When he burned the Misery into the world as a last defence, he proved as much.

A small battalion of administrators, clerks and serving staff got in my way and repeatedly told me that the commander was busy. I ignored their protests, pushed past sputtering officials. Crowfoot's direct intervention made this urgent. The Nameless don't waste a drop of their power unless it matters. Hoard it closer than gold. I almost made it to the commander's chamber before a few soldiers stopped me and I got threatened with chains. I snarled at them some. It didn't make me feel any better, and it didn't make them let me through.

Blackwing is a small organisation, if we can even be called that. There's no coordination between us, no uniformity of purpose. I knew the names of seven others, but three of those names were false and I had no idea where any of them were. We were Crowfoot's shadowed hands, his eyes and his enforcers. We were both beyond and beneath the military, operatives bearing the silent commands of the Nameless – when they bothered to give them. I'd gone five years without a real order. Free to work my own way with whatever resources I could scrape together. The men I'd taken into the Misery were hired hands, little better than mercenaries. Probably worse. Those clerks should have been stumbling over themselves to get me what I wanted, but during Crowfoot's prolonged absence, fear of the Blackwing had waned thin.

He was back now. Their fear would return.

'What in the hells is he doing that can't wait?' I demanded.

'See those carriages out front?' an unintimidated captain asked, his uniform so clean it seemed he never went outdoors. 'Commander's in with some she-devil who's been raising hell the last two hours. She's some big cream Spinner, a count's sister. Got connections to Prince Herono.' He looked me over with a critical eye. Maybe I had the dark wings on my shoulder but they lay beneath the dirt of three days' travel. I'd brought home a lot of dust and dried sweat, and my breath probably stank from all the liquorice root I'd chewed out there. He agreed he'd send someone to find me when the commander was done with the lady. Also suggested that I take a bath before presenting myself.

I suggested that he could take his suggestion and shove it somewhere unmentionable.

Expletives aside, I didn't have any way to get to see the commander short of cracking skulls, and even Crowfoot's instruction wasn't a licence to grack folks when I got pissed off. At least if Crowfoot's mystery woman was in there with the commander she was safe enough for now.

'Who's the cream?' I asked.

'Nobody I ever met before.' The captain didn't want to engage with me, but he enjoyed knowing more than I did. He shrugged. 'Lady Tanza, I think it was.'

I felt the name like a sledgehammer to the chest. Nearly staggered. Swallowed hard and tried to get my thoughts into order.

'Ezabeth Tanza? A woman about my age, dark hair?'

'That's her name. No idea what she looks like. Wears a veil, like they do in the south.'

The Misery shakes were starting to get to me. I told myself it was definitely the Misery shakes, nothing more. I bothered the quartermaster for liquorice – better than beer for keeping the shakes at bay – and chewed a root as I headed towards the roof. Liquorice, half a bottle of brandy and cold night air, can't beat all three together.

I headed upwards, always best to head up if you need to clear your head. The glass light-tubes were running at just half power on the upper levels, leaving the stairwells and corridors depressingly shadowed. Some prince was slacking on his obligations. These days they put their silver into silks and vineyards, marble palaces and buying indulgences for their concubines instead of maintaining the stations they were responsible for. Memories are short. Away from the frontier it was easy to forget that the enemy's desire to wipe us out hadn't slackened just because we had Nall's Engine to protect us. We had never defeated the Deep Kings, hadn't even come close. They were the hurricane and we'd found

22

a parasol. Eighty years of stalemate were nothing to them, they'd been ancient long before their eyes ever turned to our land.

I passed a wide arch of double doors, heavy black iron chains strung across their face, heavier locks securing them. I stopped, an old commander's instinct making me pause. This was the operating chamber from which the arching projectors of Nall's Engine — what Nenn had called the jester's fronds — could be activated. Dust lay in a light film over the chain. Nobody had been in to oil the machinery for a while. Nall's Engine was our only real defence if the drudge or their masters ever came at us in force. Any child knew that.

In the time of my grandfather's grandfather, with the Dhojaran legions and the Deep Kings marching victorious against the last nine free cities, Crowfoot had unleashed the Heart of the Void. It was a weapon, or it was an event. Maybe a spell, damned if I know. Some things you never want to learn. Whatever it had been, it was bad. A weapon the like of which the world had never seen before, or, thank the spirits, since. He used the Heart of the Void to blast the Misery into existence. Tore cracks in the sky, choked the land with poisoned dust. Hills burned, fields boiled, rivers ran to stone. The cities of Adrogorsk and Clear were ours, and turned in a screaming instant from centres of learning and culture to collateral damage in a tempest of unleashed power. They melted and burned, their citizens warped and died. The Deep Kings reeled, wounded by the attack, but they were not defeated. When they regathered their strength the war continued across what had become the Misery, the Deep Kings hurling their numberless armies against our dwindling resources. We could not have held. But the lives of a generation of young men and women bought time for another of the Nameless, Nall, to raise his Engine along the border. The Engine destroyed King Nivias and threw the drudge back for a second time. Stalemate ensued. Peace, of a sort, ensured by the Engine and the stations: outlying control points from which our vigilant commanders could remotely activate the Engine should the Deep Kings ever send their forces into range. They'd only tried it once, well before I was born. The Engine had blasted new craters across the Misery. They had not tried again. And now it was dusty. Forgotten. The station commander was a fool to put it beyond easy reach. Just because the wolf pack fears your sling doesn't mean you stop carrying stones.

The warden had already pissed me off by not seeing me directly and my mood was blackening by the second. I'd report his laxness to the marshal when I got back to Valengrad. Nobody likes a telltale, but they like the city states being overrun by the drudge even less. The station commander was an idiot. It was a petty revenge to take for making me wait, but the older I got the pettier I found myself becoming, and the less I found myself caring.

I breathed the night up along the battlements, knocking back warm slugs from my bottle and wishing I'd paid less money for better liquor. The sun had set, Clada's sour blue light keeping the night cool and dim. Now and then the Misery made a click or a crack as the earth shifted and groaned. The fading light revealed the rims of the larger craters, testament to the devastating power that the Engine would unleash on any army stupid enough to enter the Range. It was here, along this line of fortresses, that a hundred years of war had been ground to a standstill. The blasts that had created that stalemate had left their scars deep in the earth. Nobody and nothing moved out there in the poisoned lands of the Misery.

Are you out there, Gleck? I thought. *Out there, somewhere? Did you lose that much of your mind?* The smartest part of me, the part that had got me out alive at Adrogorsk and kept my head on my shoulders over two decades ranging the Misery, told me that I was speaking to a dead man. Gleck Maldon had got strange, maybe mad. It happened with Spinners, sometimes. He'd been a good man, as sorcerers went. He hadn't gone north, hadn't gone west. South was looking increasingly unlikely. I looked down at the liberal spread of inked skulls on my left arm, picked out a spot to remember him.

Ezabeth fucking Tanza. Not a memory I'd wanted to dredge up again. Decades had crumbled away since I first sat across the table from her. I'd been trying to purge the memory ever since. Twenty years, a wife, children and years of stalking through the nightmare wasteland behind me and still her name could deliver an uppercut right to the balls. I had no doubt I had to escort her to Valengrad. If I'd thought Crowfoot had any kind of human emotion in him, I'd have thought it was some kind of sick fucking joke.

A drinking song drifted up from the food hall. Off duty soldiers sang about a sailor leaving his bonny lass behind and getting himself drowned. We were a long way from the sea.

I lit a heavy cigar, drew and blew a cloud of smoke. Drink. Smoke. Chew liquorice root. Forget. Done and distant, a sour memory of something that never happened. Hadn't heard a whisper of her since. She likely had a husband. Children. What she was doing out at a Range Station I couldn't guess. Didn't want to try.

Sad fact was, she probably wouldn't even recognise me. Twenty years. A different name. A broken nose, scarred cheeks, scarred jaw. She sure as hell wouldn't be expecting that lace-frilled boy to be doing this crap for a living. I tossed the butt of my cigar out over the wall, had another swig.

I looked down into the yard. The gate sergeant yawned, stretched. The last of the summer evening's warmth had fled upwards, and he had a blanket around his shoulders. The singing had grown louder, even more discordant, which was incredible. The gateman sat down on a stool and shivered. A lonely, boring job on a cold night. If it were me, I'd have been drunk. Or asleep. Probably both.

A little kid walked out of the keep and started rolling a small keg over towards the gateman. I wondered if it was the dying one. Didn't look dying, if it was strong enough to roll a heavy-looking barrel. The presence of children was another thing I'd have to report. The Range stations were supposed to be military positions, but over the years things had got slack. First they started letting in the whores, then those whores became wives, and both whores and wives made babies and somehow Nall's stations had turned into small communities. Was it really so long ago that we'd been fighting the drudge out in the Misery? Didn't seem so long to me.

The gateman got up, looked over at the child, who stopped some feet away. He stiffened slightly. The child spoke, pointed down at the barrel. The sergeant seemed to shiver, then he took the barrel, hefted it and set it down by the portcullis. By the weak light of the tubes above the gate, I saw the red rolling down the sergeant's face, bleeding from nose, from eye, from ear. He hammered the keg open and dark sand spilled over his feet. His jaw hung open as the red dripped down his front and into the blasting powder.

The chill of realisation struck me. The child – the Darling – was running. I started to run too as the sergeant reached up and smashed open a lighting tube. Sparks spat around him in a bright shower. I saw them descending, white and beautiful, almost lazy in their fall.

I clapped my hands over my ears.

The gate exploded.

3

Even through my hands the detonation was deafening. The rush of air bowled into me all the way up on the battlements, set me staggering. The immensity of the sound lingered, the shadow of something terrible passing into silence.

For a few moments nobody on the battlements moved, and then we all snapped into action as if life had just been punched into us.

A sentry ran to the alarm crank on the wall and began winding it. Rust flaked away as he struggled with the lever, but then phos hissed and the siren began to bray across Station Twelve. His companion was running for the stairs, leaving his weapon behind. I crossed to it, lifted the match-lock.

'Powder and shot?' I yelled at the cranking soldier. Everything sounded dim, distant. The soldier was green-white, too young to be in the military at all. He ceased cranking for a moment to unhook the bandolier around his neck and throw it to me.

Down below I saw the little bastard come out to inspect his handiwork. He looked like a boy of ten years, but he would be far older than that. He grinned at the twisted portcullis, the remnants of broken wood hanging from twisted hinges. In the light of flames his face had a hellish cast.

I loaded quickly. Tore open a powder charge, loaded black grit into the flash pan. Dropped a lead ball into the matchlock's barrel, poured powder, spat paper, thumped the butt to secure it all. I broke open a light tube, used the hot rush of power from within to get the match cord lit. Far, far too long to load. Too slow. The kid was gone. That didn't mean there was nobody to shoot.

Drudge came in through the gate. Dressed for war, blank eyes and noseless faces, their spears were levelled and shields raised. The captain at their fore had crimson mottling to mark him out, and he slowed up as they pushed through the flames and smoke. They expected some kind of resistance. This was a Range station after all. There should have been soldiers. Should have been defiance. Instead they took the gate without a fight. Blank as his face was, I could see his confusion.

They expected a fight. I'd start one.

I aimed low, wanting to hit the thing in the head, but knowing the recoil would drag my aim higher. I sighted, prayed and squeezed the firing lever.

The gun fired with a dragon's roar of smoke. I waved it out of my way to see what damage I'd managed to do. The shot was good; the lead drudge staggered with a hole in its chest, and a bigger, fist-sized hole blown out of its back. Ribs splayed outwards, fragments of red bone scattered across the courtyard. Slow to load maybe, but a matchlock sure could make a hole in something. The drudge staggered a few steps before collapsing against a wall. Those that followed it looked up at me and raised crossbows. Half a dozen bolts hissed up as I threw myself down flat along the walkway. They sailed overhead but the green-white sentry went down squealing, a bolt through his leg.

A trio of our soldiers emerged from the keep and rushed towards the drudge in the gate, got halfway to them and then turned and scampered back the way they'd come.

'Fucking hells.' What kind of soldiers were these supposed to be? 'Fucking hells!' Complacency, honed by months, years of inactivity, meant that the garrison weren't even working shifts and there was nobody to respond as warriors began to pour in through the gates, dark shapes shedding heavy cloaks and drawing steel. My nerve threatened to recede before a rising wave of panic. I fought to stay ahead of the swell: it would drag me under if I let it. How many of them were there? They went after whoever they saw, soldier or civilian, they didn't care. A dazed young man holding a pair of smelting tongs, a woman carrying buckets trying to back against a wall. She threw one at the approaching drudge with a shriek. The warrior swatted it out of the way and then they moved in quick as cats, got wet and red and turned to the keep. The drudge were clearing the courtyard.

'Spirits of good, spirits of mercy, take pity on us poor souls,' the sentry whimpered. I threw him his matchlock and started for the stairs that led into the keep.

'Go! You have to retake the gate tower,' I yelled at the dismayed-looking wall sentries as they struggled to load their weapons. I didn't wait to see if they heeded me before I left the wall and entered the keep. I'd left all my gear with my baggage, but this was a fortress and the lords of castles like to hang weapons on the walls. I grabbed an old sword with a cruciform guard, tested the edge with my finger. Not very sharp.

Sharp enough.

I snatched a leather-fronted buckler from another wall mounting further down the corridor and then I was looking for staircases. There was shouting below, the tinny clicking of blades meeting one another.

If Station Twelve fell, we'd lose control of Nall's Engine but I'd moved beyond panic, like the terror was going to kick in at some later more convenient time. I imagined the enemy legions, tens of thousands of grey-faced, hollow-eyed things, streaming across the Misery towards Station Twelve. We could never match the drudge in the open field.

29

It was only the terrors of Nall's Engine that had held them back. Lose Station Twelve and we'd lose the war.

This should have been impossible. Unthinkable.

Someone lost a limb down below; I'd heard that kind of shriek before. I took the stairs three at a time, went too fast and bounced off a wall as I careered around the stairs and found myself in a corridor where the hells were breaking loose.

Two men were dead on the floor, one of ours, one of theirs, each a mess of wounds that they'd inflicted on each other with knives. With the courtyard taken, the enemy were already cutting a bloody path to the higher levels. A pair of them, noseless faces slick and grey, were doing some work on a man they'd forced up against a wall with short-bladed swords. He was already done for, they were just making a meal out of finishing him off. The drudge never show any kind of emotion, but there was savage enthusiasm in the way they were sticking him, over and over. I was about to slip into a side corridor, look for a way past when Nenn emerged behind them. She dripped with some other man's red, the bared teeth below her wooden nose less fierce than the savagery in her eyes. My Nenn was a fighter to the core, the bloodiest and hardest woman this side of the hells. Sword in her right hand, dagger warding the left, if the drudge warriors underestimated her then only one was able to re-evaluate his prejudice, as she parried the first strike aside and split a head. The surviving drudge tried to make a duel of it but I came up behind him and between us he found himself full of holes. He slithered heavily off my borrowed sword.

'What the fuck is going on?' Nenn asked.

'We're in Shit City, that's what,' I said. 'Where are the others? Where's Tnota?'

'Got separated,' Nenn said. She was breathing hard, face red with exertion and slick with sweat. 'I ran up the stairs. Think they fell back into a pantry.'

'You get a count of them?'

'Could be a thousand out there for all I saw.'

I wiped drudge blood from my hands, ran my tongue over my teeth. Shook my head.

'That many couldn't have sneaked this close. My guess is more than fifty, less than a hundred. We haven't lost yet. Come on.'

The garrison was scattered through the halls, half drunk, half green, terrified and lacking orders. Most of them had probably never seen the drudge up close before. They weren't pretty.

'We need to go down. Join up with the garrison,' I said without enthusiasm. I don't like fighting if I'm not getting paid, but we were all in the shit if Twelve went down. Nenn shook her head firmly, grabbed a heavy stairway door and pulled it closed, barring it with a dust-covered beam. All castle stairwells can be shut off like that if the builders are smart. This one had been.

'Not that way. There's ten or more down in the kitchen. Or there was. What the fuck are they doing here?'

'Trying to take control of Nall's Engine,' I said. 'What else?'

'With fifty men? They'd never hold it. I'm no general, captain, but even I can see that.'

The sound of feet tramping up the stairs rose behind the door. No telling whether they were friend or foe. Nobody was screaming any more, which did not bode well.

'Worry about the "why" later. Let's try not to get gracked now.' We retraced my steps, but at the next stair I heard voices from below, the click-and-babble language of old Dhojara. We closed that door and barred it too, tried a third route.

'Running out of options here, captain,' Nenn said. I knew that already, so I ignored her.

'We need to get out of here,' I said.

'We're not going down now?'

I hesitated. My pulse was slamming against my half-deaf ears. The enemy held the gate and they were moving up through the fortress, killing everything in their path. I was separated from my crew, and they might all be dead already.

'We don't get paid if we're dead,' I said.

We rounded a corner and came face to face with a bunch of drudge emerging from a stairwell. There were four of them, and we were just two. Bad odds. I don't fight out-numbered and I don't fight for lost causes. I would have started running if the first of them hadn't charged straight at me.

It hadn't been long since the Deep Kings changed him. All the drudge were people before they were drudge, and he could still have passed himself off as one of us. The build of a farmer, the blank eyes of the enthralled. Little strips of prayer cloth around his forearms and calves fluttered out behind him as he came at me. Chop, whack, done. Two seconds of brutality and his story was over. I didn't wait for him to realise he was dead, cut him twice more as he went down. I stepped back, crouching low and bringing my buckler up between me and the others, but they weren't attacking. Nenn growled low in her throat, and then I saw the figure behind them.

The boy. Just a normal-looking little boy, soft and small enough to be ten years old. Nenn cried out, the sound of her despair more terrible than the violence I'd just worked on the twitching, dying drudge. I turned to run but something speared into my mind, tearing the strength from my legs. I went to my knees. An ice that came from the child began working its way into my being, a creeping, burrowing mag-got. It entered my thoughts, my will and, if I had one, my soul. Pressure began to build behind my eyes, blood ran from my nose and I sure as hell knew who'd done for the poor bastards we'd found out in the Misery.

I screamed as he began to work through my mind, the ice worm driving into my memories. I convulsed with the pain, sending a puddle of brown vomit onto the floor.

Absurd though it was, I regretted the waste of the brandy.

The black evil that stems from the deep, dark cold beneath the ocean wrapped me, pierced the marrow of my bones. A marionette on the child's dark strings, I rose to face my half-sized master. A Darling. Hair shorn close, face plump with puppy fat, it was dressed in a tattered doublet two sizes too large and breeches torn through at the knees like some kind of pauper prince. The awful malice around its mouth, the cruel hunger in its eyes told me that I was about to die. It was going to hurt.

'I want the lady!' the Darling declared. Precocious child tones, but the weight of command belied its true age. Its magic had me by throat and soul both. I growled. Tried to fight it, but there's fuck all you can do against a Darling. Nenn was choking as invisible hands slowly crushed her throat. We were both well and truly gracked now it had its spells into us. The soul-worm turned through my brain, causing me to spasm and I went down in a heap of uncontrolled limbs, arms and legs just a tangle of meat sticks.

It rifled through my memories. My first cigar. Getting sunburned. Riding a donkey cart to market. It pried through them, disordered, scattered, looking for something.

'Where is she?' The pressure grew tight around my balls. My spine protested as invisible hands began to twist me. Steam rose from the walls, hissing and spitting sparks as the worm twisted back and forth in my mind. Bones grated in ways that they aren't intended to.

I was glad I didn't know. I'd have confessed anything just then.

Some poor, unknowing heroes arrived along another corridor. A young lieutenant and a few stout hearts attacked with no idea what they were facing. They fired off their matchlocks, managed to down one of the drudge before the Darling turned its attention to them.

The pressure released and the worm slithered out of my mind. I seized up my scavenged weapons and dragged Nenn with me, down a corridor and towards a stairwell. Behind us I heard the screams as our rescuers learned their mistake.

Clashes of steel and shouting had renewed somewhere below us. That was good. We hadn't lost yet, but I only had escape on what remained of my mind. We were heading back up now, away from the monstrous little creature and his magic. You can kill a Darling just like anyone else, but you need numbers, you need luck and you damn well can't let them see you coming. Fight the battles you can win, run from those you can't. Good words to keep you alive.

We reached the Nall's Engine operating room. Somebody should have been in there, firing it up and getting ready to throw the lever. This attack only made sense if there were a hundred thousand soldiers streaming across the Misery towards us, but whoever was meant to be operating the machine was probably dead already. We had to find the keys to those locks, get it into motion. When we threw the lever, everything twenty miles east of the Range would disintegrate in a firestorm that would make the hells look like a summer's afternoon. I spent a few frustrating moments scraping skin from my palms before I gave up yanking at the chains. Whoever had chained the room was fucking dead when this was over, if he wasn't already, which he probably was. I'd have to settle for giving his corpse a good kicking.

The drudge weren't far behind us. Seemed like they had the same idea that we did. The commander's office lay close by, the door locked from the inside. Drudge piled into the corridor behind us, the child's petulant orders bouncing from stone walls.

'Let us fucking in! We're not fucking drudge!' I yelled, not expecting anyone to answer. I slammed the door with

34

my palm once, twice. No way out. The drudge started moving down the corridor towards us, swords and axes ready for the kill. I tried kicking the door in. Hurt my foot.

There was a scrabbling behind the lock.

'Hurry up!' The warriors approached, cautious. I fended away a blow, sliced open the arm that had struck it. They could only come at us one at a time along the corridor and my wounded assailant staggered back, but Nenn doesn't like to let the wounded ones go. She nipped forwards, her blade sawed out and she took his leg above the knee.

A voice from behind us.

'Get down!'

I didn't see the source but a light flared up behind us. Years of experience told me that there was a Spinner behind me, charged up and ready to blaze. Nenn and I hit the ground and covered our eyes. Usually smart to do that with a Spinner. When we opened them again they'd done something terrifying, because the warriors who'd filled the corridor were lying in smoking pieces along its length. Half a drudge groaned in pain.

We scrambled up and into the commander's office. As I slammed the door behind us, more drudge crowded into the corridor.

The office was all dark wood and polish, shelves of leather-bound books that nobody had, or would, ever read. An oversized padded chair, a vast mahogany desk, both too small for the blubbering whale of a man I figured had to be the commander. Clammy white skin and vast reams of flab adorned the idiot who'd let his station fall. He stared at me, mouth opening and closing like a fish, his extravagantly frilled shirt soaked through with pig-sweat. Fucking disgrace of a soldier. His companion, the Spinner who'd just gracked six Dhojaran warriors, was a tiny snip of a thing, five foot nothing. She was hooded and gowned in royal blue, but when I saw her face it was as if I'd been hit with a spell more potent than the Darling's.

Ezabeth Tanza. She looked exactly as she had some twenty years ago. Face smooth with youth, the slender lines of a girl no longer a child, not yet wearied by womanhood. She was stunningly, heart-rendingly beautiful, a face so perfect that it had to have been shaped for some holy purpose. She should have been greying, but she hadn't aged a day. The hair that pushed out from her hood was still silk and shine. Despite the fact that we were under attack, that people were dying somewhere beneath us, I still stopped to stare like a complete idiot, mouth hanging open.

She was looking at me uncertainly, but only for a moment. She glanced at Nenn.

'I'd hoped there would be more of you,' she said. A strong voice. Used to giving orders.

'Just us,' I said. Ezabeth turned away from me, and when she looked back she had drawn a blue cloth mask up over her face. Between hood and mask, only her eyes remained visible.

'What do we do?' the commander wailed.

'You know the law,' I snarled. 'Range Marshal Venzer's orders. Take no chances. First sign of attack, activate Nall's Engine. Give me the key.'

'What's going on out there?' the commander blubbered. He'd pissed himself. Can't blame a man for doing that in times of terror, but it made me hate his guts even more. I had half a mind to run him through myself, but we needed him. I looked around. The office had no exits; we'd run right into a trap. So much for activating Nall's Engine.

'You got a sword?' I asked him. He blinked, looked around as though the thought hadn't occurred to him before. He saw an ornate weapon with a gilded hilt up on the wall, went and retrieved it. He held it like it was a turd. I doubt he'd picked it up since someone had gifted it to him. He was

36

an administrator, a button counter, the kind of man you put in charge of supplies, not a spirits-damned Range station. Too much peace had turned our grit to jelly. I told him to keep out of the way. He'd be more likely to hurt himself than the enemy.

Beyond the door I could hear a clamouring sound, a lot of footsteps. The drudge knew what they were doing, and my head was starting to clear.

'It wants to take you, lady,' I said.

'It can try,' she said. Defiant.

'You got any canisters?'

'No.'

'You can't have much light left,' I said.

'Almost nothing,' she agreed. 'I have no skill at this. I'm not a warrior.' She stood by the window, her fingers tracing bright lines through the air, drawing the moonlight as best she could. It wouldn't give her much. She needed a loom, hours to spin enough phos to charge herself up. That working in the corridor must have used most of her reserves but she gathered what she could in the seconds we had.

I heard a voice outside, amongst the buzzing Dhojaran nonsense. The Darling was here. That was very, very bad for us. Even if she'd had charged canisters to draw from, a Spinner is not a match for a Darling. The sorcery is different, but the Darling is stronger. The standard Range manual for officers says that you don't engage a Darling without three Spinners to take it down. We had one, and she was pretty much out of phos. About as useful as an empty scabbard.

While I'd been asking pointless questions, Nenn had toppled a bookshelf behind the door. I helped her overturn another behind it. This hadn't been the plan, but plans change from time to time.

'We're going to die!' the station commander squealed. He was fanning himself with a sheaf of paperwork, streams of sweat like rain across his skin.

I didn't hear Nenn's response. A great crash sounded against the door, fallen furniture shaking. The warriors had improvised a ram of some kind, and they wanted in.

'Hope you're ready for this,' I said to Nenn. I tried to give her a grin, but it came out like a leer. Nenn's expression wasn't much more pleasant.

'Can't say I wanted to go out this way, captain,' she said. She spat on an expensive book. Something hard and heavy smashed into the door again. The barricade held. 'Always thought I'd die of something stupid, like syphilis or the shits. Or eating bad meat. Normal stuff, stupid stuff, you know what I mean?' I nodded my agreement. There had always been an out before, always a way we could run for it. I'd abandoned my post in losing situations, or refused to charge into hopeless causes when I had to. That was how I'd stayed alive this long. And now we were going to get our minds prised open by some bastard child because we'd stopped in the wrong place for the night? Somehow that seemed unfair.

Smash against the door again. The voices outside rose and fell, a quick discussion, and then the table and bookcase we'd stacked against the door began to smoke, little sparks pipping away.

'Here we go,' I said. 'I want to take at least one of them with me.'

'I'm aiming for two,' Nenn said. She pulled off her wooden nose to breathe more easily. At least I got to be with Nenn when we died. That was something.

The makeshift barricade began to dissolve, wood turning soft and gooey, melting from the outside. Fucking magical powers. The station commander began to weep, big fat tears on his stupid fat face. I almost punched him.

Ezabeth strode across the room and whipped back a cloth, revealing an empty crystal prism atop a brass pedestal. 'You have a communicator,' she said, disbelieving and angry.

'You didn't send a message to the Command Council?' I said incredulously.

'It all happened so fast,' the commander squealed. 'I can't operate it. I don't know how. Only a Talent can operate it.' If I'd wanted to smash him in his stupid face before, my fists were begging me now.

'Don't think we have time for messages,' I said. Ezabeth shook her head. She was looking beneath the inert crystal prism at the base. Copper and bronze wires curled around the shaft.

'No. But these things require a vast amount of light to operate. Can you remove the prism?'

I walked over, jammed my sword under it, prised it away easily enough. Wild streaks of hot light began jetting out from the ruptured machinery. Ezabeth put her hand over the hole. Her hand lit up, then her arm. Phos flowed through her, brilliant, glaring.

'If you got something you can do, best do it now,' Nenn snarled. The bookcases were dissolving into puddles of cold liquid wood. The door was going the same way. Darling magic.

No time to think on what Ezabeth was doing. The last of the bookcase abruptly turned to slop and fell away in a wooden puddle as the door collapsed inwards. Dhojaran warriors crossed the threshold, and we met them with steel. Nenn shrieked, hacked, struck. I thrust, cut and back-cut but they were many and we were two. I roared, cut, parried, struck. A drudge died and it meant nothing at all.

Ezabeth's light surged. The warriors were cast into brightness by the glow of the woman behind me, and as the light flared in intensity they shielded their blank eyes from the glare. I managed to hack halfway through a hand, smashed my buckler into a face. Nenn went down somewhere in the brilliant glow. Beyond the doorway I caught sight of the Darling, small and furious.

It screamed something in Dhojaran that could only have

been 'Kill the woman!' Its voice was so boyish and thin that for a moment I pitied it in its desperation, but the warriors could barely look in our direction now, the light too intense. The bravest of the drudge tried it and I sent him back with blood gushing from his face, and the others cowered. The Darling raised its hands, sent its mind-worms towards us but whatever this light was it defied the child-sorcerer's power.

The Darling screamed in fury, looked left and right seeking an escape that didn't exist. I caught its eye, saw some kind of black recognition there for just a moment before the world turned to searing white brightness.

Sound disappeared. Everything went blank, all sense of balance disappeared and I felt my face land against a fallen book as I hit the ground. For a horrible moment I thought I was dead, and that I'd been lied to. Was this death, an eternity spent in whiteness, aware but unable to move, speak, nothing but the pale bright void around you?

I knew that I was still alive when I smelled cooked meat.

It wasn't the first time that I'd caught seared flesh on the wind. I burned men at Adrogorsk with hot oil, and interrogations sometimes make hard demands of the men who perform them. This was worse, somehow.

I rolled over. My eyes hurt, my head was worse. Shapes began to form in my vision. I pushed myself up against the table. Sounds, quiet and muffled, tapped around. Nobody was speaking, or screaming, or crying, so that was something. I fumbled on the over-bright floor, found the hilt of my pilfered sword, couldn't see clear enough to stab anyone. I backed up against a wall. Waited.

The commander was dead. The Dhojaran warriors were dead too, but the station commander was more dead than they were. The drudge lay fallen as men should when they get gracked, limbs splayed awkwardly, eyes staring blankly. Some of them had sword-holes that I'd put into them, some of them could have been sleeping if not for the blankness of their faces and the stillness of their chests. Whatever Lady Tanza had done, it was beyond anything I'd ever seen a Spinner accomplish before. Not even Gleck Maldon could have done that. The remnants of the commander were the source of the smell, though. He was a blackened, smoking skeleton shrouded in charred tatters of cloth and sat upright in a chair, though none would have recognised it for the man that had been there mere moments – minutes? – before. Whatever Ezabeth had done to glow like a candle had burned him up like one.

I looked for the body of the Darling, but it was missing. Bastard sorcerers. They always have a way out.

Ezabeth Tanza had collapsed alongside the charcoal-brittle bones of Station Twelve's commander. A few of the skeleton's finger bones fell away to rattle on the floor. Nenn was slumped against a wall too. She hadn't recovered, but with a lurch worse than when I'd fallen I realised that it wasn't the flare of light that had brought her down.

I was by her side in a moment, trying to grab the hand that she clutched over the line of her belt. She looked up at me, deep brown eyes either side of the hole in her face where she should have had a nose. Her teeth were gritted against pain, her expression lost between determination and fear, unsure which way to go. Eventually she settled on anger.

'Fucking bastard got me just before she cooked them,' Nenn said, each word pressed from pain like oil from an olive. 'I hit him in the face but he just ignored it, came in low. Fuck. Bastard gracked me, Ryhalt.'

'You aren't gracked,' I said. 'Not yet. We'll get you help.'

'Nah,' Nenn said, pressing her eyes closed and letting her head fall back. 'Reckon I'm bloody done. Fuck me, it hurts.'

'Let me see.'

She did, and I wished she hadn't. Low enough in the

body to miss the organs that would see her die quickly. A thrust. I looked for the sword that had made it, saw the bloody end. At least five red inches had gone into her. She might bleed to death right there and then, and if not, it was a slow death from gangrene and infection. Pain and stinking pus, blackened flesh and white weeping. The worst kind of death. Better to be burned out by a Spinner than that.

Nenn caught me fingering the hilt of my knife. Our eyes met.

'Do it,' she grunted. She reached out to take my hand, but the touch of her cold fingers against my sweat-slicked skin made me stop.

'No. We'll get you fixed.'

'There's no fixing this,' Nenn said. The blood had welled over her fingers. Her words came stunted, hard. 'We both know what happens next. Lots of pain. Lots of dying.'

'Saravor can fix it,' I said.

'No,' Nenn said, voice a wheeze of pained breath, 'not that bastard. I'm not having that.'

'You hear me giving you a choice? You're going to live.'

'His price is too high.'

'I got credit,' I lied. She was right. His price was always too high, but it might save my friend. My sister. I'd find a way. There was always a way if there was no depth you wouldn't stoop to. I shed morality like a too-warm cloak. Whatever that bastard Saravor needed, he'd get it if he could make my Nenn well again.

I moved the sword out of Nenn's reach just in case she decided to turn rebel on me. Everything seemed to have gone quiet. No more drudge had made it up to us.

'I need to see if anyone else is still alive,' I said. The doorway was still open, but it was silent out there now. The whole station was dark. Whatever Ezabeth had done had drained all the power from the light tubes.

I went to her, found she was still alive. Conscious, but so

42

weak she could barely move. The lights had dimmed to almost nothing. She'd sapped the whole damn station's stores of phos to work that magic. I got her to sit up against the wall. She eventually managed to prise her eyes open to look at me, and beneath the cloth mask over her face I thought she was smiling. Even in the madness, with the bodies of enemies all around me, blood not yet dry on my hands and my oldest companion mortally wounded on the floor, those eyes still held me. For a moment I was tangled in their spell, a youth lost in a better time. She couldn't quite focus on me.

'How very odd to meet you here, Master Galharrow,' she slurred. 'Are we going riding now?' Sounded drunk. She laughed, tinkling, broken. I felt a lump lodge in my throat, a pain deep behind my heart.

'You hurt?' I asked.

'No. I don't want to go riding, thank you. I think I will sleep now. Thank you, Master Galharrow,' she said. She closed her eyes and did just that.

The garrison had fought, but they hadn't fought well. 'Got slaughtered' served to describe it better. There were bodies all over, some dead where they fell, others slumped up against walls where they'd dragged themselves to bleed out. Some didn't have a mark on them, like their lives had just been snuffed out. Wasn't just the drudge that Tanza's magic had hit. I guess that's the power you get when a Spinner empties a Range station's worth of phos in one go. The girl had managed to summon up a force maybe even Crowfoot would have been impressed by. Or not.

It wasn't until the lower levels that I began to find the living. Gasping and mewling on the ground floor. Wounded fighters, two of them, both Dhojaran and both beyond help. One was trying to drag himself towards the door on his belly. At the rate he moved he might have made it when spring arrived. I wanted to know how many of my men were gracked before I decided how to kill them.

Tnota was alive, and so was Wheedle, hiding out with half a dozen cooks and garrison soldiers who'd hidden in the kitchen and barred it good.

'The Big Dog told me you'd make it,' Tnota said when I let them out. He tapped his fingers to his lips then both eyes, glancing up towards the heavens.

'Sure he did. We got a deal, him and me,' I said. 'Who's not getting back up?'

'Who is? Ida legged it the moment she saw the drudge. Cowardly bitch. Not sure if she got away,' Tnota sighed. He'd come through pretty unscathed, but he'd probably been first into the pantry. Probably hadn't even drawn his knife. 'You see Nenn? I figured she went looking for you.'

'Got shanked pretty bad. Dead soon, probably,' I said, hardening my voice as much as possible. Bastard words shook anyway. Tnota had been with us longer than most. He knew how thick we were.

'Go be with her,' he said. 'I'll sort this shit here out.'

'No,' I said with a shake of my head. 'Get that fancy carriage outside ready. We're taking Nenn to Valengrad. Going to pay a trip to the Fixer.' Tnota's black face darkened. It wasn't just his religion that said that what I proposed was wrong. He had common sense.

'You don't want to get in with that creature again,' he said. 'He don't do favours.'

'And Nenn doesn't do dying,' I said. 'Get it ready. We're leaving as soon as I get her down the stairs.'

I would have been lying if I said that what I proposed didn't scare me. I forced it back out of my mind, tried to keep my thoughts on the here and now. I didn't want to be in with Saravor. He'd charge me all the coin I had and then three times more, and it still wouldn't be all he wanted from me. But there are some things that, no matter how foolish, no matter how much you know you're going to regret it, you choose to do anyway. Because it's the only option you got.

4

Saw a lot of people come and go over half a lifetime on the Range. Some of them came and went, some of them came and died, and the ones that did neither weren't often the kind you wanted around. First time you lose a friend, feels like you'll never be the same again. Lose enough of them, you realise that you aren't the same, but you've forgotten how to be whatever it was you were before. Sometimes when you read the obituary it's some arsehole you cheated over the tile board and you're glad he caught a shiv or got eaten by a dulcher, but sometimes – not often, but sometimes – it was someone you gave half a stale piss for, and you'd tear down the gates of the afterworld to get them back.

I wanted Nenn back. She was foul-mouthed, hard-hearted and she cut throats like a pirate, but she was my pirate, and I'd be flayed through every level of hell before I'd let some gut wound sap the kill out of her. We stretchered her across to one of the gaudy carriages and the curses we endured would have blistered a priest's soul. I was only worried when they faded away into gasps and grimaces.

'You need to eat less cock,' I said, 'you're heavy as fuck.' Nenn's snarl told me she'd have made some savage retort if breathing didn't hurt so bad.

Tnota pulled the carriage door open. The carriage was massive, enough to seat eight people within its lavender-fragranced interior. Nenn screamed when we lifted her onto the seat. Not the most stable platform to die on but it was the best we had. We needed to go fast and the spring mounting on the carriage was better than any of the military wagons.

'Three days up the Range to Valengrad,' I said to Tnota. 'We need to get moving. Find us a team of horses. Anyone tries to stop you ...' I thought of saying to refer them to me, but I had shit to do. No. 'Shank them.'

Tnota, despite everything that had happened, grinned. He couldn't keep that smile off his face for long, not even if the Deep Kings themselves were stomping over the Range.

Station Twelve was in shock. Surviving soldiers and weeping civilians stumbled about, unable to believe what they'd seen. Couldn't blame them, wasn't far from disbelief myself. The chain of command was in tatters. The commander's remains were still hot to the touch, and nobody in the station had ever fulfilled any serious combat duties. For most of these poor kids it was the first time they'd seen a person killed. Sure, they'd all have slaughtered animals back home, and even the greenest of them had seen dead bodies. Dead babies, grandmas who didn't make it through the winter, victims of the various summer pestilences that carry off your neighbours. Death was the way of the world. Still, there's a difference between seeing an uncle pass from a wet cough, and seeing your mates get opened up by grey-skinned monsters born right out of the void.

I crouched down beside one of the monsters lying dead in the courtyard. No two drudge are totally alike. They all started off as people, before the Kings change them and make them part of their plan. Not much human left in this one. Its face was noseless, smooth as marble, a mottled grey-rust colouring to the skin. The eyes were big, round, almost entirely pupil. The eyes of a thing born in the freezing dark. The drudge still wore the tattered clothes of the person it had been, stained with dirt, sweat and other fluids, but the armour it wore was a recent addition. Good steel, scavenged from some other defeated nation. I prised off its helm, looking for the mark. There's always a mark. Had to strip it down to find it in the end, cutting away the straps of its breastplate revealed the clammy, flabby flesh of its arms and legs. Turned out this one had been a woman. Found the mark on the small of its back, a glyph far more complex than the lettering of our own script. We didn't know how they made them, it was neither ink nor brand, but it served the same purpose and each of the Deep Kings marked their creatures in some way. What function it played in the magic, we didn't know, but the mark told me who'd orchestrated this attack on us. This one bore Shavada's glyph. None of the Kings has a good reputation amongst the people of Dortmark, but Shavada was probably the most despised. Philon was the most cunning tactician, Iddin the most powerful and Acradius commanded the greatest numbers, but Shavada won hands down for cruelty. I needed to pass the information to Crowfoot as soon as I was able.

I traipsed back through the station. Blood on the walls, blood on the stairs. Drudge bodies lying slumped where they'd fallen. Empty-eyed soldiers dead on the floor. It all stank, the ripe tang of the drudge thicker than the smell of voided bowels. Back in the commander's office I ignored the charcoal of softly smoking bones and checked out the communicator. No chance there. The Spinner had sucked all the juice from it and fused all the wires together in the process. I suspected that the battery coils they stored the phos in wouldn't be in much better shape.

'I have to get to Valengrad,' Ezabeth said. Her voice was a scratchy whisper, muffled all the more by her mask. I knelt down beside her and went to remove it. She turned her head, made feeble attempts to swat my hand away. 'Leave it,' she said, pained. It was stupid, but I hadn't the energy to argue.

Crowfoot had sent me here to make sure that she

survived. He'd known, somehow, that she was in danger. How had he known? Might as well try to guess the coming of the wind as ask how the Nameless learned their secrets. I'd nearly failed. Was arguable I'd not done much to help at all, and it'd cost me eight men, including a new kid. He'd been scared in the Misery. He should have been scared here too. We'd all forgotten that.

'I'm going that way,' I said. 'Besides. I'm taking your ride.'

She didn't object. She'd passed out.

I carried the unconscious noblewoman down to the courtyard. I'd lifted heavier shields. Tnota had worked efficiently. He and Wheedle were getting the horses into their traces, a half-dozen broad-chested beasts with white splashes across black noses. I laid Tanza down on the bench across from Nenn.

'I have to ride with that witch?' Nenn grunted. Her face was red, sweaty. Bad signs.

'You never cared that Gleck was a Spinner,' I said.

'And he didn't care that he was born with silver spilling out his arse. If she starts trying to lord it over me I'm kicking her out.'

'It's her carriage.'

'It's my death. I'm not doing curtsies while I die.'

She looked half dead already. I guess she was. That she still had some fight in her gave me hope we'd make it to Saravor before her own body poisoned her. It was when Nenn got quiet you had to worry.

Before we left I found the captain who'd refused to admit me to see the commander just a handful of hours ago. He'd survived with a few scratches, had managed to gather some of his soldiers and retaken the gate. By then the drudge had been inside, but it had been the right thing to do. Not as useless as I'd figured him after all. His two best men were already hurtling north to Station Thirteen to request reinforcements and to get a communicator to send a message to Valengrad. Range Marshal Venzer was going to shit chickens when he heard what had happened. Part of me wished I could report it to the Iron Goat myself. Maybe I'd send him a report when I made it to Valengrad. For now I'd leave it to the regulars and see to my own.

The road was bumpy, the passengers shuddered in pain. I drove the carriage myself, barely rested. We followed the supply road north along the Range. Everything to the west was Dortmark, farmland, towns, forests, life. To the east, the empty red sands and cracked sky of the Misery. We sped along a frontier that divided different worlds.

One of the horses died in the traces. We cut it free and pushed the remaining five harder. Ten miles from Valengrad another spewed froth, went down and broke the legs of a third. Powerful as they were, three alone couldn't drag the carriage. A merchant train was passing so Tnota and I took their horses. They gave them over quietly and we didn't have to kill anyone.

I lashed the new horses hard. The city appeared, smoke and steam belching from the factories, the night illuminated by thousands of phos lights. Across the great citadel the word COURAGE blazed redly through the smog. East of the city, the poisoned desert pressed close to Valengrad's vast walls, but for once, the Misery wasn't the most terrible thing I'd have to deal with.

5

Every big city has a Spills. Stuff enough roofs within a set of walls and the crud and the crap will accumulate in one place. The poor, the lame, the foreign, the shunned, they all gather together to seek mutual succour from the successful, who hate them for stirring their compassion. The dangerous, the scarred, the cruel, the cunning, they sit atop the piles of shit and send out their orders like rat-kings, legions of lepers, whores, thieves and scammers milling about in filth-encrusted regiments. You know the places I'm talking about. The kind that need a mission, but even the missionaries think are beyond help. In Valengrad, the great fortress-city that anchored the centre line of the Range, we called that accumulation of damp, poorly built houses and damp, poorly mannered creatures the Spills. That's where we took Nenn. Where else would you find a sorcerer who deals in flesh?

The absurdly blue and gold carriage drew a hundred eager eyes but common sense and the naked steel lying across my lap turned them aside. I drove the dying horses past the butchers' yards and the stink of new blood into a row of tenement houses. Beggars and out of work mercenaries got out of the way quick enough. I wasn't slowing our pace for risk of crushing the legs of some scabby white-leaf addict. Minutes were more valuable than gold dust just then. I knew the way to Saravor's hole clear enough and the big town house loomed up between two blocks of tenements, as out of place in this rat-hole as our carriage. I brought the ride to a standstill and moments later my fist was banging against the front door.

A grey-skinned child answered. I felt a sudden lurch in my chest and my hand was on my sword's hilt before I took in that it wasn't a Darling and certainly wasn't a threat. Just a sickly, blind child. A bandage was wrapped above his nose, damp patches where eyes should have been. I hadn't known Saravor had brought children into his schemes. For a moment, the revulsion I felt almost clouded my sanity and I thought about turning away. No, it was no good. There were only a handful of sorcerers in Valengrad and no school-trained Light Spinner could give me what I needed. I didn't know if what Saravor did was illegal, but it wasn't going to win him any grand awards at the Lennisgrad University. The child said nothing. Hard to see the purpose of a blind doorman. I told him Ryhalt Galharrow was there to see Saravor and he disappeared into the shadows as silently as if he were one of them.

When I opened the carriage door, the last doubt I'd had about using Saravor's dark services was washed away by the wave of foulness that billowed out. The Spills has some pretty vile odours leaking out of its alleyways, but that day Nenn's gut wound routed them back into the gutters. It amazed me that Ezabeth hadn't choked on it, cooped up in there. She'd slept nearly the whole journey, which had probably been a mercy.

'Nenn's out of it,' Tnota told me. 'Fever delirium. Talking bullshit. She got an hour at best. Then she's gracked.'

'Then we better hope Saravor is home,' I said. I took my end of the stretcher and, doing my best not to inhale, began to carry Nenn through the open door.

'You don't have to do this,' Tnota told me. He fixed me in the eye with his yellow whites, always trying to needle and play counsellor to my conscience. 'Big Dog says if it's too late it's too late. Some prices shouldn't be paid.'

It was the same discussion we'd had a dozen times on the three days spent whipping the carriage back towards Valengrad. I'd thought about it. Sometimes you just got to stop thinking and act.

'She'd do the same for me,' I said. Tnota snorted at that.

'She'd have looted the gold from your teeth before you were cold,' he said. It was a joke, just not a funny one. We lugged Nenn into the reception room. This had been a merchant's house at one time. The reception room was dim, smelled of mould. Didn't look to get a lot of use. Saravor wasn't the kind to entertain visitors.

'Set a limit. Don't go higher,' Tnota said. I shook my head, put a finger to my lips. The walls might have ears in this place. It's not often you can say that and mean it literally.

The blind child returned and indicated that I alone should ascend. I wasn't sure whether the kid had genuinely lost his eyes or whether it was just some ploy of Saravor's to curdle my guts before we talked shop. He probably knew we were coming. Just because he wasn't Nameless didn't make it smart to underestimate him; a knife may not be a longsword, but the edge will cut you all the same.

Saravor's workshop was on the first floor, dark and bitter with the stink of white-leaf smoke, though none burned now. Work surfaces lay cluttered with instruments and stains better left unnoticed. Stacks of shelves lined the walls but long velvet curtains hid them from sight. One curtain had been intentionally left open. I saw jars of ageing meat in greenish-yellow fluid, a tub that may have contained fingers. Where there were no shelves, delicately drawn canvasses showed the internal workings of the human body, anatomy as taught at universities. Saravor was not there, so the boy bid me wait. I drummed my fingers. Didn't have time for these theatrics. I took a seat at one of the work benches and did my best not to look at anything that I wouldn't want to remember later.

The sorcerer came down eventually, sniffing the air like a hound.

'That's phos residue,' I heard him say, even before he rounded the corner, 'I can smell it on you thicker than dung.' He emerged from the stairwell grinning like a circus jester. 'You've been involved in some serious mystical fracas!' Bare-chested, a towel hanging around his shoulders, Saravor's ribs showed through the mottled skin of his torso. Part black, part white, part golden skin, nobody knew where Saravor had come from originally. One of his eyes was summer-sky blue, the other a darker shade, as though he'd tried to find a match and come up short. His lean torso was entirely hairless, his skin a patchwork of different racial colourings, a pale northern shoulder, night-dark biceps, stomach the amber of Pyre. I was half a foot over six, but he was well over seven.

'Had a run-in,' I said. 'I have a problem.'

'So you do. Care to share a drink with an old friend?'

Saravor wasn't an old friend, but this wasn't the first time we'd done business. He seated himself on the opposite side of the workbench and selected a bottle and two wooden beakers. He gave them a sniff, decided that whatever he'd put in them before didn't need cleaning out, and poured for me. I hadn't the willpower to resist once he uncorked the brandy. The cup he pushed towards me looked to have teeth marks in the rim. Everything in a sorcerer's house is strange.

'You really do stink of phos,' he said. 'Must have been some strong stuff. Been poking around in the Nall's Engine control chamber?'

'No,' I said. 'Had some trouble down south.'

'Trouble?'

'Darling trouble,' I said. 'But we lucked out. There was a Spinner with the garrison. She did something. Something I hadn't seen before. Whatever it was, it fried a lot of the drudge.'

'Dhoja across the Range? Attacking into Dortmark?' Saravor said. He tried to put an expression of shock onto his patchwork face, but it seemed like the muscles on one side weren't well connected and he only managed to look deranged. The sinews could probably only be blamed for half of that.

'You didn't hear it from me,' I said. 'I figure the marshal will probably keep it close to his chest until he has time to summon the princes for a formal council. This wasn't just some poke. They have something planned.' Saravor's smile was a bitter thing, the colour of autumn cold.

'But you share this information with me?'

'I need a favour. The information is a gift. Good faith.' Saravor nodded. Sorcerers might love gold but they like knowing things more. We knocked our brandy cups together and I took a drink. It was good. Times were good for the sorcerer, to afford wash like that. All-out war had rescinded in living memory, but there were still plenty of men in need of a fix – a pierced arm, a mangled hand.

'Ryhalt, we've done good business before,' Saravor said as he refilled the cups. 'I already know what you're going to ask me. You have a woman with a soured belly. I can smell it even above the light-stink all over you. That's not easy work, even for someone as skilled in the healing arts as I.' Healing arts. That was rich. I kept my face impassive. I'd had to deal with Saravor twice before, but never in as bad a strait as this, and I'd had coin on those occasions. Hadn't been worth it either time. Molovich took an arrow in the throat not two weeks after the sorcerer meddled with him. If Nenn survived I'd do a better job of keeping her upright than I had him.

'I need this on credit,' I said. Saravor's half-gold, half-cream mouth twisted in a mockery of a smile.

'Oh, come now. You didn't truly come to beg for help, did you?'

'I'm not begging. Asking. You give credit, and you know I'm good for it.'

'Hmph.' Saravor didn't blink. Those eyes, mismatched beneath hairless brows, didn't falter. 'And here you are telling me that you're getting mixed up with Darlings and Light-Spinners. Suppose I do credit you. You aren't some butcher who lopped off his finger with a misplaced cleaver. You breathe Misery dust and go first into the breach. Suppose I front you, and you get yourself killed. This is not an attractive proposition.' He shook his head. 'I do not work for free.'

'I don't have time to argue,' I said. 'You know that as well. Cut to it. What will I owe you for fixing her up?'

A sound on the stairway drew my attention. Another grey child, hairless, spindle-limbed, eyes over-wide, wandered down the stairway. This one wasn't blind, but there was a grotesquely empty look to his face. Maybe eight, nine years old. Saravor looked around and garbled something at the boy in a language that I didn't understand. The boy didn't look at him, but slowly turned and walked back the way he had come.

'Your son?' I asked.

'I was responsible for making him, after a fashion.' Saravor's lip twitched as though he intended to smile. I wasn't smiling. For a moment I almost walked out. Whether the boy was his servant or something else, that wasn't why I was here. I wasn't some lawman out to change the world for the better. I just wanted Nenn to live.

We haggled. I tried, anyway. Saravor laid out his terms. I tried to argue them down, he refused to budge, and I agreed. By the time he was done, there were no smiles around the table. The pretence of friendship had dissipated into the odour of white-leaf smoke clustering at the edges of the room. There is not a worse human being in Valengrad than Saravor, of that I was sure, but since I wasn't sure that he

55

was still human, that thought was worth as little as piss in the wind. I agreed to leave Nenn in his care until he got a message to me. I didn't ask how he'd do that, and he didn't ask where to find me. Fucking sorcerers.

6

I woke in the grey haze of a fading afternoon. Fatigue had stolen any memory of how I'd got to my apartment. If elves had carried me there, then they certainly hadn't decided to tidy the place. I'd left Valengrad in enough of a hurry not to have emptied the bucket of night soil, so it stank, literally, like shit. As I threw open the narrow windows I dimly recalled telling Tnota to deal with the carriage and team. I'd probably meant that he should stable it up somewhere, but knowing Tnota he'd have sold it for a couple of jars of ale and a rented arse.

I'd slept a whole day. Factory smog crawled through the damp streets as I stepped briskly into the gloom. I'd already lost time.

Lady Ezabeth Tanza had been gone when we emerged from Saravor's hovel. On the journey she'd seemed barely able to prop herself up, had sipped at water and eaten nothing. Then right there in the Spills she'd just disappeared. Felt like a blow to the gut. Maybe I'd imagined that we'd talk of old times, the few brief months when we'd been barely older than children. She clearly didn't share my sentimentality. Probably for the best.

The open doors of taverns called longingly to me as I crossed the city, sirens trying to lure me from my purpose. I hardened my heart against them, and the scent of dark ale that would sing me to the rocks. The citadel rose through the murky sky ahead of me, her neon words telling me to keep heart.

I rented a small office on a dismal street not far from the citadel. I called in on my way, the key stiff in the lock, the door frame stiff. The roof had been leaking and the floor was wet. A damp miasma rose to greet me, but I'd smelled a lot worse the last few days. A few items of mail had been shoved through the door, damp and ink-smeared. I sat in the beat-up chair and leafed through them.

When I'd first struck my deal and Crowfoot marked me, I'd known that a captaincy in Blackwing was not going to be sunshine and daisies. Why did he pick me? I had skills that he wanted, and I didn't die easy. That mattered to his kind. Crowfoot was a wizard. Not a common sorcerer like Ezabeth or Gleck Maldon, or even a rare freak like Saravor. He made them look like children – no. Like mice. A hundred Ezabeths couldn't have made him break a sweat. Gleck explained it to me once. How sorcerers had to draw power from something but wizards had the power inside them, always growing, swelling. They hoarded it jealously, never used a drop they didn't have to. It built to colossal levels, let them work miracles. Or cataclysms. It was for the day-to-day brutality that the seven captains of Blackwing came in. I and those few others foolish enough to accept a wizard's bargain.

On rare occasions he remembered that tossing me money was useful. A decade back he'd left a pair of gold bricks on my doorstep in a dirty old sack. Money was a human concern too far below his notice to matter. He wouldn't even have noticed the roof was leaking. Wouldn't have grasped why it would bother me.

I reported only to Crowfoot, if he ever showed up, and his mandate was a simple one: protect the Range. Sniff out the bad seeds, the profiteers and the officers who took bribes. Locate the silver-tongues, shut down the Brides, silence the doomsayers. While I was waiting for Crowfoot to throw me another priceless artefact, the courts paid good money for the heads of the traitors I brought them and asked no questions as long as they were marked. A Blackwing captain held no military rank, but *The Range Officer's Manual* required that all officers below the rank of colonel should concede the road to me. Those who got in my way didn't stay there for long.

I leafed through the papers that had come through the door in my absence. First up was a request for me to lead prayers at a meeting of the Avian Brotherhood. A cult of idiots who wanted to believe that Crowfoot was some kind of incarnation of the Spirit of Mercy, which I guess made me their prophet. It was no secret that Blackwing did Crowfoot's work, but even these fools didn't know the depth of his hold over its captains. Even to the soldiery the Nameless seemed half myth, distant as emperors of old. It was the Avian Brotherhood's third request. The only reason I'd not stamped on them yet was that my master would probably have thought they were funny. Second was an anonymous note informing me about potential sympathisers and cultists in the mercantile district. I got a lot of those. Most were nothing but spite and envy. Still worth checking out. I pocketed it for later.

Last was a bill saying that I owed money for the rent of the horses we'd had to leave at Station Twelve. I scowled at it. That was all I needed. I crumpled it, tossed it into the cold fire grate and headed to the citadel.

'The marshal's not here,' the reception clerk told me. I'd washed and put on a clean white shirt and my best leather waistcoat, but by the disdain on her face she didn't appreciate the effort. Her uniform was immaculate, buttons gleaming. She probably thought that she was doing a better job of being a soldier than I was, but I'd go and prostrate myself before Shavada and beg him to mark me before I'd wear a uniform for Dortmark's Grand Alliance again. The clerk didn't ask to see any identification of my rank, but given my height and the muscle that sits along my bones, even prissy clerks tend not to want to upset me.

'Where is he?'

'Gone south along the Range.'

He'd gone to see Station Twelve for himself. Of course he had. Our marshal had come up through the ranks, and no matter what authority and golden medals they pinned to his bony old chest, he was still a soldier. But Venzer was an old man and he'd be taking a canal barge, not the potholed, bone-jerking carriage ride by road. It would be days before he got back. I asked the clerk for a pen and ink and settled for writing a lengthy report on the events at Twelve. There was nobody else I was prepared to trust the information to. Some idiot part of me had started to believe that Crowfoot and his commands were over. Had hoped he might have let me go, finally. Scraping an existence out of other men's blood wasn't much of a life, but it was what I had, and the taverns never turn you away. Not like the ungrateful bitch who hadn't even thanked us for transporting her to the city.

She'd survived. The order had been given and I'd done what had been asked. If Lady Tanza chose to go wandering off into the city alone now, that was her business. She had the means to look after herself. My work was done, and that had to be for the best.

Thoughts of Spinners got my mind back to the sympathisers we'd found at Dust Gorge. She'd been a Talent, one of the barely capable Spinners who worked one of the big light mills. It was one thing for some cartwright or cutler to get himself a case of Bride-fever and decide that joining the Deep Kings' thralls was a life ambition, quite another if they were getting their hooks into our Talents.

Crowfoot had been silent for five years and no part of me was glad he had returned. I'd have preferred to crawl into a tavern with whatever bottle was cheapest and do my best not to think about what I'd done to Nenn, but the inked bird on my arm demanded that I get my arse moving. It reminded me of the fate of the last Blackwing captain who'd failed in his duty. Crowfoot had made it last for days. He'd only made me watch for one.

It was time to go pay the phos mill's owner a visit, and that meant paying a call on a prince. Corruption doesn't take root in isolation, it embeds itself where the soil is fertile. Without a hard-working army of Talents spinning phos to pump into its heart, the Engine was just so much iron and oil. I'd never known a Talent turn sympathiser before, and since I'd brought her head back to Valengrad in a sack she wasn't going to be talking. Her name had been Lesse, a Talent of no special accomplishment. She and her husband had been reading illegal verses, a heretical book of lies called *The Deep Songs*. There's a change comes over people when they start getting a head full of darkness. Erratic behaviours, strange moods. The mill's owner, Prince Herono, should have noticed it sooner. Lesse might have brought other Talents into her sedition and that put everyone in danger. Herono might have had royal blood, but she'd answer my questions all the same.

The phos mill in Valengrad was not particularly bountiful. From what little I understood of light spinning, there were certain places where gathering light was easier, or more efficient. It was all related to lunar orbits and atmospheric pressures, but what that ultimately meant was that the spot chosen for the phos mill was the best for some hundred miles, which was why when Nall had erected his Engine he'd anchored its heart here, and founded Valengrad to surround it. The heart of the Engine might have been well protected beneath the citadel, but the phos mill lay on the outskirts of the city. While some factories clank and grind and make a lot of noise, they kept the mill aside because it required quiet. Spinning was an art, best kept distant from the rest of the city.

The light was fading as I approached the mill's broad domes. Two flags wavered limply, one bearing the nine-pillared temple that signified the Grand Alliance of Dortmark's city states, the second bearing the personal arms of Prince Herono of Heirengrad. The Alliance had come together in the days when the Deep Kings had brought the armies of the empire to crush the west. There had been nine cities once, before Crowfoot's weapon destroyed Adrogorsk and Clear. The seven remaining states each nominated an elector prince, by whose votes the grand prince was selected. The number of votes each prince could cast was based on the number of men and supplies they fed to the Range each year, the alliance only serving to provide communal protection. The Grand Alliance was as corrupt and empty as most political systems, and the grand prince was always elected from Lennisgrad since they could afford the best bribes and supplied the most soldiers. For the most part the princes were self-serving, cowering in the west in their pale marbled estates, thinking of sunny days dodging bees in the vineyard or buggering some poor concubine. And yet, amongst the crap and the crud, some like Prince Herono rose as a beacon of what a prince could be. She, at least, understood the darkness that encroached onto our world and, for as long as I could remember, had put herself directly in its path.

Lately my life seemed to have become a series of encounters with underlings, trying to get through to see someone of importance, but the reception clerk was surprisingly helpful. He buzzed a short-range communicator and after he'd tapped out a message, a bell rang and a man came to collect me.

'Leave your swords at the desk,' the man said. He was neither as tall nor as broad as me and was even older, but he still had a tough, life-bitten look about him. His scalp was razored smooth but his moustache curled outwards like the horns of a steer. The fingers that took my sword belt and dirk were thick and heavy. I fancied he had the look of a butcher, or a bulldog. He wore a uniform, slashed to show the blue silk lining and bearing the word 'Stannard' across the left breast, which I guessed was his name.

'Follow me and don't touch a thing, there's a good chap,' he said, and led me into the mill. It would have been a mistake to take his politeness to mean he'd made a request rather than given an order.

The main workshop floor was crowded with machinery, but few people. The room itself was bigger than any banqueting hall I'd ever been in, at least two hundred paces long and half as wide. There was no light save for that coming from the moons. Row upon row of phos looms sat beneath chimneys, within which huge focusing lenses directed the moonlight down towards the looms, leaving the entire vast work floor shadowed and half dark.

'Where are all the workers?' I asked. My voice sounded tinny against the machinery.

'Got eyes, don't you? Look around,' Stannard grunted. Walked on.

Talents, weakly gifted Spinners, worked the looms. They wore heavy, many-lensed goggles, the better to see the colours of light they wanted to draw from the air. Within the looms they plucked at the air as though playing an invisible harp, drawing threads of coloured light towards battery coils on either side. They worked intently, steadily and methodically, separating red from blue, gold from white. It was not a flashy form of magic, and I'd seen it done before, but there was still something faintly enchanting about the glowing threads they drew from nothing. This was the source of power for the light tubes that illuminated Valengrad, the communicators that tapped messages to the Range stations. Even the big communal ovens in Mews had a spark powered by the phos being harvested here. But it wasn't for the ovens that I'd come.

63

We passed between the Talents as unnoticed as ghosts. They were intent on their work, never glancing away from the living phos around their fingers. None of them were older than thirty. The ability usually manifested around the age of twenty and the mill took its toll. A man can only stare into the light for so long before he breaks. Every Talent bore some kind of scarring, usually on the fingers or the palms, though some were more seriously disfigured. The first discovery of their ability, the radiance, was seldom kind. Scars didn't bother me. I'd seen enough of those in my time.

Four out of every five looms sat empty. I didn't like it. Uneasy ghost-fingers crawled along my spine.

The workroom was nearly silent save for the occasional clank or click as a wheel was turned or a new battery coil plugged in at the loom. Stannard led me between machines and as we passed I ran a finger across the gears. The dust had settled on them a while back, and some had tarpaulins thrown across them. Here, so close to Nall's Engine's heart, the workers should have been at their most numerous. It didn't make sense.

'This is Prince Herono's office,' Stannard told me. A similarly aged man stood outside, a broad-bladed cutlass on his belt, a guard. 'You do anything makes us think you're a threat, we'll cut you apart faster than a hog on feast day. You understand? Anything at all. Bad words, bad attitude, bad moves.'

'I'm terrified,' I said drily. 'I guess you boys were part of Herono's Blue Brigade back before she got taken. This your reward for those years of service? Playing doorman?'

'Always an honour to serve the prince,' Stannard said, narrowing his eyes. He thought he was a tough guy, only I was bigger than him, and he didn't like it. 'And wouldn't be a pain to send you on to the hells neither, so watch your step and your mouth. Got that straight, old boy?'

'Sounds fair,' I agreed. Truth be told, I was glad she had

servants this loyal. Of all the cream in Valengrad, she was the only one with a real sack of guts. I walked into the office of a living legend.

The walls were dark wood panels behind suits of polished armour. They dwarfed the shrivelled wasp of a woman sitting behind the vast desk. A hard, narrow face with sunken cheeks and the lines of fifty years looked out over a collar of silk and ruffles. Her single eye was bright and fixed on me, the snarled twist of flesh in the second socket seeing nothing. Scars lay across her face like fallen leaves, some deep, some shallow. The drudge had made something of a mess of her but she was smiling when I walked in. Neither the Blackwing name nor my iron seal would intimidate her. My licence enabled me to root out sympathisers and malcontents amongst the general population, but even a Blackwing agent bowed before a prince.

'Your grace,' I said, bowing low. 'Thank you for the audience.'

'No need to fawn, Captain Galharrow. We're both agents of the populace, after all. Will you sit?'

I took a high-backed chair across the desk from the prince. The desk was a huge thing, a near immovable block of wood cut from some immense tree. Ancestors glared down at me from oil portraits across the walls.

'I have been expecting you,' she said. She took a canvas bag from a purse and threw it across the desk to land with a hard, coin-filled clink on my side. 'I am not one for barter and bargains. I think you will find that I have been generous.'

I'd come here to enquire about her Talents getting turned against us by the Deep Kings. I'd expected denial, outrage, cursing. I sure as the hells hadn't expected a bribe.

'I like silver as much as the next man,' I said, 'but what are you trying to buy here, your grace?'

'Buy? I don't need to buy anything from you, *Galharrow*,' Herono said. She seemed to enjoy twisting my name and her one eye twinkled with amusement. 'This is payment for the service you performed for my cousin.'

'Your cousin?'

'Second cousin, really. Lady Tanza. She informed me that you returned her safely to us.'

I hadn't known that Ezabeth was related to Prince Herono, however distant the relationship. Curious that my parents had never told me that. Maybe they'd wanted to see how we matched without political connections getting in the way.

'Where is she now, your grace?'

'Her brother, Count Dantry, has a small property in town. I had assumed that you would be seeking compensation for bringing her back safely.'

'No, your grace. I'm not here for money—' I said. But I didn't pass it back.

'And here I'd heard that there's no job you won't take if the money's good. No, don't be insulted. Money is the grease that oils the cogs of the world. It's men like you that keep things turning. Take it anyway, a token of my thanks. Ezabeth is a strange woman, but I am glad that she survived the ordeal. So, if you didn't come for payment, then what can I do for you?'

This was going to be difficult.

'I'm here on Blackwing business. I tracked two sympathisers into the Misery. One of them was a Talent, worked at your mill. Name was Lesse. You know her?'

Herono shook her head.

'It rings no bells with me, but I probably don't know half the Talents working the looms right now. They transfer in and transfer out.' She activated her communicator, asked the clerk to send someone through.

'Not a lot of them working tonight,' I said.

'There is a surplus of phos in storage right now, more than Valengrad needs.'

'Doesn't the law require all low-grade Spinners to work

as mill Talents?' I didn't make it an accusation, but Herono's single eye narrowed. 'Forgive me, your grace, but there's a lot of empty seats out there. I'm no engineer but even I know that Nall's Engine needs a constant supply of light to keep operational. Seems to me you should have a body at every one of those looms, especially on a night when all three moons are ascending.'

'Captain, not only do I run the largest mill in Valengrad and three others around Heirengrad, I am a chief councillor for the Order of Aetherial Engineers. Nall's Engine is in part my responsibility. Do not concern yourself with it.'

'Is the marshal aware that most of the mill is dark?' I pressed.

'You try my patience, captain. I do not tell you how to run men down in the Misery, and neither do I need to be questioned on the running of my mill. Should I explain to you why the moons' alignment is causing poor refraction tonight? Perhaps if you have time you can undertake an advanced degree in lunarism and we can compare strategies. But until you have my expertise, I do not answer to you. Few still living have given as much to Dortmark as I.' She placed a fingertip into the empty hollow where her eye used to be. 'You may trust me when I say that I grasp the full importance of supplying the Engine.'

I was not deterred.

'I don't doubt your resolve, your grace. But at Station Twelve they were running at half power and the mill is half empty,' I said. 'Why are the stations underpowered if Valengrad has a surplus?'

Herono frowned.

'Ezabeth said the same and you are right. It does warrant further investigation.'

A clerk appeared with a ledger.

'Do we employ a Talent here by the name of Lesse?' Herono asked.

'We did, your grace. She left your employ nearly a year ago. I believe that she was transferred to a mill in Lennisgrad.' The prince nodded, the clerk disappeared.

'Have many Talents left your employ in the last year?' I asked.

'As you say, Talents are required by law to work at mills. Nall's Engine must be fed, and it is voracious. But it's not easy for any of us, looking at that broken sky every day, hearing the scowls and screams of the Misery. It reminds us that we're all mortal, that there are things out there and beyond that seek to destroy us. Talents often transfer away, to other mills.'

'Lesse didn't get far,' I said. 'She headed straight into the Misery and whatever information she was taking out there she took to her grave, but what I want to know is how she and her man got recruited. If there's a Bride in the city I want its head on a spike. If there are silver-tongues in the taverns, I want them hanging from Heckle Gate. And if they're getting to your Talents then the corruption is spreading unchecked.'

The air between us had grown black and hard. I wasn't accusing her of anything, but the inference was clear enough. She took a slow breath, then relaxed.

'I shall make enquiries, captain,' Herono said. 'I am as invested as you are in the defence of the Range. I know the price we would all pay if the drudge were to prevail.'

Her glare dared me to argue. I didn't. Herono had fought the drudge for a decade, leading her fabled Blue Brigade in cavalry actions deep into the Misery, cutting down enemy patrols and destroying their attempts to erect outposts. Then came a day when the Blue Brigade fell, the men were slaughtered in the ambush and Herono captured. The torture she suffered took her eye and crippled her leg. The story of her escape was told over tavern tables across the states.

'My thanks, your grace. I'll leave an address with your

clerk. If any further information comes your way, I'd like to hear it,' I said. 'One other thing,' I said as I opened the door, 'Gleck Maldon served with the Blue Brigade for a time, didn't he?'

Herono nodded sadly. 'Gleck Maldon was a good man, and a brilliant Spinner. You and he were close, I understand.'

'Heard anything of him since he broke out of the Maud?'

'I wish that I had. It's a tragedy when a Spinner loses their mind. Especially one as talented as Gleck, but he always did like to push the boundaries.'

There was truth in that. I bowed, turned to go.

'Captain? I've always wondered. Marshal Venzer would gladly welcome you back as an officer, yet you reject the offer. Why choose this meagre existence, hunting bounties out in the muck?'

I didn't look back, but I paused in the doorway. Didn't have an answer for her.

'Good night, your grace.'

Stannard accompanied me back across the mill's work floor.

'If you think of coming here aggravating the prince again, my advice would be to think better of it. She has enough enemies out in the Misery,' the stocky old veteran said as the receptionist handed back my sword. Not exactly a threat, not exactly anything else either.

'Just a concerned citizen doing his part,' I said. I gave him a lazy smile, the kind that irritates the hell out of the unimaginative.

'Maybe you don't want to be so concerned. We veterans get mighty protective when it comes to our prince. You come poking around trying to stir up dirt, you won't see us coming. Do we have an understanding, old boy?'

I don't waste words on idiots. And we didn't.

7

Three hours after dawn I headed out to Willows, a false place full of false people. I visited the barbershop for a pretence at respectability before I crossed the artificial moat surrounding the enclave of Valengrad's ever-changing stock of nobility. Willows' boulevards were wide enough for a trio of carriages to pass, well swept and free of wild pigs and stray dogs. A man in smart livery moved down the road with a hand barrow and a spade, scooping up horse manure. Out in Willows even the shit shovellers looked the part.

Count Tanza's residence was a monstrosity of unnecessary buttresses and over-tended rose gardens. A fraught-looking butler saw me inside and asked whether he could take my sword. I said he didn't need to, but he cleared his throat and with a look made it clear that he wasn't going anywhere until it was in his possession. I wasn't sure what exactly I thought I was doing, paying a call on a count's sister, but I figured she owed me. She owed me for keeping her alive, she owed me because Nenn had taken a gut wound protecting her, and she owed me because she'd disappeared without a word twenty years ago and I should have been worth more to her than that. Should have been, but probably wasn't.

'I asked if she'd see you, but she didn't seem to hear me.' The butler looked like he was having a bad day, sweat stains around his collar and beneath his arms. 'If I'm honest, sir,

I don't think she's very well. Perhaps you can persuade her to see a physician?'

I had thought to find her abed, pale and possibly dying, but a night in an actual bed seemed to have done her some good. The dining room would have seated twenty-four people on each side of the table, maybe thirty if they were prepared to bump elbows. The walls sported portraits of broody ancestors in the frill-necked fashions of the past, while the phos lights were mounted in elaborate black iron chandeliers, suspended from the high ceiling. Glass panes were set into the ceiling to allow moonlight to filter down. Ezabeth sat directly beneath one of them, intent on a mess of papers strewn across the table. She wore a long white gown, golden brocade flowers glimmering across its surface, but still wore the same summer-blue hood and veil. Beneath the papers I saw the remains of a large breakfast – bones, rinds and crusts.

'It's good to see you up and about, lady,' I said, trying not to sound bitter. 'When you disappeared I feared for your safety.'

Ezabeth looked up at me, knuckled at her eye. I saw then that she was maimed, missing the fourth and fifth fingers of that hand. Must have been an old injury. Strange that I'd not noticed it in all the ride to Valengrad. I found it hard to focus on.

'Yes,' she said. 'I suppose you would have.'

Her eyes moved back to the papers on the table. I saw that there were lunar charts amongst them, some of them apparently torn from books. Mathematical calculations covered the pages, graphs and diagrams. A lot more complex than the little lunarism I'd studied at the university. I waited for her to say something else. Maybe to thank me for saving her life. Maybe to say that since we were no longer in mortal peril perhaps we should talk. She did neither. She seemed to have forgotten me.

71

'May I offer my thanks? For what you did, back at Station Twelve,' I found myself saying.

'What I did was idiotic,' she said without looking up. Her tone was flinty.

'You saved us,' I said.

'I doubt the commander shares your appreciation,' she said. She sat back in her chair, brushed her papers aside, sending a few sheets fluttering down to the floor. 'It's no use. I can't do it. I don't know enough without his papers, and they burned. So what am I to do now? Do you know? Do you?'

She stared at me intently, big eyes wide, full of passion. For a moment I wondered whether her spinning had driven her out of her mind. I'd never known anyone do anything like she had back at Twelve. Never even heard of it. If it hadn't driven her crazy then it probably should have.

'I don't know what you're talking about, lady,' I said.

'Of course you don't,' she said, attention immediately flitting back to the paperwork. She picked up an astronomical chart and held it up. 'I don't either, and I'm an expert. The expert. And I had his papers, and now they're all ash and I didn't even understand them when I had them. Where does that leave us?'

'That makes nothing clearer to me,' I said. I took a seat opposite her. She didn't seem to notice. She picked up a quill pen, dipped it in ink and began writing messily. Her hand left black ink smears across the page. There was something sad about the frantic urgency she wrote with.

'What papers were burned, lady?' I asked.

'It's what they all want to know,' she said. 'It's what the Darling was after. I can't tell you of course. Can't tell anybody yet. Don't want to make a fuss and a panic if I'm wrong. But I'm not wrong.'

She sniffed the air, squinted at me over her veil.

'Have you been drinking?' she asked. Shook her head

disdainfully. 'At this hour? How preposterous. What were you thinking, captain?'

I stared a hard moment. She didn't have to see the faces. Didn't have to smell the blood. Didn't see the Misery raise up the shade of a wife and children only to show you their dying moments every time it thought your guard was down, a ghost play repeated, over and over. She hadn't seen that.

I'd drink whenever I fucking wanted.

'Just small beer, lady,' I said, but I'd already lost her attention. I was lying, of course. It had been a dark beer, and then a brandy to round out the shakes. Still getting the Misery shakes, three days after we got out. Told myself that's what it was, anyway.

'I can't abide a drunk,' she said, shaking her head. She began to write some kind of mathematical formula alongside the observations she'd made, sketching in what I guessed represented lines of light weaving. The complexity was far beyond any calculations I could make. Ezabeth finished her page, stopped and stared at it for several moments. Then she made a snarling noise, feral as a wildcat, and tore the paper to pieces. She threw them in the air, let them rain down around her.

'I had them and now they're burned,' she declared angrily. 'I can't remember them. I don't remember them. So what now?'

Mad, then. Mad and angry with it, and powerful as a Battle Spinner. She was dangerous. They locked people in the Maud, Valengrad's asylum, if they posed a danger. Like Gleck Maldon, though it hadn't done much of a job of holding him. Maybe she'd end up there too. Time plays cruel games with us all. The carefree girl I'd once courted, my summer love, had been treated no kindlier by fate's hand than I, slapped this way and that and ending up bruised and broken. My heart leaned towards her. The little wisdom I possessed held me back.

73

'If I can offer a word of advice? You've been through a lot. Take some rest. Maybe have a drink yourself, get calm. Whatever you're working on, it can wait.'

She looked at me like I was mad, made a slightly crazy cackling sound, shook her head.

'Lessons from the drunk,' she said. 'I must make a point to write them down. Publish them in a memoir. Thank you, captain. If I need to know where to buy cheap brandy at this time of day, I shall be sure to ask.'

An angry retort swept to my lips ready to slam back against her. I caught it, trapped it in a held breath. In the end I just looked away in shame.

Ezabeth didn't seem to notice as I got up to leave. She said nothing, fixated on her papers, their equations and diagrams. I'd done what Crowfoot had asked of me, got her to Valengrad. I didn't see what use she was supposed to be, but he'd have his reasons. The Nameless don't share their plans, they just strike the tune for us to dance to.

I glanced back once. Shreds of angrily torn pages surrounded her, a good couple hundred marks worth of white scraps. I had nothing to say to her that she might want to hear. Whatever strange surge of boyhood fantasy had barked into my mind, the young girl who'd sung for me, who'd danced in the meadow, she was not this woman. A little piece of me retreated into the dark edges of my mind, let me harden up, raise my shield again. She was just another Spinner, and a mad one at that. My mission for Crowfoot was over.

Of course I knew, deep down, that it was never over. It never would be.

8

The sky was sobbing, long purrs of sharp, cold nightmare as the dawn broke. At least the rain had abated. I headed across town, cold beneath the great dark shadow cast by the Engine and set to getting the office back into shape. I had errands to run and bills to pay, so with the money I'd made from the sympathisers' heads I paid a carpenter and a few street kids to sort it out for me while I went out to mollify the banks I owed the most money. The money I'd taken from Herono was a guilty weight in my pocket that thcy wouldn't see any of. I'd asked the prince my questions but I still felt like I'd been bought off. It didn't matter. I owed Saravor half a fortune and I couldn't afford to get all righteous about it.

When I got back one of the kids had run off with a pewter candlestick, but it was worth less than I'd been planning to pay him. The carpenter fixed the leaks, the kids scrubbed the mould from the wall. Cheap labour. I paid out shares to Tnota and Wheedle, who'd I'd left behind at Twelve. Nenn's I kept. The court had paid well, but even with Herono's silver I was still a long way from making my first payment to Saravor. Most of what I kept I'd need to invest into another job.

I was drinking coffee. Coffee. Not even anything stronger in it. Just coffee. It didn't feel right.

Saravor was a problem. I didn't regret my choice, but

the consequences were suddenly pressing. The banks could hang for what I owed them as long as that monster was getting paid. With Nenn out of action and most of my usual hired hands in a mass grave at Station Twelve I needed manpower. I'd picked up a job, a dangerous one, but it needed the right kind of people.

I passed by the taverns frequented by out of work soldiers first. There tends to be a reason that a man can't find soldiering work in a place like the Range. An old man approached me for work, but he couldn't have restrained a puppy let alone a panicking deserter. I felt bad for him and bought him a drink. The next was a strong-looking woman but she was hiding a broken foot. If a woman can't run, she can't fight, and I told her so. She got angry and started fingering her dagger. When the blade came out things got ugly, furniture got broken and it was time to try a different tavern.

I ended up hitting the debtor's gaol to find fresh recruits. Doesn't seem fair to hire prisoners when there's free men looking for honest killing, but soldiers take on debts more often than they take on an enemy, and gambling breaks a man's fortune more often than it makes it. I found ten men with experience willing to have their shares paid against their debts. Some of them even had experience in the Misery.

'We have work to do,' I told Tnota as the week drew to a close. He was carving a little image of his god into the table in my office. 'Gather everyone up. No firearms. Ready to ride in the hour.'

'Where are we getting the horses?'

'Prince Herono is providing them but she wants Blackwing arses on the saddles. She's keeping the citadel out of it.'

'She doesn't trust the Iron Goat's men not to squeal?' Tnota grouched.

'It's a big fish and she wants it landed properly. They'd only fuck it up.'

I shrugged the dust jackets from a suit of half armour. Considered putting it on. A close inspection showed me that a couple of the straps needed replacing. Poor-fitting armour is worse than no armour at all in most situations.

'We need new kit,' I said.

'Ask your boss for another aid parcel,' Tnota said. 'Maybe a diamond tiara, or a priceless vase. A prize concubine. Whatever he thinks we can sell.'

'I will if he ever shows up.'

'Big Dog says he paid you a visit not long ago. Maybe diverted us to Station Twelve, when we should have been headed home and clear,' Tnota said. He didn't look at me, kept on scratching at the table. 'Think it was worth it?'

I thought of Nenn. Thought of what I'd bought her and the price that I'd yet to pay for it. I had no idea how I was going to find one hundred thousand marks.

'What's anything worth? Come on. We're going to marry a Bride to an axe.'

When going into a job that might prove dangerous, a prudent captain sends the new boys in first.

The sledgehammer smashed the padlock from the trapdoor, splintering the boards. Two new recruits kicked the bar aside and clattered down into the brightly lit cellar as startled shrieks and fearful cries rose from below. I let six men and women go down ahead of me, a noble vanguard leading the way. The steps creaked beneath my weight, but I didn't draw the cutlass from my belt. Too many naked swords down there for my liking already, and not the kind I enjoyed holding.

Twelve worshippers squealed, naked and frantic as they cowered back against the cellar's gloomy walls. Light tubes running around the ceiling were set low, but phos light is always pale, waxy and never sensual. They wore prayer charms wound around their arms and legs, hiding nothing.

Some of them were still upright, though the abrupt arrival of heavily armed soldiers was wilting them to flaccidity. The women tried to cover themselves, save one who sprawled languorously across cushions and rugs in all her flabby splendour. She dominated the cellar with her vastness, skin tiger-striped with stretch marks as it sought to contain its pulsating contents. She smiled. My nose was plugged with wax and cotton but I'd still have been stupid to look into that smile.

Sexual appetite rose in me at once. The Bride's size spoke of health and fertility rather than gluttony and morbidity. The sweat dripping beneath her heaving arms was sweet and energising, the rolls of flesh around her neck guarded a throat from which a sensual, droning buzz began to emanate. She'd singled me out as the largest, the most powerful of her assailants and she wanted me. If I'd been able to smell her sugar and cinnamon odour I'd have been well in her grasp. It was a struggle not to throw myself onto her as it was.

The Bride's head exploded into halves as Wheedle hewed through it with an axe. She flailed her sausage-finger hands at him and he got angry as he cut one away. The babbling droning sound continued until he fully decapitated her, but her body kicked and swung its weeping stump around a good minute longer. As her death throes subsided, Wheedle, red and wet, grinned at me and raised up the largest bit of head by its lice-ridden hair. I adjusted the problem that had been developing in my trousers and gave him a nod. He'd earned an extra share by taking on the most dangerous job, but with Nenn laid up he'd really been the only choice.

'By the spirits, what right have you to be here? What have you done?' one of the men demanded, feigning panicked fury as he tried to drag the prayer cloths from his arms. He was tall and lean, his beard elaborately curled with oils and ribbons, black hair receding halfway across his head. There were six other men and five women, most of them tanned the amber of Pyre. There were a lot of sad guts and saggy tits on display. None of them would have fetched more than a few grinnies in a brothel.

'You'll be Count Digada,' I said as my men hemmed the cavorters up against the brickwork. I pulled the nose plugs out, but regretted it at once. The Bride's smell was still thick in the air, though it was rapidly turning sour. There wasn't much in the cellar, a collection of old furniture had been pushed up against the walls to make room for their antics and some kind of sigil inscribed across the floor. The count tried to grab some breeches but Wheedle backed him up with a poke of his sword. Everybody not in my employ looked set to shit themselves. I hoped they wouldn't, if only so I wouldn't have to smell it. The cellar had a hot, sweaty stink, too many human juices mixing. It was nauseating and, sadly, not the first time I'd broken my way into this kind of cesspit.

'What in the name of the Alliance do you think you're doing? Who are you? I shall have the marshal drag you all up in ropes and hanged from the Heckle Gate, I tell you, hanged!'

He was a tall man, but I was taller and broader by far. The steel I was wearing probably didn't hurt my powers of intimidation either and he cringed back away from me.

'Threats would be more impressive if we hadn't just had to cut a Bride into pieces. You're all under arrest as Dhojaran sympathisers, and for practising rites of the illegal Cult of the Deep. I count a dozen hangings coming up, unless anyone wants to save us the bother and just get it over with now? Count, how about you?'

I hooked my thumbs through my belt, let him see how absolutely few fucks I gave about his threats.

'We couldn't resist! The marshal will grant mercy, won't he? I only did it for the sex!' A southerner sobbed his bullshit to uncaring ears. There are always more sympathisers amongst the southerners. The Deep Kings hadn't managed to get their armies down into Fraca yet, but they had missionaries there proclaiming their rule was the true coming of divinity. The Deep Kings sure as the hells weren't human but they understood what bent men to their will.

'Yeah, you're just a poor victim of a cultist sex party,' I said. 'Far as Venzer's concerned, cultists are traitors. And traitors get stretched.'

They knew they'd fucked themselves good and proper, but it was hard not to feel sorry for them. Without the Bride's influence they were just so many sweating, middle-aged fools. But once the Bride got her passions into someone, they could never truly go back. Eventually, they'd start seeking out a new cult, a new Bride to fulfil their longing.

The Brides were the Deep Kings' favoured way of recruiting spies within our cities. They started out looking like young women – had probably originally been young women – and slowly they built their network of lovers. The magic of the Bride is more addictive than white-leaf, the draw stronger than pollen. The men brought their friends, and she gradually became part preacher, part sexual predator. As the Bride's influence grew, so she swelled in body. This one had been fat as a house – she'd been operating a while. Long enough to get hold of a count.

'You can't do this,' Count Digada protested. But I could, and we were.

'Cry it to the marshal, if he even turns up to watch you swing,' I said. One of the women hissed at me, but she made me sad, not angry. The Bride was only part of their ruin. The men she took knew what she was, but even in her grasp they needn't have brought their wives, their daughters into this. I could hate the men who could warp a woman's mind this way, but the women just seemed like victims. I shook my head as I gave the orders. 'Don't clothe them. Leave the prayer strips on their arms and legs. March them through the streets. The marshal wants examples made.'

My crew of killers rounded them up and began to lead them out one by one, a trail of wasted human life. What an irony that I'd found most of my new recruits in the city gaol.

Prince Herono and Stannard were waiting for me as I came out of the cellar last. The prince leaned on her cane, her man on the haft of a poleaxe. We were two miles from the city, a short ride out into the countryside, a big old farm house the count had purchased for his orgies. The naked cultists were going to get cold on the walk back to Valengrad, but it wasn't an unpleasant evening. The midges rising from the long grass were probably going to trouble them more.

'I trust that you are happy with the result, captain?' Herono asked. I gave a bow, and for once, I meant it. I owed Herono a mental apology. The half-empty mill had made me suspicious. I didn't doubt her loyalty any more. Taking down a Bride was a huge win for us. My only regret was that Herono would be claiming most of the bounty. Maybe I'd been doing this too long if I'd started seeing enemies amongst our greatest heroes.

'We got the big fish. Where did you get the information?'

'I had some of my people investigate Lesse's husband, an artilleryman. He'd come up from Station Four just a short time before Lesse left my employ. I found his connection to Count Digada.'

'Had to put a couple of his maids to the question to get it out of them, but they squealed in the end,' Stannard said. He slapped his fist against his palm, a man who enjoyed his work. Herono's scarred face was as blank and dry as the Misery.

'A cruelty, but one that has yielded great results.'

'It's good to see the circle closed. Doesn't often feel like we're winning out here on the Range, but today we took something back.'

Money is money, whatever the cut you take. I was scraping my way to making the first payment to Saravor. If things continued this well I'd not only still have my eyes at the year's end, but Blackwing might just keep the Range standing a little longer as well.

9

Tnota lived a handful of streets over from me in Mews. The rain soaked me through as I half dragged, half carried him along the road, feet stumbling, swaying left and right with half a keg of brandy inside me, the other half inside him. It wasn't late, but I tried to look alert all the same. Through my staggering and Tnota's stumbling I doubt it was convincing. Still, I got him home, found another Fracan man in his apartment who didn't speak Dort, and he helped me carry Tnota inside. Tnota often had one or more of his countrymen staying, whether they were family passing through or casual fucks I didn't know and he never spoke about them. We laid him out in his bed, surrounded by dozens of long-faced wooden statues that had a roughly canine cast to their features. He collected them, these reminders of his far-away southern country, buying them up wherever he found them as if he intended to return them all to their rightful place in Fraca one day.

'No buggery while he's asleep,' I warned the young Fracan man, but he didn't understand me, and I figured I hadn't much choice but to leave him there.

I swaggered off home, finding that the rain had driven all of the late-night pie hawkers inside and I couldn't get any ballast for my stomach. I climbed the stairs to my own third-storey apartment, noting the small, damp footprints on the stairs that preceded mine. It looked like some kid had gone up ahead of me, but there were no kids living in the tenement that I knew of. If that Darling had shown up again I'd box its ears and put a blade between its eyes, said my drunk brain, quite incapable of worrying about my capacity to do that sober, let alone drunk, and so I put a hand to the hilt of my ten-inch knife as I tried to move quietly up the stairs. Creeping isn't easy when you're my size, and once you put a bottle and a half of Dortmark's worst brandy behind it. I might as well have strapped kettles all over my body and danced a jig. I made it to the top of the stairs making slightly less noise than a volley of cannon fire and found that all my words had left me.

I don't know where she'd got the stool from. My apartment was the only one along this hall and it wasn't my stool. Made me think she'd been there a while. I couldn't exactly recognise her on account of the mask and hood over her face, but I recognised those all right. Egglebat? Ezalda? Something like that. Her name wasn't forthcoming through my fog of booze.

'Why are you sitting there?' I asked. A slight puddle had formed beneath her as the water slid from the double thick rain cloak around her shoulders. Dark eyes watched me in the pale tube-light. 'I don't have your carriage.'

The woman stood up.

'You're drunk,' she said.

'And you're in the way,' I said, my inability to easily find words indicating that she was entirely right. I staggered across to the door and tried to find my key in my pockets, which proved much harder than I'd anticipated.

'It's open already,' Ezzraberta or Enerva said. 'Perhaps you forgot to lock up.' She turned the handle and showed me that this was indeed the case.

'Don't you go opening my door,' I said. Even to me it sounded ridiculous, and I was the drunk one. I walked hard into the door frame as I blundered into the depressing little

84

kingdom of crap that I'd accumulated over the years.

My apartment wasn't much to look at, or be in, or live in for that matter. Bedroom, kitchen, reception room – they all roll together into one, but at least the privy had its own room. I was aware of the smell as I stepped inside, of old wet clothes and unwashed crockery, the bitter odour of damp on the walls. I didn't spend much time here, truth be told. A leak in the roof was dripping water onto the stained wooden floor, but I had too much of a drunk on me to care. It was probably like that every night. Fuckin' leaks ev'rywhere these days.

'A nice place,' Eggleton said.

'Pro'lly not what you're used to,' I said. I had forgotten why she was there. Had she told me why she was there? Probably? Hard to tell. Maybe it was for sex. I doubted I'd be any use to her. Maybe she'd brought me some more brandy.

'I need to talk to you,' she said curtly, stepping into the apartment and trying not to touch anything.

'You can talk, just so long as you don't mind me sleeping,' I said. I staggered over to the bed, sat down and started trying to get one of my boots off.

'This is important,' she said. 'Vitally important.'

'Sleep's important,' I said. Bloody boots, why do they make them so hard to remove?

'I can't abide a drunk,' the short woman said with a voice that snapped at me like a whip. Why was this boot so difficult to get off? I was sure I'd taken boots off before without so much trouble.

'Best piss off then,' I said. Rude of me. Wait, had I invited her in? Beneath that veil she was prettier than all the hells. I was being rude. Tried to think of some words that would set things right, but she was coming towards me. She moved slowly, like I was some kind of skittish animal that might snap at her. Didn't say a whole lot for me, I guess. My boots had got tangled in my sword belt as I took it off. Why had I only taken it half off at first? I pressed my fingers against my eyes, feeling the full unpleasantness of being too drunk to function. Small, gentle fingers pressed against my forehead.

'This might sting a bit.'

It probably would have stung a damn sight more if I hadn't been so out of my skull, and since a moment later I was sober as day, it did hurt a damn sight more. I saw a brilliant white-gold light, as if a six-spun light tube had been illuminated right before my eyes, brilliant even through closed eyelids. A fire seemed to pass through me, a venom of heat that rushed down and then back up, and then I shuddered and fell back onto the bed. Caught my head on the wall as well, and it was the sharp pain of that which made me realise that Ezabeth Tanza had just sobered me up completely.

'What the fuck did you just do?' I said. My mouth was coated with the flavour of brandy, but somehow it tasted like vomit.

'Good. Thinking straight again now?' Ezabeth took a step back, hands planted on her hips. No more than five feet tall but somehow she filled the room with her presence. Beneath the heavy rain cloak I saw she wore a blue dress. Suddenly dry-brained as a holy sister, I wanted to take her veil off so that I could see her face.

'You just made me sober?' I asked. Ezabeth was checking a small steel device strapped to her belt. It looked a lot like a drinking canteen, but I knew it as a phos canister, home to a portable battery coil.

'It will take me two nights of spinning to replenish all the phos I just wasted getting your brain working.' She sounded annoyed, but I hadn't asked her to do it. I had no idea that a Spinner could use light to do that. Always surprising what Spinners can do, though. I estimated the amount of phos she'd just burned on me to be worth a little over two thousand marks. Spun light wasn't cheap. She had my attention.

It must have been a while since I'd seen this place sober. If I hadn't known better I'd have figured I felt suddenly ashamed of the shit-sty I lived in. The sink held a series of unwashed dishes and old scraps of food – inedible pie crusts, mouldering heels of bread, a bowl of what was either unwanted soup or something else reproduced as vomit – littered the surfaces. The bed linen probably hadn't been changed in a year. Maybe more. It all stank.

'Why are you here?'

'I need your help. Are you sober enough to talk, now?'

'I think you've seen to that,' I said. I got up from the bed, crossed to the tap and pumped it a couple of times. Up on the roof the barrel was getting filled by all the rain and I got a good stream of it into a cup. Seemed a strange thing to be drinking water at this time of the night. 'Why don't you take off that veil? It can't be all that comfortable,' I suggested. I was thinking of her comfort. Nothing to do with my desire to see her face again. Nothing at all.

She hesitated.

'I might not look as you remember me,' she said.

'It's not like I memorised your face,' I said, though the reverse was true. Briefly as I'd seen it, I'd have been able to paint her in oils if I'd needed to. If I could paint, which I couldn't. I wanted to see her again. As she reached up to unclasp it I thought I detected a brief trembling in her fingers. She drew it back, and looked precisely as she had back at Station Twelve. As she had twenty-four years ago. A vision, the sweetness of perfect youth and elegance com-bined. I had to hold down the sound that fought to rise in my throat, fight the longing that welled in me. I swallowed it. She was close to my age but could have passed for the sixteen-year-old who had sat across the table from me all those years ago. For a moment she seemed concerned, and then she relaxed.

'Thank you,' she said, 'it is nice to be able to remove it once in a while.' She pushed back her hood as well revealing flowing chestnut waves of hair, shining with vitality. No wonder she'd captured my heart so completely when we were just kids. It was as if the years hadn't touched her in the slightest, not a single grey hair, not a line. She took a seat at my table after pushing a sweat-stained old shirt onto the floor.

'Why do you wear it at all?'

She hesitated again.

'A courtly fashion. Modesty is preferred in high society.' A courtly fashion thirty years out of date, maybe. My grandmother had worn one, but I hadn't been paying much attention to corsets and codpieces lately.

'What do you need?'

'I'm looking for Gleck Maldon. I'm told you knew him.' She didn't beat around the bush. That surprised me.

'I knew him,' I said.

'Know, or knew?'

'Knew,' I said. 'He's dead.'

Ezabeth's expression, tightly controlled until now, gave the tiniest sag.

'You know that for certain?'

'When he first got loose they sent me after him. Offered a lot of money if I could get him back and I was looking anyway. But, he isn't here and he didn't travel in any direction that has a road, so that only leaves east. And if he went east then he's dead. What are you, some kind of lunatic-hunter sent to try to bring him back to the Maud? Send a Spinner to catch a Spinner?'

'No,' she said. She paused, frowning. 'I was assisting him with his research. I need to find him.'

'Well good luck with that,' I said. 'They asked me to find

him, and I turned over every brick and rock I could think of. You want my opinion? He probably blasted himself to ash trying to escape the Maud.' I took long, hardening gulps of water. It tasted metallic, chemical, the taint of the purifiers.

'He was your friend?'

I sighed, leaned back. My head was starting to stab. The light burn she'd effected on me had taken away the intoxication and left me with the damned hangover.

'Out here, on the frontier, sometimes people are more than just friends. Gleck was the Battle Spinner assigned to my battalion when I served under the marshal. He was a cocky, snub-nosed git. Older than me, and he didn't like that I'd been put in charge. But you get a respect for someone once they save your arse a few times, and we did that. I left the army and became Blackwing and sometimes you need a Spinner. Gleck was like living artillery for hire, but he didn't need the money. Just liked to blow shit up. Best Battle Spinner in Valengrad. Or was, before his mind went. I could see the cracks forming, over the last two years. Saw him less and less.'

'I'm sorry for your friend,' Ezabeth said. She was one of those rare people able to express sympathy and genuinely feel it.

'We're all sorry for something,' I said. 'What were you helping him with?'

Ezabeth knuckled her lips with her three-fingered glove. She looked over at me and her eyes were asking whether I could be trusted. I wanted that trust. Needed it.

'You don't have to tell me,' I said.

'I understand that you're a Blackwing captain, for whatever that's worth,' she said. 'You were a soldier before that. Your whole life is dedicated to defending the Range.'

'It's how my cards fell,' I said. 'I just play the hand.'

She snorted at that.

'I have information vital to the defence of the Range. Or

the lack of it. Or I did, before I lost it. Months of work. The calculations alone took me half a year.' She began muttering to herself, counting things off on her fingers. I let her ramble a few moments. She no longer seemed aware of where she was or who she was with. It had been this way with Gleck. If she wasn't cracked already, she wasn't an ocean away from it.

'What if I were to tell you that Nall's Engine no longer functions?' she asked abruptly.

The cold of the apartment suddenly felt deeper, harder. My whole body went rigid and all I could do was stare at her. She waited, brows drawn seriously. I sat back in my chair.

'I'd say that you were a heretic,' I said. 'And if I heard it on the street I'd send you to the white cells on sedition charges.'

'Maldon discovered it first. He came to me because he'd read some of my early work, my thesis on light refractors. Mine and my brothers,' she said. She stood and walked to the dirt-caked window. Looked out at the city lights glowing blue and red through the darkness. 'Do you know how many battery coils it takes to activate something like Nall's Engine?'

'You'd have to ask someone in the Order of Aetherial Engineers,' I said.

'I did, and they lied. Gleck had managed to get his hands on the original schematics. It takes seven hundred and twelve thousand fully charged coils. Making those calculations alone took us half a year. I lost them all at Station Twelve.' It was her turn to scowl. 'I cannot recreate them alone.'

I shrugged.

'So what?'

'For the last six years the Order was only supplied with one hundred and twelve thousand battery coils. A fraction of the power required to activate it.'

I didn't like where she was going with this. I hadn't been joking when I'd mentioned cells. This was the kind of prime treason that Doomsayer cults came out with. Valengrad was a fragile colony, beset by a wailing sky and the smell of the tainted sands. It bred pessimism and conspiracy. But my mind was dragged back to the empty looms at Herono's mill. I recalled the chain across the operating room door at Station Twelve and the dim corridors. I rubbed at dry, stinging eyes. I was too tired for this. I had enough problems just now.

'And why do you think they'd be doing that?' I said.

'Why does anyone do anything?' Ezabeth said. 'Profit? Greed? The princes work the mill Talents until their minds shatter like glass. And for what? For light tubes? For ovens? For water purifiers? They justify it by claiming that it's all for the Engine. That only a tiny fraction of the phos goes into the public services. But they're producing it, across the states, and it's not coming here.'

'You have proof, or is this just speculation?'

She faltered. Squared her shoulders.

'Before he disappeared, Gleck sent me a message. Incomprehensible, nonsensical in places, babble about disproving a paradox. He'd uncovered something about the Engine but refused to put it in writing. He disappeared the day after he wrote it. I have to find him.'

I was at war with myself.

I remembered this woman as a young girl, carefree, light on her toes. Only an echo of her remained, but the young man that had dreamed of her was still somewhere within me. At the same time a greater shadow bent its wings over me. I was Blackwing, or I was nothing. It was the choice I had made. I'd sent men to the gallows for less treasonous claims than Ezabeth was making.

To be Blackwing didn't mean wearing a uniform and following someone else's rules. Blackwing meant following my instinct. My instinct was telling me to listen.

If she was right then it went far beyond abuse of a few thousand Talents. If she was right then Nall's Engine itself was unarmed, unpowered and useless. It meant that we were defenceless and the Deep Kings had nothing to fear. It meant that Dortmark's Grand Alliance was well and truly gracked if the enemy ever chose to look in our direction. Crowfoot and the Lady of Waves could not stand against six Deep Kings, not alone.

'Who else knows about this?'

'When Range Marshal Venzer arrives back in the city tomorrow, a meeting of the Council of Masters of the Order of Aetherial Engineers will be held. We shall see what they say then.' She shook her head. 'It has taken this long just to get them to agree to meet us. A moat of bureaucracy denies me.'

A treacherous voice rose from my gut, demanded that I help her. The more reasoned part of my brain came down on it hard, insisting that she was spouting sedition and indulging her wasn't going to make it any better. I asked myself how I would have responded had anyone else turned up making the same wild, dangerous claims.

'You will get yourself hanged,' I said. 'I didn't drag you all the way here so that I could be the one to do it. I owe you for what you did back at Station Twelve but that's not a licence for heresy.'

Ezabeth dismissed that as only an idealist can. She'd been hiding it well but I sensed then that she was still frantic, simmering with energy and a desire to act.

'The mill Talents are suffering. Even while we talk, they bleed and wither and die,' Ezabeth said. She began buttoning her cloak closed with sharp little movements, ready to face the rain again. 'I must find Maldon. If you learn anything, if you find anything out, please, contact me. You will find me at Willows.'

She left me. I dimmed the light tubes and lay back on my

revolting bed. I'd kept calm on the outside but my heart was thumping louder than a broadside beneath my ribs. The chain. Every time I closed my eyes, there was that damned chain across the operating room door. Gleck hadn't been the same for months, even before they'd declared he was mad. Even before he'd set fire to that tailor's shop. What had he learned? What did he know?

Then there was the second problem. How in the name of the spirits of mercy did you go to sleep when you were sober?

10

A thumping at my door told me why I was no longer asleep. I hate the sound of a fist against the door. I figure that one day Death herself is going to come wake me up that way, just to make me go through the torment of waking up before I die. I figure she'd be that kind of arsehole.

A message runner dropped me a note and then scarpered. Range Marshal Venzer was back and wanted to see me. About bloody time. I pulled on my best clothes, which wasn't to say that they were good but the shirt was mostly white, the leather waistcoat didn't have too many holes and the breeches almost matched the stockings. Nothing the court would call fashionable. Even a mercenary has to have standards.

The citadel is an immense structure that dominates the city, part of the great curtain wall that encompasses slums, wealth and parade grounds alike and shields us from the edge of the Misery. Venzer's citadel is the heart of the Range, and beneath it lies the crackling heart of Nall's Engine. The citadel is a symbol of defiance, of ingenuity, of magic twisted into machinery, and there are far too many steps on the way to Venzer's offices.

'You don't want to go in there.' Venzer's bodyguard stopped me at the door. He was a Battle Spinner, heavy light canisters strapped to his belt.

'Do I look like I'm paying a social call?'

'You look like shit,' the guard said. Venzer's Spinners fell outside the normal chain of command. Being able to draw power from moonlight was a pretty big deal, but to be honest being a well-regarded baker was a bigger deal than being Captain of Nobodies.

'Can't argue with that. Who's in there?'

The Spinner curled his lip.

'Lady of Waves is who.'

Even though it was just a name, it sent a shiver down my back.

'You tweaking my tail?' I asked. He shook his head, face blackly serious.

Along the Range there were maybe a couple of hundred lesser sorcerers, not counting the indentured Talents at work in the mills. Somehow they were all running head-long into my life. The Lady of Waves never left her island citadel on Pyre, and since Cold and Songlope were dead and Shallowgrave and Nall had vanished years ago, she and Crowfoot were the last of the Nameless. And here I was, only separated from the stranger of the two by a wall and some oak.

'Here's something I've always wondered,' the Spinner mused. 'Why do they call them Nameless when they got names?'

'You think those are their real names?' I asked. 'You think that someone called their kid Crowfoot when he was born? Or Shallowgrave? They don't have names. Those are just things we call them.'

'Everyone has a name,' the Spinner grouched, but I'd won the point. Made me feel slightly better. I looked down at the tattoo on my arm, the raven nestled amongst all the ordinary inks. The skin there was peeling, like it was re-covering from sunburn. The raven was nearly his full dark again.

When the call came for me to enter, I'd been debating

making an excuse and legging it back down the over-long stairs. It had only been the Spinner's snide expression that kept my feet planted.

The Iron Goat was slouched in a chair twice as wide as he needed. I'd seen him stiff-backed at attention for formal inspections and parades, but on the whole Venzer didn't stand on ceremony. He'd come up through the ranks in the days when the fighting on the front was at its hottest, when officer training meant a five-week vacation in the college before an inevitable and unpleasant death on the front lines. He'd broken the walls at Viteska, and had escaped Shavada's clutches when the Deep King led a legion to pursue him halfway across the Misery. But for all that the grand prince had heaped the marshal with the gold and jewels they mined in the colonies out to the west, he was still the muddy-boots and bloody-moods soldier who'd signed up as a private. He might be missing some fingers, half an ear and most of the teeth on the left side of his face, but none of us stay pretty for ever. Some of us don't even start that way.

Venzer had a big metal cup in his hand. I guessed that whatever he was drinking it probably wasn't milk. He looked tired. Worse, exhausted. I wondered whether he'd slept. The wide desk was littered with stacks of papers, log books, ledgers, a plate of untouched food, a paper knife jammed point first into the wood. The clutter lacked Venzer's usual austere particularity. Despite his maiming and the age that had wrinkled and leathered every scrap of skin, the marshal usually had a fearsome vitality about him. When Venzer strode through an autumn forest, you expected a wind to follow in his wake casting leaves into the air. The same bright intelligence lurked in his eyes but the flesh was drained. I'd seen healthier-looking Talents wired into their seats at the mill.

Fucking wizards. Bastards will do that to you, I guess.

'Don't worry. She's gone,' the marshal said. His voice

96

was half-slurred, a result of his flapping lips and toothless gums. One story went that a horse had kicked them out, another claimed a Darling's spell had ricocheted into his face. The Dhoja had tried to take him alive on more than one occasion. They'd even sent Shavada himself, and the Deep Kings don't often risk themselves in the Misery. Our living legend was a sorry sight that morning despite his oversized, red-brimmed hat. I'd never seen him without that hat. It had become more of a symbol of his position than the medals hanging from his epaulettes.

'Gone?' I asked. Venzer nodded.

'She never stays long. Hates to leave her island even for a few heartbeats. Count yourself lucky you don't have to deal with her too, Galharrow. Nothing good ever comes from it.'

I didn't say anything, but I nodded. Only a handful of people knew the truth of my relationship with Crowfoot. To the common populace, Blackwing were monster hunters and enforcers, investigators with a special licence to root out corruption and cauterise the wound. Men to be feared, but just men. What else would they believe? I had only trusted a scant handful with the truth. Venzer, Nenn, Tnota and Maldon understood how deep Crowfoot's claws lay into my flesh. I'd only met four of the other six captains. I could live without meeting the other two.

Venzer waved me into a chair and pointed towards the half-empty bottle on the table. I thanked him and poured a draught of bright yellow liquid, thick as milk.

'Apricot hard-wine,' Venzer said. 'Seventy marks a shot. The Prince of Whitelande sent me two dozen bottles of the stuff. He doesn't send me the soldiers I need, but he sends me alcohol.'

'Well, at least it's something.'

The Range Marshal chuckled, knocked back the spirit. He was at ease with me, as I was with him. We'd known each other a long time.

'I believe that congratulations are in order. Prince Herono informs me that you dealt with a Bride in my absence. I knew there was one somewhere, though I'd not have expected it of Digada. Always seemed such a sensible, bland man.'

'A dead man, now.'

'It's not a good living, out here, is it?' Venzer mused. Despite the bad blood and the mistakes that had separated us, he still spoke to me as an equal.

'Never was, probably never will be,' I acknowledged. The marshal sat more upright in his chair.

'I should have retired years ago,' he said. 'I have estates in four principalities, all of them run by my sons. Young men now, I suppose, but I haven't seen any of them since they were boys. If you lined them up, I wouldn't know which was which.'

Maudlin, drunk old men embarrass themselves. I tried to move to business.

'You received my report?' I asked.

'I read it. I heard all about it at Station Twelve, too. Made a good show of yourself, they tell me.'

'I killed some drudge.'

'Of course you did. These are black times, Galharrow, when Darlings think they can creep into our fortresses and slaughter my men. Black, dark times.'

'Why was the Engine's operating room chained?' I said. I couldn't hold the question back. 'There were drudge attacking the Range and the Engine had been put beyond use. Why?'

'On my orders,' Venzer said. 'And you would find the same at every station along the Range.'

'With all due respect, sir, why in the spirits-damned hells would you order that?'

Venzer sighed, rubbed at knuckles that had been warped by age.

'You are a rarity, Galharrow. You are a man who chooses to perform the worst of tasks in the Misery. Hunting down deserters, hanging sympathisers. Tearing husbands from weeping wives, cutting the heads from monsters. And you refuse every bit of aid that I offer you. You could be financed properly, you know that. I've offered you a salary, staff, an office within the citadel. No more chasing bounties just to keep your head above water.'

Spirits knew I needed the money. More than I ever had before. But there are promises you make to yourself, vows you place your pride in. Some things are worth the struggle.

'You offer it every time I see you,' I said.

'Yes, and you spit it back in my face every time.' Venzer pointed a finger at me. 'And all because you won't wear a uniform. Did it ever occur to you that Blackwing would better serve the republic without relying on mercenary bounties?'

'I've been part of the war machine before,' I said. 'We both know how that turned out. Not so well for me, or for Torolo Mancono. Or his wife, or his children. Blackwing gets by.' We were treading dry old ground, stepping between old footprints. I'd sooner be damned than have to take orders from princes again. 'What does this have to do with Station Twelve?'

'What did you make of Station Twelve's commander, Jerrick?' Venzer asked. 'A competent man? Selfless? Hardy?'

'Incompent. A glutton. A fool.'

'Though the Spirit of Mercy bids us speak well of the dead, the best that I can say about him is that he is dead and now I can put someone else in his place,' Venzer said. 'Would it surprise you to know that Jerrick bought his position? Of course not. Your father bought you a battalion, after all. The princes send me their bastards and their nieces, their fifth-born simpletons and their least capable cousins. I cannot trust the operation of Nall's Engine to their twitching fingers. One false activation could be a disaster, I don't have to tell you that. So I put the Engine beyond their use. They have communicators. In the face of a full assault the Engine is operated from here, from the heart of the Engine. I trust no other to throw the firing lever.'

It made a significant amount of good sense. That was the thing about Venzer. He made things work, even if he was building with slops and straw.

'That was not Nall's design,' I said. Venzer grunted.

'Nall is gone. If he deigns to return then he can put me right. Until then, the Range is mine to defend.' The Iron Goat may not have liked the Nameless, but he was not intimidated by them. One of the few men in the world that wasn't. 'Now, what do you know about this proposition Ezabeth Tanza is putting forward later today at the council meeting?' Of all the questions I'd expected him to ask, this wasn't one. He should have wanted to know more about the little bastard Darling. He should have been eager to learn about Ezabeth Tanza's conflagration and how we'd avoided losing a Range station by the narrowest of margins.

'It's none of my business,' I said. Which was true.

'I understand that she came to visit you last night,' Venzer said.

'You got a tail on her? Why?'

'If I wanted you to ask questions of me, I'd have tossed you this hat when you came in. I ask them, you answer. She came to your apartment?'

It was rare that Venzer showed me this face. He hadn't pulled rank on me in years, not since I'd bloodied the nose of a brigadier in a street brawl and he'd had to pull me up for it. I put it down to the bruise-like hollows beneath his eyes and the meeting he'd just endured with the Lady of Waves. Coming face to face with a wizard will make anyone's head ache, and the Lady wasn't as easy to bear as Nall. Nall had always been the best of them in my mind, meaning that when he dealt with his enemies the torture only lasted a day or two. Since he'd disappeared, by all accounts the last two Nameless had become worse. Some said they were going mad.

Venzer's questions were quick, basic, clean, just the way he ran his army. I felt like some low-grade leaf pusher getting shaken down for information. What did she want? What did she talk about? How long did she stay? Did she mention anything to do with her work? Why did she seek me out?

I hadn't walked into the office intending to cover for her. Blackwing I might be, but Venzer was the Range Marshal and he outranked anyone short of a prince, and even they bowed to his superior wisdom where the Range was concerned. Ezabeth threatened that. If I was going to drop in the ditch it needed to be now.

I gave him nothing.

'She may just be a middle-rate university academic, but she's still a Spinner, and she's dangerous,' Venzer said when he ran out of questions. 'I fear the light blindness that took Maldon has broken Ezabeth Tanza's mind too. She's fomenting unrest, causing trouble, getting the wrong people angry. If she manages to spread her mistaken rumours there'll be rioting in the streets. A panic. She's half mad, or maybe all mad, but she's related to Prince Herono so I can't just lock her away without good reason. If she comes to you again, for anything, let me know. Will you do that for me, Galharrow?'

'You want information about Darlings in your Range stations, call on me. If it's pretty girls you want to know about, there's madams on Silk Street can help you out. I have work to do.'

Venzer watched me coldly.

'When I first rose to command, Blackwing captains were respected. Well-connected officers aspired to carry the iron seal. Now? You, Silpur, Vasilov – you're all glorified heads-men.'

I rose from my seat. I wasn't dismissed yet, but I hadn't anything more to say. The Iron Goat waited a few moments before waving me away.

'You've fallen a long way,' he said coldly as I turned the door handle. 'Do you regret your choices, when you're between bottles?'

'When you realise the mountain you've been climbing is just a heap of shit, the fall doesn't feel so far.'

As I pulled at the door a communicator operator burst through. He paid me no heed, gave no salute or care for rank as he rushed to Venzer's desk and began unwinding a great long strip of communicator paper, marked with dashes, dots and clicks. The clerk was a southerner with the cast of Pyre, but his skin had turned paler than mine, a gleaming sheen of sweat slicking it.

'See? See?' the operator stammered.

'Yes, yes it's a message, I can see that,' Venzer said angrily. 'A bloody long one. What does it say?'

'It's from Marshal Wechsel, at Station Three-Six,' he said. 'Kings have entered the Misery. Deep Kings, two of them! Shavada and Philon are heading west, with an army.'

Venzer peered past me to where worried-looking clerks were trying to look into the room. 'Summon the Command Council at once. I don't care if they're sleeping, shitting or fucking their horses, get them here now.'

11

Kids these days are jumpier than hell.

Venzer's Command Council leaked more than my roof, so I got it all the details from one mouth or another. The drudge had started to occupy the old settlements in their half of the Misery in numbers we hadn't seen in two decades. They were planning something. Something big. Exaggerated reports counted a hundred thousand warriors, and even more dubious scouts' reports said they were trying to build a road. Worse, they confirmed that both Philon and Shavada were there in person. It had been a long time since any of the Deep Kings were willing to risk venturing so deep into the Misery.

For two days, that meant that we had to endure something akin to panic in the streets.

Everything would be fine. We had the Engine to protect us. The drudge could do what they wanted out there in the sand and play at laying a road, or they could get themselves dissolved by the huge jellyfish thing that lived under the sand in the Misery's far north and it wouldn't make a mouse-fart of difference to Dortmark. The land would twist and change and one day they'd lay a stone and find that it met another stone earlier down the road. The Misery was like that. The Deep Kings could posture however they wanted out there, but they'd never step into range of Nall's Engine. Everything would be fine.

At least it would be, as long as Nall's Engine was getting the power it needed.

I kept myself indoors, wringing Ezabeth's seditious words through my mind over and over. The streets flowed with streams of wan-faced soldiers and an equal number of clerks, servants, grooms, merchants and doxies, all traipsing north alongside cart after cart of supplies and the barges slowly navigating the clogged canals. I estimated Venzer was sending three-quarters of the strength of Valengrad, both the heavy cavalry divisions, the best of the big free companies and more state troops than I could count. I hadn't seen mobilisation like this in ten years. The city deflated as the soldiers flowed away, a withered, milkless teat.

'You know, whatever you did to me, it seems I can't get drunk any more,' I said when Ezabeth turned up on my doorstep.

She was cowled in a long black cloak, face veiled, hood up against the night. I'd been expecting another visit, had felt it in the arches of my feet. I let her in. She scanned the room, maybe noting that I'd cleared the empty bottles into a pile and my sheets had been laundered.

'It will fade in time,' she said without apology. She eyed my armour, breastplate laid out on the table where I'd been giving it a good scouring alongside my matchlock, dagger and sword. I hated that she wore that veil; it made reading her impossible. Somehow I still felt she was being con-descending. The sad truth was, I'd been hoping she'd come by again. I was an idiot. I didn't even like her. She was like squeezing a zit. It was satisfying to apply pressure, even if I knew I'd look stupid for days to come.

She stood awkwardly in the middle of my apartment. It didn't smell so bad since I'd had the washerwomen scrub my sheets and the pile of old clothing had mostly been fed into the fire. Women make you do the strangest things.

'Any reason you're here? It's past twelve.'

'I need you to help me break into Gleck Maldon's house.'

I blinked at that. She seemed torn about something, but then reached up and unclasped the veil, revealed her face. Her sweetness had me stunned for a moment.

'Gleck's house belongs to the recipients of his will. His bastards, probably. He might have been a womaniser and half mad, but he wasn't corrupted. It's not my business.' Hard to get my words out right. It didn't make sense that after twenty years she hadn't aged a day while I'd aged twice that and more.

'You're Blackwing,' she said airily. 'You can make it your business.'

'Folk who abuse their power don't tend to hold onto it long. I won't cast a shadow of suspicion over Gleck's memory. He's owed better than that. He might have been crazy, but he was loyal to the core.' *And if I assist you with this line of enquiry then I'll be as guilty of sedition as you are.*

Ezabeth stiffened her posture, tilted her chin.

'People say you'll do anything, if the price is right.'

'People are arseholes.' If my reputation was hitting that point then I'd lost track of popular opinion. I'd always prided myself that my crew kept itself honourable, for all that it was made of lice and pond crud. Yes, we took the pay for savage work, but a man's got to eat. A sensation like shame demanded that I dismiss it before it rose any further. Even a mercenary has to have standards.

'Yes. Princes and marshals most of all. But I need his research. Prince Herono has vowed to investigate the phos supply discrepancies, but I can tell she doesn't believe me. I did not know she had been raised to the inner council of the Order of Aetherial Engineers and now I don't know how far I can trust her. I'm hitting dead ends. I need the original papers Maldon was working from. When my brother returns from the Misery we can pull it all together, maybe show the princes and ... Well, I don't know what, then. But they have to be shown.'

'Haven't you already argued your case to the Order?'

Ezabeth's brows drew in like battle lines.

'Something is not right amongst the Order. They aren't Spinners; they're bureaucrats and accountants. They think that so long as enough battery coils come in from the mills they can forget about everything else. When I insisted that they provide me access to all of Maldon's work they told me it was the property of the Order, that "No university wench is going to come and take over years of investment." They are fools. They have no grasp of what they're dealing with.'

'You're asking me to do a lot on faith, here,' I said. 'You're asking me to help you subvert the Order. Go behind even Venzer's back. That's a lot to ask just because ...' I almost said it aloud. Because we'd known each other a lifetime ago. But that was only my side of the deal. I may have been an agent of the crow, but I was little more than a mercenary to her. Whatever she'd felt for me, if she'd ever felt anything at all, it was buried behind years of dust and a handful of madness.

Ezabeth shook her head.

'I ask nothing on faith. I'll pay before we go. Take me to Gleck Maldon's house, help me break in quietly and act as my lookout while I'm in there. It won't take long.'

'You know the marshal has men following you?' I said.

'Not tonight. I sent those clod-footed hogs following an impression of me down towards the walls.'

Not many Spinners could weave that kind of illusion. She was rare all right.

'And you chose me for this because ...?'

She took out a small but heavy purse and counted out heavy coins. Ten gold discs, fifty marks a piece, gleamed salaciously in the phos light.

'Because I have the money, and you're the only person

I know with a history of breaking into people's houses at night.'

Cat burglary wasn't amongst my usual skill set, but for her it seemed I'd make an exception.

Maldon's huge wooden mansion rose three storeys over the moat of dirty streets and alleys that kept polite company at bay. He could have chosen to live out in Willows if he'd been able to stomach his peers, but he couldn't, so he'd set himself up amongst the down and outs, the night soil lying in the street, the flickering phos lights and sleazy neon signs advertising girls, guns, gambling.

'And you're quite certain there's no night watchman?' Ezabeth asked.

'Certain? No, but I doubt it. A couple of the old house staff come by in the day. That's all.'

We walked past the front looking for signs of life but the street was dark, tranquil in moonlight. Getting in quietly was going to be the problem, or so I'd thought. Fortune favoured us: one of the servants had left a window slightly ajar. It was high in the wall, but I boosted Ezabeth up. I hadn't expected her to have such agility. She was light on her feet, dropping down gently into the room beyond. I'm a big bastard and although I can say without ego that I'm stronger than most big bastards, heaving my weight noiselessly through small spaces wasn't a skill I intended practising. I flinched at a noise along the alley, but then Ezabeth appeared, waving me in through an unlocked door.

'Lucky they left it unlatched,' I muttered.

'They didn't. Someone forced it,' Ezabeth said. I scowled, a wasted expression in the dark. If anyone was going to be breaking Gleck's stuff it should have been me.

Light emanated dully from a portable phos globe in Ezabeth's three-fingered hand. I had never been in Maldon's observatory before. A large, square room with a tower-height ceiling far above, into which a number of huge glass lenses were set. A phos loom rested on iron runners set into the floor.

'Amazing,' Ezabeth said, her voice filled with wonder. 'It's a modification of the Timus Sixth model. What do these nodes do? Something to do with impurity filtering maybe. And these extra straining wires ... there should be nine, but he has twelve, and this cross wire here? Why?'

She babbled on about the eight-foot-tall phos loom. I didn't understand much of it. I expected some folk felt the same when I got energised explaining the differences between brandy from Whitelande and brandy from Lennisgrad.

'... and this track it's on. The whole loom can be moved around the room to sit beneath the different lenses, depending on which moons are in ascendance on any given night.' She caught a breath, put a hand to her chest. 'This is remarkable.'

'Yeah. Only it's not what we're here for. Let's do this quick.'

Ezabeth seemed reluctant to leave the magnificent loom and its fireproof cut-stone chamber, but I got her moving. We went through the wood-panelled hallway and then a reception room that led to a back staircase. I eyed a half-empty bottle of finest Lennisgrad brandy on the table.

There really was a difference.

I doubted Gleck would have begrudged me. If things looked really bad with Saravor then I might be able to come back and rob the place. If he was dead, Gleck could hardly complain, and if he wasn't then he owed me for all the time I'd spent trying to find him. Mercenary logic.

'What was that?' Ezabeth whispered through her veil.

'I didn't hear anything,' I said, but I'd not been listening. She bade me be still and I heard it then. The gentle creak of a floorboard, somewhere above us in the house.

'Maybe there is a night watchman.'

'Or maybe whoever got that window open is still here.'

Ezabeth drew down her veil and sniffed the air. I didn't have much of a sense of smell; my nose had been rearranged too many times and the cartilage up there was more twisted than a priest's conscience. Strong as it was, I got a whiff of what she was picking up. Something like the jars of rancid fish the marketeers sold for a pittance at the end of a day baking in summer's heat.

I don't like things that don't make sense. Not until I've put a knife in them.

'You want to get out of here?' I asked, dropping my voice to a hush. Ezabeth looked at me pointedly as she rearranged her veil.

'Do you?'

I almost grinned at her.

We climbed a second staircase to the upper storey and that's when I heard the telltale whoosh of flame taking bite. That's when I smelled burning paper and the acrid tang of fuel. That's when I realised that the fish odour was whale oil, and we'd stumbled into an act of arson.

Smoke was already pouring from the doorway to Maldon's library. Many folk didn't have a house as big as his book-room-cum-study, which occupied most of the upper storey. I skidded to a halt against the door frame. Books had been dragged down and dumped in piles, and the discarded oil flasks lay scattered around them like primitive tribesfolk, worshipping the pyres. Between the two largest piles, two man-shapes were shrouded in smoke and shadow.

They saw me. I looked at them. A mutual feeling that we were not friends asserted itself.

The flames crackled and hissed, the orange light throbbed across the books. Backs to the fires, the men were just dark shapes but one of them grabbed the silhouette of a heavy military crossbow from a table. Not a hunting bow, not a gentleman's duelling bow, it was a charge-stopper, the kind of bow that punches a hole through an armoured horse. I wasn't close enough to stop him and at that range, if he had any kind of skill, he couldn't miss. I started moving but I knew it was already too late. The bolt that thing could launch would pin me to the wall and I'd go up in flames with the house.

I figured he was going to put it straight through me. I was the threat, sure enough, not tiny Ezabeth Tanza, and I threw myself down behind a desk as he wheeled it around.

He swung it on Ezabeth and pulled the lever. There was a solid thwack as the pent-up energy in the string released. At that range, dodging it was impossible. A breastplate of finest Whitelande steel couldn't have stopped it. I closed my eyes, couldn't look. I expected a shriek, a cry of anguish.

There was nothing.

I opened my eyes.

The bolt had stopped, rotating in the air a couple of feet from Ezabeth's chest, but it trembled as the crossbow's string thrummed. Her eyes were wild, her body shook and fizzing sparks blazed at the bolt's point, as though the tip was pushed up against a sharpener's wheel. She had directed her light against the bolt and it was pitted up against the full energy of the crossbow's release. The amount of light she was focusing to counteract the full force of the crossbow must have been colossal. Her assailant, a man wearing an executioner's hood, seemed frozen on the spot in disbelief.

'Well fuck me,' he said.

The bolt burst. The metal head shattered, spraying the door frame with dozens of tiny, glowing red shards. The shaft detonated from within in a cloud of sawdust and splinters. Ezabeth flew backwards, striking the wall with a meat-on-wood thud and collapsing to the ground.

Speed, training and a policy of relentless savagery are what make a man dangerous. I was on my feet before she dropped. I ignored the man with the spent bow as his pal made to draw his sword like an amateur. When you draw a sword you do it away from your opponent, or smart men like me do what I did and grab hold of your arm before the blade clears the scabbard. I barrelled into him, forcing his sword arm away from me, and my dagger was out and doing its work. I drove him against the bookcase and stuck him twice in the side, a third in the meat of his shoulder, more. He never got his sword clear of the scabbard.

The hooded man had more instinct than his dying companion and hurled the heavy crossbow at me. There was no question of him loading it for a second shot before my knife work was done. The heavy wood frame smashed painfully against my elbow. When I looked back, the executioner had drawn a rapier, long steel blade held out across the desk to ward me off. I let the first man sink to the ground. By the sound he was making, the soft, wet whimpering, I'd got him in the lungs at least once. Goodbye, shitbag. Hood-Face had hesitated, maybe unnerved by Ezabeth's magic or maybe by the brutality his partner had just died of, but his eyes were narrowed and his hand didn't tremble. He moved like a man who knew the sword, wasting no breath on needless words. I took his partner's weapon, a cutlass with a hand guard shaped like a clam shell. It was a half-foot shorter than Hood-Face's rapier, but I always preferred a heavier cutting edge.

The rapier against the cutlass is a brief and lethal game. The rapier has the advantage in the thrust and if he was fast enough he could strike and retreat before I could bring my own weapon to bear, but if I got my blade against his then his long, slender weapon had no leverage to win in the bind. I danced my sword in the air, kept it moving, couldn't let him know when I was going to come down against his sword. He snarled against the growing fog of paper-smoke, blinked away tears as it stung his eyes, kept his point low, away from my blade. All I had to do was get our blades together, and I'd be able to step within his guard, let my heavier edge bring about its devastation. We prowled across the floor of scattered books, short steps and long as we each sought to draw the other from his guard into a false and deadly range. Some men will tell you the rapier has all the advantages, but then men say many stupid things and I've killed a lot of them for their mistakes.

Couldn't see for shit. The smoke was growing thicker as the piles of books sent bright yellow flames higher, towers of fluttering gold.

'Who sent you?' I demanded, but the hooded man said nothing. He waved smoke from his face, kept his rapier point moving. A steady man, a cautious man, a man of experience and those are always the deadliest. It's not the loud and ostentatious fighter you fear, it's the man who bides his time, waits for his opening.

Down on the floor, the man I'd worked on with the knife was making wet, dying sounds. His friend paid him a glance, his lips drew back in anger for a fallen comrade. His bare forearms were worked with detailed tattoos, roses and thorns coiling about them in circles. I saw the tensing of his shoulders and then he came for me.

I parried the thrust but he was fast and before I could make real contact he'd rolled his wrist to cut at me from above. My deflection was skilless and frantic but I made it. As I dashed his sword aside, I launched forward in a full lunge, cutlass carving a trail in the black fog but either he was fast or I was half blind because somehow I didn't manage to hit him.

'We don't both have to die here, captain,' I heard him say. Heart drumming in my ears I realised that the fire had taken across the carpet, the curtains framed the windows in arches of flame, and the bookshelves were taking. I felt the heat on my skin, through my breeches.

'No,' I said. 'Only you.'

'Whatever pay you're on, it can't be worth this.'

'Not everything's about the money.' I wasn't just show-ing grit. Ezabeth lay back by the doorway somewhere, and this man had tried to put a crossbow bolt through her chest. Stopping it had taken everything she had. Back behind where my heart should have been I harboured a fury hotter than any pile of burning literature could ever produce, a rage born of fear and pain and longing. I needed to see a head roll across the floor, and I needed it to be his.

Fate conspires against us constantly, never satisfied to provide that which she owes us. The arsonist realised that a room as large as the library had more than one exit, and he ran for a second door leading to a different wing of the house. I'd have followed, but Ezabeth was still prone as the fire crept towards her. The man in the mask glanced back at me once, and then he was gone.

'Captain, the fire,' Ezabeth wheezed. The flame was crawling over every surface, eating across the desk, devour-ing paper.

'Nothing we can do,' I said. I bent to lift her to her feet but she pushed me away.

'Save whatever you can,' she wheezed. 'Do it!'

My first victim had begun to make louder death rattles as the flames began finding purchase in his oil-wet clothes. He probably had a family somewhere. He probably had a girl. Probably hadn't envisaged ending up this way. Not my problem. He'd made his bed, and it was one of blades and fire.

Getting burned for paper is stupid but the look in a woman's eyes is another thing. It was all I could see of her face, but the panic, the need in her eyes was too great to ignore. Damn, but I can be a fool for a face.

That she was a half-mad, tart-mouthed bitch who had no respect for me didn't enter into it.

I raced the fire across to the writing desk and scooped up as many leather-covered notebooks and papers as I could. Beneath the notebooks were sheets of crumpled old wax-paper covered with faint blue lines. They were yellowed, old, probably totally useless but I didn't have time to be picky. I tossed everything out into the hallway, and shut the door on the blaze as the black smoke clawed at my eyes. I lifted Ezabeth, books and all, and headed out of the house by a different door than we'd entered. I kept the sword in my hand until we were clear in case the hooded bastard had stayed around for another pop at us, but he'd scarpered. His work was done, and as we left I could see the roof was beginning to burn. It might spread to other houses nearby if the wind scattered enough embers.

Soon as she was recovered enough to walk I took Ezabeth back to my grotty little apartment, somehow feeling more ashamed of it than ever. I put her in a chair as I washed the blood from my hand and cleaned my dagger. I dried it carefully, wiped it down with an oily rag and tossed the sword into the cupboard. It was standard military issue, which told me nothing about its former owner. There were thousands like it floating around in the hands of the retired and the pawn shops.

'It's all gone,' Ezabeth said. She sounded as though she were crying, but her eyes were clear. That frightened, frantic look she'd worn back at her residence was back.

'Maybe there's something in those books,' I said, though the chances of anything worthwhile appearing in a few random notebooks seemed unlikely. I took her a cup of water, even filled one for myself. I hate water.

'They were there to destroy them,' she said. I didn't admit the obvious. 'Don't you see what this means?' I shrugged. She said, 'Someone doesn't want me getting my hands on Maldon's research. There has to be something to it. There must be.'

'Well, it's gone now.'

'Tomorrow I'll go to the marshal directly,' she said. She meant to speak with force but her exertions had robbed her of strength.

'What you did with that bolt. That was pretty impressive,' I said.

'Yes,' she said. Too tired for more.

I felt awkward. Stupid, but that's how it goes sometimes.

'Come on. You can sleep here tonight. You need rest.'

She protested, but I lifted her like she was a kitten and slid her into my freshly laundered sheets. She tried to protest but her words grew indistinct, and then she was making an absurdly loud snoring sound for such a small body. I'd chosen, I realised that now. Against my better judgement, against the law, against my bargain with the raven. I'd chosen and somehow the recklessness of my actions didn't taste as bitter as I'd anticipated. The choice had only been illusionary. Call it sentimentality, call it intuition, but whether she was right or wrong I'd been on her side from the moment she came back into my life. It had just taken me this long to admit it. Ezabeth's opposition wasn't just some theorem. Tonight, her enemies had tried to stop her. If they could get to her, then they would kill her.

I sat facing the door all night, sword across my knees.

Just let them try.

12

When I woke, stiff and gum-eyed in my chair, she was gone. Stolen out in the night like a regretful lover. The guilt and disappointment I felt were the same as if she had been.

Her money watched me from the table like some cheap whore on display. Somehow it had lost its shine. Unable to stomach its accusatory gaze I threw on a coat and headed out into a chilling wind.

'Big Dog says you shouldn't be getting mixed up with the cream again,' Tnota said when I laid out my woes. It was only an hour past dawn but he'd just opened a jar of black ale. Would have been rude not to partake.

'Sounds suspiciously like your advice put into the jaws of a god,' I grunted at him. I put my boots up on the opposite bench.

'Good advice no matter where it comes from, captain,' Nenn said, joining us, yawning sleepily. She scratched at the discoloured spot on her belly. 'She must have been paying you well.'

'Well enough.'

The good news of the day was that Nenn was back on her feet, stomach a darker shade of flesh than it had been but intact and not stinking. She had a cluster of large red chillies in a brown paper bag. She took one out and crunched into it, seeds and all. She saw me wince, shrugged and stuffed another into her mouth.

'I can't help it. Ever since I got fixed, it's all I want to eat. Mouth's on fucking fire.' I declined the large red fruit she tried to offer me.

'At least your only witness isn't going to go spreading his mouth,' Tnota said. 'Should probably wash your hands though.' He was right. Crusts of dark blood lurked beneath my fingernails. Putting a knife through a man's ribs isn't clean work.

'Any chance the one you stabbed up could have crawled out of there?' Nenn asked. Practical as ever.

'None. He burned.' I allowed myself a satisfied nod. Burning was a bad way to go, but my reserves of empathy were usually exhausted on orphans and puppies, a lot higher up the list than arsonists and arseholes. 'But the other man, the one with roses around his arms – he knew me. Recognised me at least.'

'How do you know?'

'He called me "captain". Slip of the tongue, maybe.'

'Anyone who's been around Valengrad the past twenty years would know you,' Nenn said. She snorted back chilli-induced snot, eyes streaming. Then she bit into another. 'Boys from the Spills. Soldiers. Mercenaries. Hells, they could have been shopkeepers.'

'Pretty good with a sword for a shopkeep. And they weren't looting, they went to Gleck's to destroy. Those books had to be worth thousands. Only time men go trash a place that way, they've had orders. I want to know whose.'

Nenn gave me a sour look.

'The witch paying you to ask around or you taking this on yourself?' Nenn asked. She thumped down on the bench and poured herself a generous quantity of the ale. There was hostility in her tone. I felt the urge to arch my back like a hissing cat, go on the defensive.

'Always worth knowing who the man you fought is,' I said. 'You know my policy on unfinished business.'

'Kill it with knives,' Tnota added helpfully.

'Knives, axes, fire. Don't care as long as it gets finished. Loose ends tend to unravel things. Besides, the bastard burned Gleck's house to the ground. It was a good house. If Gleck comes back, he's going to be pissed as hell.'

We mulled that over for a while. The early day drinking made it easy to be maudlin and Gleck had been one of us. If he'd still been around he'd probably have been sat drinking at that table.

A bare-chested young man stumbled from out of the back of Tnota's apartments. He was Fracan like Tnota, the same thick, curly black hair, but half his age. He gabbled something at Tnota in their nasal language, and Tnota barked something back at him, annoyed. The Fracan shrugged and shuffled away again. Nenn and I shared a look. We'd long ago stopped asking Tnota about his ever-changing stream of guests. Some kind of Fracan custom we'd never understand.

'Maybe I should go find Ezabeth,' I suggested.

'You're not deep enough in her latrine already?' Nenn snapped. Her eyes were streaming from the chillies. I could feel their heat in my nostrils, and I hadn't even touched them. Crazy bitch. Fixing had that effect sometimes. Changed people.

'I know you don't like the cream, but I feel like I ought to help her out. On account that she used to work with Gleck. Feels like I should get involved somehow.'

'Leave that three-fingered bitch well alone. She'll rain nothing but turds down on you,' Nenn said. She alternated between clenching her jaw and sucking in cold air to fight back against the chillies. Nenn had never had any love for the nobility, but even by her own standards she seemed hostile.

'Never met a cream was up to something good,' Tnota said, bridging the void he saw growing between us. He gave me one of his yellow-toothed grins. 'Easy to forget which side of the milk you were born on, though, captain.'

I'd never told them that I'd known Ezabeth before. To them she was just some noblewoman Spinner whose carriage we'd borrowed. Tried to remind myself that that was all she was to me as well. Didn't matter that she was beautiful and powerful and had a spine woven from ropes of steel. Didn't matter that when I was around her I felt something in me lift. She was rich and energised, brilliant and dazzling. This morning she'd be working on her theorems, and here I was getting drunk before nine in the morning with a southern queer and a noseless she-wolf.

'You think your girlfriend will tell the Iron Goat you were there when Gleck's house burned?' Nenn asked. She wiped tears from burning eyes.

'Fucking hope not. The less he's involved the better. Last time I saw him he didn't look good either. Cracking under the pressure, maybe.'

'Can't blame him.' Tnota stretched out, treating us to the odour of his armpits. 'Marshal Wechsel and his boys up at Three-Six must be shitting themselves. You think there's any truth to it? About the drudge making a push?'

I shook my head. Wished I had the confidence to say it out loud.

I spent the day finding whisper-men in the Spills, trying to get any information I could on a man for hire with roses tattooed around his arms. One false lead and a wasted day later, the sky was fully dark as I made my way home. I was surprised to see a small child approaching; most beggar children hid through the night, with good reason. I don't like children. They remind me of what should have been. What was taken from me. This one walked right up to me. I thought it was a girl, but then I realised it was a boy in a dress. One of Saravor's grey-skinned things, blank staring eyes, no fear. The kid held out its hand as if to pass me something. I stopped, swallowed and opened my palm.

The child dropped the head of a starling into my hand, then wandered away into the dark. No wonder it had no fear. Going home to that madhouse was probably worse than anything that happened out on the streets.

The bird's head stared up at me. Then in a high, piping voice, it chirruped, 'Ten days until your first instalment is due! Twenty thousand, cash or bankers note.'

'Any chance I can get an extension?' I muttered. I didn't expect a reply, but the bird head somehow coughed out a final word.

'No.'

I swear that somehow it was grinning.

13

A dismal week of stinking grey rain and cheap inebriation passed before Prince Herono's man came to find me.

'You're wanted,' Stannard told me. 'Best not to keep the prince waiting, there's a good chap.'

I didn't like Stannard. He had too much wax in his moustache, and since he carried a prince's authority, he knew that he'd done well for himself. It showed in the way he puffed out his fading chest, and that made me want to say no.

I was anxious as I climbed aboard the carriage. Either she had work for me, which would be good as I desperately needed to find a way to pay Saravor, or she'd found out that I'd been at Maldon's house the night it burned. I could hear fate's coin spinning above my head.

The carriage bounced and jarred me across town and out. I'd thought to be taken back to the phos mill, but this time it was the Willows. We passed the Tanza residence, the windows curtained, the building dark.

'Try to make yourself presentable, there's a good fellow,' Stannard said. 'You smell like you've been in that shit stain of a tavern for a full week.' A spookily accurate assessment. I allowed the rest of the journey to pass in friendless silence. No point wasting good conversation on a grunt risen above his station.

The roads into Willows were as smooth as they come,

which is to say that I felt every jostle and bounce and the booze in my guts sloshed around like water in the bilge of a ship.

Herono's Valengrad residence made the Tanza house seem a hovel. Vast white pillars of the classical style ranked up along a frontage wider than most streets are long. Semi-nude statues of long-abandoned deities struck dramatic poses over gardens of hedgerow mazes and late summer flowers. I guessed correctly that she'd have suits of polished, antiquated armour standing watch along her red-carpeted hallways and portraits of princes past glaring down from above.

Funny how the princes could afford to finance their monuments to excess while Marshal Venzer was crying out for soldiers, munitions and supplies.

'You know the rules already,' Stannard said as he admitted me. 'First sound of trouble and I'll be in there with half a dozen boys. You understand.'

I ignored him. I figured that Stannard's growls and threats were what he mistook for power. Men of his calibre didn't understand that real power goes unspoken. A man like Marshal Venzer didn't bluster and threaten his enemies, he simply told them what he expected of them. They either fell in or found themselves broken, crushed, reduced to nothing beneath the weight of his efficiency. No brags about his victories, no crowing over the vanquished. Real power shows itself through the disregard one has for those that defy it.

I found the prince sitting in an office beneath a vast oil painting of herself. It showed her in her prime, two eyes in her head, a sabre across one shoulder and a scroll in her hand. Might and learning, the great balance of princedom. The painter had shown the broken Misery in the background. His paints hadn't quite conveyed the endless depth of the fierce white-bronze cracks in the sky, the life within them. Maybe nobody could.

'Captain. Take a seat,' Herono said. I took the seat.

'What can I do for you, your grace?'

'My cousin has gone missing,' Herono said. 'Disappeared. Three days past she failed to return home. Her servants were expecting her for dinner, but she failed to materialise. I am deeply concerned about what may have befallen her.'

I felt a little twist inside, a turning of my heart. I tried not to let it show on my face. It was a week since that night at Gleck's house when the arsonists had turned the crossbow on her. My back was rigid at the thought that the hooded man might have decided to finish the job.

'I don't know anything of her whereabouts, your grace,' I said.

'Of course not. But you do have great experience in hunting men down. The men on my payroll have done their best to locate her, but while Stannard and the old brigade are very good at following orders they are not men of initiative. You'll be rewarded, handsomely, if you can locate and rescue her.' Prince Herono leaned back in her chair, her single eye bright and unblinking. 'And should someone have done her harm, then bring her abusers to me. I will see to it that they understand the fullness of their error. No one casts their dice against my house lightly.'

I negotiated a steep price for my services and Herono tossed coins at me like they were so many flakes of sawdust, but the real gold was a letter granting me her authority. She put her weight behind me, heavier than lead. With a letter like that in my pocket I could order a whole regiment to strip naked and dance for me if I wanted to. I wouldn't, but I could have. I agreed to contact her as soon as I had anything worthwhile to report. As I left her abode, the broken sky in the Misery let forth a long, ululating howl, mirroring the trembling in my guts.

*

People always think that finding them will be hard, but people are creatures of habit. We all have basic necessities of existence that must be fulfilled. We eat, seek shelter, sleep, drink, crap. Everything we do has to exist within that framework, you just have to figure out what makes a person unique from their countrymen, pry open the details that make them vulnerable to discovery. I didn't know Ezabeth well, but she had hers as much as anyone.

I couldn't believe that someone had got to her without Herono hearing about it. Ezabeth was cautious. Resourceful. When it came to her magic, very powerful. If she'd seen them coming, she wouldn't have gone quietly. I was thinking flares of light, detonations. Folks would have heard, talked, and even a simple man like Stannard would have got wind of it. That meant either she hadn't seen it coming, or, more likely, that her disappearance was a choice.

Ezabeth had enemies, but she could have turned to her cousin for protection. Only Prince Adenauer and Marshal Venzer could match Herono for power in Valengrad and her Blue Brigade veterans were tough old boys. Why would she vanish? I welcomed Herono's money but I'd have looked for Ezabeth anyway. I'd already gone in on this hand.

When you want to track someone down, you start at their home. Ezabeth hadn't been in Valengrad long, but the Tanza property still had servants. We paid them a visit.

An aged woman with a hunched back and a twitch in her eye admitted us with a measure of reluctance that the boot I wedged in the door overcame. I had her summon the other staff: a cook, a gardener and two maids. From their disgruntled looks it was evident that they considered our presence an intrusion but they were fearful enough not to voice it.

'I can only tell you what I told the prince's men,' the old woman told us. 'The mistress set off in the early morning, as she did most days, and never returned. There's nowt more to be told.'

Stannard and his men had done a number on some of the staff, tried to batter the information out of them. They were simple soldiers, though, hardly great thinkers and they didn't understand Ezabeth.

It took me less than ten minutes to find a locked box in her room. Her private papers were more or less exactly what I'd expected. Lots of diagrams of lunar orbits, mathematical calculations, theories laid out in neat lines of black ink. But there were letters she had received amongst them, dating back more than a year. The letters wasted no time with pleasantries save her name, and their contents was the same phos-spinning babble that her other writing presented, but each was signed simply 'O.L.' On its own that wasn't enough, but it was something to work with.

'Nenn, get me a list of every Spinner in Valengrad and find one with the initials O.L. If you don't find anyone, then a list of every Talent in the mills as well. Can't be just anyone who understands this crap. Seems Ezabeth had a friend here after all.'

As Nenn departed I leafed to the next document in the pile. A pamphlet, the kind that got pinned all over church doors and street corners. Such leaflets weren't uncommon. Clerics, doomsayers, even merchants used them to advertise their bargains. This was different, though. The title read: THE SLAVES OF THE ENGINE. Familiar blasphemy leapt off the page at me. *The Talents are worked until their minds shatter like glass. Their lives are sold for profit and greed!*

The pamphlet showed tomorrow's date

'Damn it.'

The paper crumpled in my fist. She hadn't picked it up, she'd written it herself. She was planning to hurl caution from the battlements. If this hit the streets I'd be given another commission to find her, but I'd be dragging her to a gallows instead of home. I was already in too deep to let that happen.

Shit on fire. I was probably one of the only people in the city who thought she wasn't light-blind already, and even I thought that was madness. She had to be stopped.

Trails are not always formed of footprints. I knew where to go.

The ink on the page was smeared. Not unusual for many of the small press pamphleteers, eager to get their poorly spelt messages out to a largely uncaring public. I crossed town, walking briskly into the biting wind and the ever present simmer of bad nerves that spread around me like a musk. The pamphlet proudly proclaimed the printer to be Pieter Dytwin, but after having read the contents it was a wonder he'd allowed his name to be attached to it. Ezabeth named the princes as traitors, subverting the supply of phos that should have been going into the Engine. She wrote about the plight of the Talents, their mistreatment. She called Marshal Venzer a conspirator. If copies of the pamphlet hit the street then Pieter Dytwin would find a new residence in the darkest, deepest cells of the citadel – if he retained his grip on mortality for long enough to get there.

The printing shop was clanking and pumping, phos-powered presses stamping sheets with carefully laid type. Nobody challenged me when I entered the workshop, the young three typesetters too occupied with placing the rows of standardised letters into the blocks while two journeyman printers worked the press. As I waited for them to complete their batch I picked up one of the freshly finished sheets they were working on. Mother Aggie's Recipe For Spiced Mutton Pie. Spirits alone knew who'd be looking to turn a profit putting that out when all the sheep had been driven up to Three-Six to feed Marshal Wechsel and his army, but printers weren't fussy about your message as long as they were getting paid.

There were limits to that greed, though, and Pieter Dytwin should have known them.

At length a man whose hands were ink-black from fingertips to elbows noticed me and walked over with a concerned look on his narrow, common face.

'Can I help you, sir?'

'Looking for Pieter Dytwin,' I said.

'That's me,' he said. He didn't like the breadth of my shoulders or the cutlass at my belt, but when he saw the Blackwing insignia on my shoulder, he nearly shat himself. 'What can I do for you?'

'I'm Captain Galharrow, here on Prince Herono's business,' I said. 'There was a woman came to see you not long ago. Cream, likely wore a modesty veil and gloves. Lady Tanza.'

Mention of the prince made him nervous; mention of Tanza made him shrivel. I'd put him on the defensive, and I evidently wasn't a customer. The tightening of his expression became a look close to panic, and I knew I'd come to the right place.

'I don't think I know anyone of that name,' he managed.

'That's odd,' I said. Sighed, dramatic as a pantomime player. 'Seems that someone must have sneaked in and started putting these out from your press then.' I held up the pamphlet that bore his name, but Pieter had already recognised it. There was a fearful glimmer in his eyes. He knew exactly what he'd printed, and he knew just where it was likely to land him. The apprentices behind him had sensed something was wrong.

'No need to make a scene. You aren't under arrest. And neither are they. Not yet.'

Pieter seemed to welcome my gentleness, grasped it as though it were a sign of things to come.

'Please, step into my office.'

The door closed behind us, shutting out the concerned looks from the apprentices. Pieter pressed his fingertips to his eyes, shook his head with a shiver.

'I want her grace to know that I was never a willing party to this,' he said. 'I know how wrong those pamphlets were. But how was I to refuse a relation of the prince? A count's sister? She assured me that she had the prince's authority.'

'So you ran the pamphlet?'

Pieter nodded, twisting his cap between his hands. He was a narrow man, forties, well worn by the arduous work at the press but his ink-black hands trembled in a manner unworthy of his age.

'Of course. She paid up front. That's rare, you know, very rare. Most customers, they want to see the finished products. Ink smears, paper gets jammed, sometimes the type is too faint. You know. But she paid them all up front.'

'How many copies did you run?' I kept my voice low, level. It's important to judge a man when you want to know what he knows. Threats and violence will motivate the reluctant, but Pieter was all too willing to spill. Sweat rolled snail tracks down his face. Prince Herono was a kindlier soul than some of her peers but even she would string him up for this – especially if it were true. Nobody with a capacity to bear insults wins a princedom. Pieter was terrified that what he said now would bury him neck deep in the midden. I couldn't tell him that it wouldn't.

'We'd run two hundred copies when I came to my senses and refused to publish any more without a letter of instruction from the citadel. I know, sir, I know that it was wrong. I see that now. I should never have trusted a woman who wouldn't show her face.'

He had a point there. Maybe I was no smarter than he was, though just then, I still felt it.

'What happened to the copies?'

'Destroyed,' he said. 'I threw them on the fire. I didn't think any still existed. May I ask ... where you got that?'

I felt he might risk making a grab for it, try to shred the evidence of his slip-up. So I folded the pamphlet, tucked it into my pocket. Always best to hold something back for insurance.

'You know what this pamphlet claims?'

'Yes, sir.'

'Tell me.'

'Sir?'

'Tell me what you printed.'

Pieter cringed, but he obeyed.

'It says that the phos that is spun in the mills isn't used to power Nall's Engine. It says that the princes are abusing the mill Talents and subverting the phos supply for their own ends. It calls them corrupt war profiteers.' He swallowed hard. 'Of course, I never believed it! I put my trust in Nall, in the Order and in the princes. Of course I do. I pay my taxes, a good citizen.'

I let him babble his innocence a while longer. I made no move to accept or argue the case. I wasn't here for him; he was careless, but no traitor that I could see. And he'd helped Ezabeth which, ridiculous as it was, earned him some kind of merit in my eyes.

'Does she know that you destroyed the copies?'

'Yes. When the boy came to collect them, I said I'd never printed them. They were already on the fire. It was a waste of very good paper. I had to pay them—'

'What boy?'

'A boy servant. Not hers. He had a jacket showing the emblem of the Order of Aetherial Engineers. Please, captain, you see? She even had a friend in the Order. I thought it strange at the time, that it seemed to go against the Order's work but I'm just a simple printer ...'

I had what I needed. He couldn't give me a name, but it

was going to be easy enough from there. I told the hapless printer that he should pay a fine of two thousand marks. It was a small price to pay to escape Prince Herono's retribution, and he ran to fetch it like an eager child. Business must have been good because he had the money in his strongbox, and in exchange I let him burn the pamphlet on his fire. Two thousand marks to char a bit of paper. I told him that I'd deliver the money to the prince on his behalf, for which he thanked me. He shouldn't have, since I intended to use it to pay Saravor off, but he couldn't have known that.

The Order of Aetherial Engineers are the scholars, machinists and ironworkers with the near-holy duty of maintaining Nall's Engine. Though the great weapon had been contrived and laid down by the Nameless, its daily oiling and polishing had been left to a small army of underlings. There was prestige in being accepted into the Order, and the Lennisgrad university regularly sent its brightest and best to swell the Order's green-robed ranks. Physicists, Spinners, mathematicians, the inquisitive of all disciplines sought positions of authority in order to gain access to the secret writings Nall had left behind with instructions about the running of his contraption. Mostly, they were a bunch of arrogant pricks.

I went to the citadel for the information I needed. Prince Herono might have supplied it, but I didn't want to let her know what her kinswoman had been up to, or with whom, just yet. I'd seen no proof that Ezabeth's pamphlets were right, and maybe it was just gut-driven intuition but if Ezabeth was on to something then it wasn't just her business, it was Blackwing's too. I still found it hard to imagine Herono as a simple profiteer. She'd more money than scars, and she didn't lack for those. If we didn't see things the same way it was because the drudge had torn an eye from her face, not because she was hungry for coin. Herono had come through for me when she located the Bride but something about that just hadn't sat right. Count Digada had been careful – very careful – but she'd uncovered his cult in a matter of days. That Bride had gone unnoticed for years to have grown so large. Maybe I just didn't like the idea that she was more capable than I was. The unease lingered. For now, whatever I was being paid, I'd deal with Ezabeth myself.

First I had to ensure that Ezabeth was safe and after that I could try to dissuade her from her course of self-destruction. If she'd managed to get those leaflets into circulation then her rank wouldn't have protected her. Venzer would see her actions as treachery, propaganda working against morale and with the situation up at Three-Six, we needed all the good spirits we could dredge up. This was well beyond the provocation he needed to order an execution.

One helpful thing about the uptight, self-aggrandising Order was that when they gained the honour of being enrolled, they got their names written into a great big book of pompously embellished letters. It took me fifteen minutes to find a name that matched the initials 'O.L.', and a cross reference with another of the citadel's records gave me his address ten minutes later. Eleven and I was out the door and crossing the city.

The Order paid its money-movers well, if Otto Lindrick's house was anything to go by. Not as luxurious as Maldon's had been but lying in a distinctly better part of town, I didn't bother clanging the bell at the low surrounding wall and hopped over it instead. Darkness had fallen but phos light glowed within. Five heavy thumps on the door led to movement inside and a momentary face peeking between curtains. I thumped on the door again for good measure.

A boy answered, at that awkward child-man age where nobody's quite sure where he stands. A cruel swarm of angry white-headed pimples blistered his cheeks and fore-head and by the bleeders I could see he'd been picking at them.

'Your master here?'

'No, sir, he's at his work,' the boy said.

'You his kid or his boy?'

'His apprentice, sir.'

'Think he'll mind if I beat some truth out of you?'

'Sir?' He looked as though he wanted to try to slam the heavy oak door but I was already too far in to stop, and his fourteen or so years had lent him only bony stringiness. I pushed past, caught sight of the pudgy man peering around a door frame. He tried to bolt, but he was middle-aged and composed of dough and butter. I went after him, caught him as he tried to draw back the bolt across the door and threw him against the wall. He flailed his pudgy hands at me, and I drove a fist into his soft gut.

The apprentice cried out as his master fell breathless to the floor. He seized a poker from the fireplace, then looked between my cutlass and his improvised weapon. Not much of a match. The black iron rod clanged as he let it drop.

Lindrick was struggling to get a breath. I hauled him up and threw him into a chair. He was fat but short, something like the shape of an apple. I had a general disdain for those that squandered the bodies they'd been given on gluttony. That was going to make this easier.

'Kid, sit down,' I said, then when he didn't move, 'sit down or I'll fucking make you.' He sat.

Lindrick managed to drag in a breath as I removed my gloves. Standard issue combat gloves, the bands of iron over the knuckles might do more damage than I wanted just yet.

'Feeling guilty?' I asked. Otto looked mortally afraid. I suppose that was fair. I pushed his face back, took a look at him. Spectacles, clean-shaven, remnants of pale brown hair sporadically decorating his scalp. I shook my head. 'Let's start with the basics,' I said. 'I'm Blackwing Captain Ryhalt Galharrow. I'm here to beat the living shit out of you until you tell me what I need to know. Let's start with the big question. Where is Ezabeth Tanza?'

'I don't know who that is,' Lindrick said.

I struck backhanded with the ball of my fist. I'd broken knuckles in fist fights before, and wasn't going to risk cracking one against Lindrick's thick skull. The force of the blow was almost enough to knock him from the chair, weak as he was.

'Leave him alone!' the kid shouted. 'I'll get the alderman!'

'Go ahead. I'm here on a prince's authority so go and get all the fucking aldermen you want. Maybe we can all go and see Pieter Dytwin at his printing press.'

The kid shut up.

I asked questions, and Lindrick lied to me. Claimed he didn't know Ezabeth, claimed he didn't know anything about Pieter Dytwin and his printing press. Claimed he was innocent. His face was bleeding from cuts above and below the eyes, and one of them began to swell over. I'd cracked his teeth and bloodied his ear. Part of me, a weak part, began to wonder if I'd got it wrong. Could he have been telling the truth? I steeled myself against doubt. In a torturer's mind there can be no room for confusion. Trust that the information is there.

I grabbed Otto by the throat. His eyes bulged fearfully as I lifted him, blubber, bloodied clothes and all, from his chair.

'Running out of time, Otto,' I growled. Squeezed. 'If you won't tell me what you've done to her then there are men in Prince Herono's employ who'll make this look like a whore's massage.' I tightened my grip. 'Hot irons. The rack. Knives. Go easy on yourself and tell me what I want to know.'

'He'll tell you!' the boy suddenly blurted. 'Stop hurting him!'

I dumped Otto back into the chair.

'You want to tell me, kid?' I asked.

Lindrick shook his head, but the kid was ready to spill. He would have, had the front door not opened as Ezabeth Tanza let herself in.

I was, admittedly, taken aback.

'Captain Galharrow?' she said questioningly, and then, seeing Lindrick, she let out a little cry and rushed over to him. 'What happened? Who did this to you?'

Things got pretty awkward after that. The kid, whose name turned out to be Destran, spilled the story straight away, and Ezabeth wasn't pleased. She threw furious looks at me as she tended Lindrick's purpling face.

'I'd started to think your reputation as a cut-throat was misplaced but I see my optimism was misplaced. You've fallen far from what you once promised to be, captain.'

I scowled right back. It was a low blow. Probably didn't hurt as much as Otto's face did, though.

'Few of us live up to the promise of our youth,' I said. I suggested we talk in private but Ezabeth wouldn't leave Lindrick and insisted on mopping at his face with a wet cloth. I ignored her attempts to send me away. 'Let me lay this out straight for you,' I said. 'Come and see Prince Herono right now. She's not happy that her kinswoman has vanished.'

'Tell her I'm fine. I have too much work to do.'

'Like spreading sedition and treachery?'

Ezabeth's chin jutted proudly through her veil.

'Spreading the truth.'

'You don't have proof,' I said. 'You have theories. That's all. You have ideas and lines on paper. Neither will keep you from the scaffold. I indulged you at Maldon's place, but this has to end. You're going to get yourself locked up, at best. But probably just dead.'

Ezabeth and Otto shared a knowing look.

'At this point, that may not matter a great deal.'

'What do you know about the Engine, captain?'

We were in the cool of Otto's parlour. The boy had brought coffee. I hadn't touched it. I didn't sit.

'I know what everyone knows. It's a weapon. If the drudge come into its range, a lever gets thrown. The projectors spin. The drudge burn. We cheer.'

'Do you know anything of the way in which it operates?'

'It runs on phos. That's all anyone knows. The Engine is vast, and the Order of Aetherial Engineers care for those parts that lie above ground. The projectors, the power conduits, the miles of cabling between the Range stations. But the heart of the Engine is beneath the citadel and nobody has been in there since Nall sealed it. The Order maintains a permanent guard unit, but they're largely ceremonial. Nall protected the heart with his own wards, impenetrable to the likes of us.'

'Not even the Order knows how the heart operates,' Ezabeth said. 'At least, nobody *did*. Not until Gleck Maldon found this.' She produced a broad sheet of crumpled, yellow paper and rolled it out onto a table. It was covered with thousands of thin, connected blue lines with numbers and calculations written tight within the intersections. The whole reminded me of a thousand-faceted jewel. Tidy lines of minute script ran around the edges, but the language didn't use any letters that I knew. One corner of the diagram had been circled in red ink, dark and new, stark against the faded lines and yellowed paper. The edges were singed: I'd swiped it from Maldon's desk as we fled the burning library.

'This is supposed to mean something to me?'

'This is Nall's original schematic for the heart of the Engine.'

A bold claim. It certainly looked old enough, and some of the Nameless had written things down. The Lady of Waves had published a mountain of self-praising sonnets and verses in her own honour and I'd read a military treatise by Cold, but he'd managed to get himself surrounded and destroyed in battle and he'd been wrong about most things. He just didn't understand people enough to grasp strategy. If Ezabeth was right, the schematic for the Engine would have value beyond price. Princes would have knifed their grandmothers for it – or for a great deal less.

'How in the hells would he have got his hands on that?'

'That's one of the things I want to ask him. But this language?' She indicated the unreadable characters around the edges of the page. 'It's Tet. Nobody has spoken it for a thousand years. It only exists on old statues in the northern mountains, on artefacts in museums. I can't read it, but the numbers – the schematic, those I do understand. This is Songlope's Matrix. These intersections represent mirrors and prisms. Refractors. These lines? They're the focused and refocused phos as it travels. As the power meets itself, it magnifies and intensifies. It turns one hundred batteries' power into a thousand.'

'I may not be the most educated man in the room,' I said, 'but I did study at university. Isn't there a law that says that can't happen?'

'There is, and it's true for most matrices of this type. But this isn't an ordinary light matrix. Do you know who Songlope was?'

I was reaching back into my history lessons now. Lady Tanza was giving my brain the kind of workout it hadn't suffered in years.

'He was Nameless. The Deep Kings took him down just before Nall used the Engine against them. Destroying Songlope was the victory that allowed them to assault the Range.'

I took a small and unjust amount of pleasure from answering her questions.

'Quite. Songlope was also the father of all of our

136

understanding of phos technology. Most of modern mathematics and science as well. Being hundreds of years old allows a lot of time for study. Songlope left behind a paradox that has never been solved. When phos is discharged, there is a backlash of power. You will recall the fate of the unfortunate Commander Jerrick at Station Twelve? I had to focus the backlash of the light discharge into something and he was the nearest and most stable expendable thing I could find. Similarly, the light canisters carried by Spinners detonate outwards as a result of a high expenditure of light. The phos-light network vents its discharge as heat, into the communal ovens and so on.'

'Sure.'

'As more phos is used, the size of the backlash increases exponentially. As we approach higher quantities of phos, let's say two hundred coils, the backlash is roughly equal to the discharged energy. At four hundred coils, it's three times as much. At six hundred coils it's twelve times as much.'

'Then how can something like the Engine control the backlash? It uses far more.'

'That's the beauty of it. The paradox allows the backlash to be reharnessed into more and more power. It breaks all of Songlope's other laws of physics. Nall used the paradox to create the Engine. He forged a weapon that allowed ordinary men to bring down the power of a god by throwing a lever.'

I didn't have time to go and study for an advanced degree in mathematics. Otto was nodding along as though he thought it entirely plausible. I decided to trust that they were getting it right.

'So how is this a problem?'

Otto's nodding stopped. His mouth drooped and he looked at his feet. Destran came and topped up the coffee that nobody was touching. Ezabeth raised her chin, strong, ready to be challenged.

'I've run the equations on it. It took me two days to plot them. Bear in mind that this is far, far beyond any light matrix that I've seen calculated before. But what I calculated was that for this matrix to operate effectively it would require precisely seven hundred and twelve thousand battery coils to maintain its efficiency for a full year. Don't you see? It's *precisely* the amount they were feeding into the Engine. Coincidences don't occur on this scale. This *is* the heart of the Engine.'

'Well it had to work somehow,' I said. 'I'm not seeing the problem.'

'Here,' Ezabeth said, pointing to the intersection of five lines that had been circled in red. 'Maldon had ringed this intersection. I removed this line from the calculation and ran the numbers again. If this section fails, the chains begin to collapse. The light never rerefracts, you see?'

I didn't see. I shrugged.

'Take my word for it,' Ezabeth continued. 'Without it, the calculation comes out differently. When this section is removed, the matrix will only accept one hundred and twelve thousand coils.'

'Which is the exact number of coils supplied to the Engine for the last six years,' Otto said. He winced as he put his fingers into his mouth and waggled a tooth that I'd knocked loose. 'Maldon must have worked through every single angle on that schematic to identify it.'

'Do you understand what this means, captain?' Ezabeth said gently.

They let me have silence while that sank in. What they were implying went beyond any claim of profiteering. If they were right then what Gleck Maldon had discovered was that the Engine wasn't just underpowered. It was dying.

'Did somebody do this? Sabotage?' I asked.

'Highly doubtful,' Otto said firmly. 'We're talking about the heart of the Engine. It was constructed by the Nameless and Nall warded the only entrance with his most dreadful magic. But without venturing inside, it's impossible to say.'

'It can't be ruled out,' I said. The thought of a traitor gaining access to the Engine's heart sent cold liquid iron through my veins, heavy and black. 'They're feeding the Engine only what it can take. Who controls the flow of power into the heart?'

'I'm not certain,' Otto said. He pursed his lips as he thought. 'The Order guards its secrets closely. The inner council comprises the three master engineers, the chief librarian, Princes Adenauer and Herono, Marshal Venzer and two master lunarists. One of them controls the phos supply to the Engine's heart. At least one of them must know.'

'But they won't act,' Ezabeth said. 'They won't even listen.'

'What kind of output would the Engine have at one hundred and twelve thousand coils?' I said. 'If they threw the lever, today. With the power stored within it right now. What would it do?'

'That's the worst part,' Ezabeth said. 'You can put phos into a matrix like this, but it's not going to behave as you wanted it to. Imagine a cart that's running away down a hill. Now imagine that three of the wheels disappear. The cart won't carry on more slowly. At best, it halts quickly. At worst? Everything it's carrying is hurled outwards, thrown uncontrollably. If the Engine were activated it might do nothing, or it might release all that power across Valengrad. One hundred and twelve thousand coils is still enough to raze the city to the ground if it were to backlash against us. But I'm guessing. I've never seen calculations that use quantities of phos on this scale before. Nobody has. Light behaves differently the more you amass.'

'So activating the Engine might kill us all?'

'Yes.'

I picked up the coffee and drank the whole cup in a series of swallows. Held it out for more. I could not be sure that there was a traitor on the council, but if there was? We might be throwing ourselves into the dragon's maw.

'Who else knows about this?'

'Nobody. Not yet,' Ezabeth said. 'I must confront the Order for a second time. They must help me access the heart of the Engine and see this for myself. Help me, Captain Galharrow. Use your influence to get me into the Engine's heart.'

I sat silently, staring at the raven tattooed into my arm. Now would have been a damn good time for him to emerge. I had questions for him. I needed to know if we were as dead as I thought we were. The Engine was our only real defence against the Deep Kings and their numberless thralls.

We could use your help about now, I thought. *There are a hundred thousand drudge setting up in the Misery and our only real weapon's on its last leg. Get here, damn you. This is your war. And we're losing.*

14

'It will all come to a head soon,' Ezabeth mused. A dull morning sky hung over the city as we took coffee on the roof terrace. Eala was the only moon rising, her golden light faint and dusty. A cold day for summer's end.

'What will, lady?' I asked.

'All of this,' she said, gesturing across the rooftops of the steaming city. 'A century ago this was nothing but pastures and fields. A village, maybe. This war has gone on too long. It will end soon.'

'You say that like it's a good thing.'

She shrugged. 'I don't know any more. I don't want the Deep Kings to win, but sometimes I wonder if we're any better. The states are all but bled dry by the never-ending need to throw men and weapons into this bloody strip of land. The harvest won't be strong this year, not when Rioque has cast such long shadows. There will be famine.'

'Valengrad seems to be surviving,' I said.

'Of course it is. The princes all know that they must send sufficient wealth to the Range or lose their lands. Lose their titles, their riches. They meet their quotas, but only just. What wealth they have to spare they hoard. There is no charity, nary a glance to the Spirit of Mercy. Sometimes I wonder what we're fighting for.'

'Sometimes, so do I,' I agreed. 'Sometimes it feels like this is all someone else's war. The Kings and the Nameless could have it out somewhere in the Misery and that would be the end of it. When you think of it that way, it all seems pointless. I don't want to become drudge, though. That much I can tell you.'

'There are cults that seek surrender to the Deep Kings. Why would anyone want to be changed like that?' Ezabeth frowned.

'They aren't all strange-looking. Some of them take on colours, bright ones. Some of them don't look so different to you and me. The drudge you saw at Station Twelve, they were standard soldier breeds. Thick skin, resilient, don't need a lot of water. Like the Kings designed them for the Misery. But if you were to cross the Misery and see what lies beyond, where old Dhojara used to be, they're different. They have artists, philosophers, artisans.'

'You've seen them?'

'Seen a lot of things.'

'Is that what took your pity? Otto hasn't got out of bed this morning. His apprentice is still shaken by what you did.'

'Pity gets men killed along the Misery,' I said. 'Stay long enough and you'll find morality doesn't survive sandstorms, clouds of arrows or Darling magic any better than flesh.'

'You've a hard soul, captain.'

'I do.'

'Do you ever wish you were different?'

'I wish everything was different.'

For a few moments, I felt like we were those kids back in the summer of our youth, walking along river banks and blowing the heads from the dandelion clocks. Like I hadn't a thousand lives soaked red beneath my fingernails and like she wasn't a traitor and most likely mad.

'I wish my brother were here,' Ezabeth said eventually. 'He was always the philosopher in the family. I could use his mathematics more than his morality, though. But he's out there in the Misery.'

142

'He's become a soldier?'

'No,' she laughed. It sounded odd through her veil. 'Though I think he might like to be.'

'Takes nerve to walk ten paces into the Misery. He must have some grit.'

'He has a cause,' Ezabeth said. 'Perhaps that's the same thing.'

'And you? You were willing to risk your name. Your life. Why?'

Ezabeth turned her back on me. She looked out over the factories, seeking, until she pointed towards Herono's phos mill, distant on the edge of the city.

'There are one hundred and thirty-three phos mills throughout the city states,' she said. 'Some are big. Some are small. They give us light and warmth and water purifiers and communicators. But we forget that for every trickle of power there's a person behind a loom. Night after night, worked until their back breaks and their mind cracks. Then somebody puts a pistol to the back of their head and sends their family what passes for compensation for the loss of a loved one. I started helping Maldon because I wanted to help the Talents. To make sure their sacrifice was not in vain.'

'Nobody likes what happens to the Talents,' I said. 'But what choice is there?' Ezabeth shook her head.

'I had a friend at the university. A girl called Tessa. She came from common stock, but she was bright, oh, so clever that girl. She'd won herself a scholarship. And then she had her radiance. A little spur of magic, right there in the classroom. She burned off an eyebrow. The next day they took her to a mill because the law demanded it.' Ezabeth put her arms around herself, rubbed at her elbows. 'She only lasted four years, and there wasn't much left to bury. She wasted away to skin and bone. She didn't know her parents any more. The light even took them from her.'

I am not much good at comforting people. I just nodded.

'I'm not so naive that I don't understand the importance of the Talents' work,' she said. 'Many have given their lives for the Range. But no life should be squandered to line a rich man's pockets.'

Otto Lindrick appeared then, being helped along by his spotty apprentice. He didn't look happy to have me back in his house. Couldn't blame him.

Ezabeth had explained their connection. Lindrick had transferred into the city from a small countryside phos mill after the death of the accountant. The circumstances were suspicious. And when Lindrick was made responsible for the importation of battery coils from the outer mills, for the heart of the Engine, he discovered discrepancies. Problems with the supply. He had leaked the phos-battery records to Maldon, an expert light Spinner known for his dislike of the governing class. A man he could trust. He couldn't have known what Maldon would discover, or what it would do to his mind.

'You didn't tell Prince Herono where Lady Tanza is,' Lindrick said. I'd gone home and slept on it. I needed her money, but Ezabeth's approval seemed to matter more.

'I'm not one to stab a person in the back while they're sleeping. If I think you're fighting the wrong cause, you'll see me coming head-on.' Actually, I'd stabbed more than one man in the back, but it sounded good. 'Someone with power sent those men to Maldon's house. Right now I'm not prepared to trust anybody. We move slow. Steady. We eliminate the options one by one, not charge in firing off cannon.'

'The Order refused to convene the council to hear her again,' Lindrick said.

'Marshal Venzer refused to give me an audience as well,' Ezabeth said. 'Even my cousin, who claims to be supportive of my concerns, offers me no assistance. If they will not heed me, I will take more direct action. I will make what I know public, if they give me no other choice.'

'I understand your urgency,' I said at length. 'You might be onto something big. I get it. Maybe you are. Or maybe you're wrong, maybe your calculations are off. But if you print that stuff, what do you think it would do to the people?'

'They have to know,' she said sternly. As unbendable as an iron bar.

'People don't need to know shit,' I said. 'Even if it's true, which I fucking well hope it isn't. You can't say things like that to ordinary people. They don't have the brains for it.'

'Have you no respect for your countrymen?' Lindrick said stiffly. The irony of his question was not lost on me, given what I'd done to him yesterday.

'People are sheep,' I said. 'They do as you tell them. They believe what they want to, or whatever frightens them the most. If they don't like it, they reject it or they ignore it. It's natural. Can't blame them for it. Can't tell them they're stupid either. They don't understand that they're sheep. How could they? The sheep don't realise the shepherd is smarter than they are.'

'You sound like the Nameless,' Ezabeth said, frosty as midwinter.

'Yeah, well,' I grunted. 'I spent some time around one or two of them. There's a point you realise those bastards, whatever they are, they're more than you and me. Not just a little, but a lot more. Where we think in days and months, they think in centuries. Play a long game. Maybe that comes with immortality. Maybe it's just part of whatever it is that they are.'

'You have such confidence in them? You're so sure?' she asked.

'As sure as I need to be.'

For a long moment nobody spoke.

'Perhaps it is time to put your faith elsewhere. The Nameless have failed us. Abandoned us in our hour of need. I do not think that Crowfoot will return. Perhaps he sees the Engine has failed and seeks new allies across the ocean. Perhaps the Lady of Waves shall retreat with him there and they will wage their war with new minions at their disposal.' A dark anger lurked in her eyes. 'As you say, they think in centuries, not months. What does it matter to the Nameless if we all perish?'

I thought about it. I didn't like the sound of it, and it had a disturbingly likely ring of truth to it. For a moment it seemed all too plausible.

'Then we're all fucked anyway. Why engender a panic that will only get you hanged?'

'Because the truth is bigger than I am.'

'Most things are bigger than you,' I said. She didn't laugh. Lindrick didn't laugh. Nenn would have laughed, and I wished she was there. 'What would it take to prove to the Command Council that you're right?'

Ezabeth thought about it. She rubbed at the stumps of her missing fingers.

'Get me access to the heart.'

'Nobody enters the heart,' I said. 'Not even Crowfoot.'

'How would you know?' she said. I knew because he'd told me once, years ago. I didn't choose to share that. I shrugged. Ezabeth glanced down at my arm, then cocked her head and a new understanding narrowed her eyes.

'You belong to him,' she said. She gripped my arm between eight hard little fingers as I tried to turn away from her. The touch of her gloves froze me faster than any icy stare she'd given. I let her turn it back, fingers tracing across the skin. Suddenly I was sixteen again and Ezabeth was dressed in a light summer dress, all linen and shades of air. She had stroked her fingers along my arm, daring me to flinch from her tickling touch. We lay in the meadow, side by side, staring up at the sky. Desperate to touch one another, our youthful lust held in check by the dour-faced chaperone at her needlework nearby. A cruel game, to thrust children together to see if their excitement kindled and then insist they deny every natural urge. The memory soured my mood and I brought my arm back. That hopeful boy was gone, dead and buried beneath a tide of stinking bodies and enough black days to darken even our broken sky.

'I don't belong to anybody,' I snapped. She was not convinced. 'The heart's beneath the citadel, and not even Crowfoot knows how to breach the locking mechanism. There's a bunch of panels, a sequence that has to be adhered to. Get it wrong and you burn. Nobody gets in without Nall. You should know that.'

'Of course I do,' Ezabeth said. 'But I'm at a dead end without Maldon. I need to know what he knew. If the Order will not answer me then I must enter the heart and see for myself. I don't claim that I can fix what the Nameless forged, but I can try. And I'm better qualified than anyone else in the Alliance.'

'The Order will never allow it,' I said.

'Of course they won't,' Ezabeth said, banging down her fist. 'The fools block me at every turn. Regardless, I don't care for their permission.' I sensed a shifting beneath her veil as though she were smiling. 'I will gain the access I need, whether they open the door for me or I have to blast open a new one.'

15

I woke to a tearing pain in my arm, burning heat and a sense of violation. I cried out, grabbed my arm and gritted my teeth as the skin thrust outwards, lances of agony through my flesh as it ripped open. The bird that struggled out was huge, too big to have been in my arm, its shining black plumage oily and slick with my blood. I tried not to scream as gore dripped across my sheets.

The bird spread its wings wide, opened its beak wide.

'GET HER OUT!' it bellowed, a furious roar that rattled the bed in its frame. The voice was tinged with the raven's croak but the rage was all too human. 'GET HER OUT! GET HER OUT!'

I'd have preferred a more cogent message, but Crowfoot didn't favour me with any details. The big bird flapped its wings once, twice, looked around in puzzlement as if wondering where it was. Its message clearly delivered, I backhanded the bloody thing off the bed. A few moments later, the raven's eyes crackled with inner fire, smoke billowed from beneath the wings and jetted in a little plume from its beak as it collapsed. I grasped my arm and swore through gritted teeth. Fucking birds. Fucking wizards.

I rolled from the bed. The wound in my arm would close of its own accord, but it was fucking up my cleanish sheets. I wrapped a strip of bandage around it and threw on the first clothes that came to hand. No time to waste. Act fast, move quick, stay bright. I glanced between the weapons in my cupboard. The cutlass was good and practical, but instead I took my longsword, half weapon, half warning. A man doesn't strap on a longsword unless he means to carve somebody in two. Crowfoot seldom sent me a mission without there being a good chance that I'd have to sever someone from their mortality.

Would have helped if he'd told me where to go, or who I was supposed to be getting out of what, but I could guess at the who, at least. I ran to a local stable, hired a horse and saddle with money I couldn't afford. Nenn's place was on the way, so I hammered on her door. She glanced out the window, saw the battle gear and joined me dressed in edges. Didn't ask me any questions, maybe saw the set of my jaw. She rode double behind me.

I tried Lindrick's house first, but it was dark and quiet. No sign of a struggle, nothing to suggest anything untoward had happened. I tried the front and the back, banged my fist against the doors a few times, but nobody was home. Nenn frowned at me, but I didn't explain and we went on to the Willows.

Nothing seemed out of the ordinary. The guards on the bridge spanning the moat waved us through. Servants moved along the streets with covered baskets or rolled sealed kegs. We galloped past them until I came into view of Herono's vast house. The groom took charge of my horse but looked uncertainly at me.

'You won't find much work today, I think, sir,' he said. 'Some bad business.'

I didn't fancy getting answers from a groom anyway. I found the steward, who looked flustered and too hot beneath his starched collar. I should have asked for the prince.

'I need to see Prince Herono,' I demanded. Shot him a black, kill-everyone type of look. The steward looked me over, noted the steels at my belt. He insisted that I disarm and that Nenn wait in a reception room, then led me through the house.

'Is your arm hurt, sir?' he asked.

'Nothing that won't get better,' I said. The thin bandage had bled through, the red stain darkening to brown. Crowfoot hadn't been careful as he tore me open. My arm hurt like a bastard but the anger in that croaking voice was more dangerous.

Herono was reading through sheaves of paperwork in a palatial chamber, fully one whole wall of which was panels of glass. It faced west, away from the Misery. Better to see the true blue of the sky when you had the choice. The prince looked old. Her skin weathered, mouth a tight, pursed line. The steward ushered me in and left me there. Herono's one eye was on the wrong side of her head to see me; she had not noticed me enter.

'Your grace,' I bowed. She looked up. I thought she seemed tired. Irritated. She ushered me to the seat opposite.

'You have no doubt heard, then?' she said. I chose my words carefully.

'I should prefer to hear it from you, your grace.'

'Ezabeth reappeared at her family residence this morning. Spirits alone know where she was hiding,' she said. 'The marshal's men took her. She has been declared a dangerous lunatic and incarcerated in the Maud.'

It didn't come as a shock. I felt cold. Empty. Slowly, a tide rose telling me I'd helped put her there. Instead of locking her down, I'd encouraged her.

'She went with them quietly?'

'Oh, no,' Herono sighed. 'She was quite ready to burn them all. She had portable battery coils and battle canisters stacked around her bed. Spirits know where she got them from. The soldiers were well warned, though. Professional. They brought sufficient sorcerers to lock her down.'

'I see.' Too many thoughts were flying by for any of them

to take hold long enough for me to think on it. I swallowed. Tried to get myself in order. 'I ...' Words abandoned me. Herono must have seen the look on my face.

'I suppose that to bring her all this way from Station Twelve only to find her unhinged must be a great disappointment,' Herono said. I nodded. Yeah. That made sense, a good enough story.

'Yes, your grace.'

'Mercy knows where she has been these last days,' Herono said. 'I've some of her writings here. Some of what she has written is quite bizarre.' She wore a faintly amused little smile. 'See this? Here, I'll read it for you. "The Steps Of Nall, as I recall them. The heart is black, the heart is cold. Only a song could be so bold." It's a children's rhyme. Do you know it?'

I felt a great sinking feeling. Like when you learn that despite what they told you, nobody has really seen the holy spirits, that you have to take them on faith, and then realise that none of it makes any bloody sense at all. Like that, but worse.

'I know it,' I said. It was a nonsense rhyme, the kind that you sing to a child. My mother had taught it to me. It went on, 'The day draws long, the night comes soon, only a child can seek the moon.' I ran my hands across my face.

It *was* nonsense. But Gleck Maldon had lost his mind and been right all the same.

'I had hoped she would come to her senses, stop before she pushed too far,' Herono said grimly. 'Even when she called me a conspirator in front of the Council, still I hoped. Now, at least she cannot harm herself.'

'What will happen to her now?'

'She'll stay there, I suppose,' Herono said. 'Perhaps it is for the best.'

I pursed my lips. I would not allow that to happen. I'd seen Ezabeth at her most frantic, so absorbed in her scribbling she'd not known I was there, and I'd doubted her. But I'd also seen her calm, methodical, wonderful. The spinning coin could have fallen to either side but the Maud sure as spit wasn't the place for it to land. She needed answers, and so did I.

'Surely you could use your influence to have her freed, your grace? Have her sent to some quiet place where she could be tended? Somewhere more suitable for a woman of her rank?'

'The situation prevents me from intervening,' Herono said. 'Ezabeth has been rather too active and vocal. Allegedly she tried to publish seditious material, making treasonous claims. Were I to intervene now I'd be seen to be taking her side. You can imagine the difficulties that would present if the allegations proved true. They took her this morning and judging by her writings perhaps it is a mercy. By keeping her in the mad house I can at least protect her. The mad cannot be held to account by law.'

'Do you believe she intended treason, your grace?'

I had to walk a careful line. I doubted that Ezabeth had sold me out for helping her, but I couldn't show any sign that I might be in agreement with her.

'Between you and me?' Herono checked the doorway to ensure that we were alone. 'The girl may have lost her mind, but I was rather hoping she'd finish her research. The results would have been very interesting.' She shrugged. 'But what's done is done. Mistakes were made. I shall ensure she is well cared for. Perhaps she can even continue her research behind the Maud's safe walls. Imagine if she were right?'

I knew she was right. I felt it now, solid as a stone in my gut. Crowfoot's direct intervention had confirmed it for me. He'd had me help her at Station Twelve because she mattered. I shuffled my cards, got ready to play the round. They held all the high cards, but those only matter if you're playing the same game.

I took my leave.

'All this fuss over that little witch?' Nenn said as we rode swiftly back into town.

'Seems so.'

'What's so special about her?'

'She's figured things out. Important things. Things people don't like. Shit on it all, we have to get her out of there.'

Maybe Nenn was giving me a look, but since she was behind me all I could feel was the tightening of her fists balled up in my shirt. Nenn never liked the cream, hated to take their part in anything. Maybe I'd been wrong to bring her. Needed her, though. Better to ride carefully.

The Maud was an old building, older than most in Valengrad. Big stone walls with two high storeys. Above the wide double doors a legend stated the name of the man who had commissioned it, some long-dead colonel. It hadn't always been an asylum, but the need for somewhere to house the crazies was pretty great in Valengrad.

The orderlies and physicians who staffed the Maud wore long green robes and brown aprons, delicate gloves and little cloth face masks, as though lunacy was something that could be caught. Maybe it could. That would certainly explain some of the things I'd been doing lately. Nenn said that at least with all those covered faces Ezabeth wouldn't feel out of place. She had a point.

I showed the fat matron the letter of authority Herono had given me. She seemed surprised, but she admitted us. I'd met her before on previous visits.

'When Maldon was a guest here we had the rooms prepared for him,' the matron told me cheerfully as she waddled along. 'Bricked up the windows completely. We had rather expected that he would be here for a long time, and he could afford a comfortable existence so we agreed to pay for the brickwork. We had kept him down in the dark rooms until it was ready, but we finished the work and not a day later he broke out. Such a waste!'

I thought it a waste too, just not of the money.

There were guards on the door. Ordinary-looking men wearing black citadel uniforms. They didn't look pleased to see us, but the matron was the boss. I wondered how long they were going to be staying around for. It couldn't be normal to post guards in the Maud, not even for a patient of status.

The chambers beyond were more comfortable than my own place, thick plush rugs and beautiful wall hangings showing the works of the spirits. The furniture was older, probably sold cheap by some noble who'd had enough of the Range and decided to pack up and run back west. The whole room was lit only with oil lamps. The stench of the whale oil was repugnant, but only moonlight could be spun into phos. If Ezabeth tried to spin this artificial glow she'd get sick. The big matron looked like she wanted to linger, to hear what we were to discuss, but I asked for privacy and she granted it. Ezabeth appeared from a side room, fixing her veil into place as if she'd been disturbed.

'They got me,' she said bitterly. Angry rather than un-nerved. 'I returned to my house in Willows as you advised, and the next morning I wake up with swords at my throat.'

'I'm sorry,' I said. I could have said that I'd warned her, but there was no use. She didn't look any the worse for wear. She wore a long dress of burnt orange trimmed with black, the knee-length fashion with long boots beneath. She seemed altogether less distressed than her situation warranted.

'I remember you,' Ezabeth said, looking at Nenn. 'You were at Station Twelve. You fought alongside the captain. You have my thanks for your help.'

Nenn shrugged. It was rude of her, but then, maybe social rank didn't count once you've been declared a mad woman. By Nenn's expression she intended to be ruder than usual.

'I have to get you out of here,' I said. 'Orders from the top.'

'From Marshal Venzer?' Ezabeth asked.

'Higher,' I said. I stroked my arm. It still hurt, although the flesh there was smooth and unbroken again. I never quite understood how that magic works. It doesn't heal, it's just not damaged any more. Like it never happened.

'Both higher and lower,' Ezabeth murmured. I nodded.

'You're both crazy,' Nenn said. She slumped down into a chair, annoyed that we were talking about something she didn't understand. Nenn didn't understand a lot of things, but she was used to me not explaining them. Ezabeth narrowed her eyes at me, a tight smile on her lips.

'Don't you see, though? If *he's* on my side, it means I must be right.'

'I don't think he's on anyone's side except his own,' I said. 'We need you out of here. How do we make that happen?'

'Fear not, I will be out soon,' Ezabeth said. 'My cousin will be furious. I had rather expected her to set me free by now. She won't tolerate the insult to her family long. You know my cousin.'

So that explained her lack of concern.

'I wouldn't look for help from that quarter,' I said. I ran a few things through my mind. Herono's absence, the prince's easy acceptance of Ezabeth's incarceration. 'It serves Herono's interests to have you locked in here,' I said eventually. 'Your ideas are dangerous. As a phos mill owner and councillor for the Order, you're spouting poison to her interests. We have to assume she's no longer an ally.'

'We?' Ezabeth said. Her eyes flashed. I'd have sworn there was a feline grin beneath her mask.

'We?' Nenn said. Her eyes glowered. She'd have scrunched up her nose if she'd had one.

'Never mind that,' I snapped. I took a deep breath. 'I need you out of here. I can get you out. If you're willing.' I placed a hand on the pommel of my longsword. The age-old signal that you're willing to start painting the walls red. Ezabeth met my eye and she didn't even consider it.

'No innocents. Let's say you kill the guards at the door and cut a path through the orderlies. To what end? I'd have no chance of presenting my work to the marshal, the Order's inner circle, any of them. I'd be a dangerous criminal, a fugitive. No. I must be freed, legally. I'm on to something, and I'm close to it. They want it buried.' She glared at the walls. 'This buries me.'

I thought back to the sad little rhyme that Herono had showed me. *The heart is black, the heart is cold.* I wish I could have been surer that I was doing the right thing. Still had to go with it. What Crowfoot ordered, I did. Even if Ezabeth didn't want to, even if it made me an outlaw, I'd cut her a path. If Crowfoot had told me to cut off both my own arms I'd have tried to do it. Failing him was not an option.

'Aren't you some high-up cream?' Nenn asked. Sourness in her tone.

'Lady Tanza's brother is Count Tanza,' I said.

'Get him to free you,' Nenn said with a shrug. I guess that to Nenn, down on the ground, it seemed like the cream could do whatever they wanted. But she had a point.

'The Maud isn't the last word in incarceration,' I said. 'They say you're crazy, but if your brother insisted on taking you into his own care, there's little they could do about it. It wouldn't give you the freedom of the city, but it would get you out of here.'

'Yes,' Ezabeth agreed. 'But he's in the Misery. He came here to help Maldon with his calculations weeks ago, and then went to study Cold's Crater.'

There was a certain expectant silence. Nenn turned to look at me and I avoided looking back. She stared at me until I met her eye.

'Don't say it, captain,' she said. Terse. Warning. Without

knowing why, a kind of grin began to creep onto my face. Maybe because it was going to annoy Nenn, and we had that kind of relationship.

'Maybe we have to.'

'You're as crazy as she is.'

'Maybe. But I think we still have to.' I looked back to Ezabeth. It made this easier that not only was it Crowfoot's order, it was what I wanted to do. This whale-oil stinking chamber was no place for my lady. For a lady. *Get your fucking words straight, Galharrow.*

'Have to what?' she asked.

'I know Cold's Crater. Been there before. It's deep into the Misery, but if Tnota can get a good lunar alignment we can be there and back within a week. If we move fast and don't get gracked on the way. Or on the way back.' I glanced at Nenn. 'What do you think?'

'I think you're a cock,' Nenn said.

'Sure. A week, though?' She thought about it. We'd spent an unpleasant summer of skirmishes around that crater some five years before.

'It's bullshit, but it can be done.'

It was decided. Nobody ever wants to go into the Misery, but sometimes you just got to follow the trickle of fate's piss.

'And that other problem? The one where you get your ghost owned, or your balls cut off?' Nenn said angrily. 'Don't act like you don't got problems of your own to sort out. You don't have the time to be doing this, captain.'

'Sometimes you got to rest your own problems.'

'Sometimes they won't rest! Problems like owing Saravor big time. Yeah, Tnota told me. You need to get yourself clear with him, not go running off into the Misery because—' She restrained herself, like she was dragging back on her own leash. I suspect some kind of vicious description of Ezabeth would have followed. Nenn's dislike for my potentially insane friend wore no silks.

157

'Saravor,' Ezabeth said, turning the name over like it was a fine wine on the tongue. 'I've heard of him. He was ... recommended to me, a long time ago. I heard bad things about him. You owe him money?'

I wouldn't have admitted it. Would have kept it to my chest as close as I could. I didn't want Ezabeth knowing the deals I'd made with that scrap of evil. I don't believe in good and evil, but if I had, then Saravor was as close to evil as I'd ever encountered. That I'd done business with him didn't say a whole lot in my favour.

'Captain paid him to save my life,' Nenn said. She jerked up her shirt, showed the patch of discoloured brown skin that formed part of her abdomen. Her chin jutted proudly. 'He saved my life and got himself tangled in more debt than he can pay. Needs twenty thousand marks by tomorrow or Saravor isn't going to be happy. And that don't go well for nobody.'

'Enough, Nenn,' I said. Stupid to feel embarrassed, but there it was. 'What I owe is my business and nobody else's. I've raised fifteen so far,' I said. 'I hoped it wouldn't come to this, but I can pawn my armour to make the first payment. I'll get at least five thousand. It's old, but it's worth at least ten.' I hoped so, anyway.

'Five thousand?' Ezabeth said. She rose, left the room. When she returned she had writing equipment. 'I'll stand you the money,' she said. 'Payment in advance for bringing my brother back here. He left me the family seal; there is a bank named Ostkov and Sons. They will give you the money.'

'That fancy bank with the marbles? They'll sure as the hells be glad to see us,' Nenn said.

They weren't. They were pissed at having to give me anything, but they gave me the money. I was still afloat.

Not dead yet.

16

I sent Nenn to get Tnota ready. They'd meet me at the Bell after I'd made my visit. The pockets of my coat hung heavy with gold and silver. I could hardly believe that I'd managed to get away with this. Somehow Galharrow was going to manage a rare win. Can't always be losing.

The Spills was as vile as ever. Ugly, sore-lipped whores called to me from their windows, sagging teets displayed above their stretch marks. Nasty young lads left their shirts open to display the skinny chests and abdomens that they were so proud of, and the pickpocket children hovered like flies around shit. They saw my weapons as a challenge; if they could rob an armed soldier like me they'd be earning themselves some kind of reputation. The first one that tried it was a girl approaching her teens. I hit her hard enough to send her sprawling in the gutter and the rest stayed well clear after that. I pity the young, but when they try to steal from me they force the hand that clubs them.

One of Saravor's grey-skinned little child creatures opened the door as usual. I said I'd wait down in the reception room, took a seat on a worn old sofa the colour of bad olives. The whole place smelled damp, like nobody really lived there. I'd read about sea creatures that in part look like plants, luring in their prey. Wouldn't have surprised me if Saravor's whole house was a deception, ready to reach out and swallow me.

The sorcerer appeared. He looked paler, waxier than he

had before, or at least the white bits of him did. Hard to see the whole picture with a patchwork man whose flesh ranges the spectrum. He brought a bottle of vodka down with him, as though we were old friends meeting socially. I accepted a small glass none the less.

'You have money for me?' he said. He sounded amused.

'You ever doubt it?' I said. I stacked the coins out onto the table, gold and silver in fat, heavy discs. Saravor ran his eyes over it.

'I did, actually,' he said. He didn't sound as disappointed as I thought he would. He ran his triple-jointed fingers along the stacks, counting and assessing the value of the marks. When he was happy he summoned one of his dead-eyed children to scoop it into a large sack. Twenty thousand marks is not a fortune, but a regular soldier would take a year to struggle that together. Many men would have killed many other men for less.

'We're done for now then,' I said. 'Maybe I'll have your next instalment after I get back. Else it's a month, right?'

'Back?' Saravor frowned. 'I don't like the sound of that. Where are you going?'

'Got a job in the Misery,' I said. 'Trust me, I don't like it either.'

'But there are skweams out there,' Saravor said in mock horror. 'Dulchers. Even the gillings can be lethal, and that's not to mention this increased activity from the drudge. The ground might just open up and swallow you whole. I find this ... bad for my business.'

'Yeah? Well there's fuck all you can do about it,' I said. I knocked back the vodka. Hard-hitting stuff. Awful, awful taste, but at least you knew it was doing the job.

'Maybe. Maybe not.' He was frowning. 'Ryhalt, I enjoy the control that my influence allows me. I fear that if you were to go traipsing off into the Misery I might never see you again. Where then would that leave me?'

'Not my place to care.' I got up. 'You got your first payment. I'll be good for the second just the same. That's all I came to say.'

Saravor rose as well. Seven and a half feet tall, he had to stoop to avoid knocking his hairless head on the ceiling. I hate not being the biggest man in a room.

'I have a proposition for you,' the sorcerer said.

'Not interested.'

'Maybe you will be. I'm prepared to knock fifteen thousand from your debt.'

OK. Maybe I was interested. My pride warred against the insanity of entering into further deals with the patchwork man.

'Talk.'

'Oh, Ryhalt, so surly! Such a brooder, aren't you? It's really very simple. Allow me to put a little glamour upon you, to know where you are – and most notably, if you're dead – and I'll trim your debt. Call it insurance. If you die out there on whatever foolish lost cause you think you're supporting, then I can pursue reparations from your estate.' He smiled widely at me, displaying his perfect teeth. More rows of them than a human should have.

'Why all the deals?' I said. 'Why the money? You don't need it. You don't spend it. What the fuck is it you want, making us dance for you?'

'Money turns the earth, as they say, but you're right. It's of little importance to me. I don't even keep it. But I would have thought that you would understand. You being of Blackwing, after all.'

'You'll have to spell it out for me.'

'What does anybody truly want in life? There is only one currency worth trading in. Control. Power. The farmers try to tame the earth, bend it to their will. The nobility bend the peasants, and in turn are bent to the will of princes. All bow before the Nameless, and even they wrestle against the Deep Kings. And for what? So that they can tell the peasants how to wall their fields and grow their beans? We all desire to control the world around us. I am little different from your master.'

'No,' I said. 'You might be emperor of the Spills, but to him you're of no more importance than a tick. You're not Nameless.'

'Not yet.' His teeth gleamed pearlescent.

'That's what you want? To be like them?'

Saravor waved the conversation aside. We were back to business.

'Today all I want is to make a deal.'

Making deals with sorcerers is bad, but when you're already twisted up in one, how bad can it hurt? I thought about it some. Made my decision.

'Knock off half the debt,' I said. 'Half the debt, and you can track me.'

'Let's be serious,' Saravor said with his irritating self-assuredness. We haggled, agreed on twenty thousand marks. A lot of money. I accepted.

'Fine,' I said. 'We're done then.' I got up to leave.

'A moment.' Saravor smiled. Before I could stop him, he reached out and put one of his long, nobbled fingers against my chest.

I remember hitting the wall. I remember the intrusion, as though something dark and terrible were working its way down my throat. Maybe I screamed, but nobody would come running towards the dark sounds that escaped Saravor's lair. It entered me somehow, turning from black to tarnished silver as it took form and residence in my chest. In my mind's eye I saw it as a dragon, silver and serpentine, curled around my heart. Something cold and clear, slumbering but very much alive.

When I had recovered sufficiently to stand, my vision clearing, I was alone. The door to the street was open, telling me where to go. I staggered upright, unclear as to what had just happened but sure that I had somehow managed to make things very much worse.

As a Blackwing captain I had the right to ride out into the Misery whenever the need arose. It was a rule made half pointless because anyone could just head a little north or south and then ride into the Misery anyway, and even more pointless because nobody would ride out there unless they were cracked in the head.

Only one gate leads directly out of Valengrad and into the Misery. The walls of the city are forty feet of packed stone and gravel, built to withstand the power of guns and sorcery. The single passageway through those walls was tight and narrow, barely big enough for a couple of men to ride abreast. It was meant that way. The walls were there to keep the Dhojarans out, not to process traffic. I fretted beside the gate, looking over the provisions saddled up on the rented horses, checking over my kit as we waited for a message from Ezabeth. She wanted to send a letter to her brother, thought she could get it to us before we departed.

'Looking fine today, captain,' Nenn said. Like me she was wearing half-plate, good armour where it was vital and mobility where it wasn't. Holsters on our saddles carried poleaxes, blades, matchlocks, ammunition. I was hoping that we wouldn't need our arsenal, but it isn't just the drudge in the Misery that require a dose of steel to keep quiet. Wheedle sulked close by, annoyed that he was missing out on a paying job. More greed than common sense in that one.

Otto Lindrick and his scrappy apprentice appeared along the road, mounted on a pair of donkeys. I frowned and he scowled back at me, hardly surprising given the yellow and purple mess I'd made of his face. At least I'd not ruined any good looks.

'I am come from the Maud,' he said. 'I find it hard to

believe, but I am told you are to be trusted.' He scowled as he produced a leather case from within his robe, but held it close to his body.

'That's for her brother?' I asked, held out my hand for it.

'Are you truly on her side, captain? You've shown me the colour of your fist before. And you were swinging it for the other side.'

'I don't fly anyone else's flag. I just care about getting paid, and today she's paying me.'

'If it's any consolation, the captain only beats the tar out of people for the money,' Nenn said. She spat blacksap in his general direction.

'Shut your mouth,' I snapped. Nenn wasn't always helpful. She took out her jar of blacksap and pointedly stuffed a fresh wad between her teeth.

Destran whispered something to his master, casting nervous looks in our direction. He was a shifty-looking kid, more of the Spills about him than Willows. His master conferred quietly with him.

'How can I know that you won't take this missive straight to Prince Herono?' Lindrick said.

'Can't prove it,' I said. 'But we're going to fetch Count Dantry Tanza, and our mutual friend told you to give that to me. I can take the message or not. If you don't want to give it to us, well delivering it isn't the main purpose of the mission. You can come with us and deliver it yourself if you want. A week in the Misery would do you good. Might shake that body lean.'

He thought about it for all of two heartbeats, then passed the letter case to the boy, who had the task of delivering it into my hand. He nudged his heels against his donkey's flanks the moment it was in my hand, glad to be away. I stored the message safely away in my saddle pack. Lindrick stayed to watch us heading out. I ushered Nenn and Tnota to go ahead of me, turned to the engineer.

'For what it's worth, sorry about your face,' I said.

'You apologise, but you'd do it again if it served your purpose.'

'I'm a soldier,' I said. 'That's how it works. Look after the girl, if you can. She's not as strong as she wants you to think.'

'You do her a disservice. I've rarely met a woman of such will,' Lindrick said.

'I know. But she'd have you believe she can go head to head with princes and Kings. She has her limits, just like any of us.'

'And you, captain? What are your limits?'

I gave him a mirthless grin.

'Usually from wherever I start to the end of the bar.' I turned my horse to go.

'Captain? Why are you doing this?'

'Getting paid,' I said.

'And that's it? You don't share her vision. Her belief?'

I gave him a long, appraising look. I'd underestimated him before. The whimpering, the cowering, that had been an act. There was something strong inside Otto Lindrick, something like the steel in Ezabeth Tanza's spine. Part of me wished that I'd not made him my enemy.

'Look after her,' I said again, and trotted into the darkness of the tunnel.

17

The Misery began less than half a mile from Valengrad's walls. Hadn't been so close when they made the city, but it grew, like the corruption was some kind of spreading mould. The horses shied and objected as they sensed the unnatural land we were about to enter. We spoke soft words, fed them sugar until they calmed. They could feel the magic in the air, the essence of distortion. It begins as a sensation on the skin, like the dry stretch when you get sunburned. Everything a little too tight, its placement somehow wrong. Then comes the feeling in the throat, the lungs, like your body doesn't want to breathe Misery air, and a feeling behind your eyes as though what they're seeing isn't quite true. There's nothing like it in all the world that I've known, and for that, I thank whatever spirits might give enough fucks to listen.

The early going was easy, the land having chosen to lie flat and sandy. No plants, no trees, just red-brown sand and clumps of glistening black rock. The stones dotted the landscape like huge lumps of tar. Best not to touch them. Best not to touch anything in the Misery that you don't have to. Nenn and Tnota said nothing. They'd both ridden the Misery enough times that this wasn't anything new to them. Tnota kept his eyes mostly skywards, assessing the positioning of the moons against his astrolabe, keeping us on course for Cold's Crater. The land began to roll, low hills and dips, and the smog and phos lights of Valengrad disappeared from view. Here and there, when the earth fell low, we saw clusters of stone that had once been the walls of some farmstead or maybe even a townhouse. Impossible to know which. They may have travelled a hundred miles since Crowfoot's weapon cracked the sky and tore the Misery into existence. Hard to judge, the way the earth could shift.

'Why we doing this, captain? Not exactly Blackwing work is it?' Nenn asked as we passed what looked like a dried-up river bed. No water flowed there now.

'Seemed important,' I said.

'The fancy skirt. You tapping that?' Something in her tone warned me to tread sensitively. I didn't look at her.

'Wouldn't be your business if I was, Private Nenn.'

'Risking all our necks for a fuck? Seems to me it would be,' she said.

'You're risking your necks because you owe me more favours than you owe me beers, and you'd have to buy out a brewery to pay that tab.'

'Hush,' Tnota said. Trying to act as peacemaker. 'This is the Misery. Don't talk unless you have to. No telling what's listening.'

It was good advice. Nenn and I are similar in our inability to heed good advice.

'She's doing something important. I got orders from the top. Not Herono, the real top. You know what Blackwing really is. You've hired out to me long enough to know that when the raven caws, we act. This isn't something I chose to do.'

'You sure about that?'

'Yes.' I wasn't.

'Shit,' Nenn grunted. 'It's been years. Thought you were finished with that bastard bird.'

I kicked my horse ahead to end the conversation. I looked up at the rifts running through the bloody-bruise-coloured sky. Maybe Nenn was right. Maybe I shouldn't have involved her at all. An intense white-bronze light glowed through the cracks overhead, like some part of the heavens was shining down on us, but I couldn't have thought of a place heaven would be less likely to glow for than the Misery. As if to punctuate my thoughts, the sky gave one of its great, wounded cries, a soaring, empty song of pain and despair. My master had demanded I do whatever was required to get her free. Eighty years ago he'd unleashed the Heart of the Void here, what used to be territory belonging to the cities of Adrogorsk and Clear. Nobody knew how many thousands of lives he'd sacrificed to drive back the Deep Kings. Some might think the likes of Prince Herono ruthless, but compared to the Nameless she was nothing but a novice. If Crowfoot told me to cross ten oceans to pick a dying flower, I'd have done it.

Late in the afternoon, distantly to the north-west, I saw something large in the sky. Too distant to make it out beyond the dark of its wings and the long tail trailing behind it. None of us had seen anything like that out here before. We stayed quiet and hoped that it wouldn't come in our direction. It flew on north and we lost sight of it.

Rioque, the red moon, began rising just as the sky was growing dark. It never gets fully dark in the Misery even if all of the moons are sleeping. The stark crack-light never fades away, but Rioque cast a gory shine across the red sands. We found a cluster of the black tar-rocks, smoothed the sands down to make something like a sleeping space and divvied up the watches. I drew first, took my ration of rum and a couple of sticks of liquorice and sat watching the land around us. There's nothing duller than sentry duty in peaceful lands, but in the Misery some of the night creatures will keep you busy. One of the horses alerted me to the approach of a flat, twelve-legged thing, less than a foot high and half that wide, insect feelers tasting the air ahead of it. The eyes were all too human. It scuttled towards where Tnota slept, so I speared it with the butt end of my poleaxe and tossed it some way from our camp. Never saw anything like it before, probably never would again. Took some care to clean the end of my weapon of the treacle-dark stuff that came out of its broken carapace. Knowing that things like that are scuttling around in the dark doesn't help sleep come easy. When it was my turn to roll under a blanket I lay awake, listening to the things that lurked in the blood and silver sheen of the night.

As soon as there was decent light we saddled the horses and ate breakfast as we rode. The red moon had sunk away, her gold and blue sisters rising to take position in the south and the west.

'Good moons for navigating,' Tnota told me as he checked marks off against his astrolabe. He consulted a dog-eared notebook. No words in there, just lots of arrows and diagrams. Tnota had inherited it from a navigator who'd retired after twenty years walking these coarse sands. He was unusually sombre despite his assessment.

'What's tugging your dangler?' I asked. He chewed the answer over.

'Nothing in particular. Maybe just feeling the Misery more than I used to. We're getting old, Ryhalt. Feel it in the bones.'

'Fuck off,' I said. 'Old my arse. I'm barely forty.'

'Well I'm that, and half a ten on top of it. When's the last time you saw a man my age in active duties? My back is kicking me after just one day in the saddle. Can feel it all the way from shoulder to the arse bone.'

'The amount of action your arse sees I'd have thought it would be hard as saddle leather by now,' I said.

'Captain has a point,' Nenn agreed.

'Cock sores to both of you,' Tnota grunted. He rolled his shoulders. 'There was a lad up from Pyre, one of those amber-skinned types with the big wide eyes. Never been sure what he wanted before, just wanted to try some things out. I made him a convert, and if I weren't riding around out here I'd be breaking him in like a wild pony. Just jump on and hold fast.'

'A convert,' I mused, finding a rare smile. 'To the church of bumming and depraved fornication.'

'Only fucking church I know, captain.' Tnota grinned back. He looked over at Nenn. 'You should try it some time. Heard you got a cock down there after all.'

'If I did, I'd stick it somewhere cleaner than your stinking arse,' Nenn shot back. Her retort lacked mirth. Tnota didn't push it.

We came to a sea of grass, as I'd known we would. The grass in the Misery is clear, made from some kind of glass. The tinkling chimes as it brushes against itself can be heard a mile distant, even though there's little wind in the Misery. The grass is smooth and knee high, but to walk through it is to break it, and broken edges are sharper than razors. You won't even know you've cut yourself until you feel the blood running down your legs. I remembered this grass sea well. We'd be skirting it for several miles.

'Captain,' Nenn called my attention. She took a swig from her canteen, pointed back the way we'd come. I squinted. Whatever she could see, it changed into a fuzz for me, just the blur of the land. 'Could be riders. Some little dark shapes. Can't make 'em out well.'

'One of the marshal's patrols?'

'Could be.'

'You think so?'

'Could be. Could also be drudge poking closer than they should. Could be something else.' She shrugged. Tnota couldn't see that far either.

'How many?'

'Can't tell. Not many.'

170

'No reason to imagine that they're friendly,' I said. 'Let's pick the pace up. Keep your eyes west and stay bright.'

The grass gave way to the desert again, and then to a chasm. Tnota kissed his teeth, looked up at the moons and frowned.

'Chasm shifted,' he said. 'Should be another hour east.'

I peered over the edge. Two hundred feet deep. Hot, dry air rose from down below. There were chasms like this across the Misery here and there, great knife wound gashes in the land. We'd have to descend and then come back up, somehow.

'How far to the southern end? We can go around?'

'Maybe, but we'd likely have to go through the grass.'

'Not an option then. Let's look for the slopes.' We rode north a way along the chasm's edge. Nenn lost sight of whatever it had been she'd seen before. In my mind it was a dulcher, or maybe some of those insect things I'd skewered last night, grown to the size of horses. There were some things in the Misery like dulchers and skweams that had earned themselves names, but there were many others, one of a kind things that had no names. Kimi Holst, the man who'd held the Blackwing office in Valengrad before me, had once told me he'd seen a thing like a man, twelve feet tall and covered in eyes, that simply ran around shrieking, falling over, getting up and shrieking some more. According to Kimi it hadn't been dangerous, just unnerving, and they left it alone to run and howl in its terror. I like to think I'd have killed it regardless. Everything in the Misery was something else before, like the drudge. They were men before they got changed. Some of them might even still be called men, they're close enough. When the magic's that deep into you, got its hooks biting that strong, it's a kind-ness to send them on to the hells. Of course, Kimi was often as not full of shit, so he'd probably dreamed it up. He'd lost both legs out here. I snapped myself out of my pondering and tried to get bright.

171

We found a way down into the chasm, then followed its floor for a mile until we reached the narrow ledge that would gradually lead us back up. We led the horses. As we went, I saw ghosts. That happens in the Misery too. I saw a pretty young noblewoman, a pair of beautiful children in her arms, standing atop the ledge ahead of us. She laughed as she flung the ghost babies off into the abyss, then hurled herself after them. I tried to ignore them. I learned long ago that the ghosts you see aren't really ghosts, it's just the magic inside you seizing hold of something and twisting it, making it play out for you. It had to be, because I hadn't been there to see them die.

'Not mine,' Nenn said as the phantom children tumbled through the air.

'Obviously not mine either,' Tnota said. Any ghosts he saw were either dark like him or male. He had no interest in pale-skinned women and their brats.

'My wife. My children,' I said.

'Shit,' Nenn said. 'Sorry, captain.'

'Wasn't your fault,' I said. My heart felt heavy. I tried to keep my face impassive, but seeing that always hurt.

'Wasn't yours either.' Tnota put a consoling hand on my shoulder. I shrugged it off.

'You're right, so stop looking at me like I just lost my kitten. Come on. We've still a long way to go.'

It would be pleasant to be able to believe what I was saying once in a while. Lies, lies and more lies all compounded into some great pretence. The Misery might try to deceive us, but we also do a damn good job of deceiving ourselves.

My eyes burned. Told myself it was just the dust.

Lies upon lies upon lies.

18

'Gillings,' Tnota said.

Third day in the Misery. I'd expected them before now. We'd passed by a lake that stank like acid and shimmered with a silvery film, and the ghost of Tnota's grandfather had followed us for a couple of miles, gibbering in his southern language of clicks and sucks, but overall we'd been blessed with uneventful sand dunes and black tar-rocks.

'Hate the fucking things,' Nenn said. Everybody who'd spent some time in the Misery hated gillings.

We were riding through a gully when they emerged eagerly from burrows in the rock. Naked, pot-bellied and red as a raw burn, they toddled out. The biggest were two feet tall, but they were all hairless and yellow-eyed. Instead of five fingers and toes they had only two, wide and sharp.

'Evening, master, care for a good time?' one of them called in its comically high voice, only there was nothing comical about its twin rows of spiny teeth.

'The roads are a mess, the governors take no care,' a second called.

'Evening, master, care for a good time?' repeated a third. There were a lot of them, more than fifteen. A concerning number. Gillings were cowardly things, and they wouldn't attack someone who saw them coming, but in numbers they could pose a threat.

'Fucking weird things,' Nenn said. One of them had

strayed a little close to her horse. She used the butt of her poleaxe to send it scampering away.

'How many of the phrases have you heard them say, captain?' Tnota asked.

'Only five,' I said. I had unslung my own poleaxe. The gillings followed along with us, most of them keeping a good distance. They wouldn't cause real trouble until they thought we were sleeping. The yellow liquid gleaming on their teeth was an anaesthetic strong enough to numb whatever they sank them into. It was said that the most likely death in the Misery came from a gilling chewing off your foot during the night. That was how Kimi Holst had lost his legs.

'I've heard "Evening, master" and "The roads are a mess",' Tnota said. 'Then there's "He's a good boy, just don't anger him", and "Seventy-three, seventy-two".' He frowned. 'What are the others?'

The gillings all know exactly the same phrases. There are only six variations, but they speak them as though they understand them, which they don't. Meaningless phrases stolen from another time. I believed that as the wave of power sent by the Heart of the Void tore apart the laws of reality, some poor bastards were caught and twisted, the words of the moment locked into the deformed little bodies of the gillings. Somehow the original words passed on to the rest of them. It was eighty years since the Heart of the Void had been unleashed, but who knew if gillings aged?

'I've heard them say "If you don't stack it on the lee side it'll be no use come winter",' Nenn put in.

'I never heard that one,' I said.

'So what's the sixth?' Tnota asked. I sighed. I'd only heard them say it once, on one of the nights after we began the retreat from Adrogorsk with the drudge snapping at our heels.

'They say "Spirits be merciful",' I said. 'They don't say

it much. And who knows why they say whatever they say? Fucking strange little bastards.' I flicked my axe haft at one that had strayed closer to my horse's leg than I was comfortable with. It scampered back, claiming that someone was a good boy.

I hadn't given the full quotation. They said "Spirits be merciful. The Nameless have betrayed us. Death comes." Didn't seem like a great time to be mentioning that, though.

Before we made camp we caught and killed a few of the gillings and hung their fat little red bodies up on spurs of rock around our camp. It was an old method of keeping them at bay, and one that only ever offered limited success. We lay up against one another, partly for warmth but also because it's easier for the sentry to watch over two people together than one. Clada and Eala both chose to stay high in the night sky, casting a soft ghost light. It's never easy to sleep in the Misery, but we managed some. Can't go on for ever without it. We woke to find that we all still had our limbs and appendages, which was a positive way to start the day. Breakfast was cold sausages and crunchy peas, washed down with vodka, small beer and finished with sticks of liquorice.

I could feel it inside me. You soak it up. The magic, the wrongness. It gets into your clothes, your limbs. Your eyes itch with it and the world stinks of it. As though I were absorbing some kind of grease into my skin, taking it in. It was ever present, always teasing at the edges. You breathe it, you smell it, can't help but exist as part of it. How had Crowfoot managed this? Nobody knew what the Heart of the Void had been, but we could all see what it had done. Had he found it, or had he crafted it? If the latter, why couldn't he create another one now, in this dark hour when the Deep Kings resumed their advance? The Misery was testament to his callousness when it came to sacrificing the lives of tens of thousands of ordinary people and soldiers alike. It was a reminder to the Deep Kings that powerful as they were, the Nameless had power too. Perhaps that was why Crowfoot had wrought it so.

Four days in we saw Cold's Crater appear through the mist. The hour wasn't late but our breath was still steaming in the air. The depression appeared as a dark shadow, then as we drew nearer we could make out the edges.

The crater was nearly three miles wide, maybe two hundred feet deep at its centre. The floor of the crater was coated in a gritty, silvery dust that reminded me of metal filings. We knew to keep clear of it. Men who'd touched that stuff would find their hands developing a painful weeping rash. Like most things in the Misery, Cold's Crater was best avoided. I breathed deeply through my nose, drawing in the tainted air. We'd made it fast as I'd thought. I chewed on Misery-filth and spat it over the crater's edge. After a few moments my spittle grew legs and scuttled off deeper into the crater.

'Let's grab this cream and get moving again,' Nenn said. I nodded my agreement. I had no desire to linger longer than necessary.

The banners of the Grand Alliance flew over the bastion erected alongside Cold's Crater. It made little sense to try to build in the Misery, given the way that it could change from moment to moment, but some places seemed to be fixed. The crater never changed. The ruins of Adrogorsk and Clear were static, as was Dust Gorge. The Endless Devoid to the south was a landmark feature. It was between those static points that the lunar navigation could be conducted, fixed points amongst the madness. So it was that soldiers of Dortmark had managed to construct something akin to a small fortress along the edge of the crater. It was crude, not much more than rocks stacked up to form low walls, but in terms of Misery fortifications, it was artisan craftsman-ship. The banners flew from long poles jutting up from the centre. I had no doubt that whatever sentries were watching had already spotted us and would be waiting with weapons cocked.

Five soldiers came out to escort us in. None of them looked pleased to see a Blackwing captain. We rode into the fort, if it could be called that, to the high-pitched whirring of the moisture extractors. It was hardly well put together, crude lumps of stone arrayed into walls, the gaps packed with dirt and canvas roofs roped over. Not much to call home, but walls would keep the gillings and the scuttling things out at night. The whining sound was coming from a bank of metal drums, black steel cans with wide, paper-thin silver dishes drawing what moisture they could from the air. There's no running water in the Misery, and I wouldn't have drunk any even if there was. The extractors were powered by phos. Old technology they'd been using on ships for a few hundred years put to new purpose when the Misery was born. Annoying fucking sound, and it would go on all day and all night. The sooner we were gone the better.

'How long you been stationed here?' I asked the sergeant.

'Nearly two months,' he said. 'Too long. Much too long.'

'You haven't seen a Spinner come this way, name of Gleck Maldon?' The longest of long shots.

'Gleck? Nah, he's not been here. We had some new blood come up a few weeks back. We heard Gleck had got light-blind.'

'I guess he did,' I said. 'Just wondered.'

The fort had a stable, and we passed our mounts over there and went to see Major Bernst. He was young for his post, handsome with a well-waxed moustache. His eyes were bloodshot. Walls or no, he wasn't getting much sleep. He just wanted to know why we were there, whether we'd be consuming any of his rations and whether we'd brought fresh orders.

'Why hasn't Venzer pulled you back yet?' I asked.

'Drudge are pushing hard in the north. Wouldn't take much to overrun what you got here.'

'Static patrol. Making sure the drudge aren't pushing into our half of the Misery,' Bernst said. He had the look of one of those academy kids, a paid commission that granted rank without experience. I would have bet that given the choice, he'd have ripped the crescents from his uniform and taken back his gold.

'See much of them?' I asked. I wasn't there for strategy, but I couldn't help but take an interest. Old habits, hard deaths.

'More than leaves me comfortable,' Bernst said. 'Their long patrols seem to be coming closer to the crater. Not many, just ten at a time. We chased them off a couple of times. No engagements, but it's never good to see the drudge.'

'I guess not.'

'How are things back west?' he asked, longing in his voice. I assured him everything was well. Gold grade bullshit.

'I'm here for Count Tanza,' I said. 'If I can grab him and be gone before noon, that'd be for the best.'

'Spirits of mercy know how he ended up out here,' the major said, shaking his head. 'You'll find him and his man out by the crater. Does his own thing. It's just as well you've come for him. He'd likely get himself eaten by a skweam or fall in the bloody pit if he stayed here much longer.'

'You want my advice? Get your horses saddled and keep them ready to ride. Drudge will be here in force before the year's out. Probably sooner.'

'The marshal would hide my arse if I abandoned this post without a direct order.'

He was right. I'd probably get commissioned to track him down.

I left the gear with Nenn and Tnota and went to find Ezabeth Tanza's brother. I vaguely remembered him, but he'd only been six, maybe seven when his family had visited my own. I had been dazzled by the spirit and vitality of his sister, had paid the kid no attention. Near enough twenty years had ground by since then. As I walked out towards the crater's raised lip, I wondered what kind of man they'd have shaped. My first impressions were not encouraging.

Two men stood beside a brass tripod mounted with a trio of devices. One of them held it steady while the second packed earth beneath one of its legs. The crouched man had twenty years on me, white-haired and skin baked brown by the sun, his tattered livery too large for his skinny frame. It had probably fit him when they entered the Misery. A few weeks of lean rations and not enough water does that to you. The younger man, who I presumed was the count, would have been right up Tnota's alley. Or the other way around. Lithe and long-limbed, the kind of wavy yellow hair that would be fashionable in some place where people were idiots. Despite the ordure of the Misery, he was clean-shaven and handsome in an aristocratic way. The frilled lace around the sleeves and collar of a five-hundred-mark shirt had been torn, stained and ruined by working in the dirt and dust. He looked up as I approached.

'Here, give Glost a hand would you, be a good fellow?'

Something about aristocrats makes me want to punch them. The enlisted officers are bad enough, but landed gentry without military rank seem to be demanding knuckles against their noses.

'No time for that today, Count Dantry,' I said. 'We're leaving. I have orders to bring you back to Valengrad.'

Not strictly true. Not entirely a lie either.

'To Valengrad? Today? I don't think so.' He looked me over, a puzzled frown above his fine cheekbones. His eyes narrowed as he tried to work out whether he'd seen me before. From up on the pedestals, we all look the same below but my bulk makes me memorable. Or maybe it's my ugliness.

'He's a new arrival, my lord,' the servant said deferentially. 'Not one of the stationed men.' He got up from his knees. He winced at pain in his joints. Too old to be out in the hell-lands, but who wasn't?

'I can't leave now, private,' he said. 'Too much work to do.'

'It's "captain". And let's get out of this wind,' I said. Low sheets of grit and dust were blowing in from the south, the wind sending them into the crater. The wind only blows into Cold's Crater, never out. Doesn't matter which side of the edge you're on. 'We can talk in the fort. It concerns your sister.'

Dantry's face changed. He blanked for a moment before actual human concern appeared there. Earnestness. I refused to speak further until we'd traipsed back over to the fort and got behind some walls. Over our heads, the cold song of the broken sky mocked our retreat.

'Speak,' Dantry said. 'Is she well? Has she come to harm?'

'In a sense.' I didn't like having the servant on hand, but what can you do? I gave him the bones of it. Ezabeth had been sent to the Maud for lunacy. He was the only one who could get her out.

'Has my cousin, Prince Herono, not moved to resolve such nonsense?' Dantry protested. I thought of Ezabeth's writings, the childish rhymes amidst her impossible calculations. *Only a song could be so bold.* Nonsense was subjective.

'The prince feels she is obliged to stay out of personal matters involving the Order,' I said. 'Her position won't allow it. Or she won't allow herself. Whichever the case, she isn't going to do anything.'

'She was so amiable, so helpful when I stayed with her,' Dantry said, wounded. Like a first love who just learned his girl kisses all the other boys too.

'Politics. Always a shit storm,' I said. Dantry squinted at me.

'Forgive me, sir, I have not asked you your name.'

'Captain Ryhalt Galharrow. Blackwing.'

He hesitated only momentarily, then reached out and shook my hand.

'Do you know what Ezabeth has done to get herself locked away? What is your involvement?'

I didn't go into the details of either. No point getting things more complicated than you have to.

'What matters is that I get you back there fast as possible,' I said. 'I know your sister. She wants you to get her out. Whatever you're doing out here, ditch it. It doesn't matter. She does.' I took out her letter, passed it over. The count read it, breath ceasing and eyes growing wider as he did so.

He looked to the servant. Asked him to leave us. Glost looked pissed about it but he obliged.

'Do you know what this says?' he asked.

'I didn't read it, if that's what you mean. But I could guess. Light. The Engine. The heart. Paradoxes. That's about the thick of it?'

Dantry nodded. He read the letter through twice more, then began tearing it into tiny pieces, each shred no bigger than a fingernail. Very thorough. He sat looking forlorn, and to my embarrassment, a tear rolled down his face. He made no move to wipe it away, no move to speak. The feelings he was experiencing were writ plain on his young, noble face. No politician this one, for all that he had the rank. This soft man would be torn apart by the old beasts of the princedoms, the Heronos and Adenauers, even Marshal Venzer would chew him up and spit out the leftovers.

'Dear me,' he said softly. 'As I feared. As I feared.'

'Get your shit together and saddle up,' I said. 'The ride back isn't short and it isn't fun.'

Dantry rubbed at his forehead, pressed fingers into his eyes.

'One more day,' he said. 'We must wait a day. Allow me

to take the final readings. I'd hoped to draw phos readings for another week or two, but what I have might do. It might. But I must take readings tonight. It is the first time that all three moons will have a north-westerly ascension. It is why I am here.' He looked at me very seriously. 'I cannot leave without seeing this work done. My sister would agree, were she here.'

'I'm not sure about that,' I said.

'She would, captain,' Dantry said firmly. 'My work here is but as an assistant to her. She is the genius. I am merely a mathematician and astronomer.'

He wouldn't be argued out of it. I couldn't exactly tie him up and sling him over a horse. One extra day in the Misery. I agreed. Men have died over less.

19

Night in the Misery. I grew up around the olive groves and vineyards of my father's estates, where the cicadas never stop their endless chirruping, where the night was alive with sound and life. I don't miss them in the city, but out here in the wild I feel their absence. There are insects in the Misery, black-shell beetles and redbacks and hovering things that'll suck your blood, but none of them sing. By night the sky seems to want to share its pain more than it does in the light, the song tearing through reality's cracks, the only companion to the dry rustling of the wind. I stood on the edge of Cold's Crater taking slow, steady drags on a fat cigar between slugs from my hip flask. Nearly dry. Dantry and Glost worked with the brass instruments on the crater's edge.

'This the last one?' I asked as Dantry began aligning the rods and lenses.

'No,' Dantry said. 'One more after this.'

The old servant looked tired, worn through. Dantry didn't seem to have noticed. He and his sister weren't much alike. She was hard company at the best of times, but even though he was cream he wasn't so bad. If there was one trait they did share it was the obsessive passion for their work. I walked over, parked my cigar between my teeth and offered Glost my flask.

'Not while I am working, sir, my thanks,' he said humbly.

A lifetime spent on the knees will break a man that way. Damn stupid thing to turn away free booze when it's offered, and thrice so in the Misery.

'Why don't you head back? I can help finish up here,' I said. The old man looked keen. The master didn't look up from his device.

'The work is delicate, and Glost is well versed in its operation, captain,' Dantry said.

'Don't worry. My fingers are more delicate than they look.' I squinted at the dials on the instruments. 'You haven't corrected the lower lens to take into account Rioque being isolated. You'll get a face full of red and nothing else.'

Dantry stopped, frowned. He looked over his apparatus.

'By grief. You're right. I'd not taken you for a lunarist, captain.'

'I'm not. I've just worked one of these a few times.'

Having demonstrated a degree of competence, Dantry allowed Glost to retire.

'So how did you come to study the sky?' he asked me as he picked up a heavy ledger and began sketching up a table. His penmanship was swift, quick, scratchy numbers beginning to fill the page.

'I don't. Just picked a few things up, here and there.'

'Of course. You attended the university in Lennisgrad.'

I frowned at him.

'How did you know that?'

Dantry flushed, or maybe it was just Rioque's light catching the planes of his handsome face.

'Just a guess,' he said, but it wasn't convincing. I decided it was best to move the conversation on. My past was like a cruel grandmother: nasty, lacking in wisdom and better off buried.

'What are you and your sister trying to learn from all this?' Easy to change the subject. Dantry enjoyed talking about his work.

'Gleck Maldon wanted to understand more about this place. He thought it might be helpful to something he was studying. I volunteered.'

'I've heard of smarter choices.'

'You're aware of Songlope's Paradox?' he asked.

'The more phos you burn, the more backlash you need to contain, until the backlash is greater than the amount spent in the first place and an infinite sum is required to contain the repeated backlashes. Songlope's paradox circumvents that by reharnessing the backlash as more power without creating a new backlash itself. Yeah, I think I got it.'

'An educated man indeed,' Dantry said happily. 'Quite so. Well, look out there, captain, what do you see?'

Cold's Crater stretched out across the Misery, a great silver-sheened bowl of nothing. Nothing to see. I said as much.

'What made the crater?' Dantry prompted.

'Cold died here,' I said. He nodded.

'Yes. More than two centuries ago he led a glorious charge into the teeth of the Dhojaran horde and won time for his men to escape. He paid for it with his life. What is it?' By his expression I could tell that Dantry objected to my chuckling at his story.

'That's what they teach you in Heirenmark?' I asked. 'That's not how it went down. You should listen to the old soldiers out here, kid, they'll teach you what the universities don't. Cold was Nameless and he wasn't some glorious, mustachioed cavalryman charging into the teeth of the enemy. He was a proud, arrogant fucking idiot who got caught in a trap.'

'A trap?'

'Aye. Cold had command of four thousand knights, the Order of the Open Door. This was back before the Misery even existed, the early days of the war. His scouts told him there were a thousand Dhojaran irregulars camped out here, so instead of waiting for the other Nameless he went after them himself. Only it wasn't a thousand, it was ten thousand with four of the Deep Kings backing them up and he found himself trapped. The Kings butchered his men, spun a web of souls and then broke him down. Took them three days to get through his defences, but they did it. When they killed him, he left this crater behind.'

'Well,' Dantry said, frowning. 'They appreciate his efforts at the military academy rather more than they do his failings.'

'He was Nameless,' I said. 'We couldn't afford to lose him then. We sure as fucking hell can't afford him to be gone now. Somehow the Kings got to Songlope after Cold, and it looks like they knocked out Shallowgrave and Nall as well.'

'Yes,' Dantry said softly. 'And that's why we're here, isn't it? Because Nall's not here to run his Engine, and we don't know how it can be activated without destroying everything in creation. If it even works. What a time we live in, to base our hopes around this awful thing. The Engine is no gift from the Spirit of Mercy. It is a destroyer. No more terrible and wicked creation has ever been wrought.'

I shrugged. I felt no sympathy for the drudge. Had I the power, I'd unleash a hundred Engines against their empire and light a cigar from the embers.

Dantry turned a small dial on the apparatus, cocked an eyebrow at the result as light filtered through the lenses, created a pattern on a brass plate that was engraved with numerous lines and circles. Dantry noted the readings down in his ledger, then looked back at the sky.

'And we're here now why?' I prompted.

'When Songlope or the other Nameless have died, there has been no detonation,' Dantry said. 'If there had been, we'd know about it. There would be other craters.'

'I guess so.'

'Well, where are they? When Cold was destroyed, there

was a release of power. The biggest backlash of our age. It wasn't phos, of course, the Nameless's magic comes from some other source. Whatever it was, Ezabeth theorised that it might be comparable in some way. Perhaps the power of the Nameless shares common principles with phos spinning. Gleck Maldon had been out here. He believed that the light acted strangely around the crater, thought it worth more study.' He stood up, stretched out his back. 'Come on. I need to take readings from the last tripod.'

I picked up my poleaxe, mounted up and rode further around the crater. Within that devoid, the sand glimmered with a silky, silver sheen that bespoke magic and poison, unreality and wrongness. Even the Heart of the Void hadn't been able to displace the grave of one of the Nameless. The scar was too deep in the earth even for that. How tragically small and pointless we must have looked to them, the great wizards of the age. How meaningless our lives.

'Why did you choose this life, captain?' Dantry asked as we rode.

'Maybe it chose me,' I said. He seemed to debate saying something, then thought better of it. Frowned. 'Might as well spit it out, kid,' I said. But he chose to change the subject instead.

'I want to thank you,' he said. 'For helping us. For helping my sister. She can be difficult.'

'I'm getting paid for it. That's all that matters to me,' I said. A half truth.

'Of course,' Dantry said stiffly. He straightened his back, sat taller in the saddle. Spoke formally. 'Our house finances are not what they once were, but I shall see that one day we are able to repay you for your assistance.'

We reached Dantry's instruments. I scanned around, made sure we were alone. The night was still, just the occasional weeping of the sky interrupting the slither of the wind.

'I won't be sad to leave this place,' Dantry mused as he set to on the brass. 'Sometimes I feel like I'm choking on the air. Do you know what I mean?'

'I get it,' I agreed. 'You'll have the shakes for a week after you get out, the length of time you've been soaking this crap up.'

'A supply train arrived at the fort today,' Dantry said. I'd seen them approaching that afternoon. Probably the riders Nenn had seen coming up behind us. I hadn't thought to check the supply schedule. 'Do you know what they brought?'

'Replacement filters for the moisture extractors, I should think,' I said. 'Misery rations? Jerky and biscuits. Maybe some vodka if you're lucky.'

'Beans,' Dantry said. 'Just a lot of beans.' He shook his head, a look of incomprehension on his face. 'The dangers of the Misery. The creatures and the magic and the cracks that open in the ground. Men passed through all that, risked their lives every step of the way, to bring us sacks of beans. It's bullshit. This war, this suffering, all of it. It's a madness, a blight on the earth. It has to end.'

'Only two ways this can end,' I said. I reached out and adjusted a lens. Dantry turned it back without reprimanding me for getting it wrong.

'Does one of those ways end with us turning into drudge?'

'They both do,' I said. 'The only difference is whether it's in our lifetime or whether we die first. The Deep Kings are going to win. Don't make no mistake there. There's seven of them, and we're down to our last two Nameless. They've already won, they're just waiting for the last of our defences to wear down. No point risking yourself when you're a deathless god thing, is there? They've got an eternity to wait. They pushed their luck once before and Crowfoot punished them with the Heart of the Void.'

'What was it? The Heart?'

'Not a fucking clue,' I said.

'If they were beaten before, they can be beaten again,' Dantry said, the heat of youth in his voice. 'Someone, whoever it was in those ancient times, someone managed to imprison them beneath the ocean.'

I shrugged.

'Crowfoot's mad,' I said. 'The Lady of Waves won't leave her island. Besides, we need her there or the drudge would just make ships and come over the sea. We're just buying time. Buying time and hoping that we get old and die before we have to wear a mark.'

Dantry shuddered and looked back to his apparatus.

We got finished up and headed back to the dubious comfort of the fort. A man on a raised platform kept a watch over the moonlit land, a heavy crossbow on his knees. He called down to us for the password. Told him to go bugger himself, and he laughed and signalled to the gateman to let us in.

Nenn and Tnota had found a tile board game against a pair of soldiers, a gaunt man and a better-faring woman. There wasn't much to gamble. Why bring money out into the Misery? They played for belt buckles, rations of whisky, tradeable duties and cups of dry beans. Nenn looked to be up on the game, a small cluster of tat sitting in front of her. Tnota seemed to have put in a couple of his rings and it didn't look like he had much else to offer.

'I'll raise,' one of their opponents said. He was thin, face like a starving mule. He unclasped an earring, just a cheap bit of tin but better than nothing. The woman joined him. Nenn sacrificed two of her tiles to avoid having to pay. Tnota looked at the board and glanced up at me. He was a shockingly bad tile player, but either luck was with him or his opponents had made some serious gaffs because by the positioning of his tiles I could see that he was two moves away from taking out all three of his opponents. He and

Nenn had probably decided to play together and divvy the winnings. They were arseholes like that. He grinned, aware of my disapproval and put in a couple of hard-baked road biscuits.

Tnota blundered his second move but righted it on the fourth and then he was collecting in the kitty. The soldiers did not look pleased.

Dantry had been idling at the edge of the game. The woman looked up and seemed to notice him for the first time. There's a change comes over a woman when she sees something she likes, seen it faked a hundred hundred times by street walkers and tavern girls. Like a little jet of water goes up their arse, straightens them out, makes them all bright and keen. She smiled up at the noble boy. Maybe it was the stupid waves of his yellow hair or maybe she just liked his cheekbones. I could appreciate he was handsome enough to draw a lady's eye.

'Come join us. Play a game,' she said.

'I don't know the rules,' Dantry admitted. Hardly surprising. Tiles isn't exactly a nobleman's pastime.

'I'll show you,' she said, then brazenly patted the ground beside her. Dantry seemed to struggle with the concept of sitting on the dirt, but she was young and pretty, and he was a young man, and young and pretty wins that battle near every time.

'You want in, captain?' Nenn asked. She patted the ground beside her in the same way. I declined her offer.

'You want me to get that stuff stowed away?' I asked Dantry, nodding to the gear we'd loaded up on a horse. He thanked me and I found my way to Dantry's quarters. There wasn't much to them. He'd been lodged in what was probably one of the better rooms in the fort, but it was just four solid walls with a door and a canvas roof. I walked the horse right up to the door and opened it to find Dantry's serving man, Glost, preparing his master's travelling garb for the morning. He helped me unload the five brass tripods from the horse and stow the ledgers safely. Poor old Glost clicked and creaked as he laboured.

'You ever think you might want to retire?' I asked.

'I'm afraid I was a debtor, sir,' the old boy told me. 'The old Count Tanza, Dantry's father, he bought me out of my debts, which were very great. I'll never earn enough to pay them off completely, but I don't begrudge him. Got me out of the debtor's gaol. I'd have died in that place if not for the count.'

'How long have you been with the family?'

'Oh, a good thirty years, sir. My best years, I should say. I know I might look old, sir, but it's a good life serving the boy. Although these past weeks have been most trying.' He gave me a cautious glance, was about to speak but then changed his mind. Looked away.

'What is it?'

'We've met before, sir, though it was a long time ago.'

'We have?'

'Yes, sir. At your parents' estate. You had a different name then, of course, but I wouldn't forget you. You were a pleasant boy, we all had great hopes for you and the young mistress.'

I stiffened. There are things that should be left dead and buried in the past. Marshal Venzer and Prince Herono knew who I had been, but precious few others would recognise that long-ago boy in what I was now. It didn't matter that Glost remembered me as a kid, but if he knew who I'd been then he probably knew what I'd done, too.

'You tell Dantry?'

'No, sir. I understand sir, that after the affair with Torolo Mancono you have a desire for privacy.'

'Good. Don't tell him.'

'No, sir.'

Nenn and Tnota knew that I'd been something else

before I was their captain, but we never spoke about the details. They'd both joined up with me after I quit the state army. After the disaster at Adrogorsk I'd promised myself I'd never be beholden to a commander again. They paid for your blood and tears with nothing but more of the same. Not a good trade. It occurred to me that Glost must know why my match with Ezabeth had been called off, that I could finally ask and learn what it was that I'd done wrong. Always told myself it hadn't been my fault, that she'd liked me well enough. Probably some family political issue, maybe a marriage order had come from a prince. He'd know if Ezabeth had been married. I'd done my best to not find out. She'd never be my wife, but if she'd been anyone else's I preferred not to know.

I tried to ask, but couldn't force the words.

The small room had a bed, put together out of old cut stone with a couple of blankets on top. Glost began preparing a bedroll for himself on the floor.

'Take the bed,' I said as I put away the last of Dantry's equipment. 'I got a feeling your master isn't bunking in here tonight.' Glost gave me a shy smile as he lumped his bedroll on top of Dantry's blankets.

'Nice to be young, eh?' he said. Couldn't disagree there.

I left him to the meagre comforts of a stone bed and went to take a leak. As I exited the latrine, I caught sight of a familiar face amongst a gang of blue uniforms helping to unload a string of pack mules, freshly arrived. Older men, hard-looking veterans with scars. None of our glory days last for ever, but I guess the Blue Brigade had wanted more out of their retirement than this. A couple didn't look to have fared too well on their journey across the Misery, the shakes deep in their hands.

Stannard was black and azure in half-plate and gun oil. He saw me, narrowed his eyes.

'Fancy seeing you here, old boy,' he said. 'This is a surprise.'

'Didn't expect to see you out here either,' I said. 'Thought you Blue Brigade boys were done with this kind of muck.'

'So did I,' Stannard said with a grimace. 'Never wanted to be back out in this shit again. But the strength of Valengrad is up north at Three-Six and the state troops they left behind are too green to trek this deep. You know what we're delivering?' He gestured back towards the wagons. 'Fucking beans. Risking all the shit and poison out here to deliver fucking *beans*. Seems hard to believe.'

'Seems hard,' I agreed. Really hard. An awfully big coincidence.

'I suppose they enlisted all the free companies to do the same?' Stannard asked.

'Guess so,' I said. Left that vague. This wasn't good news. I didn't want it getting back to Herono that I'd headed out here to find Dantry Tanza, but since Stannard and a dozen of Herono's boys were suddenly on bean delivery duty, I had to wonder whether she already did.

'I heard your girlfriend got sent to the Maud.'

I didn't have anything to say to that. Felt a twitch in my finger that said I should let a fist fly. Restrained it. One of the Blue Brigade called over to come back and bloody well help with the beans.

'We're heading back to Valengrad tomorrow. You should join us. It's not that I particulary like you, captain, but numbers never hurt in the Misery.'

'I'll think on it.' I wouldn't.

I felt Stannard watching me as I walked away. Anxiety maggots began squirming through my gut. Too much fucking coincidence for Herono's boys to be out here, days into the Misery. Nenn read my expression.

'Trouble?'

'Maybe.' I filled them in.

'You think he could be telling the truth? Just got sent here delivering beans?'

'Seems like a mighty fucking coincidence. Gives my arse the itch. Where's our count got to?'

'Went off with that woman.' Nenn yawned.

'You know where?'

'No.'

'I want to leave. Tonight.'

Tnota shook his head.

'You know I can't get a nav until sunrise,' he said. 'Could end up wandering into the grass, or worse, east. Can't do it, captain.'

'You think we should sit it out tonight?'

'I'm not even sure there's a danger,' he said.

A good rule of thumb for survival is that if you have to face the fires of hell or running blind in the Misery, you pick the hells. At least that way you know where you are. We'd come in from the west, but that didn't mean it still was. No matter that I was afraid we were all the way to the eyeballs in the shit, when your navigator talks you listen. I agreed we'd leave at dawn.

I slept in the cramped room we'd been allocated, but not easily. When I woke I could see the light from a great bronze crack through the canvas ceiling, right over us like some kind of judgement. The sky was bleeding out long, discordant notes, the Misery's wake-up call. Nenn passed me a cup of water. It had the dead iron taste of the moisture extractors, like a joke that falls flat, and it suited my mood. I got up, put my armour on. Wasn't in the mood to fuck around. The sun was just cresting what may or may not have been the east when I went to find Dantry. Didn't know where he'd spent the night so I went to his room. Knocked on the flimsy door, but there was no response.

'Hey, Glost,' I said. 'Wake up. We have to get moving.'

For a few moments, nothing. Then a squeaky, high-pitched voice.

'Evening, master, care for a good time?'

I smashed the door to kindling as I charged against it, then staggered to a stop, my mouth agape and the horror a match for anything I'd seen before. Red. Red, everywhere the red. Glost lay where he'd died, mostly just bones now. Two gillings, their bellies hugely distended, sat childlike amidst the carnage, glistening and sticky. The same colour as the blood they'd splashed about the place as they bit, ate, devoured. Glost must have been sleeping. He'd never have known what was happening to him. Both of the gillings looked up at me, one of them chewing a mouthful of shoulder.

'Seventy-three, seventy-two,' one of them offered.

'Evening, master, care for a good time?'

I drew my sword. The gillings squealed and tried to scamper to the back of the room but their guts were so over-filled with the old servant's meat that they could hardly move. I vented my fury, my horror, on them. Glost's face and head had largely been left alone. He looked peaceful. The anaesthetic in their saliva meant he wouldn't even have known he was being eaten alive. It was still a fucking terrible way to die.

I squeezed my eyes very tight, clenched my fists. I wanted to scream, to hurl my anger towards the sky. I fought that urge to stillness, tried to keep everything steady. Stay bright, I told myself. I barely knew the man. Didn't know shit about him. But he'd known my name, and he'd not deserved to be torn apart like this by little fucking bastard monsters. When I opened my eyes, my breathing was normal again. And I was looking up at a hole that had been carefully cut in the canvas roof.

No doubt about it. Someone had cut a triangular flap open in the canvas and dropped the gillings through it. No other way they could have got inside. They don't climb walls and they don't carry knives to cut heavy fabric. The little bastards had been used as a living weapon against Dantry. Glost had just been caught in the crossfire.

I ran, but when I found Nenn and Tnota they'd managed to locate Dantry and he was fine, if a little tired. I didn't fancy explaining to him that a man he'd known all his life had just been eaten to death. Didn't exactly have any choice. He took it better than I'd expected. Turned white as milk, threw up, didn't pass out. Cried. We gave him some space, got the gear together quick and quiet, didn't tell anybody anything, and as soon as Tnota took a navigable reading we rode out the gates.

I looked back as we rode away, and saw Stannard watching our departure, arms crossed over a broad chest. Framed against the blood red of the dawn sky, I realised I'd seen that stocky figure framed in flame before. He'd been hooded, the library had been clogged with smoke and darkness but a lifetime of sizing up men I wanted to kill had given me an eye for physique. It wasn't the first time I'd wanted to kill him, but we don't always get what we want.

20

They didn't follow us and the Misery seemed to respect Dantry's pain and left us alone. A few uneventful days and we were back in sight of Valengrad's vast stone walls. The vivid blood-neon letters on the face of the citadel read COURAGE, and we rode towards them in weary silence. For once Dantry had stopped snivelling. The death of his servant had struck him deeper than I'd thought it would. Maybe behind all that nobility and cream he was human after all.

'We must go straight to my sister,' Dantry said. He tried to sit tall in the saddle, but even that was too much for him.

'Not straight off. Barber, bath, tailor. If we're going in with the authority of a count, you need to look like a count.'

Dantry considered my advice, running a hand through the light growth of fuzz on his cheeks.

'You look like shit,' Nenn put in helpfully. Dantry toyed with the dirt-stained cuff of his shirt and, finally, agreed.

'The bank first, then the bath house,' he said. 'I'll need to access some money, but the banks will allow credit against my holdings, I'm sure. I hate to think of Beth stuck in that place.'

As we rode in through Valengrad's single east-facing tunnel, I felt a twinge in my chest, silver and serpentlike as the dragon flexed.

Welcome home, a leathery voice mouthed into my mind.

I felt my attention dragged to one of Saravor's little grey children, watching from an alleyway. It noted my return before sliding away into the shadows.

'Any sign of drudge activity?' the lieutenant at the gate asked.

'Didn't see anything. Any news from the north?'

'Nothing good. Drudge are shuffling closer. The Iron Goat sent half our ordinance to Three-Six yesterday.'

I thanked him and rode on. The city was a muted place with half its population gone.

We dropped Dantry's brass apparatus off at my apartment. I'd already killed off the suggestion that we ride out to Willows and alert Herono to our presence. She'd abandoned the Tanzas' cause in order to protect her position, and following the events in the Misery I was conflicted. Herono was a hero, short of Venzer there was nobody on the Range with a more distinguished career, but someone had sent Stannard to commit murder, and his was one loyalty I didn't doubt.

I'd wrangled it every way that I could in my mind, but it just didn't make any fucking sense.

At my apartment I ditched my armour and grabbed a bag of liquorice root. It was hard and dry but I could already feel the Misery shakes coming on. My skin had turned clammy and there was an ache in the roof of my mouth. We sucked the roots, stopped off at a tavern and took a long drink of beer and a hot meal. Summer vegetables in a dull gravy with a hunk of soft bread. It was simple, but after a week of eating dried meat and beans I was famished enough to rip through it in minutes. The beer helped settle us all down. Nothing like a beer to take the edge off.

I sent Nenn and Tnota off, but accompanied Dantry to the bank. I offered him a clean shirt, but mine were all hopelessly large for his slim frame. I spruced myself up as best I could, but there's something that the Misery does to you that won't be covered by a fresh waistcoat and breeches.

We'd all be looking like the hells for a week at least. I wore a sword but my nerves were up so I went as far as to sling a buckler on my belt. When I'd taken Ezabeth's money I'd made her battle my own, and her enemies would find me ready to fight it. With that thought in my mind I loaded a pair of flintlock pistols and secreted them beneath my coat.

The bank security let us in when Dantry presented his ring, but the credit manager looked distinctly less enthusiastic. I was trying to look the part of servant, since no count would choose to appear without at least one man to hand. The credit manager remembered him but looked entirely too nervous. I have that affect on people sometimes, but I didn't figure it was me in this case.

'What do you mean, *exhausted*?' Dantry said. 'I have considerable estates around Heirengrad. You can't possibly decline my credit.'

'I'm most sorry, Count Tanza,' the man said. 'I have it here, in writing, from the central office.' He showed Dantry a piece of paper. I peered over his shoulder to read it. It did indeed state that the Tanza family was to be offered no further credit until a number of undisclosed matters had been resolved. Dantry argued indignantly. The manager could only spread his hands helplessly. 'I'm sorry, my lord,' he protested, 'I can but write to the central office asking whether they have made a mistake, but as you can see here, it is not within my power to extend you credit.'

'Your bank has lost my family's custom,' Dantry said fiercely. 'Fifty years we've done business, and now here I am, treated like some common guttersnipe. You should not expect to see any of our coin pass your doors, not in this lifetime. Good day!'

We stormed out with a suitably aristocratic flounce, walked across the street and tried the next banking house. After two more displayed similar letters, we didn't try a fourth.

'I cannot understand it. Can things have gone so poorly back at the estate in just a week? It's not possible.'

'It isn't possible,' I said. 'I borrowed money from your account before I left. Someone has shut you down.'

'But who?'

'There are only three people in Valengrad with the power to exert that much control over the banks. The marshal, Prince Herono and Prince Adenauer. The Order of Aetherial Engineers might also have enough clout. This was a backup plan in case they didn't get to you in the Misery. But what in the hells do they have to gain? We're all on the same spirits-damned side and if they want your sister silenced then they could have just had her hanged. They've shown they're willing to kill. It just doesn't make any sense.' I considered trying to use Herono's letter of authority to force money from the bank but there was little chance they'd release money for anything short of an official seal. Unfortunately my own black-iron seal had long ago exhausted any lines of credit with the banking houses.

No credit, but an enterprising man can make money other ways. We swung over to the Mews, found a half-decent pawn shop and took a loan on a quarter of the value of two of Dantry's rings. The kid was practically rigid with indignation that he'd be offered such a paltry sum, but it was enough to get us washed, trimmed and to outfit Dantry in last season's best fashion. He kissed his teeth as he looked at the embroidery running in lines down the sleeves. I reminded him that we had pressing business, and he nodded sombrely. By then I'd realised that getting Ezabeth out wasn't going to be as simple as I'd thought. Whoever had sent Stannard to end Dantry had also taken precautions against his return.

Stannard was not acting alone. I'd considered whether he could be marked, turned by the pleasures of a Bride or the promises of the Cult of the Deep, but he was too small a fish. Maybe his hand held the knife but it didn't provide the will that drove it. That left Prince Herono as our most likely enemy but that made even less sense. She despised the drudge. They'd captured her, subjected her to torture, torn out her eye. She'd led me to a Bride. She had nothing to gain by striking against either the Range or her own kin. But the only other person that could have done this, that could have sent Stannard out into the Misery, was the marshal. We'd had our differences but I loved that old man. I couldn't believe it of either of them. I rubbed my fingers into my eyes wishing that my problems were the simple kind that could be solved with a nice volley of cannon fire. The fat matron who ran the Maud sat at the desk as though she were waiting for us. Didn't look surprised when we walked in. She was wearing her Holy Sister's coif and was flanked by seven orderlies, all young men with hard eyes. They didn't usually carry clubs, but today they did. Every step of the way we seemed to be behind.

'Good day to you, revered Sister,' Dantry said politely. 'I'm here to see my sister. Ezabeth Tanza. I should like to be admitted to her chambers at once.'

'I'm afraid that won't be possible, my lord,' the matron said.

'Do you know who I am, Holy Sister?' Dantry asked. His eyes had narrowed, his voice turned to creamy coldness.

'I do, Count Tanza. But your sister is most unwell. We've had to move her to the cells on the lower levels, the better to keep her safe from herself.'

'You put her downstairs?' I asked, spoke hard. The cudgel men flinched, but they stood with their arms folded, trying to look menacing. They didn't do a good job of it.

'When she became seriously unwell, she became deranged. Babbled, chewed the bed hangings, tried to perform her light magic on the orderlies. She is most unwell sir, and for her safety and that of our other patients we had no choice but to lock her below.'

'I will see her at once,' Dantry said. He looked aghast. He was swallowing it like a fish on a line, while I didn't believe a fucking word of it.

'I'm sorry, my lord, but after the loss of the last Spinner who was here, we have instructions that she is to have no visitors but for our excellent team of physicians. It is a matter of security. Spinner Maldon's breakout caused so much damage that our instructions relating to any Spinners we admit now come from the citadel.'

'From the marshal?' I snapped.

'From the Office of Urban Security,' the sister said. 'But yes, they ultimately report to the marshal.'

'And yet she wasn't in the dark cells when I came here a week ago.'

'Her condition deteriorated very quickly,' the vast woman said. She sounded regretful but I wasn't buying it. I could smell a lie clear as I could smell the stink of the Misery's sands leaking from our pores. My hands were starting to shake, and I gripped my belt to steady them.

'This is an outrage!' Dantry was beginning to shout, but I took him by the arm and led him out. No point in having arguments that can't be won. A lot of people don't realise that. They shout and protest so they can claim they gave it their best shot. You don't have armed men waiting if you aren't expecting to quarrel, and I was practically growling as we stepped back outside.

I took a minute to cool off. I could have knocked the orderlies aside, let them feel my frustration, kicked Ezabeth's cell door down like some fairytale prince. But to what end? Becoming fugitives wasn't going to get us access to the Engine's heart. Official channels had to be exhausted before I could allow myself to get creative. For as long as was possible, I had to play by their rules.

'Only one place left to go,' I said. 'The citadel. Going to have to go straight for the throat.'

'And if it's the citadel that's working against us?' Dantry suggested. 'They might just … lock us in a cellar. Or shoot us!'

'Then we die now rather than die later. If the Iron Goat's selling us down the river then none of this matters anyway.' Surprise, surprise, a lot of administrative nonsense clogged our path to the marshal. I didn't have the rank to demand an immediate audience with him, and Dantry wasn't commissioned so he didn't have it either. Cream in the blood counted for a lot in society, but when it came to the marshal it didn't mean shit. Princes bowed to Range Marshal Venzer. They knew who they owed their ongoing survival to. I made it very clear that we would, however, have to see somebody from the Office of Urban Security. I gave my best psychotic murder-lust grin, showed a lot of teeth. It's the kind of look that gets people wanting to please you, or at least to get away from you. A clerk scuttled off to see who could be found.

'This already feels like a dead end,' Dantry said as we sat waiting in a pleasantly furnished reception room. Cheap tapestries and old cigar smoke decorated the walls. One of the light tubes was on the blink, buzzing with an irritating whine and flicker. 'I wish Ezabeth were here,' he went on. 'I mean, I know that's the point, but really, she'd know what to do. Much more decisive than I am. Good in a crisis.'

'That so?' I said. He smiled weakly. I could see how much the shakes were taking out of him. His hands trembled against the arms of the plush chair.

We waited an hour, then went to complain that Dantry wasn't being taken seriously. Complained again forty minutes after that. I had the feeling that, somewhere else, people were sitting in a room arguing about what to do with us. The clock on the wall had ticked around to five when a clerk came in to let us know that Heinrich Adenauer, a senior member of the Office of Urban Security, was coming to see us.

'Prince's get?'

'Adenauer's natural born son, I think,' Dantry said, brightening. 'I've not had the pleasure of meeting him. He will be able to assist us, I'm sure.'

'You think that just because someone's got cream in their veins that they're automatically going to help you?' I said. I cocked an eyebrow at him.

'Regardless of what Ezabeth may be accused of, we are both descended from old bloodlines,' Dantry said. 'Good families, you know. There is a code of honour amongst the nobility. While we might vie with one another for business and jostle for position, it is understood that on a personal level we must assist one another.'

'So that you all live a charmed fucking life, that it?'

'I don't like your tone, captain,' Dantry said. 'You show me no respect. I am of the old blood, and titled.' He stopped short of telling me that I should be using his title. His pride might be feeling poked but even he could see that he needed me.

Heinrich Adenauer was announced by a clerk. He had a wiry build, devoid of excess flesh. A man who considered putting mere food in his mouth an affront to the refinement of his palate. I figured he wasn't much younger than Dantry, and he was fully decked out in the most fashionable of absurd courtly attire. His codpiece was hugely exaggerated, the cap on his head lined with precious stones and the fabric of his doublet screamed cost if not taste. The only part of his dress that seemed suited to going outside was his rapier, simple steel, the cup hilt heavily scratched from use. Intense little eyes, and curtains of black hair framed a ratty expression. I'd known a lot of likeable, ugly men, just as many that were handsome shitbags. Heinrich Adenauer would never be the latter and I was pretty sure he wasn't going to be the former either. He brought a couple of noble types in similarly ostentatious dress with him, her in a red silk dress with long boots, the current style, him in a more reserved brown leather waistcoat. I knew their type; professional hangers-on, parasites, the mistletoe of the courtly world.

'Count Tanza. My apologies that you have had to wait,' Heinrich said in a voice that dripped with insincerity. I could already tell this would not go well, that before the conversation was done I'd be struggling to remember a reason not to lay him out.

Dantry went straight to it, credit to the man. He made his case with sincerity and a clear, calm voice. Made it plain that he had the legal right to nurse his sister himself.

'What's more, I must think of the cost to the citadel,' he said. Go for the purse. Usually a smart way of negotiating. 'Taking my sister back to our estate, I feel, would be the best course of action for all. It is clear that life on the Range has not suited her.'

'Yes, well,' Heinrich said in a tone that suggested impudence, 'would that it were so simple. I'm afraid the risk is too great to allow such a thing. I understand your position, really I do.' Every word he said dripped with mockery, talking down to the count as though he were a child. Dantry outranked him, but you wouldn't have known it. 'Times are hard,' Heinrich continued. 'I am aware that you have had some trouble with the banks, and I feel for you. Really, I do. But for now, the Lady Tanza will be better off locked where she cannot ... present herself ... so brazenly. Best for all of us, don't you think?'

'No, sir, I most sincerely do not,' Dantry said. His voice had gone very cold. 'It is an affront to my honour. To the honour of our house, to have her imprisoned like a common thief. Has there even been a trial?'

'My dear sir, there is no need for a trial! The woman is quite clearly as moonstruck as a ...' Heinrich's elegance failed as he sought an analogy. He wasn't quite sneering, wasn't quite holding it back. He wanted to offend Dantry but was afraid to do so outright. He coughed into his hand, pasted on a lazy, lopsided smile. 'Well, you know what I mean. She's perfectly mad.'

Dantry didn't see it. He'd turned red as sunset.

'Sir, you walk a fine line,' Dantry said.

'Speak to someone who isn't an arsehole,' I suggested.

'You will watch your tongue!' Heinrich spat at me. Real indignation flared in his eyes that time. 'I could have you flogged.' A prince's bastard carries a lot of clout but he didn't understand who I was. I'd been introduced as Dantry's manservant, not as Blackwing. For now I was content to allow that misconception to continue. The two hangers-on twittered their encouragement, smirking at the notion of seeing a man they didn't know flogged. The tide flowed favourably for them and they enjoyed its eddies and currents. I ignored them.

'You should watch yours, sir!' Dantry countered. 'By the spirits of mercy, you shame your father with this behaviour. I come here to request your simple assistance in extracting a noble lady from a bleak and cruel torment, to allow her to be nursed as her rank demands. As a gentleman, honour obliges you to assist me.'

Heinrich Adenauer looked at Dantry for longer than was comfortable without speaking. Eventually he reached inside his coat, removed a gold-plated pocket watch and checked the time. Slowly he breathed across the surface, buffed it upon his jacket and returned it to his pocket. The hangers-on were watching him carefully but Adenauer's bastard turned his attention to the polish of his fingernails.

'I did not wish to say this, Count Tanza, but, alas, I feel I have no option. Your sister offered herself to each and every member of the Maud's staff, thrusting her naked womanly parts at them and insisting that they take turns fucking her. She would bend over, presenting her naked backside—'

Part of me wished I'd failed to stop him. I would have valued the resounding crack as Dantry's open palm belted Heinrich Adenauer across the face. But I'd seen it coming, and I caught Dantry's wrist before he could strike the blow. Heinrich Adenauer's eyes narrowed to slits. He almost looked disappointed.

Guards arrived to escort us out. The meeting was over.

'He baited you into trying that,' I said as we stood outside, smoking cigars. Dantry sucked on his in rapid, greedy draws, smoking to get his heart back under control.

'I should not have lost control,' he said, ashamed. 'But his rudeness was intolerable. The dishonour of such a slur ... That insolent little whip! I'll put a foot of steel through his throat and send him to the hells.'

'Much as I might enjoy watching you duel, that won't get your sister out of the Maud.'

Dantry stamped up and down the street muttering furious assertions of intent and thrusting at the air. I let him blow it all out of his system. I was glad that I'd stopped him. I'd duelled a man once, and winning hadn't made anything better. Dantry wiped his ridiculous hair away from his eyes and came back to me. Slumping down on a step, he asked, 'You don't think that there's any chance? I mean, that she, well, that she ... ?'

'I'll slap you if you swallow any of that bullshit. He was goading you. Wanted you to hit him. Even brought witnesses to make sure it was recorded, although your handprint on his face would have done the job. Spirits of ire, they really don't want your sister out of there.'

'But who?' Dantry said. He looked ill. The after-effects of the Misery and fear for his sister were starting to break him down. 'Everything she and I have done, we've done it for the Alliance. For the greater good. We're trying to protect Dortmark, don't they see that?'

I knocked ash from the end of my cigar. My hand had a really bad shake to it now. Needed to find a new bag of liquorice. A new bag, a new life somewhere maybe. But not while Ezabeth languished in that grim place.

'It's what Ezabeth's got figured out. They don't want it known.'

They might not want her out, but Crowfoot sure does, I thought. He'd sent me to save Ezabeth at Station Twelve and now wanted me to fish her out of the hole she'd dug for herself. He must want her to complete her work, wherever it led. I wanted her out of there too. She wasn't a creature of the dark. Made me angry just to imagine her sitting alone in the blackness. It would be enough to drive a sane woman mad, given enough time.

21

The ale tasted flat but the mood was flatter. I sat across a forgotten tile board from Tnota, Nenn and a grey-faced count, looking into my ale and saying nothing. What was there left to say? The air hummed with the bitter regret of white-leaf smoke and the odour of abandoned ambitions. I raised my eyes from my cup, looked around the detritus drinking in the Bell. Couldn't help but feel that we were just numbered amongst them now. I'd always considered myself a cut above; I was a captain, a man of standing, and maybe I'd never managed to get as much cream out of my blood as I'd thought. The clientele were soldiers, and they were ex-soldiers, mercenaries and vagabonds. Most of them were unemployable or they'd have been off at Station Three-Six getting ready to repel the biggest invasion force we'd seen since Nall's Engine sprang up. They were the leaf addicts, the sick, the lame, the cowards and those simply too stupid to hold a pike in line.

Like them, I'd failed.

'Do you think Stannard will have made it back to Valengrad by now?' Nenn asked. Tnota scratched his arse, gave his finger a sniff.

'We had a lead. But maybe – if his navigator was half decent.'

'What happens when he does?'

It was a good question. Couldn't help but feel I'd have

Herono's men battering against my door in the morning, some kind of trumped-up charges levelled against me. I'd picked a side and it was losing. If I had made an enemy of a prince then my history with Venzer wouldn't protect me, and that was if Venzer was on my side at all. That thought rose and died quickly. I refused to consider the possibility that he was working against me. I'd followed that old man's lead for twenty years.

The raven on my arm was blank and dry, scabbed and cracked. I stared at it, willing the bird to break free, to tell me what to do. 'Get her out' hadn't been the clearest of instructions, but if Crowfoot hadn't meant it seriously he wouldn't have wasted any of his power to send me the message. He was going to need it all if the Deep Kings made it to the Range.

'Seems to me I'm fucked either way.'

'Tomorrow I shall try again to have her freed,' Dantry said. His spirits were lower than mud. Couldn't blame him. We'd been blocked and fucked over at every turn, always a step behind. Our enemy had managed to second-guess the plays we'd make, had always been a move ahead.

'Won't make any fucking difference, kid,' I said. 'Seemed to me they'd have been glad to have your sister off their hands. We played on the legality of her imprisonment, her status as your sister. But that's not it. And if they thought Ezabeth was a traitor she'd be swinging from Heckle Gate by now. So why isn't she?'

'It's not that easy to curdle the cream,' Nenn said. She shot Dantry a glance that meant she either wanted to kill him or fuck him, or maybe both.

'Count Digada would disagree, but what's left of him isn't doing any talking,' I said. 'Someone high up has gone to a lot of trouble to silence her without ending her. But why the fuck would they do that?'

We settled back into an uncomfortable silence. The

drinking wasn't helping my maudlin, but a fish will swim if you throw it back into the water. I thought of Ezabeth pouring her light into me, burning the drunkenness out of me. I was going to an awful lot of effort over a woman I could no longer claim to know. I don't know what that said about me other than that maybe I'd been lonely a long time and somehow in encountering a spectre from my youth I'd felt a kinship. Didn't seem to matter that she was a half-crazy bitch, we grasp any branch in a flood.

The cup in my hand exploded in a shower of broken pottery as a matchlock roared. A second shot followed, blowing through a second window pane as we threw ourselves to the floor. Patrons ducked beneath tables, upsetting bowls and glasses. I threw my hands futilely over my head, waited for more, but the two shots had rung out and nothing further followed. As stillness descended across the room, gun smoke wafted in through the shattered windows.

I was bleeding. Shards of jagged ceramics had nicked my chin, my fingers. Nothing that wouldn't scab over in a day or two. The instinct was to draw steel and charge, find out who was shooting at us. But that's a fool's manoeuvre. Either they'd spent their weapons and run, or they had more and were waiting for me to do just that. I stayed low and made sure I could get steel in my hand quickly if I needed it.

Against the quiet, a wail began to rise. Agonised. For a moment I pressed my eyes shut, not wanting to see. Not wanting to know how bad it was. The blackness could not last.

Below the shoulder Tnota's arm hung limp as a sock full of rocks, a tangle of shredded flesh and shattered bone. He collapsed screaming, spurting red. His arm was a mangled ruin of ugly white splinters amongst minced tatters of meat, the blood issuing from it in jets.

Nenn worked fast. She pinned him, cut a tourniquet.

'He needs a surgeon,' she said.

I sat, blank, numb. Part of my mind had recoiled at what it was seeing. There was no battle-thrill running through me. All I saw was the pain on my friend's face. My brain was cold. It ticked slowly, gears wound down.

'He won't make it,' I mumbled.

'We fucking try!' Nenn spat.

'Try,' Tnota gasped, eyes rolling wildly, 'please, captain, try.'

Men more foolish than I had ventured out the front to look for shooters, but they returned shrugging and shaking bewildered heads. We were regulars; they knew Tnota well. A couple of the boy whores brought liquor out, and a roll of bandage. Started trying to tend the mess that had been a functioning limb moments before.

My heart plummeted like a comet. Tnota never hurt anybody. This wasn't his fight. I'd dragged him into the murk and grime of court and this was how he'd been repaid. For some reason asking him to risk himself in the Misery wasn't the same. Out there, the beasts only wanted to eat you because they are hungry. Here, those bullets had been meant for Dantry and me. We were only alive because the assassins couldn't shoot for shit. Tnota met my eyes, questing, like there was something I could do for him.

'Dantry. Lads. Get him to a surgeon. One of the good ones on Copper Street. If they won't operate without payment, get violent.' I drew my pistols and placed them in Dantry's shaking hands. 'Don't stop for anyone. Make it happen. Nenn, you're with me.'

'What we going to do, captain?'

I rose to my feet, feeling the passage of fate turning around me, a river of possibility and eventuality.

'The tile board just got flipped on us. We don't have to play by their rules any more.'

22

The Maud was old back when Dortmark's biggest worries were the clan chieftains' power struggles. Bits of it were still that old brickwork, grey and pitted, flints protruding bonily from cement. The matron paled as I stalked in on a wave of rage.

'You know why I'm here,' I said. 'Bring out the girl.'

She looked like she wanted to argue, claim I needed some official papers, like the sword in my hand wasn't a sufficient mandate to act. Self-preservation won out over bureaucracy. The Holy Sister ordered a man with a big bunch of keys to go and open Ezabeth's cell.

'I ain't bringing that mad witch,' he said. His voice shook. Officials like to believe their uniforms give them some kind of authority, hide behind them, imagine that they shield them from the world. That only works if other people are playing the same game.

'You're talking about Lady Ezabeth Tanza, you fucking dog,' I told him with a snarl. Then, just because I felt like it and because adrenaline and fury were overtaking everything else, I grabbed him by the coat and threw him across his own table. Papers scattered in the air as he went crashing down. I took his keys and we went to find her. I doubted he'd try to stop us on the way out. The matron said nothing. Truth was, she just wanted to run her hospital. Probably a good woman, most of the time. Just happened to be in the way of princes and angry mercenaries. She'd be setting her orderlies on us in no time, but Nenn was a hellcat and I'd wager on our swords over their cudgels even on our worst day.

We walked fast. The outermost cells were for the gentle lunatics and those with the wealthiest relatives. Their rooms were mostly clean, the many residents free to wander about the place as long as they didn't try to leave. In a common room an old man was playing a beautiful melody on a viola, while a woman who'd plucked out her hair until she had a bald crown sat listening at his feet. Along another corridor there were children, and I wondered how anyone could tell when children were mad, since they never made sense anyway. Maybe they were the kids of the lunatics. It was neither a frightening nor an upsetting place. Not until you went down a level, where they kept the really dangerous ones.

If a lunatic was mad enough to hurt people, the law dealt with them the same way it would anyone else. Murder was murder, accidental killing was murder, and wounding someone so that they got infected and died was pretty much murder too, so there weren't that many dangerous madmen. Instead, the noisy ones tended to be the ones that hurt themselves. One closed door partially blocked away shrieks that went on and on, and through another I heard a hoarse voice croaking that she wanted her babies, over and over. The subterranean tunnels held the sounds, sent them back to their owners, the echoes repeating their madness like some dismal prayer.

Ezabeth was kept one level below the dangerous mad.

Ezabeth's room was only dimly lit by a single light tube running along the ceiling. I unlocked the door, not looking forward to what I was going to find. And it was bad. The room stank. I'd spent a lot of time in some pretty shitty places, had done my fair share of latrine digging in the ranks, and still that weren't so bad as this. The floor was wet, walls streaked with filth.

'Come in, quick,' Ezabeth said with her back to us. Didn't even turn her hood in my direction. 'Lift me up.'

Not exactly the reaction that I'd expected.

'Time for you to get out of here,' I said. 'Come on. We don't have long.'

'Not yet. Quickly. Lift me higher. Closer to the ceiling.'

'What the fuck are you on about?' I said, my spirits sinking. Maybe I'd been wrong all along. Maybe she was as mad as they said, and I'd made enemies against a foolish hope.

'I can see better with the door open. The light from the corridor helps. Do you have any more light?' She adjusted her veil to cover her face and turned around, eyes glittering blackly in the weak light. I looked upwards towards the ceiling and it was only then I realised what she was looking at.

From a distance it could be mistaken for simple dirt, but as I stepped closer I realised there was an art to it. The walls were covered in crudely drawn diagrams, lunar observances and charts, numbers and calculations, the occasional paragraph.

'What is this?'

'This is where they imprisoned Gleck Maldon,' Ezabeth said. 'And he wrote his thesis across the walls. I understand most of it, but my eyes aren't good enough to see this bit on the ceiling. Can you lift me?'

'What's it written with?'

'Shit,' she said. 'Mostly shit anyway. He must have mixed it with his urine, to make a kind of ink. Maldon must have had a chair to write on the ceiling. I imagine they saw him smearing faeces on it and took it away from him. Now lift me up.'

Well that explained the smell. We were surrounded by verse after verse of human waste written across the walls.

'Don't imagine they let me down here voluntarily,' I said.

We were already on borrowed time. The law may have been on my side, but the law didn't control the soldiers and I had no doubt that the matron had sent for them.

'Captain, lift me!'

I hesitated. A sudden fear came upon me, far greater than anything I'd felt in the Misery. Ezabeth's blue gown was grime encrusted and it stank but that wasn't the reason I swallowed hard before putting my hands on her waist. She didn't meet my eyes as she asked me again to lift her. She hardly weighed anything and I raised her up. Not the first time I'd lifted her, but a shiver ran through my shoulders all the same. This was all of her, that I held now in my hands. I braced her up on my shoulder, seated like a pet bird. Nenn scowled at me and held up a lamp. The wails of the mad echoed down the corridors as Ezabeth examined detailed calculations written in crap across the ceiling. She read off numbers, repeating them back into her memory.

'Someone's coming, captain,' Nenn said. I'd heard it too.

'Time's up.'

'Yes, put me down. I have it. But … it doesn't make sense.' I could hear the hurt in her voice. The disappointment. 'The algorithm breaks down. I don't understand. I was sure it was going in the other direction. None of it works. There must be something I'm missing.'

'Time to go,' Nenn said again. 'Come on, captain, leave the mad bitch if she won't come.' I could hear the tramp of boots in the corridor, lots of boots now. I suddenly realised I may have overestimated how long it was going to take them to come for us.

We left the stinking cell. A group of the Maud's staff had appeared with cudgels. They didn't look friendly.

'Can't let you take the prisoner, sir,' one of them said respectfully. He was a man of middle years, thin grey hair, a neat beard.

'Didn't know you kept prisoners here. Thought this was

a hospital.' I ran my eyes over them; there were nine men in all, most of them younger than me but none so young those sticks wouldn't hurt.

'I have instructions from Prince Herono herself that Lady Tanza can only leave the Maud with her express permission, and she hasn't given that yet. I don't mean to be in your way, sir, least not to take on the displeasure of a nobleman, but I don't rightly have no choice. Please step back into your chamber, my lady.'

It is the way of the world that good people try to do the right thing for the wrong people's wrong reasons. The grey-haired man looked to be one of them.

'We're leaving,' I said. 'Nenn. If these men stand in your way, you have the order to cut them down. You have Blackwing's full authority. Get out of our way, you fuckers. We're working under Crowfoot's direct orders.' It wasn't often I played my highest-ranking ally as a trump card. I doubted that he'd bother to turn up to a trial if it came to that, but it was the best I could do. I wasn't letting them take her again. Nenn grinned as she bared her steel. The orderlies readied their sticks. I left my own cutlass sheathed, though. I could see that I wouldn't need it. Nenn was a warrior, a killer, a bitch of steel and cold bloody murder. To her, cutting a path through these men was all in a day's work; to them, even standing before her sword was terror. They might use those clubs against the mad and the senile locked away here, but fighting is not the same as bullying. They edged away from her.

'Perhaps we can just all wait patient-like until the prince has been contacted?' the lead orderly requested. Vigorous nodding from his colleagues. Nenn hissed like a cat.

''Scuse me, sirs, is this the low level?'

A child had wandered down the corridor. Beyond the orderlies, standing at the foot of the stairwell. In the dim light of the flickering tubes, he looked strangely familiar.

His hair was all close shorn up against his head, his eyes wide and oddly blue.

'Off with you, lad,' the lead orderly said. He paid the boy no heed and tried again to appeal to reason. 'I'm sure that it's just a matter of paperwork ...'

He seized up mid-word like someone had grabbed him by the throat. A spasm ran through his whole body, and then another man jerked in a similar fashion, like great puppeteer's strings had suddenly attached to his shoulders and he were being pulled about. Another of the orderlies collapsed to the ground, clawing at his face.

That was no little boy. Now I knew why he was familiar. I'd met him at Station Twelve.

A lash of dark magic sliced the air of the tunnel and two of the orderlies collapsed in pieces, shrieking as they lost the use of legs and arms. The lead orderly and the other two front-runners came jerkily towards us, puppets swinging their sticks. Blood ran from their eyes and noses as they twitched forwards, bodies moving in the thrall of the creature that sought us out. Nenn beat a clumsy baton aside and opened an orderly up, her curved sword slashing deep through neck and collar bone. She kicked his twitching body off her blade, cut a hand from the leader, and growing confident as she cut a path through them, hacked the head from the third. His body went down twitching, still trying to swipe at her with the baton. I caught the handless puppet-man, hurled him back towards the others as a second blast of dark magic cut through the group, splitting another of the poor bastards in two. This strike had been aimed at Ezabeth directly but as it reached her the lash of unreality dissipated in a shower of bright sparks. She still staggered at the force of the impact. She might have saved what little light she had but it wouldn't last.

The Darling was panting; all magic took effort. I took out my knife and threw it straight at the little bastard but an orderly managed to get in the way. Those still able to give voice cried out, covering their heads with their hands and ducking, caught in a crossfire that they couldn't hope to survive.

As Nenn fended off another of the mind-wormed orderlies I saw a door further along the corridor. Beyond it, a stairway.

Ezabeth sagged against the wall. If the Darling's magic was costing it, then deflecting that blast had cost her more. I hoisted her over my shoulder and we dashed through the door. She was light as a field mouse, just skin and small bones. Nenn skittered through the doorway as the Darling launched another cutting blast; dust and chips of stone fell from the ceiling. My girl slammed the door behind her as we ascended damp stone steps. At the top another door was barred on the wrong side, locked. For a horrible moment I imagined us caught between a dead end and the creature coming at us from below. Without Ezabeth's magic we didn't stand a chance against the Darling, but Nenn shoulder-charged straight through the door in a shower of rotting boards. The lunatics on the other side gaped at us in wonder but they cleared a path before Nenn's bared sword. I tried to tell them to run, but they stared blankly and gabbled.

As we made it out into the courtyard, Prince Herono's men had just arrived. An officious-looking squawk in a starched and pressed uniform had some kind of arrest warrant in his hands.

'You there!' he called. His eyes widened at Nenn's bloody sword. His men had pikes, which they levelled at us but I recognised Battle Spinner Rovelle, a mustachioed man in a gold brocade doublet stepping down from a carriage. He'd been on the Range as long as I had.

'Stand down, captain,' Rovelle said. He let a flicker of light work its way around his fingers. 'Drop the girl. Orders from Prince Herono herself.'

'There's a Darling in the fucking Maud!' Nenn yelled. She flicked at one of the pike heads with her sword, causing the soldier to scamper back. A moment of confusion, a moment of doubt, and then there was doubt no more as a flash of sorcery whipped out and scattered the soldiers. At least two of them were strewn around in bloody pieces. It was only the Darling's poor aim that was saving us now. Battle Spinner Rovelle looked from us to the demonic little child standing in the Maud's doorway some thirty feet away. He couldn't believe what he was seeing; sorcery smoked from the Darling's skin like golden steam.

Rovelle attacked, the Darling attacked, and the world exploded in flares of light and darkness. As the magic blasted away flagstones and chewed bricks from the walls. The soldiers ran, and we ran, and we didn't stop running until the sounds of the conflict had faded.

I learned much later that Rovelle put up a good fight before the Darling took his head off.

23

Lot of things I would have liked just then. A fast stallion and enough gold to get me safely away from the Range for ever would have topped the list, but they weren't forthcoming. I'd have settled for an old nag and a beer, but fortune's a fickle bitch. We hid out at Nenn's place long enough for Ezabeth to get herself together then risked the journey across town.

The city shivered, cowered and played dead. Windows were shuttered, doors barred. Mounted soldiers pounded through the streets with sabres drawn and trembling hands as a siren wailed from the citadel. A Darling was loose in the city and the last thing those brave men wanted was to encounter it. They paused only long enough to ask whether we'd seen any children and then galloped away. Nobody was looking for us, not with a Darling on the loose. Venzer would have all of his remaining Battle Spinners together in a cabal hunting for it. I hoped they'd find it but I doubted they would. Tracking down something like that should have been my job. Losing yourself in a city is a simple affair. The horsemen were more show than effect.

Otto Lindrick's house was shabbier than I remembered it. The garden was overgrown, weeds routing the arrangements of the flowerbeds, paint flaking around the windows. I was surprised: he'd struck me as a man who cared about outward appearances.

Young Destran appeared at the door, glancing out

nervously, his face an eruption of angry pimples. Being young is hard. Our bodies seem to reject us even as they mould us into what we will one day become. He looked over the odd assortment of scarred, masked, bloody people on the doorstep and nervously beckoned us inside.

'Dear lady!' Lindrick said, appearing in a flurry of chubby fingers. 'When I heard the news I feared the worst! Oh, dear spirits above, thanks be, thanks be!' He seized her in an embrace and wet her shoulder with fat little tears. Otto was wearing courtly finery, a heavily embroidered, over-frilled shirt that would have been in fashion fifty years ago, his balding crown hidden beneath a maroon cap. He didn't give Nenn or me much of a glance.

'I need paper,' Ezabeth said, cutting aside pleasantries. 'Ink. Compasses, a rule, lunar cycling charts. He left it all written there for me, but I need to write it down before it leaves my mind.'

'Of course,' Otto said, ushering us inside, though he couldn't have known what she was referring to. 'But first you must tell me what happened at the Maud. The city is in chaos. A crier ran by shouting that there was some sort of battle there.'

'They will fill you in,' Ezabeth said. She dismissed the most troubling invasion of Valengrad in a century as though it were idle gossip. Nothing mattered to her more than her calculations. 'Ink and paper. Now.'

Otto took us into his office, the same one in which I'd put the marks on his face. I actually felt bad about it. Couldn't be easy for the engineer to have me back in his house. Dantry awaited us there, his face full of concern, but Ezabeth barely acknowledged him with a nod and a joyless smile as she swept about gathering what she needed before sitting down to work at the desk. Dantry looked hurt, but unsurprised. He watched her scribbling with weary, pained resignation.

'How was Tnota when you left him?' I asked. Steeled myself.

'Alive. Not in a good way,' Dantry said. 'I found a surgeon willing to take him against my word for future payment.'

I nodded. Didn't have the words to express how I felt. If there was one thing Valengrad's surgeons knew well, it was amputation. Tnota was in good hands. He'd live, or he'd die. I felt him as a hanging weight suspended in my chest. *Not Tnota, spirits of mercy. Please.*

Dantry looked shaken as his sister silenced him and sent us to another room. The apprentice led us to a reception room with fancy padded chairs and too many cushions. Decadence and wealth, quite contrary to the shabby exterior. Everything inside Otto's house seemed new, like it was seldom used, just on show for guests. The decanters on the drinks trolley were all full, the glasses in ordered rows.

'We can speak plain? Any household staff around?' I asked.

'It's just myself and Destran here,' Otto said. 'Tea? Coffee?' He was perfectly civil. The engineer tried to smile, but winced as his facial muscles met with the swelling my fists had dealt him. He settled for a look of smug superiority. It's not a lot of men of his height who can give a man of my height that kind of look. Maybe he figured he was acting the bigger man.

'Got anything stronger?' I asked.

'You smell like you've taken enough liquor today already,' he chastised. 'There's work to be done.'

'Seems a pissy kind of revenge to deny a man a drink.' I could see the brandy in the decanters, waiting for me to taste it. A mellow golden glow danced on the table as sunlight filtered through the bottles. Otto gave me a pitying look.

'I bear you no ill will, Captain Galharrow. The truth is, I don't blame you for this.' He indicated the mess I'd made of his face, blackberry bruising and split skin that hadn't yet healed. I avoided meeting the open-mouthed stare Dantry was giving me. 'You were following your orders, like a good soldier. Like an obedient hound.'

'Yeah. I don't like you much either.'

We all sat down and Destran brought coffee. According to Dantry it was an excellent, smooth blend, but to me all coffee tastes the same. It tastes like not-booze, which means it might as well be mud from a ditch. I told the story of our escape from the Maud, and it tasted worse than the coffee.

'A Darling in Valengrad. I never thought to hear such a thing,' Otto moaned.

'Well, you heard it now.' I ran a hand over my eyes. 'Lot of people died today. Lot of wives will be weeping before nightfall. Maybe some more kids end up in the orphanage.'

'A regrettable price, paid so that truth may find the light,' Otto said. Not a trace of emotion, like he was tallying his accounts, ticking off the profits and losses.

I looked them over, this odd pairing. Otto short, fat, as unreadable as he seemed changeable, his apprentice a gangly youth all limbs and bad skin. Destran withered uncomfortably beneath my gaze, gave that shrug that only teenagers can give, uncomfortable in his own skin. Life's no easier for the young than it is for old men like me. Destran couldn't be older than fourteen but Otto's age was harder to judge. His eyes didn't seem right to me, too bright, too young, too knowing, too old. Takes a strange man to sit sipping coffee with a cut-throat who once beat him senseless without the hate clouding his face. Never met a man could drop a grudge that easily, could weigh the lead and find the insult lighter than the benefits. I didn't sense any lust for revenge in Otto, like he was blank to it. It was like he didn't give two shits for what I'd done to him.

'You're taking one hell of a risk letting us in,' I said. I wanted to get a rise out of him, any display of emotion that wasn't that calm smugness. I didn't get it.

'I may not look like much of a hero to you, but Ezabeth needs her answers. We all need her answers. I put her in contact with Gleck Maldon knowing nothing of her, save for the papers she had published regarding the optimisation of phos technology.' He sighed. 'If not for me, none of you would be mixed up in any of this.'

I looked down at Crowfoot's ink on my arm. Wherever that Nameless bastard was, off running around in foreign lands when he should have been here, helping us, he seemed to think Ezabeth valuable. Invaluable. I still couldn't see it. There were a hundred thousand drudge warriors crossing the Misery, fortifying, building as they went. The Deep Kings were coming like they'd lost their fear of our weapons and Crowfoot had put all his stock in one veiled girl.

'Herono is family,' Dantry muttered. 'I just can't believe that she'd do anything to harm us. She hired Captain Galharrow to help my sister. To help us. We need to go to her.'

It was the sad, world-weary look that Otto directed towards Dantry that made me certain he wasn't just some rural accountant, out of his depth in a world of princes and knives. He was tough as year-old jerky. Range tough. A man who could take a beating and not hold a grudge because it didn't help his agenda. The kind of man it's usually best to grack first and wonder about later.

'Count Tanza. It is a pleasure to make your acquaintance, although I am sorry that we have not met under better circumstances than these. I have heard great things of your mathematical talents.'

'I have heard good things about you also, Master Engineer,' Dantry said. Otto's well-mannered calmness was catching. The engineer had judged how best to handle the proud young count. Smart fucking man. Too fucking smart.

'Your great aunt may be family, but ask yourself why your kinswoman did not use her influence to free your sister,' Otto said.

'What could she possibly have against my sister?' Dantry asked.

'You ask the wrong questions, my dear count.'

'Main question is, what do they want?' I said. 'What do you want?'

'What do any of us want? Safety for the city states. Safety for my wife, my children back in the west. I want the Range to stand for another thousand years, or at least until the Deep Kings turn upon one another and destroy themselves. What else?'

'Ezabeth thinks she has something new to work with. But she still needs to access the heart,' I said.

'Nobody can enter the Engine's heart,' Otto said. 'Nall ensured as much. There's a mechanism that not even the Order can open, a series of panels that must be pressed in some unknown order. Those that tried and failed are buried out beyond the walls. What was left of them, at least. He made well sure no tampering enemy could meddle with the Engine's heart. Whatever he worked in there is not for mortal eyes.'

'But Nall is gone,' I said. Otto nodded.

'And since Nall departed – or died, or whatever became of him – men like Gleck Maldon have begun to ask questions, to dig up the old equations. While Nall held the secrets none questioned them, but with him gone, curiosity grew. Maldon wanted Nall's knowledge. And nothing is more dangerous than knowledge, isn't that so, Destran?'

'Yes, master. Knowledge is power,' the apprentice said.

'They silenced Gleck Maldon. Now they want to do the same to Ezabeth.'

I needed a drink. There was a clammy sweat on my skin, the kind that comes out when I've not opened the bottle in a while. I crossed to Otto's supply and poured myself a glass. It was piss poor stuff. It should have been beneath a man like him to drink that swill. Good enough for me, though.

'If they only wanted Ezabeth silenced, it could have been done easier,' I said. 'They could have put her on trial for sedition and treason using Pieter Dytwin's testimony. She was vulnerable in the Maud, easy to get to. They tried to kill Dantry, twice. But they were keeping her alive. Why?'

'An individual can be slain. An idea is less easy to put down,' Otto said. 'By declaring Ezabeth mad, they not only stopped her wagging tongue, they invalidated her findings. They did the same to poor Gleck, though I rather suspect he had actually started to lose control of his faculties by the time they committed him.'

'But if she dies, her blasphemy dies with her,' I said.

Lindrick shook his head.

'Ideas do not succumb to the knife so easily. Imagine that Ezabeth dies in mysterious circumstances. Imagine the scandal, the attention that it would draw to her work. Dantry would have to be summoned back from the Misery, would have orchestrated an inquest. Maybe he finds enough evidence for a trial. He might have had every one of the Maud's staff racked to get to the truth.'

'I wouldn't,' Dantry said, and I believed him. Soft.

'But they couldn't know that,' Lindrick said, patting the count sympathetically on the shoulder like he was a sad dog denied a bone. 'All that attention, when attention was the last thing they want. While Ezabeth lives as a mad woman, she is a lunatic pursuing horse feathers on the wind. If she were to perish, her research passes to the next Spinner smart enough to look into it.'

'So it had to be quiet,' I said.

'It had to be legal,' Otto corrected me. 'Which seemed to be working well for them until they realised that the matter hadn't gone to rest in the Maud. You had the right of it, the law backed Dantry's request to take care of Ezabeth. And so they tried to kill Dantry, first in the Misery, then by goading him into a duel with Heinrich Adenauer – who for all his foppish appearance is a devil with a rapier. And finally when their plans had failed them, they tried to shoot him in a squalid tavern.'

'The Bell's not that squalid,' Nenn snapped.

'It's not just Prince Herono trying to keep Ezabeth silent,' I said heavily. 'It's not just Marshal Venzer. It's Prince Herono, it's Marshal Venzer and it's Prince Adenauer together. It's the spirits damned Order. It's probably every high-ranking fucker in Valengrad.'

I sagged back into the depth of the armchair, pressing my fingers up against my eyes. Politics. I hated this shit. I'd hated it back when I had a fancy name, back when I first met Ezabeth and we'd run through the meadows together. I'd hated it when I took my first commission and the other officers sneered at one another as they sought to befriend me or mock me, and I'd hated it when my wife wrote to me with snippets of gossip she thought would be to my advantage. I'd hated it when I was a general, I hated it when Torolo Mancono had died for it, and even though I'd lost my name, my command, my wife, here I was, swirling around in the shit pot with everyone else. Politicians – only the Nameless can fuck things up worse.

I needed to speak to Crowfoot. I hated what he was, and I hated what he did to me, but I needed him. It had been a long time since I'd actually wanted to speak to that feathered bastard.

Lindrick was looking at me.

'Tell me, captain. If it were down to you, would you let her continue? When the drudge come, and they are coming, would you attempt to activate Nall's Engine even if it meant the wheels fly off the cart? Would you risk the destruction of Dortmark? Maybe the destruction of the entire world?'

It was best that I didn't answer that.

'The Deep Kings already suspect,' I said. 'And they're coming. Right now. They're bringing their legions and they're going to roll over us in a wave of blades and fire. So Ezabeth better have some theory to try, because we don't have time.'

24

Nothing to do. Ezabeth worked away, scribbling down whatever hidden wisdom she'd gleaned from Maldon's shitty smearings. Nenn moved between the windows, peeking out between the shutters as if expecting a troop of soldiers to march down and arrest us. The road remained quiet, peaceful. I took a bath, washed the sweat and blood away. The house had water heaters driven by phos, Otto's own design. I wondered how Tnota was faring, whether he was still even alive. If it was bad news then I didn't want to know the answer, not yet.

As the evening drew on Destran served up vegetable soup and bread. Seated around a table like the strangest of families, at first there was an attempt at light conversation, and then it all got quiet as each retreated into their own thoughts. I didn't know what to do. It wasn't my responsibility, wasn't under my control. I'd done what was right, and I'd kept Ezabeth alive and free. That had to be something. That had to be enough.

There would be a price on my head by now. Everything was changed.

Night drew in and Lindrick needed to go to the mill. He would be missed if he didn't show up. I promised that I'd keep Ezabeth safe, and he headed off to work. He might have given us the hospitality of his home, but there was something about him that I didn't like. Maybe just that the marks on his face left me feeling guilty. It didn't matter what he'd told us, I still didn't trust him. Trusting clever people is always inadvisable. There were only four people in all the world that I could trust, three of them were in the house with me and the other was either flirting with the surgeon or riding with his Big Dog in the sky. It was a coin flip which.

I stood on the landing beside a second-storey window, looking out across Gathers. A city district flush with new money, quiet in the late hours. Smoke from a hundred hundred fires rose over the tall roofs, carrying the prayers of the city's hungry with it. For every stately mansion the likes of Lindrick enjoyed, a thousand suffering souls would go to bed hungry tonight. Valengrad wasn't a good place. Wasn't even worth saving. I didn't have to save it. Didn't have any way to save it even if I wanted to. Nobody did.

'What are you thinking?' Nenn asked as she came to stand beside me. For all that she didn't like Ezabeth, she spoke soft enough not to wake her in the next room. I doubt a fifty-gun salute could have roused her anyway. Dantry had brought her tea and found her snoring on the desk, ink blackening her fingers.

'I'm thinking we're in well over our heads and we need the Nameless to sort this out for us,' I said. 'If there's a Darling roaming Valengrad then things are worse than we'd feared. That it braved the Range the first time was bad enough. Twice, though?' I shook my head.

'But if it knows that Nall's Engine is fucked, then what does it want with your short-arse bit of cream?' Nenn said. I don't know why the quickness of Nenn's mind could still surprise me, but it always did.

'That's a fair question.'

'You really think Venzer is part of this?'

'I'm not sure. That's the next move. Got to find out whether the Iron Goat's involved or whether he's been as used as the rest of us. We're puppets, Nenn. All of us. Someone's pulling everybody's strings, and it doesn't matter if it's wizards or princes doing it, sooner or later they get tired and cut us loose.'

'You got that voice again, captain.'

'And what's that?'

'Like you think you should be in charge of the whole world, and you're pissed that you aren't.'

She grinned at me. I let the bleakness slip away for long enough to return it. Nenn had a packet of thin cigars and we smoked them one by one as we watched the shadows lengthen and the sky begin to shed its brightness. We were facing west, the cracked blood-and-bruises sky hidden from sight. That was good. Sometimes you just want to see something natural, something true.

'We need another Heart of the Void,' I said. 'Nall's Engine was never the answer. Just a bandage on a wound that won't close. Now the blood's starting to run again and if Crowfoot doesn't have an answer then we're all gracked and gone.'

'We can get out, captain,' Nenn said. 'We aren't tied here. Could go west. Find a ship at Ostermark, see what's over the sea. Maybe we settle down, get us a farm. Or maybe just go kill people some other place, where they don't have Deep Kings and Darlings and Brides. You think they got Kings and Nameless over the sea?'

'I expect they got their own problems,' I said. 'If it comes to making a stand, you'll go?'

'You won't?'

I didn't know the answer to that. The full strength of our little Range was less than forty thousand men. The Dhoja could field many times that, but the numbers wouldn't matter if the Deep Kings came at us in person. The kid stamping on ants doesn't count how many there are in the nest before he goes to work with his boot.

I knocked ash from my cigar and wished Lindrick stocked better brandy. I was drunk enough to be maudlin, but not so bad as to lose control. I wanted to be.

Destran had prepared comfortable rooms for us, but sleep didn't come easy. I wrestled with my conscience a good while before getting up to find what was left of the brandy. Before I reached the stair I saw that the door to Ezabeth's room was open, her bed empty. When I found she was not at the writing desk, I knew where she would be: up. The city was sleeping, but the night was a time for Spinners and people with dark minds, and she was one and I was the other. I found my way to the roof and stepped out onto the terraced surface.

Ezabeth sat at the far side, but her whole body was a white incandescence, a silhouette of intense light against the dark night. Her hands worked left and right, trailing through the air to draw bright strings of coloured light like feast day ribbons. Rioque was at her height, but Clada and Eala were half showing and the light pulsed green, purple, gold and crimson through her fingers, the streaming lines lingering on the eyes even once they'd faded from the air. She was spinning, but like nothing I'd ever seen before. Always I'd seen Spinners drawing phos and storing it into battery coils, but Ezabeth's whole body seemed to be afire with brilliant energy. Stunning. Inhuman.

When I was twelve, my parents took me to the symphony house in Frosk. The boat trip had taken two weeks, and by the time we arrived I and my brother had been frothing with excitement. When Lady Dovaura came onto the stage she wore a gown of bright white diamonds, thousands of stones glimmering like stars as she turned in the phos light. She had worn a collar like a peacock's tail, crowning her in emeralds and sapphires, and when she raised the viola to play, a silence had descended upon the assembled lords, ladies and princes. Within minutes she had half the audience weeping, and the other half trembling to retain their composure.

I relate this now only to say that by comparison to Ezabeth's spinning, Lady Dovaura's performance had been a tawdry circus act. I had never known the true meaning of beauty until I stepped out onto that roof top and saw the woman of light drawing colours from night air. Like a blazing ghost, a fae spirit that did not belong in the physical world but only in dreams and longings, she stopped my heart for a beat and I was felled. There was no contrivance there, no reliance upon stones cut from the earth and shaped and sewn, but a delicate display that was both utterly unnatural, magical, displaced from reality and at the same time the truest display I had ever seen.

'Ezabeth,' I said beneath my breath, and I did so not to call her attention but only to praise her, to worship. I don't know how she heard me, but she did. Her light-blank head turned towards me, and then darkness suddenly came down as the streamers of light scattered. Her radiance dissipated, I was left night-blind and blinking away the after-image. I heard her scrabbling around and by the time my eyesight came back to me she was clothed and veiled. The light had all but gone from her, save a very soft luminescence emanating from her skin. She glowed in the night.

'What are you doing up here?' she asked, voice faintly metallic.

I sought out words but found them scrambled and gone. More breathless than if I had run a dozen miles. 'Forgive me. I didn't intend to intrude. Your spinning – it was like nothing I ever saw before.'

'A technique I devised last year.' Nervous, embarrassed to have been seen. I felt more of a voyeur than if I'd spied on her bathing. She said, 'I have drawn all the phos that I can without battery coils. We should go down.'

I was suddenly aware that it was cold on the roof, that

summer's end was upon us and the last months had not retained their warmth. A cold wind was blowing in from the Misery, where the spidering cracks in the sky glowed a pale bronze-gold through the night. Ezabeth turned to look with me and we stood in silence. Distantly in the night a drunk was singing. Somewhere a child cried.

'I missed you,' I said at last, the only words I could think of. 'When they locked you away. I missed you. I'm sorry.'

'You owe me nothing, captain. Certainly not an apology,' she said. Her voice was as straight and solid as a steel bar, betrayed no emotion. 'You have done more to aid us than could have been asked. I will repay the debt, one day.'

'You owe me nothing, lady. Not a thing,' I said, and I wanted to say it right then, to tell her, and to let it all spill out, and I couldn't. Too many years of bitterness and curled lips, too many cups of bad whisky, too many lives running across my hands. I wasn't the man to say the words that I wanted to. Wasn't fit to own them, to let them be my own. To force them upon her, to let my failure cast its shadow over somebody else.

'I will see you both safely through this,' I said. 'I promise you. In that, let me serve you, Lady Tanza.'

'Call me Ezabeth,' she said.

'I don't have the rank, lady.'

'Only because you gave it up. Why did you?'

Old memories, some of them my worst, reached up to me like a sea of clutching fingers. They wanted me, would have dragged me down into their darkness if I'd let them. I'd spent a long time keeping my distance from those grasping claws. Somehow I found myself lowering back into them.

'After the disaster at Adrogorsk, after what I did to Torolo Mancono in that duel, I wasn't fit to be one of the noble born,' I said. 'My family had no choice but to disinherit me. I don't blame them.'

'So you took a new name. Tried to start again.'

234

'You say that like it was a decision, but I just kept on living. Things happened around me, and I lived with it. I rode out to Adrogorsk a nobleman. There was nothing noble about me when I came back.'

'You think you've changed so much?' she asked. Her eyes were bright. Spirits alone knew what her expression was beneath her veil.

'I did,' I choked. 'I have.'

'I've changed too,' Ezabeth said. 'We were children when we knew one another. I am glad I knew you then. Summer is a time for children. It is not meant for those like us.'

'Like us?'

'The scarred ones,' she said.

'You mean your hand?'

At its mention, Ezabeth tucked her three-fingered hand behind her back and stepped further away from me. The gap between us was growing, when I wanted it to close. We dealt in words that were meant to comfort but somehow they only brought bitterness.

'No,' she said. 'Not just my hand. All of me. I am nothing *but* scars beneath this veil. You don't understand.'

'I know that's not true,' I said. I remembered her clear as day, even now, standing beautiful and fresher than youth. Defiant, lovely, powerful. Slowly the realisation began to seep in on me. I didn't want to say it, didn't want it to be true. It was like being spun around until the dizziness gets in your eyes and nothing makes sense. Like being punched in the face by a boxer, like drinking until the world heaves you onto your side and leaves you sprawled in the gutter, desolate and alone. It was like all that, and worse.

'You saw a lie,' she whispered. 'A crafting of light. An illusion. I panicked when I saw you in that corridor. The drudge were so close … I thought that if I showed you that face, a face I thought you once loved, that you would help me. That you would protect me. Save me. I needed your help.' She turned back to me. 'Don't be angry with me. Please. But I'm not what you think. When the light first came upon me, my first radiance burned down half the manor. I was abed for two years, my skin burned away, my body weeping. Father bought every surgeon, physician and apothecary he could find to keep me alive. No Fixers. He hated the magic, what it had done to me. So they kept me alive, feeding me through a funnel. All I knew was pain. Half my hand burned away entirely when I drew the light. The rest of me is not something that anyone would wish to see. This veil is not for modesty's sake. It is for yours, and everybody else's. Nobody should have to see the horror that lies beneath.'

'I don't care,' I said.

'You would, if you saw me as I really am.'

I didn't know what to say to that. I stood silently, and so did she.

'I'm sorry,' I said at length. 'Your accident. That's why it was called off? Us, I mean. Is that why we were called off?'

'The radiance came upon me the month after I travelled home,' she said. 'Nobody knew if I would live, but they knew that if I did then I would be hideous. It wasn't fair to ask you to take me then. You would have refused.'

'I wouldn't,' I said.

'No,' she said. For a moment I thought her voice would break on the word, but she took the pain and bound it tight against her backbone. 'You would. And you would have been right to. They found you a real wife. A proper wife with whom you could be happy.'

'I wasn't happy,' I said. 'I was never happy.'

'They said you were. You had children.'

'They died.'

'I know.'

'They made me take a wife, a girl of sixteen. My family had the name, hers had money. I barely knew her. Back then all I cared about was making a name for myself as an officer, climbing ranks and polishing medals. Proving that I was worth the commission, the uniform my parents bought for me.' I shook my head. 'I should have seen what I held in my hands. Instead I let them fall through my fingers.'

'Nobody lives without regret,' Ezabeth said. 'Least of all not here, under this sky.'

I carry many painful memories. On my right arm, nestled amongst the green-ink skulls there were three small flowers, half bloomed. I put them there so that I would remember. So that I had to remember, even when I didn't want to.

'She gave me children and I was too young, too self-absorbed to appreciate how much they were worth,' I said. 'She jumped from the high tower on midsummer's eve, but it was the shame that killed her, long before that. You know the story. Everyone knows the story.'

'That blame isn't yours to claim,' Ezabeth said. 'You weren't the one that demanded the duel. Only the spirits can judge you.'

'There's times that I've thought it would have been better if I'd let Torolo Mancono run me through. I was the one that survived but my name died that night. *Our* name. My children's name. When she jumped, she took them with her as revenge, I think. Revenge for making her an outcast, wife to a monster.'

'You're no more to blame for her choices than you are for mine,' Ezabeth said. A few sparks crackled from her fingertips, drifting lazily in the night. She wasn't the first to say that to me and she would not be the last that I didn't believe. Ezabeth reached out, hesitated, lowered her hand. 'It was a cruel ending and the children were innocent. But you didn't choose it.'

'I'll always do what I must,' I said. 'There's nothing I wouldn't trade to have them back. But it's not their deaths I regret. We're born, we run and we die, and Death always wins the race in the end. It's the years they were running that I regret. The years that I could have been a father and a husband, but instead I cowered away on the Range. I found it easier to face the broken sky than to see the hope in her eyes. Because whenever I was with her, I wanted her to be you. Wanted what we'd shared. Wanted that feeling again, and it was gone.'

'We were just children,' Ezabeth said. She sounded so much older, so much wiser, and free from the bitterness that coloured my every word. 'We were just babes. Children in the summer,' she said. 'It wasn't real.'

'Then why does it feel like it still is?' I snapped.

Ezabeth tilted her veiled chin up, straightened her back. Steel ran through that spine, firmed up her posture. She radiated strength as strongly as she had light.

'I am not that girl. You are not that boy. We changed, the world changed. You remember a girl in skirts who chased butterflies and named the rabbits in the field. I remember a young man who was so pleased to show me how he could ride a horse, and who brushed his hair whenever he thought I wasn't looking. What are we now? A scarred, light-blind freak. A sodden drunk with more blood on his hands than the Spirit of Death. Life was cruel to pour our youth into such bitter moulds, but we are what we are. There is no summer for us. Not any more. The end is coming, and we both know how this will finish. With terror and death and Dhojaran soldiers trampling the fields, the marks of the Deep Kings upon the people. Harden your heart against such soft longing. We can neither of us afford it.'

I stood silent as three-week old death, new insults scraping open the old wounds. She was right, of course. I wasn't that optimistic, blind, joyous, foolish kid. I'd changed my name and become someone different. She'd changed her face and become someone else. Give a lie enough time and maybe the lie takes over the life.

Our masks were our real faces now.

Ezabeth looked at me, eyes defiant, daring me to say she was wrong. I couldn't.

I let that foolish dream of love turn hard and cold as black iron inside me. Let it crumple, shrivel and die. A fool's dream. Better to go back to my old self. There were still plenty of people needed killing.

25

I thought I was done with it all. The dreams of military honours, the glory of the charge, the adulation of the nobility. That pile of goat shit had been buried in the dirt with my wife and children long ago. I'd spent ten years crawling through the muck with men I'd rather have gracked than greeted, taking the easiest, most tedious work. I'd scraped by making just enough coin to maintain a steady inebriation beneath a leaking roof and little more. I didn't want to be mixed up with the greater schemes of the generals, the plots of the nobility or the bloody front lines against the drudge.

Sometimes, we don't get what we want. Usually, in fact. In my case, pretty much never.

Dantry had slipped out at dawn and returned to tell us that Tnota was still alive. After the surgeon had removed the tangled mess of his arm, he had fallen into a fever. He would die, or he would live, and there was fuck all any of us could do about it.

Bring him to me, Saravor's silver serpent whispered through me, or maybe it was just my imagination.

'No,' Nenn told me plainly, a shadowed look in her eyes as she traced fingers across her belly. 'I won't let you. No.' And I gave her the final say on that.

I had to see Venzer. I'd known the Iron Goat for long enough to know that no matter what Herono and Adenauer might stoop to, no matter how they manipulated the river of coin flowing through the city, he was the shield that held back the Kings and their countless legions. He was a man of honour. I might have spat mine at his feet and broken his own law, but there wasn't a better man in the states. I had to believe that. Had to cling to something.

That only left Herono. She was the only other with the power to pull this many strings against us. I didn't want to believe it, but there it was. She'd blocked Ezabeth when she went to the Order's council. She'd sent me to hunt Ezabeth when she disappeared. She'd sent Stannard into the Misery and it had been her soldiers that turned up at the Maud. She didn't need money and this had never been about profiteering, and she didn't want Ezabeth dead. No. She had wanted Ezabeth to continue her research within the Maud.

There was an army approaching Three-Six, an army like we hadn't seen in four generations, and she was seeking proof that the Engine would not activate when they came.

Was she seeking to make a deal with the enemy? The first rat off the sinking ship? Or was she just misguided? She was a damned *hero*. I felt polluted just thinking it, but I saw no other option.

I had to go to Venzer and make him see the truth. Make him take Ezabeth into his protection. The Darling's assault on the Maud surely proved that. I had to stand before him and insist that he believe me, a drunkard who refused to even wear a uniform, as I threw accusations at the most decorated prince of the republic. I had to tell him that he'd been blind, that one of our greatest commanders had tried to murder her own kin, had killed innocents in the process.

I had to tell him that somehow, beyond sense and reason, Prince Herono of Heirengrad was working against the Range.

I'd be lucky not to be thrown in the white cells.

But if I succeeded? Ezabeth had to have access to the

heart of the Engine. The Lady of the Waves was on Pyre and we might get a communicator message through to her. Implore her to come, implore her to save us. I already knew that she would not respond. But damn it to the hells, I was going to try.

I was running on fumes and blind hope now. Blind hope that the last card to turn was the one to complete the trick. An awful lot to gamble on, but I was all in at this point.

A trio of mule-drawn carts plodded slowly and inexorably away from the Misery. The familiar drab green of body bags crowded for space within the carts. A pair of soldiers drove with drawn, wan faces.

'Who got gracked?' I called to them as they grumbled along the cobbles.

'One o' the big patrols,' the lead soldier answered me. 'Lieutenant Mirkov. Fifty men. They were only twenty miles deep. Nearly in sight of the fucking walls.'

'Which battalion?' I called, but they were past me now.

'Eleventh,' he shot back over his shoulder.

The eleventh were rookies, green as algae and younger than hell. I felt more than a chill as I watched the wagons of dead pass by. The corpses were packed in tight, side by side like food in a larder. If the Kings were sending hunting patrols that close to Valengrad then things were worse than I had figured. They were practically daring us to come out for them.

Maybe they were.

Venzer only had four thousand men in Valengrad, the rest having marched north to Station Three-Six. Spirits, but we were in the shit now.

I stalked blackly towards the citadel. A light summer rain had begun to fall, a welcome relief from the humidity. I couldn't keep my thoughts from Tnota. He was one of my oldest friends, one of my only friends. That matchlock ball had been meant for Dantry, but it was my fault he was mixed up in this. I was too engrossed in my own thoughts, didn't keep myself bright.

'Captain Galharrow. I need a word, there's a good fellow.'

Whether by plan or by dark fortune, it was Stannard. I'd nearly walked into the fucker. I didn't like the way he wore his greatcoat, only the top button done up and his arms inside, as though it were a cloak. Bloody ridiculous way to wear a coat. Easy to hide what's beneath it, though.

'I'm on business for the marshal,' I sort of lied. 'Your mistress wants me, she can speak to him.'

Stannard kept pace with me. My skin was creeping cold, my fists balling. You get an instinct for trouble when it's your business to cause it. Something was about to go down. I stopped. Faced him.

'You know Prince Herono doesn't like to be denied. Funny how we end up having the same conversations, ain't it? They go around and around,' Stannard said. He smiled, empty, unctuous, wolf behind it. 'We had you looking for the girl, and now we're looking and you've got her. Where is she?'

'You want the witch and her brother? They hit some tavern in Pikes,' I said. 'Went drinking. The Open Cask, I think it was. Fucked if I know where they are now, though.'

'You really want to test my patience?' Stannard said, smiling that insipid 'I'm going to hurt you, and I'll enjoy it' smile. It was then that I saw the others, men in similar coats, loitering aimlessly at the end of the street. I took a breath, tried to get my thinking into military order. Checked the angles. Looked behind. Another pair of them were closing in that way as well, walking as casually as they could without seeming to get much nearer. Didn't want to spook me. They were professional enough that they had me surrounded, clumsy enough that they all wore matching coats and stood out like a Bride at a wedding. Soldiers, not back-alley professionals. One of them had left the hilt of a longsword poking out through the gap at the front of his coat. A man doesn't go around wearing a longsword unless he expects to use it. The sword at my side was half its length, short in the blade, single edged. None of that mattered. It doesn't matter how good you think you are with a sword, nobody wins against five men. I knew it. Stannard knew it. His men all knew it.

'Let's be honest with each other,' Stannard said, like he was reasonable and so was I. I kept my eyes moving every now and then to the men at the end of the road. They kept their distance. 'Can save us all a lot of time if you take me to them so that I can get them safely back to the prince.'

She was moving faster now, taking a direct approach. The politics were over, her cover was crumbling. She must have known I'd figure it out after her men had been the ones to show up at the Maud. If Venzer managed to get Ezabeth back he wouldn't let her out of his hands again. He'd understand her importance now. But if Stannard and his thugs got their hands on them, Dantry wouldn't survive past nightfall and I didn't want to imagine what they'd do to Ezabeth.

'I have a counter-proposal,' I said. I mimicked his smile. 'You go fuck yourself and I go see the marshal. I don't work for Herono any more.'

'Friend,' Stannard said, reaching out a hand to take my arm. As his hand pushed back the fabric of the greatcoat, I saw the naked knife blade in his other hand.

What happened next was not a conscious decision. I move purely by instinct. One moment the man was reaching for me, the next he was staggering back screaming, blood spraying from his face. Drawn and cut all in one motion, bright streaks of blood marred the dull grey steel of my cutlass. When you have to move there's no time for thought. There is only the cut, and the kill.

Stannard reeled back clutching at the flaps of his cheek,

screaming and staggering in pain. I took no chances and would have run him through between the ribs if he hadn't been wearing armour beneath that coat, but he was and my sword glanced away. The rest of the Blue Brigade came alive and tore towards me, tossing back their coats and baring edges.

I ran.

An alleyway presented itself and I skittered into it, found it blocked at one end by a shoulder-height wooden fence. Without stopping, I put my faith in shoddy carpentry and mouldy wood and smashed straight into it. The fence disintegrated at the impact, shards of wood clattering about me. I scrambled back up, black-sludge dirty from the muck. The men were charging at me with weapons drawn, two of them with longswords and the others armed similarly to me. They'd shrugged away their greatcoats, Prince Herono's livery evident now. There wasn't any decision to be made, fighting that many men was as suicidal as charging a Darling.

I'm not much of a runner, but I'm fleet-footed when I'm scared. I dashed down Loom Street and onto a cluttered road, packed with the afternoon's traffic. People got out of my way, either because I was running with a drawn, bloody sword, or because I shoved them when they didn't look behind them. One young woman went flying, her basket of linen scattering bloomers into the mud. Herono's men trampled over them in quick succession. One of them was shouting for me to stop, but none of the civilians were fool enough to try their luck against my bloodied sword.

I skidded around the corner and onto Tank Lane, only to realise that the far end of the street was a stone gatehouse, a covered archway at which two of Venzer's soldiers lounged. I'd already started running towards them when I realised my mistake. Too late now, I had to throw the dice.

'Help me,' I called. 'Those bastards are trying to kill me!'

The soldiers were already panicking because of the red-greased sword in my hand. They lowered their halberds towards me, menacing with the long steel spikes.

'They're right behind me!' I yelled, and indeed, my pursuers were not far back. I turned on them now, raising my sword to a hanging guard, feeling that with the help of two of Venzer's men I could now fend them off. Prince Herono's men slowed up. They were panting, a couple of them labouring hard to find breath. My own lungs were on fire, never should have smoked so much. I looked the first man in the eye, let him see his friend's blood on the sword. Somehow a grin – a fool's grin at that – had made its way onto my face.

'I arrest this man for attempted murder, in the name of Prince Herono of Heirengrad,' the lead man said. It suddenly occurred to me just how bad this must all look from the perspective of the guardsmen.

I felt the point of a halberd nudge me in the back.

'Give up the sword. Knife on the ground too,' one of the guardsmen said. Of course he did. I looked like a civilian, and an ugly one at that, blood on my blade, blood on my shirt sleeves. These were prince's men, dressed in fine blue and gold uniforms with the Heirengrad arms across the breast and fancy gold stitching around the cuffs and collar. Balls.

Once you're unarmed, soldiers tend to want to dish out the beating they can finally deliver safely. I wasn't on my knees two seconds before they began pummelling me. I couldn't see, but Venzer's boys probably threw a couple of blows with the poles of their halberds too. They didn't have a fucking clue what I was being arrested for, not really, but soldiers aren't paid to think for themselves. That's what makes them good soldiers.

It hurt.

They didn't have a rope, so instead they took my belt and

used it to bind my wrists behind my back. Another of them had a hood that he threw over my head. I was a known face for a lot of people who mattered. They couldn't very well go parading a Blackwing captain up and down the streets without drawing attention, but nobody would bat an eyelid at a drunk being dragged off to sober up.

'Nice knife,' one of the men said as he pocketed it. I liked that knife, Tnota had given it to me. I'd take it back after I'd killed them all.

'We'll take him from here,' another said to the soldiers, who were more than happy enough to dispense with any formal proceedings and to let the prince's men take care of it. When I tried to speak, one of them slugged me across the face. He wasn't good at punching, so it mostly didn't do anything, but even a bad punch is a punch. There wasn't much point in trying to say more. Even if I managed to convince the soldiers that Prince Herono was trying to have me murdered, or that she was trying to do the same to her own kin, even if I managed all of that – they'd probably still send me off with Herono's men. You don't wind up on civil guard duty when the might of the Dhojaran Empire is bearing down on the nation because you're blessed with an overabundance of cognitive function, capability or ingenuity.

Blind, I was dragged across the town. They didn't spare the shoves. My captors were all older men, veterans. Older men are typically better for quiet work, less likely to go spouting off after the fact, less likely to panic. Young men might get a taste for blood and slam you around just for the hell of it, but men who'd lasted as long as those grey-shot veterans would do their jobs right. Hard men, professional, the kind of men I'd have hired if they'd been looking for company work. They marched me along at a brisk step, deposited me in the back of a small carriage. I couldn't sit up with my wrists bound behind me.

The interior of the carriage smelled of lavender and spiced

oils. One of the vets slugged in beside me, not a lot of room for us both on the narrow seat. The bag came off my head, and sitting opposite me was the one-eyed prince.

'Captain,' she said by way of greeting. 'I hear you tried to kill Stannard.' Herono's single eye was cold and clear. She had a long, slender poniard in one hand, fingers tracing the elaborate engraving along the blade. Herono's maiming had taken the bluff vitality of her soldiering days, but she'd have no trouble at all putting that point into me, bound and useless as I was. She tapped the roof of the carriage and the driver started us into motion.

'Damn. I hoped I'd succeeded,' I said. I didn't flinch from her gaze or show any other outward sign that I was feeling ready to shit my breeches any moment. I was all too aware of Herono's capability for violence. She frightened me far more than her thugs.

'Where are Dantry and Ezabeth?' Straight to the point, then.

'They're safe,' I said.

'You left quite a mess behind when you took her. Quite the alarm and quite the affray,' she said, a scowl across her scarred brow. We regarded one another for a few moments. Prince Herono did not speak. I looked into her single eye and found it dead, empty and soulless. A growing tide of hatred built within me.

'What did they offer you?' I said. 'I can't believe it's just gold. Did the Deep Kings buy you? Did they offer to give you back your eye? Offer to make you immortal? What do you want so badly that you're willing to sell out your whole damn species?'

Herono allowed a slight smirk to reach her scarred face. She wasn't about to reel off a monologue for my benefit like the villain in a playhouse tragedy.

'You, Captain Galharrow, are an enemy of the states. You have assaulted one of my men in broad daylight, and two dozen observers will swear to it. You broke into the Maud and murdered the staff, led poor Battle Spinner Rovelle into a trap. Your interrogation shall commence shortly.'

'I'll have your head for this,' I said clumsily. My lip was split and swelling. Herono didn't dignify my threat with a response.

I looked out the window as we bounced along the road. The carriage wasn't going to the citadel to throw me in gaol, and it wasn't heading to Willows either. You don't drag your prisoners off to your luxury villa and parade them before your servants. You take them to some quiet part of town where everyone knows to turn a blind eye. Some dark little holding, rented under someone else's name, fit for dark work with irons and saws. I knew the kind of place. To say that I wasn't deeply, deeply worried about the future of my limbs, digits and appendages would have been a grotesque understatement.

I kept an eye on the street just in case I saw one of my crew. Nenn, Wheedle, even Lindrick would have done just then. Anyone to bring some sword-hands. Wasn't like they'd be able to go up against a prince of Heirengrad, but any hope was better than none. I'd tried to suck a drop from emptier bottles than this before, but I couldn't remember being successful.

'We can end this quickly, you know,' Herono said. She'd been silent for some time, letting events and my thoughts run their course. She toyed with the dagger, passing it between her hands. 'In all honesty, Galharrow, as frustrating as yesterday's stunt was, I understand you. You want to fuck the girl. Spirits of dread know why, with those scars, but I suppose everyone has a fetish. I always liked the blacks.' She gave a little chuckle. 'And while Stannard will probably take particular relish in cutting the information from you, I just want the girl. If you tell me where they are, I'll kick you out on the street and we'll go there now. I won't even punish you for attacking my man. You should know from our dealings that I am nothing if not pragmatic. I can even forgive your wild accusations.'

I didn't enjoy just how close to truth she was with every word. Who was I really fighting for? Ezabeth had told me how things stood. An eager little voice began suggesting that I was on the losing side. Would have been easy to accept it. I wondered how many of the traitors I'd sentenced had started by listening to that same voice.

Herono, our great warrior hero. Mill owner, councillor to the Order of Aetherial Engineers, commander of the Blue Brigade. She'd welcomed Ezabeth in and then distracted me with silver when I came asking questions. She ran a mill operating at one-fifth its capacity, supplying too little phos to an Engine that couldn't accept it all. She had the influence to deny Ezabeth access to the heart, the power to lock down Dantry's credit at the banks. Always she wanted Ezabeth under her wing, had sent me to retrieve her when she disappeared. But why had Stannard burned Maldon's house if she wanted Ezabeth to succeed? Even now, my face aching and her dagger poised, I didn't have all of the pieces.

'They're long gone,' I said. 'I put them on fast horses and told them to get the hell out of here. Six hours ago they were riding out of the city. Now, I don't even know which direction they travelled. You've missed your chance.'

'That would be bad for you.' Herono frowned, steepling her fingers. 'I would have no choice but to burn you, cut you and otherwise take you to pieces until you tell me where they can be located. Now I confess, it's possible that you genuinely don't know. If that's the case then I'll have you tortured until you either guess correctly, or expire. Unfortunately for you, that may take days. Perhaps it will be infection that does for you in the end, but until I have Ezabeth Tanza under my protection again, I have no option but to assume you are lying to me. Ah, here we are.'

The carriage rolled to a stop and I heard the soldiers disembarking outside. We were in some residential area, a workshop opposite a rundown bath house. I didn't recognise it. Herono's men had their greatcoats on again, colourless greys and browns masking the bright blue and gold of their uniforms, and the prince donned a cloak and hat to make the six-foot journey into a disused ironworks. Old odours of charcoal and hot metal lingered in the brickwork. Scavengers had picked away any anvils, tools and furniture that had been left behind, leaving bare, scorched surfaces and an empty furnace. They shut the doors, giving us a few moments of blackness before kindling lamps.

Part of me was advising that I might as well tell her now. I knew torture. Plenty of personal experience, only I'd always been on the other side of the irons. I don't claim to be a good man, and in a war, bad men do the worst things. What were the Tanzas to me? She wasn't my woman. Would never be my woman. Dantry was a good kid but I'd done my part by him. More than I needed to. This wasn't my fight.

It was always my fight.

There were no chairs in the old workshop to sit me on, but there was a post and an old bucket and propriety didn't seem all that important. Sat on the bucket, they strapped my hands behind the beam, kept me upright. Easier to get to my vitals. It's what I would have done.

Prince Herono stood over me, her sole rotten eye looking down on me with something between admiration and disgust. Maybe I was imagining the former. Always did think too much of myself.

I think that ultimately, Herono rather liked me. She genuinely would have preferred to have had me on her team. If things had only been slightly different, I probably would have been.

'We want the same thing, Galharrow,' she said. 'I won't harm Ezabeth. I've done nothing but work to keep her safe.

I paid you to find her when she was lost. I led you to a Bride, an important one. A damn big score for you. Was that not proof enough of my loyalty for you?'

I kept my mouth shut.

'Last chance,' she said. 'Speed is my only interest. Tell me now and we don't have to go through the tiresome process of cutting it out of you.'

'Go fuck yourself, Herono,' I said. 'It isn't that I love the girl. Truth is, I gave up on myself a long time ago. I've always been fucked over one way or another, and when your life's as worthless as mine you get to stop caring about it altogether. You want to know why I'm going to sit through this until you break me?'

'Enlighten me,' the prince said, pulling a suede glove onto her right fist. I saw the gleam of brass across the knuckles. Very old-fashioned.

'I know where they are. And every minute of every hour that I delay you is another minute that they might be somewhere else. I don't have to hold out for ever. I just have to hold out until they move on.'

Wham, the brass knuckles smashed into my head. For an older woman, Herono could dish out one hell of a punch. Skin split, my skull rocked on my neck and jets of cold pain spurted through my brain. My head lolled for a few moments as the bright spears ran across my face, somehow turning it both numb and aflame at once. I couldn't see for several moments, and I was so preoccupied with trying to get my vision back that I didn't realise I was throwing up over myself until I found that I wasn't breathing and had to choke a wad of bile from my mouth.

Reality began to come back into focus. Two of Herono's men had moved across to the furnace, had begun to load it.

'Tell me where to find Ezabeth Tanza,' Herono said coldly.

'Fuck yourself in hell,' I mumbled.

The next blow from those brass knuckles was ill judged. I felt my brain bounce around inside my skull, and then Herono couldn't ask me any more questions because the idiot had knocked me out cold.

26

Perception began to reaffirm itself. I didn't want it to. The blow from those brass knuckles had set my head to screaming, a sharp and brutal pain digging into the left side of my head, the worst of it just above the temple. Getting punched in the face with a metal bar will do that. The initial acknowledgement of deep, aching pain was followed by a swell of nausea and dizziness. My eyes were closed and I realised from the pain in my arms that I was hanging forwards, my wrists bound taut against the post behind me keeping me upright. I'd blacked out. It was quiet but I could hear the light, soft sounds of somebody moving not far away. Just one person, I thought. I could hear the crackle of something aflame, smell the heat of the furnace. I remained entirely still. Seemed best to play dead and keep my head down. No point in torturing an unconscious man.

Getting punched unconscious was the best thing that could have happened to me. Not many situations where that's true. I'd have to thank Herono for that. The smell of vomit was thick on my clothes.

'You can come in. I sent them all away.' That was Herono.

'This must go faster.' A young voice. Childish even. I'd heard it before. My stomach did a double clench and I had to steel my limbs against movement. It couldn't be.

'Can you wake him?'

'I could tear his mind open, but killing that Spinner cost

me. Rovelle was strong. I need to gather my reserves. He'll confess quickly enough. Galharrow's all talk. Show him pain and he'll spill.' The voice was male but unbroken. A child. It was the Darling from Station Twelve, the same one that had chased us out of the Maud. You don't forget a voice like that. It haunts your nightmares, sours your dreams, but there was something bizarrely familiar about it as well.

It was worrying that the Darling had any kind of opinion about me at all. But I had other things to worry about just then.

Herono was in league with one of the Deep Kings' creatures. For all that she'd clearly had some kind of agenda against Dantry or Ezabeth or both of them, I hadn't figured her for a sympathiser. She was a prince, noblest of blood, master of one of the richest city states in the Alliance. It didn't make sense.

'I need that girl,' the Darling said again. 'The master will not tolerate failure. You know that.'

'I know,' Herono agreed. 'They aren't going anywhere. They have no allies in Valengrad, I've made sure of that. I have men watching every gate. They are trapped here, and every resource I have is turned to finding them. Trust me.'

'If she dies, her genius dies with her,' the Darling said fiercely. 'I cannot permit that. She may only be a Spinner, but only she can tell us for certain. She must prove whether the heart of Nall's Engine still burns. If the way is safe for the Kings.'

'The only true test is to access the heart itself,' Herono said. 'Without that all we have is an incomplete theory. But Venzer guards the heart even from me, and beyond his authority lie the wards Nall placed there. There is no way to breach it.'

'Not yet,' the Darling said. Its frustration simmered hot and low in the stagnant air. 'But I will find a way, even if I have to bring the whole city down around me. Until I succeed, the master believes the girl's theory will provide the proof he needs. Ensure that he receives it.'

'You should have let me cut it out of her in the first place,' Herono said.

'No. If she is wrong, if the heart of the Engine is still afire then maintaining your position is vital. If this is not the hour for victory, it will come, eventually. The master is eternal. He is willing to wait.'

They fell silent for a time and I heard something being moved around in the forge, the rustle of ash and the collapse of some burned thing. My time like this was limited. Someone would realise I was awake and start to hurt me again. Knowing that, and being able to do something with the information were two entirely different things.

'My men are returning,' Herono said. 'You must go.'

'Burn the information out of this man, and do it now,' the Darling hissed. 'My patience grows thin. So too does our King's. She must be yours before night falls or we risk losing her altogether. I must go.'

A door closed somewhere. The main double doors clunked open and then shut again.

'Anything?'

'They didn't go to the citadel, or back to Willows, your grace,' one of the soldiers said. 'Wherever they are, they're staying low. I've got all your ears out listening but the network will take time to find anything. We gotta make this one squeal on 'em if you want to know it faster.'

'You do it,' Herono said with a resigned sigh. 'I haven't the patience to tease it out of him.'

A bucket of water went over me. It stank as badly as the vomit, probably drawn from the gutter outside. It got in my nose, and though I tried to remain still, the soldier forced my head up.

'He's awake, your grace. Aren't you, old lad?' A familiar voice.

256

Strong, calloused fingers gripped my beard and drew my head up. The first thing I saw as I opened my eyes were the roses. Roses and thorns, tattoos coiling around a strong forearm. I'd seen those before. An ugly face blurrily moved into focus. Stannard had got his face stitched together, the flesh angry, red, still weeping. He patted me on the cheek affectionately, gave me a wink.

'You fucking idiot. Herono's working for the drudge,' I growled.

'You know, your shit would be more convincing if I hadn't found you and the witch trying to steal from Maldon's place,' he said. 'We go there to make sure his blasphemy don't fall into the wrong hands, and what happens? You turn up to rob the fucking place.' He spoke from the corner of his mouth, wincing as the movement of his face tugged at the neat black stitches. 'I've been looking forward to this.' He moved off to plunge a poker into the fire. Stannard started humming to himself, music without melody, noises to keep his mind ticking over as he waited to deliver the pain. The doors opened and a troop of his cohorts showed up, nasty-looking old bastards ready for a show. A good crowd, twenty in all. A couple of them I recognised, men I'd seen around Herono's house at the Willows or in the taverns. Two of them lounged nearby, a pottery jug passing between them.

'Any chance I can get a hit of that?' I asked, but they gave me a disgusted look and kept at it. I wondered how long these men had been serving Herono, how many dark alley jobs they'd pulled for her when the candles burned low. How many Otto Lindricks had they smashed around, just as I had? If it wasn't for fortune's turn, I could have been sitting with them. A worrying thought but infinitely less worrying than what they were about to watch happen to me.

A cowardly part of me still said it was time to confess. I'd played this out for as long as I could but the glow and the stink of the forge as it devoured coals and turned the black rods red was putting one hell of a terror in me. I didn't owe the Tanzas shit. I'd done my part by them already. I ought to give them up. Spill the address, hope that was enough to spare my flesh from being roasted. I'd smelled it too often, from cannon fire, from the spells of Battle Spinners, from my own black questionings.

Stannard shifted the iron in the fire. Tears of abject terror began to well in my eyes. Only an idiot doesn't feel their breath turn cold at the prospect of torture. There's no holding out against it. I knew that I'd break, of course I would. I didn't know how many thrusts of the poker I'd take before it wasn't worth it any more. Maybe just one. In the military they don't even try to train you to endure it. There's no point. No strategy can be successful. In the end, everyone begs. In the end, everyone breaks. That's just how it works.

I should give them up. But I didn't. Couldn't have explained it any further than that.

The poker was starting to glow red at the tip. Not quite hot enough, not yet. Stannard knew his business. Wasn't his first time playing the torturer either. Prince Herono sat with a faraway look, deep in thought, somewhere else. Nice to know that my impending agonised destruction wasn't the most important thing on her mind. I could smell the iron getting hot, giving the air that forge-baked hollowness, the dry, empty flatness of scorched metal. I didn't have much more time for sanity. There was a good chance that this would break me completely. I thought back on what I ought to have done with my life. A lot of failures in there, but a couple of victories too. A lot of people had relied on me, too many for my own ability. I'd never been suited to lead, not as a general. I'd been too young for it, but I'd done my best. The dead didn't care about my best. They littered the path of the rout from Adrogorsk, nothing but empty skulls and bones picked clean beneath the bronze of the sky.

It was my kids that I had failed the most. In a sense,

my failure at Adrogorsk had killed them too. Not straight away. Defeats happened. Adrogorsk had been a position of strategic importance back then, or at least we all thought so. We held it for four months, deep in the Misery, the ruins of a once beautiful centre of art and leisure, a city crushed to rubble by Crowfoot's weapon. We held those ruins, started trying to build them into a fortification, something we could defend. The drudge didn't want that, and they sent an army. We could have fought them, could have tried to hold. For three days we bore the cannon fire and the Darlings' spells. The general took an arrow in the shoulder, into the bone, the infection turning black and stinking in a handful of fevered days. We lost a lieutenant general on the eastern wall to climbers, another to misfiring artillery. One by one the rankers dropped until I was somehow next in line, a brigadier risen to command the whole fucking force. Then word came through the communicator, a message from Crowfoot. Philon was coming in person, risking a confrontation between wizards. He'd called our bluff; the Nameless had no inclination to do battle with a King over a heap of rubble, so I signalled our retreat. I hadn't known that a second army lay in wait for us, smashing into our columns as we fell back towards Station Forty-One.

Nine thousand men weigh heavy on your conscience. But they were soldiers, and truth be told I hadn't liked any of them anyway.

It was the kids that weighed the most. I got back alive. Torolo Mancono called me an incompetent wretch so I killed the bastard for nothing more than his angry words and my pride. When my wife heard of my disgrace, she took those little lives out of the world and herself with them. Couldn't bear the dishonour, couldn't bear to live with the shame. I'd never even seen the boy, born after I returned to the front with high dreams of gilded epaulettes and cries of glory. Against the backdrop of the thousands I'd led to their deaths, against the dozens I'd led to their deaths since, with all the fucking blood that I'd felt splash against my face and every screaming bastard I'd severed from his future, it was the unseen baby that haunted me the most.

The world is a cruel mother, a matron of darkness, selfishness, greed and misery. For most, their time suckling at her breast is naught but a scramble through stinging, tearing briars before a naked, shameful collapse as the flesh gives out. And yet in the bright eyes of every newborn there lies a spark, a potential for goodness, the possibility of a life worth living. That spark deserves its chance. And though most of them will turn out to be as worthless as the parents that sired them, while the cruelty of the earth will tell them to release their innocence and join in the drawing of daggers, every now and then one manages to clutch to their beauty and refuses to release it into the dark.

I would never manage that myself, but someone else would. While the Range held, there was still that chance. No fucking way was I going to speak.

Stannard stepped forward with his glowing poker, white and yellow and red, and I gritted my teeth and tilted back my chin and I stared at him with every bitter thread of hatred, every scrap of loathing that I held deep in the black echo of my soul. The mess I'd made of his face reminded him to enjoy his work.

'Where is Ezabeth Tanza?' Prince Herono asked from across the room. Her agent waited patiently. I had to refuse to answer before he was allowed to start burning me.

The lights came on, casting the empty ironworks into the pale brightness of phos-tube light. There were still a few glass tubes running around the ceiling.

'I thought the generator was gone?' Herono said irritably to one of her soldiers. 'Why have we been sitting in the dark all this time if there was a generator all along?'

Stannard scratched at his quietly leaking stitches. His

eyes followed the tubes along the wall, where they ran downwards to an empty space. The ends of the tubes were just broken glass, and the phos light was spilling out of them there. Phos moves like water, or smoke, or whatever else needs to stay in its pipes, but this light stopped there, curling back on itself like some lazy serpent. The would-be torturer chewed his lip, wondering, but Herono didn't care enough to notice.

'Where is Ezabeth Tanza?' she asked again.

'I'm here!' she called, voice filling the room, louder than a trumpet blast. The prince's guards started up from their positions around the room, hands going to hilts. Herono's lone eye swivelled oddly in its socket.

The doors exploded inwards, not just staved in but annihilated. Shards of splintered wood filled the room, a swarm of furious, stinging hornets. Stannard lost hold of the poker as half a dozen inch-long splinters speared the meat of his arms. He shrieked as he tried to shield himself from the blast, but his loss of dignity was mirrored a dozen times across the work floor. Daylight, easily forgotten in the seclusion of the ironworks, was blinding through the open portal, a white glare.

An unmistakable silhouette appeared black against that brightness, Nenn moving fast and low in a fighting crouch. She sprang through the portal, a primed harquebus in her hands and the gunpowder roared in spite as she blasted one man from his feet. Before the smoke had cleared she was coming through it, fiercer than hell and spitting hate and fury as she slung herself at Herono's men.

The first soldier she met was a veteran. He'd fought in the Misery and he knew his swordplay but Nenn was a force of nature. She slashed with her cutlass, drawing a low parry before stepping in fast, hacking through the side of the man's head. He went down screaming, not yet dead but not long alive either.

'Protect me!' Herono cried, her business with me forgotten. More men appeared in the doorway, men with primed harquebuses, and blast followed blast followed blast as they gave fire. At such close quarters it was hard for them to miss at first, four or five of Herono's boys sent flying, ribs blown out of their backs. The discharged smoke held its place in the air, thickening and hanging, spreading as gun followed gun. I counted a dozen flash-pans fired, and then whoever had come for me rushed through with blades.

The light beaming down from the tubes died as quickly as it had come, leaving the fighters in a half-darkness of smoke and red forge light. I was forgotten. Blades rang through the fog, shapes flitting this way and that, men screamed and bodies crunched as they struck the workshop floor. My would-be torturer had dropped his poker at the first blast and taken up a longsword, charging forward into the melee with broad strokes. He disappeared into the blossoming clouds of powder smoke as he roared and set about trying to dismember somebody.

'Give us a hand, boss,' Wheedle said, appearing behind me, grinning like the fucking idiot he is. He sawed with a knife and pain shot up my forearms as they came free. He threw me the dagger, laughed once and then was off seeking prey in the chaos.

Time for anger. Time for vengeance. The treacherous bastards were about to understand why you do not, not with the backing of princes, not with the backing of Darlings or Kings or the spirits of hatred themselves, fuck with Ryhalt Galharrow.

The first man had his back to me and I put Wheedle's blade into his neck three times. As he dropped I took his longsword, a fine weapon which is as useless as a spun sugar kettle if you don't see your enemy coming. Another of Herono's veterans was locked up against one of my new recruits, each having grabbed the other's sword hand as they struggled against one another. I delivered the stroke of wrath, the longsword hewing half of Herono's man's head away, giving the kid a good soaking. I was grinning as I cleaved him, and the boy grinned back at me, hungry for the kill.

I sought Stannard out.

His sword was bloody; he'd done for some poor bastard already, suffered a light cut to the forearm for it but wasn't slowing down. The look in his eyes said he wanted to kill me. The look in mine said I meant him to suffer before he died.

He came in hard, half technique and half power, the long blade shearing the air. I stepped right, struck across his blade and blasted it from its trajectory. The art of swordsmanship is to flow, to never stop moving, and my counter swung around in a blow aimed at his head. Stannard was fast. He responded instinctively, moving right and cutting at my overhand strike in a mirror of the counter I'd just used. Sparks sprang into the air as the metal struck a chime into the fog. As the blow came back at me I struck across, lateral and high with a thwarting cut and he barely managed to stop me taking the point into his face. His moment of hesitation cost him. I wound his sword down, drove forward and was rewarded with his breathless gasp as a foot of steel punched through his gut.

Six heartbeats, maybe seven, was all it took. When the fire of hatred is hot, when there's no time for circling and feinting because you fear the sword in your back more than you fear the sword before you, attack is all there is. Stannard looked into my eyes and raised his sword high. No point in defending now, so he sought to cleave me. I may have skewered him, but dying men fight on until they're gone. I threw myself in close against him, got a nose full of unwashed armpit as I wrapped him in my arms and bore him down. We hit the ground and I rolled away as he continued to flail after me with his sword. He was gracked now, though, down on the floor, too fucked to rise again.

Hands yanked me upwards and I had a fist balled and ready to throw when I saw it was Nenn. She wore a savage grin, eyes blazing. I threw my arms around her and crushed her against me.

The smell of powder and slow match lingered in the air, masking the blood. The ironworks floor was wet with it, getting wetter as bodies bled out. Men were gasping and choking as they suffered, and someone was sobbing over a lost leg. I glanced over the victors, hazy through the smoke. Some were the lads I'd taken on, but others I didn't know. I wondered where they'd come from. I wondered how they'd found me. Too many questions for now. Those answers could wait. Nenn was smiling darkly at me, Wheedle was hissing at a gash across his collar bone but it didn't look too bad. Seven of my recruits were upright, but four had been killed and three more were down with wounds. No time now to assess how bad. Dantry Tanza was breathing hard, rapier in his hand.

'Tanza,' I said, nodding to him.

'Captain,' he said, nodding back.

'How did you do?'

'I killed two,' he said without emotion. He shrugged towards a pair of bloody bodies. I figured that one of them had suffered a mortal wound from a matchlock shot before Dantry had managed to run him through, but a kill is a kill. The men were dead and that's what mattered.

Ezabeth stood in the doorway. She held a gun in her hands, the match cord smoking at each end, but it didn't look like she'd fired it. A crow perched on her shoulder, cackling. Behind her in the street I saw dozens more of the big dark birds, a whole murder of them.

'The birds came, and I knew he'd sent them,' Ezabeth said.

I looked down at the tattoo on my arm. I didn't like to feel gratitude to Crowfoot. I guess I owed him even more, now. Nice to know he was looking out for me, somehow.

'What do we do with her?' Dantry said. His young face was more serious than a face that lineless has any right to be. He looked over towards Prince Herono of Heirengrad, who had retreated to the back of the ironworks. She was glaring towards the ragged-looking assortment of mercenaries, her single eye swivelling frantically as if trying to escape from her head.

'Her?' I asked as I picked up the poker. 'To her, we do very, very bad things.'

'Criminal or not, you can't harm an elected prince of Dortmark,' Dantry said with a frown. 'And she is our cousin.'

'She's a traitor,' I said. 'She's a bastard liar. The Darling was here, all cosy as hell with your cousin.' I narrowed my eyes, my jaw trembling with the fury, the hatred that coursed through me. When fear is taken away it has to go somewhere. Most men use it on bringing down some other poor cunt. I am not so different from other men. I considered the smoking end of the poker. The world had turned upside down in a pair of stinking, blood and gun-thunder minutes, not even long enough for the iron to have lost its glow. I had an inclination to stick it as deep as I could up Herono's arse and let her cook from the inside.

Herono had not moved from the wall. She didn't seem to be trying to escape, didn't plead. Now that I started paying her some attention, she didn't seem to be doing anything. She might have been dead, but that she was stood bolt upright, stiff as a post.

'We don't have long. Someone will rouse the aldermen and I don't want those fuckwits getting involved,' I said. I approached Herono, the longsword still in my hand, letting the point trail against the floor. It made a pleasant, tinny kind of grinding noise against the backdrop of the moans of the wounded. Dantry, Ezabeth and Nenn joined me. The others tended to the bloody or else stood well back. I guess Nenn probably hadn't mentioned whose men they were going to hit, and they were only now realising that they'd wiped out the last of the Blue Brigade.

'So,' I said to the prince. 'You've sold us out. You're in it up to your fanny with a Darling. He went to prepare for something. What's he preparing for?'

Prince Herono said nothing. As if she didn't even register that I'd been speaking.

'Something is wrong with her,' Ezabeth said firmly. The prince had turned a shade somewhere between grey and green. Her one eye twitched, seeming to strain against its own socket.

'What the fuck is going on?' Nenn spat. 'Captain, I don't like it. Permission to grack that fucker right now?'

'Denied, private,' I said quietly. 'Herono? Can you hear me? Wake up, you piece of shit.' I stepped forward and raised a hand to slap her across the face.

With a popping, sucking sound, Herono's one eye pushed out from her face on a bulbous white body. It pulsed outwards once, twice, three times, an inch with each push until suddenly the rest of it slithered out of the socket and fell to the floor. The prince collapsed to the ground and we stared down at the fat, juicy grub worming its way around on the floor. Its body resembled a bloated maggot, but the eye at one end continued to see. Of that I was sure.

A dreadful smell filled the air, far worse than the acrid burn of powder. It turned everything to nausea; the odour of things long dead, things long rotted, of things that decayed. Stagnant. Only one wizard's magic carried that vile taint with it.

'Shavada,' Ezabeth breathed, and I knew it to be true. Nenn skittered back a few steps, but the Tanzas held their ground. That took guts. I was either too weary or too surprised to move.

'Fucking wizards,' I said.

'I am free of it,' the eyeless prince whispered. She coughed, a choking sound, hoarse and hacking. She brought her fist away speckled red. 'Thank you. Thank you. At last.'

'Cousin?' Ezabeth said, kneeling beside her. I felt an absurd, irrational envy as she tenderly cupped the blind prince's face. I would still rather have put my fist through it, and the jealousy that rose in me made me want to do so even more. Instead I picked up the old bucket and put it down on top of the eye-grub, which was trying to crawl away. It bumped against the side of the bucket, nudging at it in a bid to escape. I put a foot down on top of it to be sure. This wasn't just sorcery, even of the Darling kind. This was powerful Deep King magic and I wasn't going to let it escape that easy.

'They caught me,' Herono moaned. 'Caught me in the Misery. Took my eyes. Put that thing in. Sent me back. I have been his creature for so long. I am so sorry.'

'Don't speak,' Ezabeth said. 'We'll find you a physician.'

'No,' Herono breathed. 'Dying. Not long for me, I think. Can feel it. The magic that kept me alive is returning to its master. He has seen through that thing ... has let it control me all this time. Since they caught me. In the Misery. Trapped me.'

'Rest,' she said.

'No,' Herono said. Her blind hands grasped out, caught her by the hood. 'The Darling. Planning an attack. Attack here. Soon. They believe ... believe Nall's Engine has failed us. Know that there is no power in it any more. They need you to prove it.'

'How do they know?' Ezabeth asked, prising the fingers from her hair.

'Used me,' Herono breathed. I could hear the pain in her

breaths, the laboured draw. I'd heard it before in dying men. I tried to pity her. Somehow I couldn't. 'The Order needed me to falsify ... to falsify supply records. Make the Dhoja spies believe it all still worked. To reduce the supply to a level that the Engine could still hold while ... pretending that it still functioned. Venzer ... would not say why ... But then you came. When you told the Order that you had proof that the Engine had failed ... You told Shavada what he needed to know. That's why they come. They're coming. They're coming. Tell Venzer that ...'

We never learned what Herono would have said to Venzer. She was dead.

27

I gave Stannard's corpse a grin and a pat on the cheek before attending to more serious business. The Range Marshal was not best pleased to see me.

'I thought you were killed at the Maud.'

'That seems unlikely.'

'You have made new enemies,' he said coolly. The marshal's hat hung limply over a deeply furrowed brow as he skim-read report after hastily written report.

'The list might be somewhat shorter than you're imagining,' I said. I put the heavy, covered jar I was carrying down on the floor and then took the seat across the sea of purchase orders, requisition statements and contractor contracts plaguing the marshal's desk. He stopped and looked up at me.

'Tell me why I shouldn't have you arrested, tried and hanged before sundown. I'll give you five minutes of my time to convince me that you should not die today.'

'Prince Herono has been Shavada's puppet for years. Now she's dead, there's a Darling loose in the city, and the drudge are on their way.'

The Iron Goat looked up over the paper chaos atop his desk, scowling as he lowered his monocle.

'What have you done this time, Galharrow?' Venzer sucked air through his missing teeth. I saw the remaining set had a light purple cast to them. It was still pretty early in the afternoon but he'd been drinking, an open bottle of liquorice spirit sitting guilty amongst the chaos of paper. The soldier in me wanted to reprimand him. The drunk wanted to join him. Neither won out.

'I killed some people.'

Venzer's eyes had gone very cold. There was a button on the desk, a large, half-sphere of polished white ivory set in a bronze frame. It was an alarm. If he pushed it, his tame Battle Spinner would probably burst in and ash me before asking any questions. I don't know why I flirted with fate that way, save that I was tired, my dry tongue ached for a sip of the good stuff and all my reserves of terror had been worn out. Neither of us moved.

'You killed Prince Herono?'

'Technically I think Shavada killed her. But she's dead, and I'm moderately responsible for it.'

'My patience is thinner than you might think, captain,' Venzer snapped at me. 'You may enjoy being cryptic but you only have seconds to explain why I shouldn't clap you in irons.'

I gave him the short of it. The Iron Goat sat licking at the purple stains on his teeth. He hadn't been hitting the bottle for long. The first thing you do when you got a problem like mine is get cunning. You don't sup shit that's going to make it obvious, you do it quiet, invisible, so that nobody realises. Tell yourself that you can stop whenever you want to, that it's just for today, just for the week, just until the bad time passes and you can get back to normality. Then one day you wake up and ten years have passed and you're still running the shittiest, most pointless errands for the most dismal pay. Venzer was still an amateur.

At the story's end, I placed the jar on the desk and stripped back the covering cloth. The fat little maggot creature was writhing this way and that, trying to find a way out of its confines. For all that it was a big eye on the end of a grub, it seemed blind enough now. I wondered whether Herono had felt its tail worming around in her skull, tickling up against her brain. The thought made me sick. I'd sealed the jar with a cork and then melted wax around it. The dead odour had been contained so far.

'This is Shavada,' I said, placing a hand atop the jar. Even then, I didn't trust the thing not to push out the cork and make a lunge for the marshal. It was a risk bringing it into the inner sanctum but I had to move fast. 'Or part of him, anyway. Shavada had his claws into Herono for years, ever since her capture in the Misery. What Herono knew, he knows.'

Venzer had seen a lot of weird shit in his days on the Range. The year of the witching fever, when men would laugh themselves to death, breaking their own ribs with their spasms. The cries of the gillings weren't good for a man's sanity, and dealing with Crowfoot wasn't much of a party either. The eye in the jar didn't cause him to shriek or cower. Instead he swallowed twice, then again, apple bobbing in his throat. The magnitude of the betrayal settled on him. When he found his voice he spoke in a dusty whisper.

'Her body?'

'My men have it in the Bell,' I said. 'Had to kill a lot of her boys. I guess they were as innocent as anyone gets out here, but we didn't have a lot of choice.'

Venzer got hold of himself, shook his head.

'Cover it.' I did.

'Only thing I don't get,' I said, 'is why you conspired with her to have Dantry Tanza gracked.'

'An accusation like that could see you in the stockade. Or the stocks. Or dead,' Venzer said coolly.

'Yeah, I guess. But we both know you won't. You like me too much.'

'Spirits, Galharrow, but you're a cocksure arse. It was Adenauer's plan. Ezabeth Tanza was spreading her sedition and with the influence her rank gave her, people were willing to listen. We had to do something.' He shook his head ruefully.

'You wanted Dantry killed because his sister made too much noise?'

'It was a bluff,' Venzer snapped. 'Don't you see? We've been bluffing for years.'

'You mean Nall's Engine? It is down, isn't it?'

'It's been down since Nall left us. He had us build it eighty years back, but we never understood the science. We did what he showed us, pumping millions of marks of phos into the heart beneath this citadel, and the moment he disappeared, it started leaking back out. Rejected, you could say. The Order has tried but they don't understand it. So they kept the failure secret. Only a select few had any idea. The head of the Order, the five most senior engineers. The technicians that discovered the failing were disappeared off to the west. And that was it. Not even the princes were informed. There are spies, Galharrow, spies everywhere.'

'How did Herono find out?'

'I told her,' Venzer said. He stood up and walked across to the wall-length windows, looking out at the bloody bronze-bruised sky over the Range. 'We needed her. Or needed her phos, more accurately. When we discovered we couldn't feed the heart, we reduced what we bought. What could we do with so much raw power? So much congealed magic? Gleck Maldon was our answer, at first. He absorbed what he could and then released it into the Misery. Quantities of phos that no Spinner should be meddling with. I think it's what unhinged him. What destroyed him.'

'I'm beginning to have doubts about that. But go on.'

'We had to cut the supply,' Venzer said. 'There were too many Talents spinning in the mills, not enough Spinners to make use of the power. Couldn't sell it, or the phos companies would have realised there was a grotesque surplus.

Questions would have been asked. Herono's light mills produced a third of what the heart of the Engine had consumed when Nall was present. We feared that a spy may have infiltrated the Order, that Nall's Engine had been sabotaged somehow. I brought Herono onto the inner circle of the Order's council, asked her to falsify records, to divert her phos supply carefully, secretly, as though she were profiteering from it. Exactly as Ezabeth claimed. Indeed, some of the princes believe that they *are* profiteering. Lots of little movements, all secret from one another. Of course, Herono agreed to it.'

Venzer sat back deeply in his chair. He seemed dwarfed by it, a tiny speck, a shrivelled flap of skin over bones that should have been pastured out years before. He had a core of iron, but the flesh grew brittle. I can't be too harsh about the way he looked. Herono's brass knuckles hadn't left me looking pretty either. The flesh of my face was swollen, purple and tender as calf meat. It was testament to life on the Range that Venzer hadn't even questioned it when I walked in.

'And the Tanzas?'

'You do have a soft spot for the scarred, don't you?' Venzer asked. My bad news must have been sinking in, because he reached for the liquor and poured himself a tot. He didn't offer me one. For once, I wasn't in the mood. Somewhere in the hells the wind must have been cold.

'Maldon spoke highly of Ezabeth Tanza, before all that phos drove him crazy,' Venzer said. 'But the two of them were more addled than anyone realised. It will do that, taking too much light, burns you as sure as staring into the sun. I feared for his sanity, so I brought in a few independents. Spinners and engineers from the Order, even an expert from the university. You know what they told me?'

He paused to refill his glass.

'Mad. Nonsense. Sheer, barmy craziness. Calculations

that they didn't understand, not one of them. And at the heart of it, some absurd children's rhyme. Then Maldon began talking about the Engine, something he'd come to understand about the way that it worked. Sat in here one day and told me that we were all doomed. He claimed that he'd solved some paradox. It was ridiculous babble, of course.'

'Herono's man burned his house down. It took me a while, but I think I understand it now.'

'Go on.'

'Herono wanted Ezabeth to prove that Nall's Engine was failing, but she couldn't risk her getting her hands on Nall's original papers. Couldn't risk anyone having them, in case they held the secret to getting the Engine working again. So she tried to destroy it.'

'Herono actually had us believing that it had been Ezabeth who started that blaze. Losing control, just like Maldon did. That she had to be nullified.'

Venzer shook his head. This time he didn't bother with a cup and took his liquor straight from the bottle.

'Herono always wanted Ezabeth to continue her research,' he said in a low, cold voice. 'Said it should be completed, but secretly and without fanfare. "Let her complete her work from the confines of the Maud," she said to me. "Perhaps it will be useful."' He chuckled bitterly. 'It is no wonder to me now. She'd thought it through so well. If Dantry were dead, Herono would become Ezabeth's guardian. We could imprison her indefinitely, let her provide the proof that Shavada wants. But by that time, I already knew. I tried it, you see. Three years ago. I went into the control room and I threw the lever. Nothing happened. Nothing at all.'

I was stunned. My mouth worked up and down like a fish. He'd known, all this time. Had held the secret tight against his chest. I'd seen him decaying, seen a great man buckling beneath an impossible burden. I hadn't realised quite how much weight he bore for the rest of us.

'It's what they wanted all along. Proof that the Engine has failed. The Deep Kings won't risk their sorry hides in range of it until they're certain that it's dead. But when they are certain ...'

'Yes. When they are certain.' Venzer nodded. 'When they know our great weapon lies silent, the Deep Kings will come in all their darkness.'

'Well,' I said. 'We got a real fight on our hands now.'

'A fight?' Venzer asked with an unpleasant, hysterical grimace on his face. 'No, Galharrow, there's no fight. The charade had to stand, you see? We've lost. The game is over. Nall's Engine was the only thing that held the Deep Kings back.'

'We have walls, guns, blades and brandy,' I said, turning my voice hard. 'And fuck me but those are good ingredients to whip up a fight.'

'Immaterial against the numbers the drudge can throw against us. They have their legions, they have their sorcerers. The Deep Kings are six, and we have just Crowfoot and the Lady of the Waves, if we can even count them. It was Nall's Engine that held them back since the Heart of the Void first burned the land. Our only weapon.'

It appeared that my commander had given up.

'Not our only weapon,' I said. I wanted to shake some fight back into him. 'We have a whole army stationed here. How many men do we have, including state retinues? Forty-five, fifty thousand men?'

'Thirty-two thousand, spread along the Range,' Venzer sighed. 'Twenty thousand of them at Three-Six, four thousand here, and the rest at the stations. Oh, Galharrow. Dear boy. You don't understand at all, do you? The Deep Kings come for us, and there's nothing we can do to stand in their way. Thirty-two thousand men all in one place couldn't put enough shot into the air to stop them. The communicators from the north count almost two hundred thousand Dhojaran warriors crossing the Misery. You want to know why they aren't coming at us in a charge? Because they're building a *road* across the Misery. A road, half a mile wide, paved stone, raised from the ground. There are as many engineers out there as there are soldiers. They believe they have us, they know it's over. So, the Kings won't send their men charging across blindly. Why bother? They were ancient before even Crowfoot was born. They can wait a little, be absolutely certain that the Engine has failed us. There is nothing holding them back but their own caution. The truth is, they've already won.'

'Not yet,' I said. 'Allow Ezabeth to access the heart. Let her see if she can fix whatever is wrong. It's worth a try.'

'I'll give the order. She's welcome to. You think I haven't already? I lost sixteen senior Order engineers just trying to get in. It's over, Galharrow. Even your master sees that.'

'I don't—' I began, but he cut me off.

'I don't share all the reports. Don't broadcast the worst of the news. Even if the walls at Three-Six stood up to them. Even if the princes raised another hundred thousand men and sent them to man the pikes, the Dhoja aren't afraid any-more. The Deep Kings have come in person. Real wizards, on our side of the Misery. Shavada, Philon, and now they say Acradius and Iddin are joining them. They will sweep our forces aside, swatted like bugs from the air. We have cannon, and walls and one half-mad old Nameless who has disappeared off to spirits know where when we need him the most. All of those will mean nothing when the Deep Kings choose to take their revenge for the Heart of the Void.'

28

I had no idea how long we had left, how many useless, pointless weeks before the Dhojaran army rolled up on its new road and the Deep Kings reduced the walls of Three-Six to rubble. I thought about running, about heading as far west as I could get and taking a ship. Maybe if I could get out to Hyspia, the Iscalian states, even reach the savages of Angol, I'd get far enough away to never see another one of the drudge. Maybe I could go and join Crowfoot, wherever the hell he'd got to. I had no love for the Nameless, but they were still the only ones that could stand up to a King. The rest of us, we had to run.

But I didn't. Instead I got set for a fight.

The Iron Goat offered me a commission in one of his battalions, like he always did. I brushed it off, as I always did, and set about finding work for my squadron of useless, flea-encrusted layabouts, vandals and eye-gougers. Tnota was sick. I paid him only one visit, finding him grey and unresponsive in a sweat-stained bed, though the surgeon said he came around from time to time. The fever had not diminished. I thought that he would die soon, and could not bring myself to see him again.

Ezabeth and Dantry were safe enough now. They took up residence at Otto Lindrick's house, and together they continued trying to decipher Maldon's equations. Between taking jobs dragging deserters back to be hanged, I tried calling in on them a couple of times. Only Dantry would see me, though I knew she was there as well. He said she was too deep into her studies to be disturbed, but we both knew that was bullshit.

'Well, give her my regards,' I said on one failed attempt, and turned to go.

'Captain, wait.' Dantry frowned, an uncertain look. 'I don't know what passed between you. I don't understand it. But she cries. She cries all the time.'

'That woman is harder than the hells.'

'Even so. She cries.'

'Things are bad.'

'I know. But she never cried before.'

'That supposed to make me feel better?'

'I don't know. No, I suppose not. I just thought you should know.'

Word came down from Three-Six. A scouting party had got close enough to Shavada's contingent to get a good count of the numbers, and the communicators were hammering desperately to send more men. Send more men, more guns, more fucking Battle Spinners. Like we had any of those to send.

I stopped back home one night, fuzzy-headed and lighter in the pockets than I should have been thanks to a shitty run of tiles. A little kid was waiting outside the door of my apartment, a boy, his skin grey and his eyes orange as an owl's. One of Saravor's little helpers. He didn't say anything, just held up a box about the size of a man's head, wrapped in brown paper and tied with string. I took it, felt something shift inside.

'This from Saravor?' I asked. The child nodded. 'Do I want to see what's inside?' He said nothing at all, as though he had no feelings either way, or else he didn't understand the question. 'You want to come in and sit down a while?' The child shook his head. They were always mutes, these little ones that belonged to the Fixer. I felt a curl of revulsion as I wondered whether they were allowed to keep their tongues. The boy started walking away.

'Hey, kid,' I called after him and he turned towards me. He didn't look me in the eye. 'If I killed your master, would that make you happier?'

The blank-faced child stood silent for a moment, then shook his head. No emotion at all, not so much as a blink as he turned and walked off. I frowned after him. Maybe he had no frame of reference for what a better life would be like. Maybe he'd formed that strange bond that occurs between master and slave. Or maybe a life with that sick fucking creature was better than being an orphan out on the street. Hard to imagine how, though.

I carried the box inside, stuck it on the table and slumped into a chair. Whatever Saravor had sent me, it couldn't make me feel much worse. You can always surprise yourself with just how much worse things can get, though.

The box contained a severed head. I opened it and stared down, barely surprised, not even impressed. I lifted the head and placed it on the table. It was quite dry, leathery even, the head of a man past his best years but the hair still dark and worn long like a younger man's. He'd been clean-shaven when he died, and the skin around the stump of his neck had been stitched neatly together.

'What am I meant to do with this?'

The head's eyes fluttered open. I'd half expected something like that. I sat back in my chair.

'What do you want?' I said. I wasn't talking to the head.

'I want my money, Galharrow,' Saravor said through the head's lips. The unwilling intermediary's eyes swivelled in the sockets to look at me, but his jaw didn't move at all. The sorcerer's words hissed out, sighs of corpse-breath.

'You'll get your fucking money,' I said.

'I like you, Galharrow,' Saravor said. 'You bring me work. You bring me flesh to work and shape.'

'I think you're probably worse than the Dhoja,' I said.

A hiss of air escaped the head. Maybe it was meant to be laughter.

'I like you, but when I do business, I forget who I like,' the sorcerer's pet head said. 'Time is ticking by, and word is that none of us might be here much longer. Since I do not intend to be sitting idly by waiting for the Deep Kings to invite me to their court, your deadline has been advanced. Get me my money, Galharrow, or it will go badly for you. I own you. Did you forget that?'

'You don't own me you fucking piece of—'

It is, without a doubt, ill advised to verbally abuse a sorcerer. The silver dragon in my chest stirred, reared its wicked head, and spat fire.

How to describe what he did to me? Imagine that all your skin has grown very loose, as if it were a great coat but still attached to you. Then imagine that some great giant grabs a handful of that skin and twists it around and around so that all of you is twisting, all of you is stretched and tearing and pulled in an excruciating twist, until you wonder how it's possible that you can still be covered in skin. Lastly, imagine that instead of on the outside, it's all going on inside, and it's your heart that's getting twisted and you suddenly feel the floor slamming into your face because you've blacked out for a moment and fallen over. It was like that, except the floor part which was actually that.

'Pay me, Galharrow,' Saravor hissed, the breath coming faint from the dead man's mouth. 'Pay me soon or I'll have my due from you, spirit or flesh, either will serve. Come visit me soon.'

29

The rain kicked up fiercer than the second hell as I made my way up onto the wall. The wind caught my cloak, sending it snapping around my legs, water plastered my hair slick against my face. Distant peels of thunder set the broken bronze of the sky over the Misery to clamouring with whale song, the scars in the sky flashing with light.

'You up here all night?' I asked one of the luckless guards as he hurried towards one of the shelter posts along the wall.

'Wouldn't be here if I didn't have to be,' he answered, stepping quickly and spitting rain water. 'Get down if you got any sense, matey.'

Why was I there? The rain came down on me, seeping through my cloak, my doublet, my shirt, even chilling my hands through the thick leather of my gloves and soaking me through to the underclothes. I stared out into the fading light of day, leaned my hands on the parapet wall, and blinked rain water back from my eyes. At first, it was just rain water, and then, as I let everything build upon me, it turned to half rain and half tears. A rare sensation for me. I hadn't cried in a long time. I'd wept for my children, I'd wept for their mother, or maybe that was all just for myself. Hadn't had a lot worth crying over since. I'd hardened, turned my core to something tough and dry as old oak, tried to tell myself that I didn't give a shit about anything or anyone, and for a long time I'd managed to do it. Worked hard in the day, beating heads and kicking pond-scum into line, drank harder in the night so that when I had to put my head down there was no space for thinking and the only hopes I had were for the room to stop spinning. I'd lowered myself far enough that dignity, pride, hopes for the future were all worthless things, so alien to my life than they were for other men. You can't long for the impossible.

Ezabeth Tanza had undone me. It hadn't been much of a hope, just a childish fantasy, but she'd shown me something that I wanted more than just another bottle. I'd never truly thought that I could have her, hadn't allowed myself that delusion. But for a time it had felt good to dream of something, to long for something that was far out of reach. For a time, I had felt alive again. Now she had no use for me, and that was gone, and I stood on a dark wall in Valengrad, sodden through and crying a decade's worth of pain and self-loathing and frustration into a thrashing storm that cared nothing for it. It had to come back. The emptiness, the void inside me. It had to fill the space that she had occupied. I needed that hole in my heart to be myself again. Part of me wanted her to hurt as I hurt. I hated myself even more for that.

It was as if my thoughts had summoned her. I didn't know it was her at first, through the driving grey rain as she struggled along against the battling wind, cloak rushing out behind her like some wild, thrashing demon.

'Captain Galharrow,' she said, and I could barely make out her shout over the roar of the storm. She was veiled, regarding me over the soaked fabric.

'What the fuck are you doing up here?' I said. I had to shout across the rain.

'Your men said I'd find you here. That you've been up here every day since we last spoke. I wanted to see you.'

'I'm here,' I said, 'you've seen me. What do you want?'

'I need to ask you for something.'

Ask me. Ask me for anything. I love you. No, you made me love you. I hate you. Ask and I'll refuse. I wouldn't give you an ounce of my spit. I'd give you the world.

'What do you want?'

She watched me coolly for a few moments. She reached up with her maimed left hand and tugged her hood further forward.

'Your forgiveness,' she said. The thunder echoed through the sky, forcing her to shout louder over the rain. 'I didn't say it before. I was too proud, but I owe it to you. I'm sorry, for what I did to you. I had no right.'

'I could have died because you put your light into my eyes,' I said.

'I know.'

'Made me act like a damn fool.'

'I understand.'

'Yeah? How can you understand?' I looked away. The rain seemed to be matching moods with me, and it got suddenly heavier, harder, though I'd not thought that possible. Drops the size of walnuts were crashing down across the wall. A few dedicated soldiers were moving around, carefully checking that the barrels of powder were well covered by oil cloths and that none were standing in puddles.

'Maybe I don't,' Ezabeth said. 'You've done a lot for us. You helped us when you didn't have to.'

'I got paid,' I said.

'I don't believe that was your only motivation.'

'Yeah, well around you, it's hard to know what to believe.'

She fell silent and looked out with me over the Misery. The after-effects of her phos charm were still at work, even if she'd blown out most of her power fighting Herono's men, because even knowing what I knew, however she'd deceived me, I still wanted to be around her. I was doubly a fool.

'You aren't him, you know,' she said after a while.

'Who?'

'The man you pretend to be. The hard-hearted killer. The drunkard who feels no pain. The common soldier, friend to murderers and addicts. You try hard to be him, but it's not you.'

'You think that? Who the fuck am I then?'

'I don't know,' she said. 'Maybe nobody knows. You're bitter, and you can be cruel, and you change your voice depending on who you're talking to, as if speaking like your men makes you one of them, but it doesn't. You're strong, and brave and you hide your compassion behind glares and glowers. But if you were a bad man then I'd be sorry that we met you, and I'd be more sorry still that I light-blinded you. But I'm not.'

'I thought the point of you being here was to apologise to me,' I said. I had to spit rain water from my mouth. It really was a bloody stupid place for a conversation.

'It was. It is. I don't know. Maybe I'm not as sorry as I thought I was.'

'You just keep on brightening up my life.' I turned away from her to glare across the Misery's shadowed redness, and as I did a flash of lightning lit the wasteland.

Men. Thousands of men, cloaked and hooded against the rain. They were just black shapes as they trooped across the cracked plain, still miles from the walls, but they were coming. The Dhojaran Empire was here, and they were in range of Nall's Engine, and now they had sent an army into its killing zone.

Broken hearts would have to wait.

I ran for the nearest alarm crank, released the safety bolt and began to wind it. Phos flared along power lines and a few seconds later the clamouring call rang out into the storm. It droned long and hollow, rising and falling. Lights appeared one by one in puffs of bright phos along the top of the wall and the citadel towers, shining out over the Misery. I looked towards the jester's cap projectors of Nall's Engine, but they remained dark and motionless. I hadn't expected anything else.

The wall guards streamed from their shelters to stare out at the Misery. I heard curses, gasps, and amongst them a few chuckles. No doubt those finding mirth thought that they were about to see a demonstration of the Engine's power. Those who'd been stacking gunpowder along the wall probably had a better idea of what was about to happen.

'The drudge are here?' Ezabeth said by my side.

'Bloody well looks that way,' I grunted.

The end had begun.

30

The rain did not relent. My crew stood for an hour getting wet and cold, then wetter and colder. Not that anyone minded, save maybe Nenn. It's less dangerous down in the gutters, away from anything that the drudge and their sorcerers might fling at the walls, but you also can't see shit and there's nobody to kill. Our guns might have been gracking thousands of the bastards, sending them scampering and scattering across the broken earth, or the forty-pound lumps of iron might have been like so many drops of wine spat into the ocean. No way to tell. The drudge could have stopped to draw up earthworks, or they might be coming on at full charge, ladders ready. We didn't even have a remotely reliable estimate of their numbers, current guesses ranging between five and fifty thousand. The not knowing clawed inside my skin like itching little fingers, prising to escape my body. Only the constant thumping of the guns indicated there was anything going on at all.

The bright little dragon coiled around my heart twisted painfully. A reminder not to get myself killed before I'd paid my debt. Thanks, Saravor. His profit was assuredly the prime concern on my mind.

The cannon bleated their percussive blasts again, no volley fire, the gunners loading and firing as swiftly as they were able. I couldn't be sure, but that didn't seem like a good thing.

'Nervous, captain?' Nenn asked. She'd found a decent helmet somewhere, though it didn't match the rest of her patched and often repaired armour. A layer of rust speckled the side of her breastplate, which she was trying to keep hidden from me.

'Of course I am. I'm not an idiot,' I said. I get terse when the action's getting close. I wouldn't mention the breastplate, not now when it might make her fearful. There'd be a full gear inspection if we repelled this first assault.

'What the fuck are we doing here, captain? This isn't our usual line of work.'

I shrugged.

'We're standing in as reserves. You got somewhere else you need to be?'

'I heard it's a lot of 'em,' she said.

'Sure looked like it from up there.'

'Looking forward to getting stuck into it, sir?'

'As little as ever. But we'll fight, if we're needed. And we're needed.'

'Think that there'll be danger pay for this, captain?' Wheedle asked. He was running the edge of a straight-bladed sword against a portable whetstone, the grinding whine muted by the rain, the steel too wet to shed sparks.

'There fucking well better be,' I said.

Drudge would reach the wall. It should have been unthinkable. Nall's Engine should have been blazing in action already, blasting new craters across the Misery. Men muttered to one another that maybe it was a trap to lure in more of the drudge, even as they wondered if they were going to die over it. I knew the truth, and I was still standing amongst them, so I guess that made me the stupidest.

Before long the cannon blasts were joined by the occasional, sporadic clap of a matchlock discharging. Not many gunners could fit under the cannon's awnings, so their numbers were few. I guessed that the bows would have been spitting arrows the whole time. Women of the quartermaster's division had been hurrying around the square with bags of extra shafts for some time, though now that flurry had thinned to a drizzle. That meant that either no more arrows were needed, or, more likely, that we'd sent most of our arrows north and there weren't any more to bring.

The cannon thundered their storm song, and still we stood cold and wet in the muster square, teeth chattering and feet turning numb. Water ran from helmet rims and sloped from fluted pauldrons. The stink of blasting powder mingled with the rain and a slick smog gathered in the streets as the wind brought the gun smoke back into the city, an ankle-deep mist driven low by the rain.

'What's going on up on the wall?' Dantry asked me. I don't know why he'd attached himself to my unit, but he'd found arms and armour and at least looked the part.

'Not a fucking idea,' I said. 'Firing guns, I suppose.'

'Is it always like this? War, I mean?'

'Wet?'

'The not knowing,' he said. 'I've studied the famous campaigns and battles between the princes when I was reading at university, but they all give so much … detail. Overviews. We're a hundred yards from the action and I don't know anything.'

'Oh,' I said. 'Yeah. It's pretty much like that all the time.'

'Seems like a foolish attack,' Dantry said. He was asking for reassurance. 'I mean, the walls are high and they're gunned and manned. What can the Dhojaran commanders hope to achieve?'

'My best guess?' I exhaled cold breath into the wet air. 'Valengrad is the heart of the Range, and it's where the heart of Nall's Engine is found. The Kings have always wanted Valengrad destroyed, but this is really them testing the Engine. Send an army, fifteen, twenty thousand men, and see if they can get up to the walls. The Deep Kings don't give a shit about our guns, but they give a lot of shits about Nall's Engine. They want to know if we can activate it and obliterate these men before they commit the rest of their boys up at Three-Six.'

'Twenty thousand men as ... as bait? A test?' Dantry said, aghast. It was the latest estimate we'd heard.

'You have to think like a King. They're immortal, so they don't gamble their chances like we do. They want to take Dortmark, but Nall's Engine killed one of them, once. You have to realise how big a deal that is to the rest of them. They won't come at us if they think we can fire it up.'

I could see by Dantry's expression that he and his sister knew full well the dire situation we were in.

'Do you think that the drudge can take the walls, without help from the Kings?'

'Depends how many they sent, and what gear they brought. To get this close without us spotting their advance, I'd guess it's a few thousand and they don't have heavy artillery. But I could be wrong.'

Dantry looked down at the growing puddle we stood in. His face had lost it's boyish cast in just a handful of days. He hadn't hardened up enough yet to get immune, hadn't the grit to put aside that sickening feeling that we were all going to die and there was nothing we could do about it. I patted him on the shoulder, though he'd have to take the comfort through layers of wool, leather and steel.

I saw a junior officer moving through the muster yard with a scroll case, which I figured was being used to keep orders from getting soggy as they travelled between the citadel and the wall. I flagged him down and though he was keen to make haste, he paused just long enough for a shouted exchange over the pouring rain.

'What's going on?'

'Idiots came up at us with ladders,' the squawk shouted.

'Repelled?'

'Not one drudge made the wall. Must be a few thousand dead and wounded out there.'

'All good then?'

'A slaughter.' He grinned at me, 'We're gracking them left and right. Cannon tore 'em to pieces!' And then he dashed off through the rain. The men who could hear gave something of a cheer, although the weather had sapped a lot of their enthusiasm.

It seemed too easy.

The Dhoja weren't stupid. Could they really have thought to take us by surprise because of a bit of rain? Didn't seem likely. The Deep Kings and the Nameless might be willing to toss lives away to test a theory, but the drudge had their own commanders. When the Kings twisted them into warrior form they didn't turn them stupid.

A cloaked figure had joined my men. I could tell that it was Ezabeth without seeing her veil beneath the hood because she was barely taller than a child. When she turned I saw that her dress was strapped with a War Spinner's battle harness. Ten portable battery coils in iron tanks, each the size of a loaf of bread, were buckled to the leather straps. It looked good on her, and with that veil she looked more Nameless than Spinner, one of the freaks. Our eyes met for a moment, and I gave her a slow nod. She returned it. I didn't know how many Spinners Venzer had kept in Valengrad when he sent most of the army north to Three-Six, but I'd seen her brought to bear against the drudge before. Ezabeth alone was worth as much as an artillery battery.

'Lady Tanza,' I called to her, 'are those all the canisters they'll give you?'

'They have more. This is just what I can carry, captain,' she said. Hard to hear her through both rain and veil. I thought on it a moment.

'You all topped up?'

'I'm holding as much as I can, but if I have to throw it

at the Dhoja it won't last long. Battle magic saps phos like nothing else.' She looked down at her canister belt. 'I have enough for maybe fourteen, fifteen good blasts.'

'Not enough,' I said. 'If we get any action I want you burning them like bonfire mawkins. Nenn. Oi, Nenn, listen up.' Nenn looked up at me, irritated.

'Go to the store and bring a barrow load of canisters. Enough that Tanza can throw it all night if she has to.'

'Send someone else,' Nenn said. She took out her pouch of blacksap and broke off a piece. I felt a growl rising in my throat.

'That's an order, private,' I barked. Nenn shot me one impudent look, then stalked off glowering, boots sending ripples through the growing lake around our feet. Some of the boys were looking at me as if embarrassed.

'Next time I give an order, I want it done in fucking triple time and you don't ask questions, you fucking hear me?' I yelled at them. I looked at the Tanza siblings. 'Goes for you two as well. I yell it, you do it. No exceptions.' Ezabeth nodded; Dantry actually gave me a salute.

The cannons had fallen silent. That meant one of three things: either the Dhoja were out of range, the guns were out of ammunition, or the Dhoja were packed so close to the walls that there wasn't any trajectory to fire on them.

'Fuck it, I'm going up there,' I said. 'Won't be long.'

I wasn't strictly supposed to be going up on the wall, but nobody was guarding the stairwells so it was easy enough to get up. Soldiers in black and gold uniforms were mostly stood idle. The smoke was thick and eye-watering despite the rain, and the cannon barrels glowed with fierce heat. I pushed through to the crenulations and shielded my eyes to look out.

The Dhoja had pulled back beyond the range where cannon fire would do serious damage. The broken ground beyond the walls was littered with bodies. Thousands of them, some dead, some in pieces, and some of those pieces buzzing their drudge buzz and getting no help at all. Greys and browns mottled the skin of what had formerly been men of the Dhojaran Empire. A battalion of drudge in outdated mail shirts with barbed blades on their spears lay twisted and red beside bearded men with dark skin and stretched ears, slashes of bright yellow across their flat-nosed heads. Helmets lay scattered where the artillery blasts had ripped them from heads, weapons and shields had been discarded as their owners fled. A leg lay here, a hand there, something unidentifiable wept scarlet fluid atop a rock. Furrows and dents in the earth attested to the passage of cannon balls, and arrows sprouted from both carrion and mudlike weeds.

It had been a suicidal attack. Here and there lay ladders, some of them intact but just as many smashed to pieces. I tried to picture whether they would even reach the top of the wall. Probably not. The larger pieces of drudge corpses looked emaciated, half starved. Some had barely turned, others seemed to have become misshapen. None of them carried decent equipment.

I reminded myself what this truly was. A test of Nall's Engine. They'd thrown their weakest junk at us. Lives broken by fire and iron, just to see if we'd activate our weapon. For all that there must have been five thousand corpses along the length of the wall and not a single loss on our side, it didn't feel like much of a victory.

31

The drudge sent their Darlings against us, and the bastard things melted holes in our fucking wall. The fighting went hard until Ezabeth unleashed her light against them. We plugged the holes with corpses.

We piled bodies as high as we could load them, ready for the meat carts. It kept the living busy. Men moved slowly, wearily. I'd seen rocks in the Misery with more energy. Nothing takes it out of you like fighting for your life, when you give your all in every thrust and cut in case it's your last.

The wall had fallen quiet, or at least nobody was shooting. Squawks began to appear from the wall to gape at the freshly melted tunnels. Some of them hadn't even known what was happening until it was over. Engineers assessed whether the wall above was likely to collapse, but for now it seemed to be happy enough supporting its own weight, even with all those men and cannon atop it.

'We'll have to pull down these houses and get the tunnel filled in with the rubble,' a captain with a fancy plume in his helmet was saying. Funny thing about officers, the fewer men they command, the more sense they tend to have. I didn't volunteer us.

'The other tunnels?' I asked.

'Five in total,' the captain told me. 'Two to the north of yours both collapsed in on themselves halfway along. Maybe killed the Darlings that made 'em. The furthest south was held by the Black Swan Grenadiers. The other didn't do so well.'

'How bad?'

'We lost two hundred men trying to push them back into it. Had to send three Battle Spinners to shut down the Darling, and it still killed two of 'em. Just a little kid, like it was ten years old. Same age as my boy.'

'Those little bastards are older than they look.'

'These all your boys?' the captain asked.

'Those that survived.'

The waiting started again, like it always did. The tavern on the edge of the muster square looked warm and inviting. I bought a cask for the men. The sweats were back, so I took a mug of ale too and set about washing them away. It hit the spot. Nenn hit the beer like it was going to spoil in minutes. I just did a lot of sighing, a lot of regretting and tried to avoid thinking about how I felt about anything at all.

Ezabeth and Dantry kept to a corner of the tavern. A lot of men tried to send drinks her way, thanks for what she'd done that day, but she refused them all. What in the hells had she done? I'd never seen a Spinner so powerful. I joined them. Dantry wore a long face. Ezabeth looked exhausted. She'd spread papers across the table in front of her, damp and running with ink, and had scribbled across them so fiercely she'd torn the page.

'Keep your chins up,' I said. 'We're still standing. After a day like today, there's a lot of folks can't say that.'

'Dantry worked it out,' Ezabeth said, looking up at me. Her eyes were glassy, only half seeing me. 'Maldon's thesis. All that work, and it came to nothing. Nonsense. He took a children's rhyme, codified it and then buried it in half a dozen equations to mangle it until it was incomprehensible.'

'Maybe we were expecting too much from a man who smeared his own crap on the walls,' I said. 'What's the rhyme?'

'The same one he sent me before. The heart is black, the heart is cold, only a child could be so bold. The heart is dark, the night comes soon.'

'Only a child can reach the moon,' I finished. Maldon's faecal thesis hadn't been much of a hope but it had turned out to be the literal shit it was written in. 'Don't discount anything yet. Maybe he'd lost his mind by then. But if not, he left that message for you two specifically. I doubt anyone else could have solved whatever puzzle he made of it. Stay bright. We're not dead yet.'

'Aren't we?'

We probably were, but I didn't like it when other people said it.' Aren't you supposed to be the optimist?' I said. 'Venzer gave you access to the Engine's heart. You're the only one that has a chance to make this thing work.'

She held up another sheet of paper on which she'd sketched the heart's door and its mechanism.

'If I could figure out the mechanism to open it, don't you think I'd be there right now? But Nall locked it tight. There must be a mathematical sequence to it, but what? He didn't tell us that. The door is unbreakable, and I wasted three canisters trying to blast it open. I ...' She shook her head. 'Let me be. I'll work it out. I have to.' The pen started up again.

'Let me know the moment you think you have something,' I said. 'I believe in you.'

Ezabeth paused in her scribbling and turned sad eyes to me.

'Yes. I suppose you do.'

Nobody came with messages or orders. We kept informed by taking turns to run up onto the wall, take a look out and report back to the group. We'd given the Dhoja a real bloodying. I hated the drudge, hated them for what they were even if they hadn't chosen their corruption, and even I felt sickened at the loss of life. Whoever had command out there was willing to pay a steep price for Valengrad, but while the twisted bodies at the foot of the wall were expendable, losing Darlings had to give them pause. Sorcerers weren't as cheap as those poor brave bastards they'd funnelled to their deaths. Doubt they expected to lose them. At the foot of the wall the tangle of abandoned ladders started to resemble a forest blown over in a gale, long splinters of broken wood lying haphazard across one another, bodies for foliage and blood for sap.

'Powder's all gone,' I overheard the hushed voice of a quartermaster. 'Guns stay silent now. That's come from the top.'

'What are we meant to do, throw the gun at them?' an artillery man fumed.

'You want my advice? If they sound another assault, get your horse and ride west fast as you can. Who knows what tricks they got for next time?'

'You crazy? Venzer has officers manning the western gates. Women with children are the only ones getting out. There's talk of arming the Spills, putting them up here as militia.'

Similar sentiments echoed along the wall. Morale was collapsing faster than a leaf-smoker's promises.

There was blood on the parapet. Today's drudge had come with good armour and ladders that actually reached the top of the walls. In those numbers, and with the length of the wall, in some places they'd made it. Fighting had been fierce, and we'd lost men. Guesses said something like three or four hundred were out of action up top, two hundred in the streets below, and we only started with a few thousand. The more we lost, the more we'd lose in any following assault because keeping them off the wall would only get harder. I looked up at the jester's cap fronds of the projectors of Nall's Engine towering over the citadel. We'd put too much faith in it for too long. We should have had more men. It seemed so obvious now, at the end.

The room smelled of the dying.

I sat with my head in my hands in the silence that surrounded the only other occupant. He was out of it, dreaming his slow path down towards the final darkness that awaits us all. How long did he have? Impossible to say. From the moment we're born the sands of our lives are draining through the hour glass. Living is the biggest steal we ever make, but nobody gets away with it. The city had learned to watch the minute hand rather than counting the hours as time ran down for us all. Tick, tick, tick.

'I don't know what to do,' I said, the only sound in that stinking pit. 'Tell me what to do.'

All else was silence. Even Tnota's breathing was quiet beyond hearing. The guns on the walls were still. The street beyond the shuttered window was empty. Seemed like the whole city had gone mute. Nobody had anything worth saying or enough optimism left to try saying it.

I'd found him alone. The surgeon may have been off tending more wounded, or maybe he'd done the smart thing and got the hell out already. Nobody had been in to change Tnota's dressing or to pour water between his lips for some time. He'd soiled himself and his sheets were yellow with old sweat and mucus. I could bring myself to change the bandage on his stump and squeeze moisture between his chapped lips, but I couldn't bring myself to undignify him by changing him like a baby. He was burning up and out of it. Wasn't like he cared one way or the other.

What was I doing there anyway, wasting valuable minutes? I should have been getting some sleep. I should have been taking advantage of every whore still plying her trade. I should have been checking my kit. I should have been sneaking out of the postern gates and riding west as fast as I could manage. Too many options, and all of them vinegar sour.

I didn't know why I'd come. Shouldn't have come. When my boys got hurt, I left them to it until they either came back or went into the earth. Easier that way. Lessened the guilt. What was I doing wasting what might have been my last hours here, breathing the stink of a dying man's air? I didn't know. Maybe I just needed the reassurance of an old friend's presence. There were few enough of those left.

Tnota made a sound, a grunt of distaste. Gummy eyes fought their way open a crack. He wheezed and groaned like a dog in a drought. Poor bastard. I dipped a rag into the pitcher of small beer and placed it against his lips. He responded, suckling at it, feeding like a babe in arms. I tried more and he sucked again. I squeezed a trickle into his mouth but he choked, spluttering liquid across his chin. His eyes sank closed again and his breathing returned to that pained wheeze.

Tnota had been a navigator before I met him, a good one. Could have signed on with the regulars, if he'd wanted it. He hadn't. Simple man, Tnota. Knew what he liked, made sure that he got it. Valued the simple things in life: love and ale and sticking your feet up by a fire. I'd taken him out on a job, and after that we'd stuck together. Never really understood how I managed to pick them up, the long-timers like Nenn and Tnota. No glory in working for the crow. Just a long, certain walk into darkness.

'I'm sorry,' I told him. 'You didn't deserve this. We're neither of us going to sit judgement's scales with any confidence about the outcome, but you were far from the worst of us. Never murdered a man that I knew of, and that's more than I can say for most of the sorry fuckers in this city.' I dabbed a damp cloth across his forehead. Was glad he couldn't see the glisten in my eyes. He'd never have let me live it down. 'This was my fight. You'd have been the first one to get us out of here when the shit started frying. Wasn't your fight. Never was.'

Tnota stirred enough to make a pained noise. I couldn't tell whether he could hear me or was just sounding reflexively against the pain. He murmured something and I leaned in closer.

'You want something?'

His eyes cracked open again. This time I thought he saw me.

'Stand,' he wheezed, a hiss of foul, dry breath.

'You're not even strong enough to sit up,' I said. 'Lie still. Rest.'

'Stand,' Tnota said again. His eyes widened, stared at me more intensely than I'd ever seen them.

'Not yet. When you're stronger,' I said. If he got stronger. A big 'if'.

Tnota's left arm reached up and grabbed me by the hair. He drew my face in close.

'You asked what ... you should ... do,' he said. 'Telling you ... now. Stand.'

He released me, coughed and then sank back into his slow death.

32

They let us rest through the night, and came at us again with the dawn. I awoke to clamouring sirens and the flashing of the broken sky, blood-red Rioque casting a liquid sheen to the broken reality.

The remnants of my company formed up, the survivors of the night's desertion. A junior officer squirmed for my attention, face glistening whitely with perspiration.

'The marshal will activate Nall's Engine today, won't he, sir?' he managed to ask.

'He will,' I lied, 'or he won't.'

'Why, sir? Why hasn't it been activated?'

I listened to the whining of the siren, its rise and fall timed to the drawing of breaths.

'Best not to question the higher-ups. They got their reasons and we got our jobs. See to yours.'

At the foot of the stair leading to the ramparts, Ezabeth was waiting. She had fresh canisters across her harness. Men were saluting her as they went by. I stopped, met her eyes. Beautiful eyes, dark and intelligent. No fear in them, just determination. Somehow she stilled the fear in my chest and as it dissipated I felt Saravor's dragon mocking me for my weakness. I had hoped that, giving the imminent destruction we all faced, he would have forgotten about me. What use was money going to be when the walls fell? He'd be the first rat off the ship if he wasn't already gone. But then to Saravor it had never really been about money.

I offered Ezabeth my arm and she took it. We climbed like we were the lord and lady of the company. What a fucking pair we must have made. I felt the eyes upon us. Maybe it gave the boys some hope. It did me.

The day went hard. Arrow storms lashed the Dhoja, a handful of cannon gave some pretence at volley fire before they sputtered and died away. Emboldened, the Dhoja abandoned their pavisses and charged. Ladders were the order of the day again. They must have cut down a forest back in Dhojara to bring that many across the Misery. The drudge buzzing across the field of body parts and rotting corpses marched stoically with fanaticism guiding their steps. Not one company baulked as they drew near. When the Kings changed you, you loved them for it. I never understood why that was, but those poor bastards loved their overlords more than Tnota loved cock. Which was a lot.

We fought. Blades thrust over the parapet, ladders went clattering to the ground beyond, hammers and axes sang down on helms, rocks and old bricks went tumbling down. The first drudge to make the attempt weren't in control of their own actions; the Darlings had their mind-worms into them, sending them up first to encourage the rest of their fodder to the suicide. I speared a man whose eyes had the blank, glassy stare of the condemned. Some of them were already dead, the Darlings animating the bodies without a care.

The Dhoja did not come at us in waves, they just kept coming. My arms grew heavy and I moved to the back of the wall letting other younger, fresher bodies take my place. I saw Dantry swing an axe through a hand that clasped over the crenulations. Saw a couple of men give it up and flee the wall. Saw one of my new boys get grabbed by lifeless hands, dragged over the wall to break with the bodies below.

The neon letters across the citadel still read: COURAGE.

The Darlings were reluctant to engage. They'd not expected the previous day's losses, but they must have had
their orders as well because by midday they were hurling
their sorcery at us. A dozen of my men got disintegrated
by a kid that looked maybe thirteen. He must have been
one of the oldest Darlings, turned when the Kings first took
power. Ezabeth had it out with him, his dark power and
her blasts of spun moonlight flashing back and forth across
the sky. His wild blasts took down another twenty of our
men before Ezabeth managed to bind him, burn him and
send him scampering back into the Misery with his hair
smouldering.

She fought like a legend. The dry, hard-air thumps of
her percussive sorcery blew great holes in the Dhojaran
formations. Along the wall Venzer's remaining three Battle
Spinners were sending bolts of light out against the Dhojaran
horde but their strength was nothing compared to hers.
Worse, one of them took an arrow in the chest, and another
was overcome when, maybe emboldened by Ezabeth's victory, he tried to match his skills against a Darling. The little
bastard got the mind-worms into him, turned his power
against us and we would have lost the wall if some nameless
hero hadn't managed to get a dagger into him.

The killing lasted all day. We survived it, exhausted,
battered, weary. I was lucky, didn't take any injury. Aside
from Nenn and Dantry, I could find no living man left
under my command. Maybe dead, maybe fled. No way to
tell. The Dhojaran forces scuttled back to their camp. There
were still thousands of them out there, too many to get a
true count. We couldn't kill them all, only hope that they'd
run out of ladders.

The citadel said: COMMAND COUNCIL MEETING.

I decided to go and listen to the squawks. I wasn't on
the council, but there weren't many officers left who were.
Weren't many left of anybody, in truth.

There was no fire, no gusto in that room. Nobody boasted of their kills or the performance of their men. Sallow, worn-out faces, confused expressions. There were chairs, a big table. Venzer had the head, the high-ups the chairs, and low-rankers like me stood around the edges.

'Marshal, it is time,' General Jonovech began. 'The Misery swarms with Dhojaran legions. There can be no better moment. Unleash the fire upon them. Activate Nall's Engine.'

'General Jonovech is right,' a colonel put in. 'It is now or never, marshal. Why are we holding back?'

'Crowfoot has his reasons,' Venzer said. 'Do not question me on this.'

'What else are we here for if not to question this fucking madness?' Jonovech said angrily. He was a rank-climber, a wiry and handsome man. 'If half my men haven't deserted by the time I get back to them I'll be astonished. Activate the Engine. The Nameless may have their own ideas, but I for one don't want to die here.'

They dissented. Nobody stood with Venzer. He was a fox beset by three dozen snapping hounds. He couldn't get a word in, such was the yammering, the clamour to save themselves. Couldn't blame them rightly. They didn't know what I knew: that we had no defence. And I'd chosen to defend the walls anyway.

Venzer stopped trying to talk. He grew silent, shrivelled in on himself. I'd never seen so sad a sight in my life. He was the best soldier I knew, a hero, a warrior, a strategic mastermind and just then he was nothing more than a powerless old man, feeling the aches and pains that come with age. I met his eye only briefly, and I was the one that turned away. He must have known this was coming.

'Give me the key.' General Jonovech stood over Venzer, hand out. The officers bayed for it, howling as they sensed their quarry tiring. 'Marshal,' he went on, 'with all of the respect I've had in serving you these past twenty years. Give me the key.'

He wasn't a bad man. He was just doing what he thought was right. Maybe he was right. He'd just relieved Venzer of his command.

'Activate it, then. If you can,' Venzer said. He passed Jonovech the heavy iron key that symbolised control of the Engine. The general straightened up, knowing that he, now, was the man in charge. The rest of them all looked to him. He signalled to a junior officer.

'Get on the communicator to Three-Six. Inform them that I will activate Nall's Engine at midday.' As the lieutenant scampered out, Jonovech looked sadly across to Former Range Marshal Venzer. 'I am sorry, sir,' he said.

'You will be sorrier come nightfall,' Venzer said coldly.

The officers began to discuss their preparations for activating the Engine. I couldn't bear to listen to it. I walked out.

In the office outside I guess the juniors had been listening in. They were grabbing what little there was of worth, throwing it into cloaks-turned-sacks and getting out. I guess they'd intercepted enough communications to have a good idea what Venzer knew. When your own side launches a coup, it's time to run. Everyone runs, in the end.

It was over. I couldn't believe it, but it was over. This war, everything I had known. All things turn to dust when the years have passed, but we never think to see that turning in our own lifetime. The man I'd been before the Range? He was gone, just as Ezabeth had said. No summers last for old men like me. What would I do? Surrender, prostrate myself and wait for the changes to take hold? Would I serve the enemy that I'd fought all those years, a thrall sent to conquer new lands and spread their evil further? I'd sooner have died. Those seemed to be the two options.

I sought out Ezabeth. Didn't explain myself, just took her by her malformed hand and dragged her up the stairs to one of the tavern's spare rooms. Some of the men cheered, thinking I was planning some soon-to-die desperation sex.

'What is it?'

'They just kicked the Iron Goat from his perch,' I said. I'd run some of the way, my face red and sheened with sweat. 'Bastards launched a bloody coup!' I swung a fist at the bed. It was unsatisfyingly springy.

Ezabeth slumped down into a chair. She drew a hand over her eyes.

'Maybe they have to. The marshal will never surrender, never withdraw from the Range. Even if it costs the lives of every man, woman and child.'

'Surrender is not an option.'

'Do we have a choice?' she said, glancing up at me from behind that mask. 'I've tried, spirits know I've tried. But I don't know how to open the Engine's heart. I can't break the wards of the Nameless. Maybe with more time, with the Order's resources, I might have a chance to work it out … But here, today? Nall's Engine is nothing but a lie. Maybe it was always a lie.'

I slumped down on the bed, rested my head in my hands. The air was too heavy, too hot around my eyes, too cold in my throat. I felt sick, depleted, sour. I still didn't have it in me to give up. Not yet.

'I need answers,' I said. 'I need you to help me to get them.'

'I'll do what I can.' Just like that. So assured, so poised, so ready to work. I felt her strength fill some void within me, heavier in my chest than she was in the flesh.

I drew back my sleeve, showed her the raven on my arm. The bird's talons wrapped the blade of a longsword but it was the raven that glowered with threat.

'I need to speak with Crowfoot. Can you summon him?'

Ezabeth reached out, pinched at my forearm. She ran her fingers over the scabbed, worn-out skin.

'Spirits of mercy,' she said. 'Why did he do this to you?'

'A debt I had to pay,' I said. 'I need him now. Can you use it to summon him?'

'This is the magic of the Nameless. It's nothing like a Spinner's. I don't know what I can do.'

'Can you try?'

She thought about it, fingers tracing along the lines of black ink. Just for a moment I lost myself in the gentle touch of her fingers across my arm. She reached down, adjusted a light canister on her belt.

'I can try to burn him out of you,' she said. She hesitated. 'It will hurt.'

I took my belt off, tied it around my arm like I was fitting a tourniquet and she was about to amputate my limb. Maybe she was.

'What do I have to lose, right?' Our eyes met. So much certainty within hers. I almost forgot what we were doing.

Light blazed into my arm. She didn't wait for me to be ready, didn't wait for any signal, just got on with the job. It hurt. A lot. Spun moonlight rushed into my flesh, pulled through the canister to her to me, and somehow though my arm shone white and gold I knew that this light had been spun from Clada's ascendance, blue and cool and soft upon the earth. Nothing soft in it now, not with this intensity. Ezabeth smoked with the light as she forced it into my arm, the energy hissing, and then above it I thought I detected a terrible, bestial snarl.

The raven's head erupted from my flesh, sticky, black and evil as the night, beady eyes swivelling in all directions. The bird tore itself free as Ezabeth was bowled backwards from her chair by an airless thump of energy. She struck the ground and began convulsing, her small body spasming. I was thrown away too, but the great black bird that tore itself from my arm went straight for her. It landed on her chest, wings spread wide, beak as wide as the gates of hell.

'WHO DARES?' it cried in Crowfoot's terrible snarl.

'Lord,' I gasped. The raven swivelled its black head. Birds don't have expressions, but I thought I saw contempt.

'Galharrow?'

'Don't harm her,' I croaked. The air had turned dry, hot as a furnace. My breath burned in my lungs. 'She's the one you sent me after. The one to protect. To get out.'

The bird cocked its head at me, my own blood dripping sticky from its beak, sizzling against the steaming wood of the floor. It flapped its wings out, once, twice.

'What do you want? Don't you have a wall to be standing on?'

'Nall's Engine failed,' I said. 'It failed and we're all dead men. Help us. Please. Please help us.'

'I never took you for a begging worm,' Crowfoot said. The bird barked three chokes of laughter. I bowed my head, felt the hot blood coursing from the rupture in my arm and dripping down over my fingers. A bit of arm-meat decorated the raven's feathers. It pecked it up, swallowed it down. Behind it, Ezabeth's fit had subsided. She rolled over onto her side.

'Have you abandoned us, lord?' I asked.

'Do I answer to you? To anyone? Just do as you're fucking told, Galharrow,' the raven glowered. 'You impudent sot. You interrupt me for this, at this crucial moment? I should destroy you where you stand for your impudence.'

I pushed back with my heels to sit against the wall.

'But you won't,' I said. The air was so hot I had to close my eyes. 'You won't, because you need me for something. You need her for something.'

'You presume to second-guess me?' Crowfoot cawed. 'Do you know why I despise you? You and all your snivelling kind? It's your impudence. The sheer gall. The arrogance. I was old when your grandfather was sucking teats. I have been fighting the Deep Kings before your kind had language to name them. Do you know how long this war has been waged? You can't even imagine.'

'We're all going to die if we don't get help,' I said.

'Ants will be born, ants will die. The colony collapses but the species perseveres,' Crowfoot said. 'Your whole life, every experience you have had or ever will have, is just a gust of wind across the plain. Fleeting, momentary, barely more than a dream and less well remembered.'

The raven turned away from me, shaking its black feathers free of the gore that clung to them. It stalked towards Ezabeth. She sat up.

'Don't you have work to be doing?' it cawed at her.

'My work is done. All it shows,' Ezabeth said slowly, her voice trembling, 'is that Nall's Engine is a lie.'

The raven had already swung its head back to me, its interest in her gone.

'Shavada is coming for you,' Crowfoot said. 'But he won't attack while he believes that Nall's Engine can still harm him. Delay him for as long as you can.'

'Shavada?' I said. My heart froze in my chest, my jaw locked rigid. 'One of the Deep Kings is coming here?'

He didn't answer. As though it had been stuffed with woodchips and left to blow over in a wind, the raven teetered to one side and then lay stock-still. It burst into unenthusiastic flames a couple of moments later, sizzling and popping with greasy smoke. I looked down, saw my arm was greasy with blood but the raven was back in his place, the torn flesh smoothed over. The heat of the room was sucked into that raven's body, leaving a sudden chill in its place. My eyes were drier than Misery sand.

'Are you all right?' Ezabeth said. She'd recovered better than I had. I could only sit and stare into space.

'Shavada is coming,' I said. 'Shavada. Coming here. A Deep King.'

'I know,' she said. 'We have to stop him.'

'We can't,' I whispered. 'We can't stop him. He'll come and he'll take us. Mark us. Turn us into his creatures.'

Ezabeth mopped blood from my arm with a bed sheet. Again she traced her fingers across the raven tattoo.

'You ever think that maybe the Nameless and the Deep Kings are just two sides of a coin? Seems to me one of them already has you marked.'

I couldn't argue with that. She cleaned my arm while I stared off out of a window, watching the bright bronze scars flashing above the Misery. A few thousand soldiers, a weapon that didn't work and one unnaturally powerful Battle Spinner. Not much to throw in the face of a Deep King. A frog would stand a better chance against an otter, a mouse against a lion.

Bad odds.

33

Midday rolled around faster than I'd have liked. The drudge let us be and the blazing red letters across the citadel changed.

NALL'S ENGINE TO FIRE AT NOON

I wondered whether it was wise to advertise it. Decided it didn't matter. At best it would send the drudge into a panic, maybe even make them back off. Not likely. From their current position they couldn't have escaped the kill zone. At worst it would make them throw everything they had at us to try to take the walls before we blasted them all into the hells.

None of it mattered. I didn't care any more. I couldn't find it within me.

Ezabeth watched me from the stairs, her eyes dark above the veil. She clutched a sheaf of ink-smeared pages in one hand. Couldn't read what she was thinking. I'd never been able to read what she was thinking. There was only so much bitterness that I could hold, and I let what I'd felt for her leak out like a slow fart. She'd used me because she'd needed me.

I had no company left, just Nenn and Dantry. I told him to go help his sister – he was more use to us with a pen than a sword. Despite his annoying hair and naivety I knew that I'd be sorry when he got killed. Nenn couldn't be dissuaded from manning the wall and went to join those that still fought. I wondered whether I would ever see her again. As the hour of our defeat approached, entering the heart of the Engine was our only chance. I didn't have a good plan, barely a plan at all. If the Order's best engineers had died in their attempts to breach the seal, what chance did I have?

Any chance was better than none. I set out for the citadel.

The city was silent save for the creaking of shop signs in a wind kicking up from the west. Somewhere a goat brayed, forgotten in its shed. Windows had been boarded up, as though that would stop the drudge from staving them in and taking beds and pans and drapes for their own. Did the drudge care for such things? I guess nobody really knew. They got changed, they became what they became and then they served their masters. I'd always assumed they had no real will of their own, pawns in the grasp of the Kings, like Herono had been. I scratched at my arm. Best not to think about it.

I passed familiar places turned strange. The bath houses, a barber's I had frequented a few years before, half a dozen taverns whose owners would serve my drink without asking, the big weaver's, the small light mill on Time Row. None of them seemed themselves. Bricks, stone, wood and thatch, just bits of the earth. They weren't what they had been. Without people, they were just shapes in mud and stone. Only the citadel retained its true identity, the great iron projector arms hanging out beyond the battlements. At this last dreadful hour, the only thing that stayed true to its character was the one crafted by inhuman hands.

As I approached the citadel, something lay sprawled dead in the road. A man in uniform, gold-trimmed black. He was still, the city was silent, and my heart started pulsing faster in my chest, *thump, thump, thump*. I jogged to the end of the road, knelt. Something had cut him through the chest, ribs sheared through. His eyes stared blankly at the scudding clouds overhead.

Sword in hand, I moved on towards the citadel. The body was the first of many. Civilians and servants dressed warm against the weather in oilskins and fur collars lay scattered like tiles struck from a board. A few lay crumpled with blood still slick on their lips and jaw, others had felt the bite of power more sharply, sliced in two. Half a dozen soldiers lay amidst broken matchlocks and pikes. The tendons in my neck had turned hard as wet rope. Not many things in this world are capable of doing that kind of damage. The orderlies back at the Maud had been cut to pieces by the same power. The Darling was here.

Only one place it could be going.

I entered the citadel's wide courtyard. The gatemen had tried to shut it out, but a hole had been melted through the iron portcullis and the guards had felt the bite of mind-worms. A severed arm floated in a trough; a soldier lay dead against a wall with her matchlock across her legs. I had to hurry. I hadn't any kind of a plan, and when you don't have a plan, killing something is usually a good place to start. I picked up the dead woman's harquebus and checked it over. Primed and ready, but the soldier hadn't got her slow match lit in time to discharge. Bloody useless weapons. I sparked the cord to life, blew it to sizzling and cocked the firing lever. Slow to load, clumsy to aim, I still couldn't argue with the holes they could made in things, though.

Thump, thump, thump beat the drum within my chest. Breath came dry and short, narrow draws of hard air. Sweat on the skin, down the back. My hand wasn't steady on the firing lever.

I didn't need the trail of bodies to follow the Darling's passage, but it had left one for me to follow. The bastard thing was burning power fast. Darlings don't need to charge up like Spinners, but they had their limits all the same. Or at least I thought they did. This one was dispensing his indiscriminately. I entered the citadel, rounded corners, the barrel of my smoking harquebus nosing ahead. A few courtier types, a pair of noble ladies, a junior officer. The last clung to life, bloody bubbles on his lips, terror in his eyes. I left him to his death and hurried down the stairs. A couple of Order engineers lay with their hands around one another's throats, choked the life from each other under the grip of mind-worms. I found another matchlock in the lifeless hands of a soldier, cord smoking but undischarged. I added it to my arsenal.

The soldiers who should have been here were all manning the walls. Jonovech had taken command of the walls but he'd forgotten that the city was never the prize. It was the Engine that mattered and he'd left it defenceless. Stupid, stupid, stupid.

Down, along corridors and through abandoned guard rooms and down again. I descended. Beneath me lay the operating chamber, and beneath that the heart of Nall's Engine.

The soldiers were all off facing the horde in the Misery, but even in times of desperation and war, the Order of Aetherial Engineers had maintained its elite guards at the operating room's door. Blackened steel armour with intricate gold scrollwork, swords with gleaming lion's head pommels, halberds with ornately decorated blades. The pieces of their grandeur lay strewn around the guard chamber. They'd done their duty and died where they stood. The door to the operating room lay open surrounded by shreds of muscle and entrail that told the story of the Order's last failure to protect us.

The Command Council had convened here. They had sought to activate Nall's Engine. They had advertised the fact on the side of the fucking citadel and told the Darling precisely where and when to hit them. Fucking idiocy.

The stench was worse than it had been outside. Thirty men in a cramped room, their insides opened to the musty air. Some, but not many, had drawn their swords. I stepped in amidst the human wreckage, the match cord sending ghosts of smoke into the wretched air. The operating room was silent as the grave, which it had become for our military elite. The panels of dials and levers were splashed red, speckled with lumps of brain and bone. The killings outside had been fast, efficient, single slashes of power to dismember and disable. In here it was different. I could read the glee the Darling had taken as it decimated the poor bastards. A fox let loose inside a coup, and the chickens had panicked and pecked and been torn apart.

I glanced at the faces, the pieces of faces. The officer elite of Valengrad: majors, colonels, brigadiers, the robes of a half-dozen Order engineers amongst them. Some of them had been good men. Some of them had been arseholes. Now they were all just torn meat and bone, clutter for someone else to clean up. I didn't see General Jonovech amongst them, but as I scanned the charnel house my eyes fell onto the largest of the levers. A great black iron arm protruding from the floor, six safeguarding locks around it unclasped. The knob was shaped like a golden hand, reaching out to be taken in a manly grasp. The operating lever that would activate Nall's Engine at every station along the Range. A bloody smear stained the gold hand and I saw with a final disappointment that the lever had been thrown. They'd tried and they'd failed. What terrible knowledge that must have been to hold as the Darling moved in for the kill. The Command Council had been shredded, cleaved and burst apart knowing that all was lost. Life is cruel.

I'd known it was over. It didn't come as any kind of a shock, but seeing something always makes it worse. For a moment I thought the tear ducts were starting to work behind my eyes but I snarled them down and gritted my teeth against it. No time for weakness. Not now, not ever. I had a monstrosity to destroy.

Amidst the devastation, the firearms I carried seemed pitiful things, snowballs against the avalanche. A voice I'd been ignoring said that I should turn back. *Listen to the heat of your skin, the clenched muscles in your neck. Observe that churning in your guts and remember that this isn't your responsibility*, it told me. *Run*, it begged.

I'd been good at ignoring my own best advice for a long time. Only one other archway led from the operating room, a dark stair falling deeper into the cold earth. The Engine's heart lay below.

Thump, thump, thump, said my own.

Not a good idea to go up against a Darling alone, but I was damned if I was going to let it get at the heart of Nall's Engine. It invaded my mind at Station Twelve. It tried to kill Ezabeth, tried to kill me, and even if hope was draining fast, there was still revenge. If I had to, I'd settle for that small victory. If I got lucky I could put a lead ball through its brain. Sometimes that was enough to kill one. Not always, but I had two tries at it.

Wet red footprints guided me. One pair small, one large, together they had pressed on beneath the sputtering light tubes. A series of iron doors had impeded them only briefly. They hung from their hinges or lay in torn and blasted pieces in the cramped corridors beyond. Nall's Engine had been designed to be guarded, protected. I wondered what Nall had envisioned, should this day ever come. Had he imagined corridors packed with soldiers and Battle Spinners? The winding passages and stairs formed choke points, easy for a lone man to defend against limitless opposition. But before he'd left us, Nall had failed to foresee the short-sighted greed of the princes. The great mistake of man is to believe that other men can live up to the ideals that we set them.

I rounded another corner with a sweep of my gun. Nobody there. I'd grown so accustomed to the scattered bodies that their absence made me nervous. Had I reached the end of the trail? Sweat rolled down my brow, stinging into my eyes. I had no spit left, and the great cold lump of leaden fear in my throat was making very reasonable points. Suicide, it said. I knew it was right and still something made me go on. The fight was lost, the battle over. The drudge had won, and Dortmark was part of Dhojara, but somehow I couldn't let it go. Not yet. I'd believe it when I was dead. Maybe not even then. As long as I could still spit I was going to fight. I owed it to Tnota, to Herono, to every man, woman and child who'd given everything before me. In the end we're nothing but the impression we leave behind and I'd rather die screaming and defiant than sink quietly into defeat. And despite everything, I hadn't given up on Ezabeth Tanza.

Not dead yet.

I swept around another corner and they were in front of me, their backs turned. One of them was the Darling that I'd first met at Station Twelve, the same that had chased us from the Maud, the same that had advised torturing me. Someone had shot it in the arm but it didn't seem to care. A small, slight figure alongside General Jonovech. They both were looking at a great round portal, a round door covered with symbols.

'How can you not know how?' the Darling muttered in a voice too wise, too bitter for the body it came from.

'None of us knew,' Jonovech said, voice strained, hoarse.

'There has to be a way to open it,' the Darling said. He gestured, just a flick of the fingers and Jonovech fell to his knees screaming. I saw his face then, the blood running from his nose, the corners of his eyes, his ears. The mind-worms had burrowed deep. He belonged to them completely.

I ducked back around the corner, *thump, thump, thump.* I would only get one shot. If I missed, if I didn't hit him dead centre of the brain then I was going down with all the rest of the Command Council. A shot to the body wouldn't stop it, not even the heart. The Darlings didn't need their organs quite the same way mortals did. Anywhere but the brain and I was going to get split in two like the rest of the poor fuckers back there.

'Lord Shavada demands an answer!' the Darling demanded and Jonovech shrieked in agony. I risked a glance, saw him thrashing around on the floor like a landed trout. Limbs flopped, legs bucked. The general's crescent moon lapel pin fell from his shoulders and rolled across the bare stone tiles. 'I must know!' the Darling barked. 'Tell me!'

The cries subsided. Maybe the Darling had pushed too far.

'A door is just a door, no matter what mysticism the Nameless worked on it,' the Darling said. 'There must be some trick to open it. There must be a sequence.'

The circular door was covered with small discs. Each disc bore some kind of carved image: a sun, a rabbit, a clock. Maybe fifty of them, each a hand span wide.

'What happens if I get the sequence wrong?' the Darling asked. A rhetorical question, revealing its nerves. A locking mechanism this elaborate wasn't likely to ask it politely to depart. The Nameless didn't go for half measures.

Thump, thump, thump in my chest, *drip, drip, drip* down my back. I drew a long breath, checked the match cord was properly aligned. Had to make this count. Had to give it one last shot. Not for Dortmark, or Venzer, or even the countless thousands who were going to get made into drudge. I had to do this because this was my fucking city, my fucking Engine, and the Darling was an invader, a cancer within my walls. I brought the matchlock to my shoulder as I rounded the corner. Aimed low to account for the recoil.

There was a roar as the flashpan ignited, the kickback slamming the stock into my shoulder. A great smoke cloud billowed before me and I could see nothing of what I'd done, the smoke white and heavy in the windless air. I tossed it down, swung the second matchlock up and rushed through, gun up. I'd hit it, shot it right through the face, but its shriek told me it wasn't done. I hadn't done the damage I needed but I had made a hole a palm's breadth wide where the Darling's eyes should have been and it'd fallen back against the wall. It howled in agony. I brought the barrel up at it but suddenly Jonovech hurled himself at me. I swung the gun between us, crashed into the wall. The general was a strong man, a real soldier, and the mind-worms had taken him completely. We wrestled the gun between us and I put my elbow into his face once, twice, rocking his head back on his shoulders. He didn't let go, instead tried to go for his knife. I put a boot in his gut, kicked him back, brought the gun to bear. I hesitated. Only one shot left and Jonovech wasn't the real enemy.

The Darling lashed out blind, an arc of deadly power. Somehow I got out the way as the slashing air carved a line through the stones. It launched a second spell, shrieking in pain and fury. Jonovech staggered, then the top half of his torso collapsed forwards. I'd blown the little bastard's eyes clean away and left it blind and its third attack flashed right through the doorway. Somehow its blinding seemed fitting revenge for what they'd done to Herono. In its frustration the Darling lashed a blast horizontally. I pressed myself down into the stone floor as it threw piercing lines of magic out into the unseen world. My heart pounded far too loud: surely the sorcerer could hear it beating, so loud the drums must be heard across the city walls, *thump, tha-thump, tha-thump*.

The Darling drew heaving, ragged breaths. The young face, too youthful ever to have felt the touch of a razor, had turned a sickly yellow where it wasn't black and red with the wreckage of what had been eyes. Sweat drenched it, rolled in rivers. It sat back against the wall, small legs extended out in front of it. In each ragged breath I heard the pain of its failure.

Of course, if it figured out where I was lying, it'd split me in two in a heartbeat. Slowly, so slowly, I began to reach for the harquebus.

The Darling reached its hands up to the broken bone and blood across its face. It was shivering, whether it was fear or pain or fury that shook it I didn't know. Maybe all. I nearly had my fingers on the gun. He was listening.

'I know you're still there,' it said. 'I should have had you killed when Herono caught you.'

Don't know how it recognised me without any eyes. It wanted me to answer. Wanted to hear where I was so it could send its killing spells.

'You always were a hard man to kill, Galharrow,' it said. Even though its face was ruined, the Darling managed a sneer. 'Too bloody hard by far.' Something familiar in the voice. The way it turned its words. I squinted at that little boy's face. And I realised that I'd seen it before, long before Station Twelve.

I'd known him for years, only he'd been forty years older and fighting on our side.

'Gleck,' I said. The word escaped me without thinking. I realised what I'd done the moment I said it. To my immense surprise the Darling did nothing.

'Nice to be with an old friend,' the child said. 'Haven't a lot of those left any more.'

Time changes us so much. When we age we lose that softness, that childish beauty. They'd found Gleck Maldon and made him one of their creatures.

'No. You don't have any.'

'No, maybe not. I'd say I was sorry if I could still feel sorrow. Nothing personal, of course. It's just how things work out.' He gathered blood from the back of his throat and spat out a sticky wad of it, black and red. Drew back a sleeve, showed me Shavada's glyph marked into his forearm. The left forearm, same as I wore the brand that made me Crowfoot's.

'What happened to you?' I asked. Couldn't help myself.

'Life,' Gleck Maldon said. 'Life and death, I suppose. It's not the time to talk it through, though. Now come on. I need you to help me open this door. I know you've been working with that Spinner. Irony is, if there's one person in this city that knows how to get into this vault, it's probably her. You probably do too.'

'I don't know shit,' I said. I had a very bad feeling.

'Well,' Maldon said, pushing himself further up against the wall. 'We'll see, won't we?'

I knew what that meant. I went for the harquebus, brought it up and made to squeeze the trigger as the coils slammed into my mind. The mind-worms hooked into me, digging into my brain, into my being. I felt Maldon's presence, Maldon and something behind him looming like a great and terrible shadow, a power so great and ancient that it eclipsed concepts of time, of morality, of humanity. They broke into my mind and began to rifle through my memories.

A child picks up his first wooden sword. It feels right in his hand, just a crossed piece of wood with string for a grip but he grins as he swipes at a dog. His mother shakes her head in disappointment, but his father is proud. The kind of son he wants begins to form before him.

A girl, sweet in her sixteen years, lies in a meadow, long grass a collapsed palisade about her and the buzzing of summer insects a song to fill the day. She wears a linen dress and a bright smile, her hair long and dark, her mouth a blaze of joy. She picks the daisies and weaves them to-gether, a wreath to lay upon a suitor's brow.

A young woman stands before him. She's sticky with the blood of the mercenary that tried to rough her up. The commander is supposed to be mad, but he's just impressed. There's something haunted about her eyes, like she's cracked on the inside. The commander is supposed to have her punished but instead he asks her name. She says it's Nenn.

'Get out of my head,' I snarled. Every word forced between my lips was an agony, like driving nails through my own limbs. I vomited. I sobbed.

The mind-worms burrowed deeper. They sought something. I felt myself losing control, felt Maldon consuming me, flowing through my whole body like smoke. He took control of my limbs. The weapon fell from my fingers as he pushed me upright with my own fucking hands. Silently I raged, silently I screamed.

A young man takes his first command, his pride shining brighter than the polished buttons on his uniform. His brother is watching. Marshal Venzer says the people of Dortmark are depending on him.

A cousin arrives to inform him that his wife and children are dead. It is the last time he will see any of his family. The cousin blames him, spits at his feet. Tells him he has no name. He has nothing to say.

He doesn't want to meet her, shuffles anxiously. She's said to be bookish, odd. What use does he have for some dowdy girl with her head bound up in mathematics? He grimaces as the door opens. Count and Countess Tanza are greeted, and then she steps into the room behind them. Breath catches. Muscles lock rigid. He has to remind himself to draw a breath because nothing will be the same again.

Maldon began to hum to himself.

'The night is dark; the night is cold. Only a song could be so bold. Of course. Of course. That's why I left the rhyme for them.'

Maldon stood, turned to the door. He reached out and placed his hands upon the stone surface, feeling across the discs. They were smooth. He spat more gore and then jerked me up onto my feet.

'You must depress the dials that correspond. Firstly, the dial that represents "dark".'

Helplessly I looked across the door. Didn't have any control of my own body now. The sigils were simple but easily recognised. A sun, a fish, a chair. I saw one that resembled a moon, but I figured that was moon rather than dark. At length I found one that seemed to be a town with cross-hatching above it. I reached out and depressed it. The stone key sank half an inch into the face of the door. Maldon hissed out a pent-up breath. He was grinning despite the blood leaking down across his ruined face.

'Good. The second is "cold".'

Within me something stirred, something that had been sleeping. It uncoiled, flexed and stretched.

I found the right key, pressed it in. It sank like the first.

'Careful now,' Maldon said. 'Get one wrong and we'll have to start over. And I'm sure Nall would have laid wards against those without the correct combination. Although there are ...' and he did some kind of calculation '... over fourteen million possiblities.'

Within my chest, Saravor's silver dragon magic had awoken. It sniffed, if a shard of spirit magic can sniff, sensing something was wrong.

'What's this?' Maldon said. His blind face turned towards me. 'What magic is this?'

Get out, Saravor's voice hissed within me, though I knew Maldon heard it. *This one is mine. Get out!*

'I own this body and the mind within it,' Maldon said. 'You will regret it if you find yourself in my way.'

No, Saravor whispered. *It is you who shall regret it.*

And then everything went mad.

34

The silver dragon reared, light gleaming from its smooth, flawless body. The beast glared but there was a savage glee to the set of its fang-filled jaws, the soft golden glow of its eye sockets. Vast wings spread across the world, bat's wings of gleaming liquid metal, rainbow colours struggling for purchase upon the shimmering surface. It bellowed defiance, a roar of pride and indignation. Nobody dared to challenge the great dragon for its property. It reared onto its hind legs, sucked in a great gust of frozen air and belched golden fire. I cowered down in the nothingness, waiting for the blazing heat that would end me.

Twisting black shapes rushed past me to engage the dragon. The mind-worms were long, fat-bodied winding coils of mouldering, rotting darkness. Their many fanged mouths whirred as they swarmed and evaded. They attacked as one, wrapping the dragon in lengths of foulness. Behind them lurked a presence, the shadow of great, dark corruption. The twisting maggots sought to bind the dragon's limbs but it tore free, slashed with mile-long claws, crunched down with jaws stronger than an earthquake, seared them with fire hotter than stars. A jet of flame splashed over me but there was no heat to it, not for me. The worms wrapped tighter, squeezing, constricting and boring with jagged, granite teeth. Blue blood spurted from beneath silver scales, great dark shreds of rotten flesh showered from the pulsing abdomens of Maldon's worms.

Where was I? I wasn't sure. The battle played out silently in front of me, wounds torn open and sealing shut as fast as they were inflicted. The creatures ripped at each other with frantic rage, shredding, gnashing, tearing. On all sides of me lay doors into corridors. I could travel in any direction, walking would take me up as easily as left and right, but there were no directions and there was no up or down either. Just space, space without rules. This wasn't the world. We were all somehow inside my mind, or maybe drawn out into the magic that connected the three of us. Threads of thought passed by like cobwebs drawn on the wind. Bursts of magic sparked and blew apart all around me. If there was pain I couldn't feel it, but then, I didn't seem to have a body either.

The dragon crashed to the non-earth, worms forcing it down. It responded with fire. The vast shadow behind those worms looked on with silent, loathing eyes. Even without true senses, I had the impression of dark tombs, of things dead so long that not even the flies would touch them. Shavada.

I finally understood what Maldon had become. He was a conduit, a vessel through which Shavada could exert his magic, an arm reaching out into the dangers of the world. Saravor could not overcome Maldon alone, not backed as he was by a Deep King. The worms sank their fangs into the jealous drake, ripping away one of its forelegs.

Just as the shadow loomed behind Maldon's worms, so Saravor had backers of his own. Small, grey-faced shapes, a half-dozen of them. They watched like ghosts in my mind, dead expressions on faces too young to know them. Saravor's children? How could they influence this? They were merely his servants. Or so I'd thought.

I'd always imagined that Saravor made slaves of those children. Perhaps it was those children that made a slave of the man.

I hated Saravor. Loathed him with every facet of my

being, in every way I could imagine. But he had to win. I started for a door. It wasn't really a door, just as the sorcerers weren't truly dragons and worms but a way for my brain to make what sense as it could of the magic coursing through me. I passed through the doorway: the battling monsters were gone and I was somewhere else.

Maldon had forced passage into my mind, but that doorway led both ways.

A dark room, not just dim but lightless, utterly black and cold. He has lived his life in pursuit of knowledge of the light, has felt it drawn into his body, has worked it into illusion and fire, into energy and joy. How long has he been down here now? There is no time. It could be years. He does not eat the food they bring him. There may be poison in it. He cannot succumb now, not when he is so close to the answer. He knows that, and so they have trapped him.

He hears the grille drawn back at the door, but whoever has come for him has not brought him the gift he most desires.

'Spinner Maldon,' a woman says. He recognises her voice. Prince Herono. He served under her command in days gone by. He tries to answer but he has not drunk water for days and his tongue will not move in his mouth.

'I wish to help you,' Herono says. 'We can go, but we must go now. I can see you free from the traitors who seek to stop your work. Will you come with me?'

He manages to croak an acceptance. She sparks a phos globe. The soft light is painful to him. It is not the clear light of day, but the deep red glow of Rioque bound in crystal. Herono's thin face watches him through the grate. One eye trembles slightly, bulbous in the socket. She smiles.

I was in Gleck's memories now, rifling them just as he had mine. I controlled nothing of what I saw, felt myself drifting apart in the pull and swell of another man's being. I snapped away and into another memory.

He stands before his classmates, unable to grasp the nuance. He doesn't care for poetry, but they look down on him, sneer at him for his lack of understanding. These ponderings are a rich child's games. What use this torturing of words into soft phrases? The mathematics, the sciences, those are worthwhile. The other boys are doing an impression of him, mocking his accent. It shouldn't hurt, but it does. He looks out of the window, tries to ignore them. Hates them. He sees a pair of bright moons rising slowly over distant forests. For the first time, he sees the blue light of Clada differently. Sees her light spilling down into the world. Almost as though he could reach out and touch it.

I moved on, stumbling. I crashed through a dozen incidents from his life, his childhood, his adolescence. I saw myself in one of them, younger, leaner but with a frightening set to my face I never knew I'd owned. I saw the doxy he'd taken to his bed, saw him kicking a beggar. I saw him lingering at a vegetable stand because he was attracted to the merchant's wife, saw him frantically pouring over mathematical texts and calculations late one night.

I could have become nothing in another man's life, another man's dreams. Through every memory I was aware of the distant thrashing of serpentine grubs, the snapping of reptilian jaws. The shadow was growing stronger, the grey children were pushed back.

He can scarcely think, he's so tired. Weariness, hunger, thirst, all of them have blurred his senses. Dimly he knows that to head into the Misery is foolish but Herono tells him her men will meet them just a short distance away. They have light canisters, she says, enough to keep him safe. He hasn't the strength to draw phos from the moons himself. The promise of those canisters is like offering whisky to a deathbed drunk. With their power he can grow strong, can take vengeance. The marshal betrayed him, imprisoned him, stole his dignity and left him to scrawl in shit in the darkness. This is the only way to lose the pursuit, Herono says. He can trust her.

He sees men ahead. There is something wrong with their faces but his mind isn't working quickly and Herono is so reassuring, tells him not to be afraid. He lets them bind him with chains and ropes, blindfold him, force water into his mouth. He doesn't understand, not until he hears their buzzing tone and realises these are not men. They're the damned drudge. And there's nothing he can do. They take him deeper into the Misery.

I jerked free of Maldon's memories. Doors and pathways shone around me as silvery strings. I could hear the distant shrieking of the dragon, the screeches of the worms, but I tried to ignore them, to focus. I was not alone. Overhead the great presence had turned its eyes upon me. I felt his breath, the foulness of the rot within. The shadow watched me. He had no power here to intervene, I thought, or he wouldn't let me be going this deep. I sensed its hatred of me and knew what I had to do. Knew where I was going, for once in my fucking life.

Deeper into the memory I plunged.

The process is slow. It is not without agony. They string him between posts in the baking sun, let the twisted magic of the Misery enter his body through a thousand small incisions. They pour something down his throat, and hanging between the posts he has no choice but to swallow and choke and gasp as the liquid sears all the way down.

A canvas awning is moved throughout the day. They never leave him in direct moonlight, never give him a chance to spin. They do not fear that he would escape. There are three Darlings in the camp, who look at him with something like envy, or loathing, or maybe both. Such malice in the faces of children. It should not be possible.

The process is not brief. Daily they lengthen the ropes that bind him. His hair falls away, his muscles shrink, somehow the bones in his limbs contract. They are changing him, turning him into one of them. He feels the core of magic within his chest growing, building with every dose of the draught they feed him. But he still has his mind. He begins to believe that there may be hope, that they will gift him these dark powers and he will be able to turn them against his captors. Let them suffer the way he has suffered.

On the tenth day, Shavada comes in person. Maldon can feel his approach from many miles away, can sense the depth of the power that resides within. He thrashes against the bindings, but his body is different now, the puny form he had when he was a boy. It is stronger, more resilient, and it is ageless but it feels foreign, alien, to him. He lives within a constant cycle of youth, the tiny dots that make up his body set into an eternal process of regeneration so that nothing can damage him, no years can claim him. The greatest gift any man could be given. He will live for ever.

Shavada arrives. His presence eats into Maldon's mind, defiling it, polluting it with his intrusion. There is the tiniest of severances and Shavada casts off a flake of his being, his weakest part, a part to live in Maldon's mind. Maldon feels drunkenness taking him, his thoughts becoming wild and wretched, and as that sliver of darkness spreads through his mind like ink in water. He screams as his will is taken from him.

There! That was the moment I needed. I grasped it. That memory, the thread, and I saw its long tail trailing off into the darkness. The shadow stood behind it, shapeless, a blot of darker black against an endless night. Shavada's attention shifted to me, the pivoting of a mountain.

I staggered beneath it. The weight of his gaze alone was enough to crush me down, down into oblivion and nothingness. Crowfoot I had experienced before, but he was merely insane, whereas Shavada's glare was filled with the malice of centuries. It told me that they had come before us, that

328

they owned this world, that we had no right to it. They had suffered at our hands, and they would visit that suffering back upon us, and they would start with me. The ire, the cruelty prickled over me, but nothing more came. Maldon was the conduit: Shavada could not exert his will against me directly.

'Saravor!' I cried out. I clutched the thread of the memory as it began to buck and twist, a line of sparkling rope in my not-hands.

The dragon was down, the mind-worms were wrapped tight around it, their coils locking up crippled, broken limbs as the fang-filled mouths bored into the flesh. The maggots' necks pumped away as they drained the dragon of blue blood, splashing it greedily. Saravor's dragon-head tried to raise, but the long neck was wrapped and coiled, the fire choked from it.

'Saravor, here!' I shouted desperately, but the dragon had fallen and Maldon held the Fixer there, a prisoner along with me, inside my own mind. The dragon gave a low, choked moan. To go up against a Darling had been a colossal display of arrogance.

The shadow looked down on me. Its hatred lifted away. Instead, I saw mockery.

I felt a tug on my non-hand. Around me the six little grey children had clustered. They all wore the same dead expressions, as though they could not understand the world around them. It tugged again, harder. I gave it a shrug. The little child pointed off along the dream-thread of the memory to the cloud of oily blackness. Then it pointed back to itself.

'What?' I asked. The lead child pointed to the darkness again, then back to itself. 'You want that?'

All six children began nodding voraciously. Their blank little faces smiled in unison. 'How can I give it to you?' I asked. The mute children simultaneously shrugged at me.

The shadow overhead had turned its vast attention back to me and the troop of grey orphans. Whatever the hell they were. They wanted the blackness, the shadow wanted them to be gone, the dragon and the worms were nearly done fighting and whatever mad dream I was in, what was left of my mind was having difficulty keeping up. I reached out along the thread, my arm stretching a hundred miles, and grasped hold of the black power.

It was alive and poisonous in my hand. I felt it writhe and twist, felt the cold darkness within. A shred of a Deep King's power, and it was mine. I could take that power and turn it against my enemies. I could become a sorcerer myself, melt stone, cut through men as though they were playthings. Could I turn the tide against the drudge? Could I use the magic against them? *Of course*, the magic whispered to me, *take me and wield me!* It hissed low, sultry, the poisoned voice of an arch temptress. It wanted me, and I wanted it.

Another tug. The children pointed to the magic. They were hungry, greedy for it.

'You want this?' I said. I looked over to the dragon. Coiled and wrapped by blood-fattened grubs though it was, the dragon had a desperate, devouring look in its eyes.

'Yes,' I heard Saravor say, closer than his dragon. 'Yes, yes, give it to me! I will take it from the Darling!'

Shavada's blackness and rage thundered across the long, binding link. My mind shook with the force and distantly I knew that in reality my nose ran with blood, my knees gave out. His anger was vast and terrible. This was something he could not allow.

'This is my debt,' I cried at Saravor. 'This is what I owe you. Take it and get the fuck out of my body.'

The children bobbed up and down excitedly.

'A deal's a deal,' Saravor said. I held out the ball of darkness, and with a snap of his silver fangs he severed it from Maldon.

Shavada's rage blossomed. A tidal wave of purest hatred crashed into me. The grey children vanished, the dragon dissipated into smoke, and the mind-worms detonated into darkness. I heard someone screaming hoarsely, and realised it was me. I blinked and found myself in the dimly flickering light of phos tubes. Jonovech's body lay close by. Maldon lay up against the wall. The slow match from the matchlocks still crept upwards into the still air. I shuddered and retched. Nothing came up, but it hurt my guts all the same.

I quested around in my chest, but Saravor had made his deal and honoured it. The silver dragon was gone. I had no time to think about what I might have done by passing that creature even a taste of a Deep King's power. One thing at a time.

I placed the barrel of the harquebus against Maldon's forehead. What would he be when he awoke? Had taking Shavada's power away been enough to free him of the Deep King's command? Could the bond be broken? My finger trembled on the trigger. Safer for all of us if I put a lead ball through his brain.

That would be the smart thing to do.

I swallowed, sighted along the barrel. In the kid's youthful cheeks and jaw I could make out the vestiges of the friend that he had once been. My best friend, at times. A comrade in arms at others. Didn't I owe him more than a blast of black powder? I looked at the ruin the first matchlock shot had made of his eyes. Clean white bone displayed like porcelain through the slick red gloss.

'Finish me,' Maldon croaked.

'I should,' I said.

'Do it.' I put my finger against the trigger. The smoke from the match cord stung my eyes, bringing tears. I let them roll down my cheeks, gritted my teeth. Shifted the butt of the stock against my shoulder.

'I will,' I said. But I didn't.

'I've nothing to live for,' Maldon said. 'And I've seen too much. I've seen into the black heart of the things that call themselves the Deep Kings. You can't imagine, Galharrow. Can't know how terrible they are. What they will do, if they win. Please. Take the pain away.'

'You can feel the pain?'

'I can now.' He spoke very quietly, his voice just a whisper in the dark tomb. He tried to manage a smile. 'Do you remember the night we bought those bottles of Whitelande Fire and drank them with the brothel girls above Enhaust's shop? A good night, wasn't it?'

'You bedded all five of them,' I said. I smiled, but I didn't move my firearm.

'You wouldn't touch a single one,' he said. He coughed, a hacking, dying sound.

'Better times,' I said.

'Look at me now,' Maldon said. 'This crippled child's body. This ruined life. They took everything from me.'

'I'm sorry,' I said. 'I wasn't there to stop them taking you. I should have been.'

'Not your fault,' he said. 'Now get on and do it.' He shifted himself against the wall, tilted back his head. 'Make it quick.'

'Nall's Engine,' I said. 'We need to activate it. Shavada is coming here.'

'Well, yes,' Maldon said. He tried a smile. 'Why do you think I want you to kill me so much? I won't be his again. He's coming. He knows that the Engine doesn't work.'

'Can we make it work? Is there a way?'

'Songlope's Paradox,' Maldon said with a shrug. 'The power of the Engine takes so much phos that the countermeasure would be too large. I did have a theory, though.'

'Go on.'

'Imagine a hollow ball, but every surface on the inside of the ball is a mirror. The light begins inside the ball and reflects back. It reflects infinitely, in fact, never able to get out unless a hole is made in the mirror. I suspected that the heart of the Engine is exactly that.'

I felt a surge of hope within my chest. It had been absent so long it made me shiver.

'So when the Engine could take no more phos, it wasn't rejecting it because it was broken. It was full. The Engine could be fully charged?'

'Maybe.'

'Then why didn't it work when Jonovech threw the lever?'

'I don't know.' Maldon's little body gave a spasm, limbs trembling. He looked to be trying to avoid having a fit. Hardly surprising with half his face shot away.

'Shavada sent you here to find out?'

'Yes. There's a spy, someone high-ranking in the Order of Aetherial Engineers. He sent word that you were getting closer to figuring it out. That Ezabeth Tanza might be able to activate Nall's Engine after all. Your Nameless have all betrayed you and fled, but the Deep Kings cannot shake their fear of Nall's Engine. Since the Heart of the Void burned the earth, only the Engine has ever managed to hurt them. Philon and Acradius remember that humiliation.'

'A spy?' I muttered. 'We dealt with Herono already.'

'No. Someone else. I don't know who,' he said. 'Does it matter?'

I stepped forward and put the barrel of my weapon against Maldon's forehead. He raised his face towards it, eager. I guess that the things he'd seen, the torture he'd been forced to bear, would make any man crave oblivion. There was no choice really. Not much use for an immortal, sightless child stripped of all his magic.

'I'm sorry, Gleck,' I said.

'Just get on with it.'

Shooting him was the safest option. No real choice there.

It would be the smart thing to do.

35

I staggered from the tunnels beneath the citadel to find the city quiet, the bodies unchanged. I hadn't been down there as long as I thought. I felt a hundred years older. There was blood in my beard.

Not everyone was dead. I got hold of a runner-girl, penned a message to Lindrick.

Tanza and I have new information. Will activate Nall's Engine when the drudge attack.

She was glad to get away from the carnage. We had nothing, of course, but I sure wanted Lindrick to think that we did.

I made my way up through the citadel. The offices were mostly deserted, the guard posts empty. Now and again a looter tried to hide from me, arms loaded with precious books, silverware, candelabras and works of art. Most of the looters wore a uniform, administrators, bookkeepers, even soldiers. Maybe they'd heard the commotion below, seen the bodies in the courtyard and decided this was the time to get out with something of value. Couldn't blame them.

The Iron Goat had decided to go as well, though there was no running for him. His withered, shrunken frame swayed in a cold wind blowing in through the windows. The plush red curtains lay in a heap on the floor. He'd used their hanging cord to form the noose, made a ceiling beam his own gallows. His eyes stared, tongue protruding from his toothless gums. I stood in the doorway, watched his cadaver sway in the wind. Before I'd come to the Range there had been stories of Range Marshal Venzer. A tactician so cunning that the Deep Kings had chased him across the Misery. A living legend, responsible for countless triumphs, a man who made every arrow go further, made every camp fire seem warmer just by sheer force of reputation. I'd have died for that man, and now he slowly swung back and forth in an uncaring wind. Just another body.

Venzer's wide-brimmed red hat had been set out on the table. Around it he'd arrayed those things that meant something to him. His cavalry sword, the bright gold pin of three interlinked moons that told his rank. A heavily worn copy of common love poems. A series of small portraits had been laid out in a row, maybe his family or old friends long since gone to the grave. Though the sword's guard was gilded and the portraits were framed with precious stones, the accumulation of memories were the summation of the man's life. He'd gone to meet the Spirit of Mercy, or else he was on his way down to the hells. Or maybe, as I suspected, he'd become nothing at all, just a swinging sack of dry meat and brittle old bones, too tired and old and sad to continue.

I cut him down and laid him out by the window. Threw the curtains over him as a shroud. Maldon had worked his way through all but one of the Command Council and Venzer had finished the job for him. For several moments I stood in silence, looking through the window. The drudge were gathering themselves for another big attack. This time they had managed to construct some kind of assault towers. The lights on them blinked and winked. Our cannon hadn't the powder left to stop them.

I picked up Venzer's hat and walked numbly into the outer office. One of the communicators was blasting a message at us from Three-Six. I listened to the taps and clicks, tried to follow what it was saying.

Dhojaran forces advancing in huge numbers. Estimate two hundred thousand. Expect assault within two days. No Nameless aiding us. Request urgent activation of Nall's Engine. Dhojaran forces advancing in huge numbers. Estimate two hundred thousand. Expect assault within two days. No Nameless aiding us.

It went on, repeating. A terrified minor squawk sat weeping behind a desk. She would have been pretty if not for the fear and the crying.

'Everyone's abandoned us. What do we do, sir?' She was trembling. 'Who's in charge?'

I thought about it for a moment. Didn't like the answer I found, but fate's a bitch and worse.

'You know how to operate a communicator?' I asked her. She nodded. Spirits, but she wasn't much older than twenty. Too young to die here with us bitter old men.

'Yes, sir,' she said.

'Then get on it. I need to send a message.'

The woman moved to obey as though my instructions were some kind of balm against a wound. She got into the chair, moved the tapping arm into place and looked at me. What to say?

I could say that we were finished. Venzer was dead, the generals were all dead, the colonels and the brigadiers were all dead. Valengrad had lost half its strength and couldn't hold its walls. Nall's Engine was a bitter lie, a false promise from a wizard who had either died or no longer cared. I could tell them to fuck off, that it wasn't our problem any more, that they needed to sort their own world into order. I could tell them that the price of putting one's faith in princes was now clear. I could tell them that I was sorry, or that I wasn't sorry, or that maybe nothing mattered.

I thought of Ezabeth, and how I wished that things had been different between us. I thought about the man I'd been when she'd loved me, all those years ago. I tried to imagine what that young man would have done. The young know better than the experienced. They see things more clearly, understand right from wrong in a way that bitterness won't let you. When that young brigadier led that rout from Adrogorsk he hadn't done it for Dortmark, or for princes or even for the war. He'd done it for his friends. He'd done it for the women and men who stood shoulder to shoulder with him, and even if he'd failed, he'd done his best to get them out of there. He saw the small picture, the one that mattered the most. Somehow I'd forgotten him, managed to get my head up into the sky, in the cracks of unreality over the Misery.

Nenn. Tnota. Ezabeth. Even Dantry was worth trying for.

'Sir?'

'You ready?'

'Yes, sir.' She sat up straight.

I set Venzer's red-brimmed hat on my head. Cleared my throat.

'This is Acting Range Marshal Ryhalt Galharrow. Hold the Range. Hold at all costs. Hold to the last man.'

36

I sent someone to find Ezabeth and Dantry, then gathered what remained of Valengrad's commanders together in a room that wasn't full of the dead. Not a lot to look at. Nobody of real rank. Lieutenants were suddenly promoted to brigadiers, sergeants to captain. They listened to me because I wore Venzer's hat and his collar pin. I didn't have much to say to them other than that we would hold until help arrived. I reassured them that the Grand Prince was on his way with fifty thousand soldiers. They were only petty squawks; they didn't know any better.

I promoted Nenn from private to general. It was absurd, but we lived in absurd times. She wasn't good at counting and couldn't read a lot more than her name, but she was good at kicking the other officers around.

If we hadn't been so deeply fucked, it would have been hilarious.

I sent everyone but Nenn away with orders to hold the walls, fortify them as best they could. They didn't need to hear the truth of the situation.

'We don't have enough men to hold the walls,' Nenn said. 'We got maybe a thousand boys, tops. No arrows, no guns. Red Flight scarpered an hour ago. The Black Drakes stopped to loot the merchant districts before they took off. The Black Swan Grenadiers and some of the better regulars make up the majority that stayed.'

'Spinners?'

'All dead except for the scarred bitch.'

'What if we fall back to the citadel itself? Think we can hold out here longer?'

'I guess we could try,' Nenn said, 'but if we lose the city walls, is there really any point? I know we don't got fifty thousand men coming in to back us up. They can just starve us out if they want. We're the rear guard while smart folks take ship and run like all the hells. Crowfoot has fucked off and the Lady of Waves won't hold her island when there are Deep Kings in Dortmark.'

'Got any better ideas?'

'Send Lady Tanza out with canisters strapped to her and see if she can blow herself up like at Cold's Crater?'

We stared at each other across the office. The pretty communications officer pretended not to sense the hostility between us. This had been simmering away for a while. Nenn's eyes were hard, the kind of look she gave men before she put a dagger in their hearts.

'You have a problem with Tanza? After she saved us, time after time?' I had to stay calm because Nenn was losing control. Stress was getting to her. 'Never saw you speak two words with one another. What exactly is your problem, general?'

Her face was hard. Severe. She wasn't wearing her wooden nose any more. Gave it up when the fighting had got heavy.

'You don't want to know.' Her eyes were hard. She met my stare unflinching.

'Maybe I need to.'

We stared it out. Eventually, Nenn narrowed her eyes and spoke.

'I forgave you for maiming me,' she said quietly. 'Wasn't your fault. Accidents happen. Could have been anyone. Maybe I shouldn't have been so close behind you. Was trying to watch your back.'

339

I nodded. I'd never apologised for it. Shit happens. I knew that I should have apologised.

'But then she appears. She comes along and your wits are gone and you stare at her like she's made of fucking starlight.'

I said nothing. There wasn't anything to say.

'Tnota isn't the best man. He's a first-rate shit some of the time, but he's dying for your new woman. Right now, in that dirty bed he's dying for you, and he's dying for you because of her. There wasn't even no profit for him to make. You asked him for everything and he gave it. And for what? Some half-mad witch he never even spoke to.'

'Tnota knew the risks,' I said. 'He was one of us.'

Hopefully still was. Could have been dead by now. Probably was. I'd mourn him later, if there was a later for any of us.

'I always wanted you to be like the rest of us,' Nenn said. 'You throw yourself down in the mud and you drink and curse and act like you understand us. But you aren't one of us. You aren't *like* us. You were born with silver flowing out of your arse and no matter how we bleed and die for you, you'll always be sitting above us. Looking down. And she's just a fucking reminder that despite everything we've been through together, you'd drop us all six storeys for the approval of your own kind.'

I listened. Sometimes there's a time for just listening. I plucked an old cigar from the ashtray, struck a match. Took a few drags. Nenn glowered at me over the table.

'You're right. You done?' I offered her the cigar.

'I'm done,' Nenn said. She took it. 'At least you can fucking admit it. Marshal.'

'Good. Now let's get on with defending this fucking country. General.'

As we talked over our options, messages came in on the

communicator. She was brave, the woman operating that machine. She bore the brunt of the despair.

Scouts predict Dhojaran assault to commence in two days' time.

Dhojaran army camped three miles beyond Nall's Engines' maximum range.

Banners suggest Philon, Balarus, Nexor. No sign of Crowfoot.

We only had two real options, hold the wall or fall back to the citadel. I had little confidence in our ability to achieve the first. The second was a death sentence.

Otto Lindrick's apprentice, Destran, brought a message from his master. He asked me to go to him urgently, to bring Ezabeth with me. I figured he'd want to see me soon enough. I wondered what the treacherous bastard would say this time. He had to be the traitor Gleck had mentioned. Maldon had killed everyone else.

Only problem was, Lindrick had genuinely helped us out, more than once. It didn't make a brick of sense, but if someone had been reporting Ezabeth's activities back to the Dhojarans it had to be Lindrick.

The drudge had been slow to rise that morning, hadn't sounded their war horns or advanced on the walls. They were waiting for something, and my message to Lindrick was the buffer holding them back. Shavada feared Nall's Engine might work, but he'd get over it eventually when we didn't activate it. I left a message directing Ezabeth and Dantry to meet me at Lindrick's house.

'You haven't legged it with the rest then?' I asked Destran as he led the way.

'No, sir, don't have nowhere to go, sir,' the apprentice said. 'Master Lindrick says the Order must stay. Work at the Engine.'

'You think that's a bad idea?' I asked. He shrugged, the

way that teenagers will. 'What do you think, kid? Think we should surrender?'

'Would that really be the worst idea?' he said.

'You have no idea how bad it would be.'

'If they do win, we'd all become part of their empire, wouldn't we, sir?'

'We would. Best not to think on it.'

Lindrick's house was the only one with phos shining from its windows.

'I found it!' he exclaimed as I entered. He was brimming with excitement, a red glow to his doughy cheeks. 'We can do this, captain. We can do this.'

I tipped my hat back.

'It's Range Marshal, now,' I said. But his words had kicked something in my gut. Something stirring that I somehow had been expecting. It was hope. False hope. He could only be misleading me. 'What did you find?'

'Here.' He passed me a small bundle of papers. 'It's the missing link. The information that Tanza needs. To activate Nall's Engine. This is what will do it.'

It wasn't what I'd expected. I'd imagined he'd want to know about the Engine, about how we could activate it. Instead he brandished paperwork as though it were a sword to cut through the enemy.

'Maldon's papers?' I said. 'Where did you get them?'

'Not Maldon.' Lindrick beamed. 'Nall's originals! I had to translate them, but *we have them*, Galharrow. We have them by the balls now!'

The writing of the Nameless? Not some half-mad deciphering, but the real deal. If we'd had these to begin with, all this could have been avoided. I would have been angry, if I hadn't felt such a sudden urge to live. To survive.

I had to calm myself. Reminded myself that Lindrick wasn't on our side. Maybe he'd been laying false trails and misleading us the whole time. Was that what this was, a lie meant to delay us, deceive us and send us chasing rainbows while Shavada closed in to crush us?

I walked to Lindrick's liquor cabinet, poured myself a much-needed glass of brandy. Long, deep swallows took it all the way down. It was the same dismal, cheap liquor he'd stocked before. Almost like he kept it just for show, something to put the right colour in the decanter. I never should have paid so much attention to booze.

I gasped and staggered forward as the blade entered my back. Crystal decanters shattered into a thousand glittering pieces as I fell into the table, sending it crashing over. I looked up, confused, to see Destran standing terrified with a vegetable knife in his hand. He was a puny little thing, but a blade equalises men. As I drew my sword he turned towards Lindrick, then charged at him. The little engineer tried to put up a defence, all flailing arms and panicked shrieks but it didn't help. The kid stabbed at him over and over, casting red arcs across the wallpaper. The knife got to the artery in his neck. Otto Lindrick went down.

I'd managed to make it to one knee. The pain threatened to absorb all other thoughts. Every movement was an agony. Destran still had to go past me. Couldn't let him. Couldn't let him get away. I got my sword all the way out of its sheath but my whole body felt weak. Had to hold it left-handed. I was between him and the door. The papers were fallen on the floor between us. He couldn't get to them without risking my sword.

'Get out of my way,' Destran said. He was terrified.

'Why you doing this, kid?' I winced. I could feel hot, wet liquid down my back.

'The Deep Kings are gods,' he said, and in his eyes I realised that there lay the madness of religion. He was a sympathiser, a fanatic. They'd sucked him in with the sex and promises.

'Trust me, they aren't any gods that you want,' I told

him. 'Believe me. I've met one. Put that down.'

'Lindrick said that Nall's Engine can be activated.' He didn't seem certain.

It was a strange standoff. Him with his little fruit knife, me with a sword I could barely hold. Things were starting to get dizzy. Had to stay bright. Had to keep him here. He thought about it a moment, the dark light of fanaticism burning in his eyes and I propelled myself at him. He'd misjudged what I was still capable of and I nearly cut him through the face. He jumped back, then realised that he didn't need the door. I staggered to my knees, grabbed at him, caught nothing but dust. Destran had vaulted through the window, disappeared out into Valengrad. The little fucking traitor.

I dragged myself to Lindrick, but it was too late. He stared blankly upwards, an inappropriate smile on his face. I tried to push the edges of his mouth down but couldn't.

Ezabeth and Dantry arrived. She took care of my wound, cauterised it with magic. Whatever she did sent warmth running through my back, repairing the muscles. I'd been lucky. The knife had been small and blunt enough that it hadn't reached anything vital. They fed me cold meat and wine, a pretty good combination for treating wounds. We hadn't the manpower to go after Destran. I had no doubt that he'd be off communicating his treachery to his masters. In a way, he might actually buy us some time.

'Here,' I said, passing them the pages. 'Maybe you can make something of it. Get Nall's Engine working for us.'

Ezabeth looked the papers over, frowned. She and Dantry put their heads together, muttering and conferring while I drank more than I should have.

By Dantry's expression I could tell that something was wrong. He wore the frown of a man who finds every garment in his wardrobe inexplicably turned inside out while he slept. He was utterly baffled.

'What does it say?' I asked. 'Something about a mirror?'

'No,' Ezabeth said finally. 'It's nothing. Useless. Just that same nonsense song.'

I shook my head in disbelief and she passed it to me. It was that same stupid rhyme that Maldon had been trying to use to open the Engine's heart.

'Why would Lindrick think that this would activate the Engine?' I asked. 'He already knew this stuff. It's nothing. Just the same fucking rhyme over and over again.' I leafed through. 'And half these pages are blank.'

'He had nothing for us,' Ezabeth said.

Otto Lindrick's body made a sound like laughter, but it was just gas escaping from his body. Ezabeth knelt down and stroked his head.

'He was a good man,' she said sadly.

'A lot of good people died already,' I said. 'And a lot more are going to. I can get you access into the heart of Nall's Engine. It's why Maldon left the rhyme for you. It's the key to opening the Engine's heart. It's our last chance.'

'It truly opens the heart?' Ezabeth said. Hope, faint as distant starlight grew in her eyes. I saw her resolve draw up, pushing back her shoulders, lifting her chin.

'I think so.'

'I'll go alone,' Ezabeth said. 'Entering the heart could be dangerous.'

'So is staying out of it. Only one of those things leaves us all dead for certain. We all go. At this stage, I'm willing to take any shot we have. One last throw of the dice.'

'Can you be spared from the wall?' Dantry asked.

'Nenn's got charge of it. She'll do what's needed.'

I summoned ten men, left instructions for them to kill anybody who tried to follow us down to the heart. They kept their matchlocks smouldering, their swords close at hand and I figured I better try trusting them. Ezabeth and Dantry followed me as we headed down into the silky luminescence of phos light.

Nall had been careful when he erected this weapon. His Engine could be activated from any of the stations, or at least it formerly could have been, but the heart was buried deep, one hundred feet beneath the fortress. This place was more than just the operating chamber for the greatest weapon the world had ever known: it was almost holy, a shrine to the power that gave us hope.

At the great circular door, I saw that the discs I'd already pressed down had remained depressed. I checked through Lindrick's papers to be sure I had the nonsense rhyme correct and finished off the last ones. It was easy enough. From behind the door came a loud clunk as a lock disengaged, a hiss of steam, sparks of light as the door moved back and then rolled out of our path.

The stairway led onto a short corridor before opening out into a vast underground chamber that stank of iron and rust. The ceiling was domed, a half sphere covered with buttressing stripes of metal. It was filled with battery coils, vast things of decaying red iron, slick with growths of slime and moss. Some of them had the static fuzz of energy about them but just as many were drained. They were plugged into pipes that dived into the floor. I wondered how many tens of thousands of hours the Talents must have laboured to fill these coils with power. Useless power, maybe. We would see.

How long had it been since anyone had entered the heart? I didn't know whether anyone had since its construction. It felt like we strode into a lost world.

Another archway led to another stair and we descended yet deeper into the earth. It was cold, unpleasantly so. My back was feeling strange and fuzzily numb.

Dantry and Ezabeth talked about moon-things that I didn't understand. We came to a vast set of double doors. The lock-wheel had settled into place over decades of immobility. Dantry struggled to turn it, and I had to put my own back into it with him before the mechanism began to grind and screech. It turned. We entered.

The chamber beyond was even larger than the first. The length of a cathedral, tall as a tower, another vast dome with the webbing of steel pipes, iron ropes and bronze wires arcing across the rounded ceiling. Phos lights lit up all along it, casting the whole dank chamber into a muted, half-light glow. This was it: the heart of Nall's Engine.

It was empty save for a small stone basin on a pedestal.

'What the hell?' My voice bounced from the walls of the chamber.

'There's nothing here,' Dantry said and the chamber took his voice and cast it back at him. *Nothing, nothing, nothing.* 'It's empty. It's not even a machine. Not anything. There's nothing.' *Nothing, nothing, nothing.*

'It *was* a lie,' Ezabeth said. Her voice, her strong, beautiful voice broke against the word. 'All just a lie.'

Nothing, nothing, nothing, lie, lie, lie.

I walked out into the centre of the room. The smooth flagstones bore a spider's web of inlaid bronze wires, incredibly intricate. I approached the stone basin. Maybe there was something there, something we hadn't counted on. It looked like the bird baths the cream had in their gardens. No gears, no levers or wheels. Just plain, rough cut stone. Inside there lay a shrivelled little black lump of something that had probably once been organic. Fossilised and ancient, it sat in honour in its little tomb. I poked it about a bit and half of it flaked away into nothing. It was not going to be our salvation.

A few oddments sat around the cavern, but they were all just as strange and useless as that first. A barrel of salt water, black and stagnant. A bowl of crumbled bird skulls. A coffin filled with fine grey dust. I tried searching through each for anything that might be useful, that might be part of some greater design, but they were barely even the sum of their parts. Just a wizard's cast-off junk.

Tanza spoke with Tanza, searched around the edges of the great dome. There was nothing else there. They didn't know what the wires were for. Couldn't see any use for an old stone basin.

Nothing.

We walked around, looking for something, anything, for the better part of an hour. We pushed at the walls, looked for a lever, a button to depress, anything. At length, Dantry rubbed his chilled arms. He looked forlorn, broken. His stupid, fashionable hair was a matted tangle around his shoulders and he looked drained. He'd thrown his last die and not even come up with a one. It had fallen right off the table, exploded into pieces and then been devoured by dogs.

'I'm going back to the wall,' he said. 'This is useless. It was all useless. All for nothing.' He walked away up the stairs, footsteps echoing.

I took out my hip flask. I'd filled it with the best brandy in the citadel, near enough the first thing I'd done after I found myself in charge.

'May I?' Ezabeth held out her good hand for the flask.

'Thought you couldn't abide a drunk?' I said. I handed her the flask anyway.

'What does it matter, now?' she said. She turned away from me to lift her veil and drank. She coughed, sputtered a little. I guess she wasn't used to drinking.

'When did any of it matter?'

'It did,' she said firmly. 'It mattered, and we fought because it mattered. You like to act as though you don't care, Ryhalt Galharrow, but you did. You do. You always have. It's why you're still here.'

'Not really,' I said. 'There was something here that I wanted.'

I took the flask back, rested it on the stone basin.

'No,' she said. This woman who commanded the very light from the sky turned away from my gaze. 'I don't understand you.'

'What is there to understand?'

'You don't understand either.'

'Why don't I explain it?' I said. 'Here we are now. At the end. It didn't work out the way we wanted, and we lost. Fucking sad, but true. So I tell you this: I am in love with you. Maybe I've always been in love with you. Loved you the first time, when we were just children, and never fell out of it. I figure I ought to let you know that, before we all end up gracked and done.'

'What is there to love?' she said, a sob in her voice. 'You don't see me. You don't know the horror that lies beneath the veil. There is nothing of a woman about me. No beauty.'

I walked to her. My hands found her shoulders, turned her towards me. She was so small, and she trembled at my touch. The drudge didn't frighten her, sorcery didn't frighten her, but this did? We humans are so strange, so fragile. I searched for my voice.

'I saw you stand,' I said. 'Saw your courage, back at Twelve. Saw the steel in your will, the power you command. You say there's nothing of woman about you? You aren't some painted vase, delicate and useless. You're a fucking lioness. The strongest damn thing that ever lived. There's nothing of you but woman.'

My arms had encircled her, drawing her into me. She wasn't the only one that was trembling now.

'I'm scarred,' she said, but the protest was weak. A leg was pressing against mine. Her eyes were wide open, meeting mine, and within them, the same longing that I felt.

'I want you,' I said. 'All of you. There may not be long left, but in the time we have, I want you to be mine. I'm already yours.'

Her voice was barely beyond a whisper.

'I've always been yours.'

I reached down to draw away the mask of cloth over her chin. Her hand shot up instinctively, protectively, the fear returning. Tears bloomed there. I took her hand away, drew the veil down. The light had not been kind when it first welled within her. She would have drawn the gaze of every poor disciplined child, the flesh misshapen and too smooth, warped. Scarred and deformed, certainly. For a moment I thought she would withdraw. She shivered and clutched at my clothing, willing herself not to run. We all have our demons. She'd carried these ones within her for a long time.

'I want it to be dark,' she said.

'No,' I said. 'I want to see you. I don't care.'

I silenced a further protest by pressing my mouth against hers. As we connected her reticence vanished and she surged against me. The scarring of her skin and lips felt strange against my face but I'd told the truth. I didn't care. Bodies are just bodies. Mine was ugly and lumped and scraped and reset from a violent life. I was just lucky that I'd never feared it as Ezabeth did her own.

Most of the left side of her body bore the same scarring, the right was just as any other woman's. I drew away her hood, finding her hair long and brown on one side, missing altogether on the other. Her left hand was mangled and misshapen. I didn't care. Her scars were the story of her power, and they were glorious. Our clothes made for poor bedding but as they came away, leaving us stark, cold and pale before one another, I didn't care about that either. We lay down together, and our bodies moved hot and low. I tried to restrain myself, gentle and careful, but when we collapsed sweating and spent, the sounds of our passion still echoed around the dome. We looked at one another, laughed at our own recast sounds. It felt good to laugh at something for once. Wasn't a sound I'd heard in some time.

'I love you,' I said.

'I love you too,' she replied.

I could have stayed there for hours, with her face pressed against my chest, my hand stroking the length of her back, up and down, but time wasn't going to wait on us. Neither were the drudge. We dressed slowly, sheepishly, as though in the putting on of our clothes we were regaining our old reticence, renewing old fears. When it came to her veil, Ezabeth trailed it through her fingers before letting it fall back to the floor. I smiled and nodded. No more masks.

We sat in silence, hardly able to believe that at this moment we'd found something so long denied to us both. Dying now didn't seem fair.

37

My arm burned as if a small sun grew beneath the skin.

'About time he showed up,' I said. The bloody raven wrenched its way out of me and flapped its wings, drops of blood spattering the wires running through the flagstones. It looked from me then to Ezabeth, then flapped awkwardly up onto the stone basin.

'Shavada comes,' it barked.

'He's coming now?'

'Now,' the raven croaked. It was bigger than usual, fuller in the body. More of Crowfoot's power in it, maybe. My blood pattered down onto the basin.

'I need to go. I should lead the defence,' I said. I got up and Ezabeth clutched my fingers in her own.

'No point,' Crowfoot cawed at us. 'Shavada comes.'

We must have been a hundred feet below the ground, but we heard it all the same. The earth shook, dust rained down from the distant ceiling. A distant roll of thunder.

'What was that?' I asked.

'Shavada just tore down a half-mile of wall,' Crowfoot croaked. 'He comes here, to ensure the destruction of the Engine.' The raven cocked its head to one side. 'Philon and Acradius are mobilising to attack Three-Six.'

'Why are you here now?' I asked bitterly. 'You come when it's too late. You abandoned us. We needed your help, all this time. You could have made the difference.'

'Hah! So confident that you know everything, Galharrow. The arrogance of it all! The gall! That's why I like you. Why I chose you for this. Tenacity! That's what mattered. Nall said to use Silpur. He's twice as smart, but hasn't your tenacity to get the job done, though.'

'I haven't achieved anything,' I said, but I'd lost the raven's attention. He cocked his head to one side, listening. Ezabeth was tending to my arm. She cut strips of cloth from her dress, wound them around the gash. It hadn't stopped bleeding and it hurt as much as you'd think having a bird force itself out of your arm would. Crowfoot seemed to have lost interest in us. I wondered what he was doing here now, at the end. I thought of reaching out and breaking the bird's neck, just to annoy him.

'Should we run?' Ezabeth asked. I took her bloody hands in my own. Smiled as gently as I could. She read it in my face. There was to be no running, not this time. There was nowhere to go and no place far enough away to be worth trying to hide. The drudge would spread their plague across Dortmark and then to the countries beyond the sea.

'Why didn't you fight them, lord?' I asked. Crowfoot was silent a few moments, then turned to me.

'What happens when two wizards fight, Galharrow?' the bird asked.

'Someone dies,' I said.

'Wrong!' Crowfoot cawed. 'Wrong! Wrong! Think of that arrogant fool, Cold. Arrogant, like you, Galharrow. It took four of the Deep Kings to bring him down. Defending is easy. Attacking is hard. It would take four Nameless to un-make a single King. Do you think that they simply prostrate themselves and ask to enter the void? Why do you think we design such elaborate weapons to use against them?'

I had nothing to say to that. We'd been lost from the start. The raven nosed around in the basin, mashing the rest of its desiccated contents into dust.

'And you can't make it work again?' I asked.

'The Engine was Nall's work, not mine,' Crowfoot said. He sounded put out. 'You want to know what's truly astonishing about all this? That anyone – anyone at all – believed that Spinners and Talents could generate enough power to drive the weapon. Those battery coils above us hold so much phos they could light every tube in Valengrad for a thousand years. But to activate something as powerful as the Engine? Men and women picking light from the air, sending it here? Sounds ridiculous when you say it out loud, doesn't it?'

'What is it then?' Ezabeth asked. 'What powers it?'

'Think!' Crowfoot barked. The bird stepped from one foot back to the other. 'For a weapon like this to operate, it's not sufficient to have a bunch of coils stored away. You need something far greater. Come on, Spinner. What else generates that much power?'

'There's nothing,' I said. But I was wrong. I could tell by Crowfoot's demeanour, by the glee he was taking in his explanation, that he wanted us to reach the conclusion.

'The death of one of you,' Ezabeth said. 'Destroy a Nameless. Cold's crater. When they killed Cold it blew a hole in the earth a mile across.' Her eyes grew wide. 'And that's why you're here? You're going to sacrifice your own life to power the Engine?'

Crowfoot's avatar burst out laughing. Laughed so hard out that the raven fell over onto his back, black and red wings flapping to either side, kicking his legs into the air. An ugly, cruel sound. He was mid-laugh when another roar echoed from above us. Dust showered down around us, covering the bird with a layer of grit. That cut his laughter short.

'That will be the citadel's outer wall,' he said. 'Try not to get in the way if you hope to survive.'

The ground shook again. A vast, terrible odour filled the

room. It billowed in thick as steam, far fouler than it had been when Herono's eye broke free, more nauseating than in my dream. It was the stench that denoted the absolute absence of life, of joy, of compassion. The poisoned air of selfishness, of lethargy, of greed turned from the abstract to the sensory. An unutterable evil, corruption leaked into the world.

My nose began to bleed. A pressure grew in my head. Ezabeth started to shake. The presence of a Deep King is a powerful thing. Men are not made to face gods.

Shavada entered.

He was not a man, perhaps not a living thing but a dark-ness. Hard to focus on, hard to interpret through human senses. There was a shape of dense shadow, vaguely like a man but towering ten feet tall, broad as an ox. Two fist-sized eyes that were a darker black than deepest night swept the room. A suit of armour, old steel engraved with a life's work of intricate coils and shapes, somehow clanked around the emptiness of the shadow, though no mortal weapon could have harmed the Deep King. A demon, a god, maybe just another wizard. Whatever the hell he was, wherever he had come from, his presence struck me hard as a charging stallion.

I fell to my knees, Ezabeth went down with me in un-intended supplication. The Deep King opened a dark maw to speak, and when his voice came forth it bore all the dark horror of the grave. He spoke with the sound of the deep things that live far below the ocean, hating the world above for the light.

'To think that for so long this is what we have been afraid of.' He stepped into the room, armour clanking about his shadowed nothingness. I'd heard stories, dismissed them as just that. They had done no justice to this monstrosity.

The shadow-creature looked past us, cowering on the ground in terror. The thing that was Shavada didn't even seem to register our presence, life forms so insignificant we were beneath his notice. What did we matter to him? We were little more than lice. He'd just swept away our walls, probably killed hundreds with a flick of his arm. I thought about making a final try. Maybe I could get my sword into that darkness, hit some mystic vital spot. It wasn't like that would kill him, I doubted a thousand swords would stop him. Maybe it was worth it just for the attempt at defiance. I had always wanted to die fighting.

The sympathisers believe that the Deep Kings are gods. Looking at the monstrosity I could believe it well enough. How had we ever thought to stand against this thing? My stomach revolted with nausea at the foulness that clogged the air. Hard to breathe.

Shavada's dark eyes noted the raven flapping over to land on the barrel of salt water across the chamber. He eyed the walls, the floor.

'How can this be it?' Black eyes narrowed in suspicion. 'There's nothing here.'

Shavada looked at the pedestal and covered the ground in a few brief strides, flowing as much as walking. Reaching down, he delicately plucked the fragment of matter from the centre of the basin, held it up. A maggot-white tongue, long as a serpent, reached from his mouth and licked it. The eyes went suddenly wide.

'Songlope,' he said. He sounded amused. 'So this is what they did to you.'

A slow clap sounded from the doorway. A ghost stood there, bloodless but standing corporeal still. Otto Lindrick. His knife wounds were gone, and he looked somehow younger, though he was still chubby and short. Quite un-afraid of the creature that dominated the room. Strolled in like this was his office.

'You,' Shavada growled. 'Where have you been hiding all these years?'

'Oh, here and there. Mostly here.' Lindrick smiled. I'd never liked his smile.

'Hiding?' Shavada gloated. 'Cowering, I suppose. You knew this day would come. Knew that one day your machine would fail you. Have you come now to watch my final victory over your people?'

Realisation clicked slowly into place. I'd been deceived. We'd all been deceived. Lindrick who was not Lindrick gave the shadow demon a patronising smile.

'Not exactly. You see, my beautiful Engine hasn't failed. It simply ran out of power. Songlope's heart wouldn't keep going for ever. But thankfully, that trial is now over. I should thank you.'

'You only ever spoke in riddles,' Shavada said, a dank growl from the darkness. 'Face it, old man. Your time is done. You don't have the strength to destroy me. Not alone.'

'No,' Nall agreed quite easily. 'Not alone. We had quite a difficulty, you see. It was Crowfoot's idea, in the beginning. We needed a heart, but they are rather difficult to come by. None of us liked Songlope very much, and while he was rather reluctant to give it up, I'm afraid that the rest of us removed it from him. Desperate times, you know. It all worked terribly well for a while, but nothing lasts for ever. You can see that for yourself, I think. You're holding it, after all.'

My nose had stopped bleeding. I spat grease and bile and forced myself into a sitting position. I pressed my hands against the sides of my throbbing head.

'Then you have nothing,' Shavada said.

'No, what we had was a problem. We needed another heart. I couldn't possibly have caught any of the Nameless unawares like we did Songlope, but I had a better idea. Invite one of you in. Bring you into Valengrad. Into this very room. To the heart of my Engine.'

'It would take all four of you to break me.'

'Yes,' Nall agreed. 'So it would.'

I'd never thought it possible for a god to show fear. Shavada's shadow hands clenched into many-fingered fists, he growled through his teeth. He scanned around, only now noticing the oddments placed around the room. Salt water, bird bones, grave dust. His eyes grew wide, flared with an amber light, sudden terror driving him to fury.

The stench erupted anew as Shavada threw his power against Nall in a wave. There was nothing to see, but it could be felt. Like a dam bursting open, Shavada tried to smash reality into his own image. Nall countered, the little man suddenly caught in a gale of force.

They appeared around the room as if they had been waiting for this moment. The Lady of the Waves came first, flowing from the salt water, coiling into something that was half woman, half ocean-dwelling thing, spiny and webbed. From the coffin dust rose Shallowgrave, and him I couldn't even see clearly, as if he were nothing more than a trick of the mind, a swirl of disturbance in a tall, vaguely man-like shape, and with him came the screaming of the afterworld. Lastly came Crowfoot, a bent old man with a hunched back and a distended bird's claw in place of his right foot.

Had to hand it to them. It was a trap twenty years in the making. I saw it all now, saw what their machinations had been from the start. Nall must have known his apprentice was a conspirator. Probably knew what had lived in Herono too. The slow drip feed of information, pushing the Tanzas, all to make it clear that the Engine had failed. Pushing fragments of information to Ezabeth, ensuring that every high-ranker in Valengrad was talking about her and her belief that Nall's Engine had broken. Drip, drip, drip the Nameless had fed their lies through Ezabeth, through me, through anyone they could use.

All our efforts. We'd been nothing more than glorified bait.

We hadn't even understood our role. Shavada would never have risked such direct action if he'd believed that we had any ability to activate the Engine. He'd pushed us to the brink and seen us fail. If the cost in lives hadn't been so absurdly high I'd have given a standing ovation. If I'd been able to stand.

A battle between beings of such vast power has no flashes, no bangs. No balls of fire, no rays of light. They were terrible, ancient beings, slow and methodical as they worked. They bound Shavada with their magic, tying his spirit in the aether, his darkness in the flesh. Soon they would slowly start to break through the layer upon layer of his protective wards, picking them apart as scavengers take stones from a ruin. The four Nameless were no less freakish and terrifying than Shavada, and they paid us no more attention than he did. I'd always known we were insignificant to them, but I felt it then more than ever.

Powers hummed in the air all around us. Shavada was frantic, lashing out at each in turn as if probing for weakness. His shadow form hissed and jerked, as if his insides strained to escape their confinement.

He roared and gnashed at them. Shavada was alone, but he was still staggeringly powerful. I saw the Lady of the Waves' image tremble, the water that formed her body rippling. Shallowgrave's fuzziness weakened and for a moment I thought I saw a famine-starved, brown old man looking out from within his living vortex. Crowfoot let out a long, slow breath and they stabilised. Shavada sagged back; he was not done. He would try again.

'You see, Galharrow!' the raven crowed triumphantly. It flapped across the room and landed on my offered arm. 'You see!'

I did see. Thousands of lives had been lost out there. Were still being lost. I thought of Nenn, Dantry and Tnota, wondered if they were dead. All those brave people shattered and broken so the Nameless could have their day. They'd been planning this so for long. What did it matter to them that the ants underfoot were crushed?

Shavada was being unmade. Nothing showy. Just the slow picking apart of his existence, the deliberate, precise extrication of his heart.

'The Engine will destroy the drudge in the Misery,' I said.

'If we're lucky we'll get Acradius and Philon as well!' Crowfoot cawed. He hopped from foot to foot. 'Even if we don't, we've managed to destroy one of them. A Deep King! We've bested one of them, done the impossible!' He was gleeful in his victory.

'Well, you got what you fucking wanted. Too late for the rest of us, though, isn't it? The Engine can't save Valengrad.' I was angry despite myself. 'There must be thousands of drudge in the streets by now. You've sacrificed the city to take out a single King.'

'I don't expect you to see how good a trade that is for us,' Crowfoot said. 'But aren't you the marshal now? Isn't it up to you to save the city?'

'I'm just one man,' I growled.

'Maybe that's all you are. What about her?' Crowfoot said. 'Seems to me the world's greatest supply of phos is sitting directly above your heads. Seems to me Tanza's got some rare talent. Come on, Galharrow, where's that tenacity I mentioned?'

Over on the other side of the room, Crowfoot's human form gave me a sneer and a wink.

Hope. It burns so intensely there's not a brandy to match it as it goes down.

'Better hurry, though,' Crowfoot said. 'The drudge are coming. They'll stop you if they can.'

Ezabeth and I shared a look. The raven flapped into the air laughing as we crawled for the door.

38

I led the way, blade held ahead of the charge. It wasn't far to the vast chamber where the battery coils were lined up, row after row of greenish metal. The air in the room was taut with static charge, the energy stored in those copper coils and iron drums eager to discharge. It was here, the phos of eighty years of Talents and mills spinning away, and it was pure and ready to be used.

'Can you do it?' I asked breathless. 'Can you save us?'

'I don't know,' Ezabeth said. 'This isn't the Engine. Look at it all. It's just a bluff, a glorious bluff. Spirits of wisdom, this has been their intention for a century.'

'The Nameless are the masters of lies,' I said. I could smell my own anger, sour sweat and bitter bile in my throat. I went to the doorway and listened. Nothing yet. The drudge must have been in the city, following their master, but I couldn't hear them. They didn't know where to look, I reminded myself. Not one of them had been in this place before. I doubted their spies were going to wait around to greet them.

Ezabeth was moving from coil to coil, running her gloved hands across them.

'Can you do it?' I asked again.

'Give me time,' she said. 'I don't know. All this power, all this energy. So much of it. Maybe.'

I told her I'd be back and ventured back up to the ruin of the operating chamber. The gold-capped lever, the dials and the meters, the wheels and gears. I wondered if any of them were connected at all. Nall had made his Engine so complex that not even those who maintained it had truly understood how it worked. A shield against spies making their way into the Order. As for Songlope's Paradox, they'd not only murdered its creator but outlawed its study. It was clear enough now why.

I stepped beyond the operating room and found the remains of the Order's elite guards. They had the weaponry I wanted. Badly fitting armour was still better than no armour, and I sifted through enough of the blood-drenched steel until I had an undamaged breastplate, an open-faced helm and gauntlets. Half armour is like a whore's dress: just enough there to cover the vitals without getting in the way of business. Most of the soldiers' weapons had been broken in Maldon's attack, but an ornamental shield hung on the wall. It would have been a common sight on a battlefield a few hundred years ago, and though an artist had spent weeks painting a beautiful scene of birds crossing between towers across its face, I was more interested in its ability to keep me alive. Good shields are heavy things and I liked its weight. I slung the shield strap over my head and gathered what little else I could. The sword I was wearing was the same that I'd taken from the wall in Station Twelve. I tried the edge with my finger. Still not very sharp.

Sharp enough.

I heard a noise from somewhere up the stairs. Didn't take more than a few seconds to identify it as the buzzing hum of the drudge language, the clatter of their weapons, the clank of harness. I hurried back down into the dark depths. The drudge had swarmed the city, were into the citadel. Not for the first time I wondered where Nenn was, if Tnota lived. I should have been with them for the end. Nothing I could do about that now except send as many drudge down to the hells as I could. I was aiming for at least two.

Ezabeth was standing very quietly in the centre of the power-room. Her scarred, too-smooth, twisted, beautiful face was wet with tears.

'Anything?'

She looked up at me. Blinked away the tears.

'I can do something. I don't know if it will be enough.'

'Anything's better than nothing,' I said.

She ran to me and put her arms around me. Despite what we'd shared, I was taken aback, unused to such intimacy. I circled her with my arms and held her against the cold steel of my breastplate. It couldn't have been comfortable, but it was all there was time for. She was trembling.

'They're coming,' I said. It didn't help. Ezabeth stepped back, wiped a hand across her face.

'Do you remember, back when we were children, the day that I took a fall from my horse?'

'I remember. You hurt your leg.'

'I tore my dress and skinned my knee,' she said with a wry smile. 'My leg was fine. I just wanted you to help me walk. It let me hold onto you.'

'I remember. I was glad you fell. It let me hold you too.'

'Thank you,' she said. 'For holding me again.'

I could hear the drudge coming now. Their buzzing echoed down the corridor. Somewhere below us their god was being dissected, his heart cut from the shadows of his chest. The Nameless would swat aside any drudge that got down to them, but up here we were very much in their path.

'I need you to do something for me,' Ezabeth said. 'There is something that might work. But I need you to keep them away while I do it. Can you do that?'

I straightened up, rolled my shoulders, clicked my neck. I nodded. That had never been in question.

She walked me across to the entrance of the battery chamber and stood me on the outside.

'They mustn't enter,' she said. 'Keep them out.'

'What are you going to do?'

'What I did at Station Twelve.'

She'd pulled it off then with just the power of a station. This was the entire might of Dortmark's mills at her disposal. There was enough power here to level the world. But I thought too of the station commander's blackened, smoking corpse. Ezabeth had funnelled the backlash of that light into him so that it wouldn't consume her and he'd been annihilated. I frowned.

'Goodbye, Ryhalt. I love you.'

'What—?'

Ezabeth pressed a panel on the wall and the door shut. I struck at the panel on my side, hammered at it but the door sealed her away from me. A half-foot of solid oak.

'No,' I said. 'Don't do it! Don't do it, Ezabeth!' I was yelling. I stopped shouting words, my cry becoming nothing more than a wordless scream of pain. Of rage. Of unfairness. 'Don't do it!' I shouted. I kicked at the door, once, twice. To come this far only to lose so much. It wasn't right. It wasn't just.

I spun around at a noise. Down the corridor, drudge in blackened steel armour were descending the stairs. They were broad-shouldered, arms thick with heavy muscle and flab, noseless faces and clammy grey skin proclaiming that these were the oldest, the most changed creatures of the Dhojaran Empire. The leader had bands of red across his armour, the streamers of prayer cloth around his arms and legs dyed the same colour. Yellow eyes regarded me.

'You. Move. Out. Way.' Its voice was distended, the warped larynx struggling with our speech.

'How about you fuck right off instead,' I suggested.

'God. Is. Below.'

'Not for long.'

The drudge's blank expression contorted into one of rage,

364

revealing a dual row of spiny teeth. It drew a sword, curved as a crescent moon, gripped the long hilt with both hands and came to end me.

Some men are born to charm ladies and spread their irresponsible seed across the land. Some exist to create the great works of art that inspire dreams and drive creativity for generations. Others are born to till the fields, put bread on the table, and raise their sons to till the fields, put bread on the table, raise sons of their own.

I was born to end lives.

I brought both sword and shield up to meet the slashing blow. As I bound his blade down with the shield my sword doubled around my head, cutting hard from my right. The drudge's helm covered only the dome of his elongated skull and his head exploded like a melon, the top cut clean away. The body clanged down with a satisfying deadness. Little good his prayer strips had done him.

The drudge behind him stared at their fallen leader. Had I just ended a captain, a general? They didn't contemplate it long, and then they too came to meet their deaths. The first led with his foot, arms cocked back and a simple lunge put my sword point through his face. He swiped down even so but the shield took his hammer easily. I threw him back into the path of the next drudge, spewing blood from his agonised face. A sword sliced the air in front of me once, twice. I made a cut out of distance to draw the next one in then knocked his thrust aside and struck his leg. I misjudged it, my sword struck armour but his lumbering drudge body wasn't fast and I burst inside his guard, my sword finding a way up beneath his chin. Another one dead. Killing two had been unambitious. This was my place in the world, my reason to live. I would be lying if I said the slaughter did not hold a passion for me.

The light tubes glowed more intensely. Behind me, beyond that portal a humming sound had begun. I bellowed my anger, my rage at the unfairness of it all. The drudge cowered, thinking I challenged them. They looked from me to the groaning, bleeding bodies in front of me. They hated us, but they didn't run eagerly to their deaths.

'Come on, you fuckers!' I taunted them. Tears stung my eyes. Ezabeth's magic was lighting the place up bright as day and it was unnerving them. The humming intensified.

'She's doing it!' Somehow that fucking raven had joined me. He flapped down onto the only drudge that had actually died from its wounds, pecked at an eye. The warriors in the corridor were packed in thick. A whole legion of them were cramming in to find and protect their lord.

'Shouldn't you be ripping the heart from their god?' I growled.

The raven laughed, started jabbing at the drudge's second eye. The other two that I'd maimed were trying to crawl away. I stepped forwards and struck one across the back of the neck. He lived through that, somehow.

'Some help, maybe?' I asked the raven, but he didn't seem to care. Probably needed to focus all his power against Shavada below.

Two drudge tried to come at me together. They had spears, but while the spear is the king of weapons, there wasn't so much they could do with them in the narrow corridor. They tried jabbing at me but I crouched low and my borrowed shield kept them at bay. The towers and birds had been scratched to shit, the priceless artwork lost to war.

No way that I could attack the spearmen except with bad language. The drudge packed up closer behind them, urging them forward, goading them on to escape the building crush. One of the spear-wielders stumbled as he was pushed across a body and I took the moment. I split his head clean through the centre, the sword hacking through his leather cap and splitting his skull like nothing before the hate that coursed through me, hotter than boiling lead. His friend slammed his spear into my shield but was caught in the shower of blood from the exploding head and as he tried to blink it away my rage dealt him a similar fate. I watched them die through a veil of bitter tears.

Breathing hard I staggered back. Fighting will exhaust you like no other work. My shield arm ached, my sword hand burned. Sweat poured down my face, stinging, into my eyes. I didn't see the arrow coming from the corridor, didn't realise what had happened until it fell away from my breastplate, the point blunted. A second arrow hummed into my shield. The drudge language buzzed in the air, the raven cawed his approval of the bloodshed and the humming of the light grew louder in my ears.

An axeman came for me. He died. A swordsman came for me. He died too. I was screaming my hate, my pain, my anger. I fought. I cut and I hewed at them, felt my head ring as a scything blade slashed across my helmet. Felt my arm jolt as I cut through a spine. I stood before a growing mound of corpses, my shield a battered, dented plate on my arm, my sword nocked and notched. Blood ran down my arm. I hadn't noticed the wound when I took it. It didn't matter. I was a god of death, the lord of destruction. The drudge could keep their gods. I was the only one needed: Death, The Long End.

A spear punched into my thigh. I cut back, claimed a few fingers. The spearman scampered away as I fell to one knee. No good! Couldn't fight from the ground. Rose again, found a big drudge taking the spearman's place, a two-handed war sword in her oversized hands and red mottling on her yellow face. She swung down on my shield and a strap broke. Weariness had found my arms and she parried my counter-strike. When she sliced at me it was only my breastplate that kept me alive. I staggered back, shaking the remnants of the shield from my arm and try-ing to menace the encroaching warriors with my sword. I saw then that the point had broken away. When had that happened? Everything was growing difficult to understand. The pain in my leg seemed distant, but then it buckled on me and I sprawled backwards onto my arse.

The drudge loomed over me, the red markings across her flat face looking like the spray of my blood that was about to decorate it. I tried one last slash but she swatted the sword to the ground, stepped on it.

The light tubes flared, far beyond their ordinary intensity. The drudge was startled. She glanced upwards as the humming stopped. Then nothing, silence. She looked down at me as I struggled with the sword beneath her foot, but she raised her war sword in two hands, ready to take my head off.

Power leapt from the tubes above, a crackle of yellow lightning. It struck the big drudge for a moment, her body spasming and then with a crunch she exploded. The drudge behind stared dumbly for a moment and then it too was struck by the lightning. The next followed, then the one behind. Along the corridor, drudge after drudge was blasted into pieces. There was no sound, just the stench of hot intestines and shit and metal.

In seconds the corridor was clear and the light faded back to dimness. Shrieks of terror rang from the stairway beyond, the popping of bodies as Ezabeth blew them to pieces. The light in the tubes started to dim. My leg was bleeding a lot. It started to hurt. I didn't need to cut bandage cloth, instead I used a strip of prayer cloth I found on a detached arm. I bound my leg up as tight as I was able to. Did the same for my arm. The end of my nose had got nicked somehow, but it wasn't too bad a cut and I hadn't been pretty to begin with.

Everything became very quiet. Silent. The light tubes grew dimmer still.

One of the drudge had been carrying a heavy axe. I was

tired, beyond tired and my limbs were lead. Didn't matter. I put the axe to work against the door. It took longer than expected, but then I didn't have a lot of strength left to use and the door had been made to be strong. When I finally got through I saw the inside was charred black with soot. Any remaining hopes I'd had were lost then. Hopes for Ezabeth, hopes for me, for us. I'd told myself that she'd survive it, that she could unleash all that power and Songlope's backlash wouldn't turn her to ash.

There was nothing left of Ezabeth Tanza. Nothing at all. The charge from the air was gone inside the coil room, the batteries were piles of half-melted, fused and twisted metal. The drums had imploded, become crumpled wrecks. Of my Ezabeth there was no sign. Not even a charred set of bones to mark her passing. I would have nothing of her to bury.

Outside, she'd killed drudge in their thousands. Blown them to pieces. I limped out into a silent city, a city of corpses and body parts. A cold rain had started to fall and I leaned against the citadel's gates, looked out towards the Misery's broken bronze sky. The sky was howling her song, a song of sorrow and defilement. The moons were slung low, a lazy line of gold, blue and scarlet beyond the ruddy-tinged clouds.

Above the citadel, the arms of the great projector slowly began to move. I watched them as Nall's Engine began to arm itself. The Nameless had done their work, they had the heart they needed. I shook my head, limped back into the fortress. I couldn't be bothered to watch any more killing.

39

'They're coming! They're coming!'

Children get so excited by change. It didn't matter that they'd seen its like before. To a ten-year-old, the world is still new and magical enough that anything will lift their spirits.

'You going to come see?' the youngest asked me. I don't know where they'd come from. Somehow the Bell had become a home to orphans and those simply abandoned when the walls went down. Most of them didn't know if their parents had fled west when the drudge swarmed the city, if they lay crushed beneath tons of rubble or if they'd died with a sword in their hand. It didn't matter anyway. One kind of gone is much the same as another.

'I think I'm better off just resting here,' I said. The kids looked disappointed. Spirits know why they liked to pester and bother me so. Maybe just because with my leg bandaged and propped up on a chair I wasn't able to swat at them or avoid their incessant chattering. 'Why don't you go and see them arrive for me, and then you can tell me all about it?' They didn't quite seem convinced. 'I expect they'll bring food with them,' I said. We were all hungry. That got them moving.

'We'll bring you something back!' they called, but they'd forget, because they were just children.

'Might be worth the trip,' Tnota said. He swayed as he

walked, not yet used to the new balance his body demanded. He placed a brimming jug of best quality ale down on the table with difficulty. The tavern's owner was gone, and we'd more or less moved in. There weren't many adults left in Valengrad to drink, not that we were stopping the children who chose to tap the barrels. As long as they left the good barrels alone, anyway.

'I've seen enough of princes to last me the rest of my lifetime. About fucking time the Grand Prince made an appearance. I hope Nenn spits in his eye.'

'Knowing her, she probably will. Poor Nenn. Big Dog says they ain't going to like her.'

'Nobody likes Nenn at first,' I said. 'But she's still a General of the Range, and she led the last defence. Your Big Dog hasn't been so hot on his predictions lately.'

'Can't expect him to be perfect. He's a dog.' Tnota grinned. He moved his lips as if to drink, then realised he hadn't lifted his cup. Using his phantom arm again. The surgeon had done a good enough job at cauterising and stitching it up at the shoulder, but my navigator was still having to get used to its loss. I'd not believed he would pull through. They breed them more resilient than rats in the south. 'Think they'll let her keep the job?'

'They can't take it away. Wartime promotions stand. Someone even filled in the paperwork and put it up in Venzer's office.'

We drank a while. Ten days since the battle for Valengrad had passed. I'd been obliterated drunk pretty much constantly since. In reality, the only thing that had changed was that we weren't paying for it any more. The kids mostly did the serving and cleaned us up when we passed out. They were good like that.

The orphans had been building their own little world in the ruins their parents had left them. They found and cared for the blind, the ones who'd stared when Nall's Engine smashed its judgement down upon the Misery. Most people had looked away, but those too terrified or stupid to turn their heads had lost their sight. We had a few of them in the tavern with us. An old woman with a bent back came by twice a day to ensure we were taking care of them and taught them to knit. We had quite the little production line going.

The door opened and Dantry entered. He crossed to the bar, poured himself wine. Came to sit.

'How's the arm?' he asked Tnota.

'Still gone.'

'And your leg, captain?'

'Doesn't look great,' I said. 'Inflamed. Could be infected beneath the scar. Could go either way.'

He nodded. At least the spear had missed the bone. If the infection was set in deep, then either my body would fight it off or my flesh would blacken and I'd die. I was a gambling man, and I didn't fancy betting on the outcome. Only thing to do was leave it propped on a chair and not think about it.

'Anything new out there?' Tnota asked.

Dantry drained his wine glass, refilled it, took half of that down as well. Shook his head.

'They have a name for it now,' he said. There'd been a haunted look about him ever since the first sighting. '"The Bright Lady".'

'No use chasing ghosts,' I said. Tried to soften my voice. I knew how he felt. I didn't feel any better.

'General Nenn is going to greet the Grand Prince?' Dantry asked. He didn't want to talk about where he'd been. Every rumour, every whisper of the Bright Shade and he went racing off. If my leg hadn't hurt like blue fuck, maybe I'd have gone too. In a way I was glad it was keeping me immobile.

'Him and his twenty thousand soldiers. Valengrad's about to get busy again. I liked it quiet.'

'You should be there. This was your victory as much as hers.'

'Let her have it,' I said. 'I didn't want to be marshal any more than I wanted a spear through the leg. She'll have to do some bowing and scraping, then she'll have to think about money and beans and building walls. I'm too old for all that.'

I could have gone before the Grand Prince. It had been my order to hold Three-Six after all. There would have been gold, fine uniforms, women, maybe even a progress through the states. I could have looked at my long lost family and spat on them as they bowed. But we had quite a lot of ale and brandy at The Bell and nobody was charging for it, and there wasn't really anything else I was interested in. No use for money, no use for women. I'd had both in my life and neither had brought me anything other than pain. Well, that wasn't quite true. In those last hours I'd found something I never thought I'd find again. That only made me all the angrier, all the surer that the bottle was a better resting place than any other.

Dantry looked harrowed, old. His hair had been singed and his nose had been broken and reset with a kink. He'd lost the softness from his cheeks, the youth from his eyes. The lively young man was gone. Tnota's hair was coming through grey and he hadn't fucked anyone since his arm had been taken. We were all of us changed in ways I'd not expected. I told myself that I hadn't, that I was going to shrug this all away too. One more bottle, one more song.

'I'm going to get some air. Don't let anyone take over our inn while I'm gone.'

I took my crutch and limped off into the daylight. It had stopped raining at least, but the Misery was howling her song. She'd grown louder since Nall's Engine had enacted the terrible vengeance of the Nameless.

I limped to what remained of the walls. Some parts of the

city had burned. Some buildings had been torn down to pack the holes the Darlings had made in the wall. Everywhere the light tubes were shattered and burst. Ezabeth had used them like a network of veins, her lightning the medicine to burn away a fever. Bits and pieces of rotting drudge meat lay ignored in the gutters. Scavengers had mostly stripped them of arms and armour. You could always trust the Spills to send out its legion of picking beetles, ready to turn a profit from some other bastard's destruction. The surviving three hundred men under Nenn's command had done a good job lumping corpses into the canals. As a result, the canals weren't exactly operable any more, but at least there wasn't plague in the streets.

Shavada hadn't just poked a hole to walk through. He'd destroyed a vast swathe of stone. There were probably a lot of bodies underneath the ruins, but Nenn hadn't the manpower to dig them out. She was doing a good job of keeping order, but then there weren't a lot of people left needing to be kept in line.

I couldn't face the stairs up the wall and instead sat on a huge block of cracked masonry in the gap, rested my crutch across my knees and looked out. The twisted land of the Misery was full of great new craters, scorched and blasted where the Engine had done its work. Nothing of the drudge remained out there.

I touched my fingers to my nose. A few drops of blood leaked across my skin.

'You don't look like a man who won.'

I wiped the blood away. Otto Lindrick – or the simulacrum that had called itself such – stepped through the rubble to take a seat alongside me.

'Do we look like we're in a city that did?'

Nall smiled. I'd never liked his smile. There'd always been something about it that set me on edge. He was in a different body, one devoid of the knife wounds his apprentice had put into it. I wondered whether he was conscious in that body alone or whether there were many iterations of him around the world, each slowly winding up the threads of his plans.

'The city is still standing,' he said.

'No thanks to you.'

'I hardly think that's fair,' Nall said with a dry chuckle. 'It was my Engine that dealt with all those legions up at Three-Six. Philon and Acradius took direct hits as well, although I don't think we've seen the last of them. Not so Shavada, though. We unpicked him right out of reality. I know, from your little point of view on the ground it doesn't always feel like a victory, but it's the big picture that we above have to look at.'

'"We above",' I said. 'I guess that's how you'd see it.'

'And so we do,' Nall agreed. 'Crowfoot wanted me to stop by. To say that you did well.'

'He decided not to come in person?'

'Crowfoot has gone to lead a campaign far to the east of here,' Nall said. 'Well beyond the Misery, beyond Dhojara. There are other nations at war with the Deep Kings and their empire, Galharrow. The Range has only ever been one front, a single battle line amongst many.'

'He needn't have bothered,' I said. I felt the bitterness welling, deep within. A well of darkness and bile. 'I didn't do it for you, or any of your plans. Not even for Dortmark.'

'You did it for her,' Nall said. 'Of course. We knew that when Crowfoot first sent you to her. We knew that you'd protect her better than anyone else. She was very important to the plan.'

'She was a pawn. She was bait. You used her.'

'Of course. But a pawn that rose to be a queen. You must understand, Galharrow, Shavada would never have dared cross the Misery if he'd believed that there was a chance my weapon could have struck at him. Acradius was barely within range and we dealt him a terrible blow. Would you

375

feel less sour if you'd known the plan at the time? Do you think you could have been more convincing? Do you think Ezabeth Tanza would have proven the impossibility of the Engine to all of Valengrad's commanders if she'd been aware it was all a hoax?'

He chuckled to himself. He was right, of course, but that only made me want to hit him.

'The ends justify the means, do they?'

'Come now,' Nall said. 'You know they do. They always have. My poor apprentice, Destran? I knew his mind had been poisoned by the cultists before I took him. For five years I had to play the role of an accountant, to ensure the illusion was solid for him. You have no idea how tedious it was.'

'My soul weeps for you,' I said. 'I get it. I understand. I can't like it. It's war and I grasp that. We just paid too high a price.'

'We? Or you?'

'Does it make a difference?'

'One allows you to weep for the world. The other means you feel sorry for yourself.'

I couldn't argue with that either. The worst thing about the Nameless, worse than the nosebleeds and the headaches and the raven in my arm and the demands for servitude, is that, ultimately, they really do know more about everything than we do.

'So what now?' I asked. 'The Lady of the Waves went back to Pyre. What happened to Shallowgrave?'

'Most of the time, not even we know where he is or what he's doing,' Nall said. 'Or what he is. It's like that with our kind. We bind ourselves to something so powerfully that we lose distinction. Speaking of which, have you by chance seen this "Bright Lady" they speak about?'

'No.'

I'd avoided hearing about it as much as I could. Dantry

was the one racing off at every mention, every sighting. Like I'd told him, chasing ghosts didn't do so much good. The Bright Lady had appeared like some kind of glowing spirit here and there around the city ever since the Engine smashed the Dhojarans.

'Maybe you should try to catch a glimpse.'

'To prove what? That the Misery is now bleeding into the city? That maybe your weapon did something worse than any of us imagined? Magic started all of this. I've yet to see it do anything that I consider worthwhile.'

'Oh, the Bright Lady is no doing of mine. She created herself, in a sense. You know the paradox, Galharrow. Songlope wasn't wrong. Imagine taking all that light, using it all at once. You didn't wonder about the backlash? Where all that misspent energy would go?'

'She died,' I said bitterly. 'And I don't want to talk about it.'

'Death is swift,' Nall said. 'But that much power has to go somewhere, and a single woman's fragile little body can hardly be said to be a fair trade. Of course, if she'd taken it with her ...'

'Whatever that shade is, it's not Ezabeth.'

'No,' Nall agreed. 'I'd say that whatever it is, it doesn't have a name. Not any more.'

He winked at me. The implication drifted between us. He wanted me to ask. The question burned on my tongue, but I knew he wouldn't tell me anyway. I let it die behind my lips.

'I have to be going,' Nall said. He glanced down. 'Your leg doesn't smell so good. I'd get it looked at if I were you.'

The Nameless walked away into the city. I looked out at the bruised bronze sky, listened to her dismal howling. Only one low-slung blue moon looked back at me. Away to the west a fanfare of trumpets had started up, heralding the arrival of the Grand Prince. He'd probably been expecting the streets lined with people to welcome him, as though his late arrival somehow made up for his failures. He'd find Nenn chewing blacksap and little more. That thought at least brought a smile to my face.

Thousands were dead. Thousands more orphaned. The city was in ruins, the canals clogged with carrion and even if we'd won for now, it was only a temporary respite. I'd seen the great evil of the Deep Kings, seen what they truly were. They couldn't let such a defeat rest. They would return.

Of course, they'd have to go up against me again. They were as close to gods as a man would ever meet in the flesh, but they weren't just up against wizards. They were against the iron-hard Venzers, the steel-willed Nenns, the Tnotas, the Tanzas. They were up against swords and walls and powder and magic, and above them all, the howling of the sky.

Bad odds.

Acknowledgements

This book is for Clare, because she is the best one. However, to see my own fantasy novel in print is the fulfilment of my life's ambition and significant thanks are also well deserved by:

Kitty Morgan, without whose feedback and advice you'd be holding a very different book.

Ben Morgan, my first and most enthusiastic reader.

Greg McDonald, whose advice proves invaluable both within the both and outside it.

Andrew Stater, the only other adventurer in a small English town. We may not roll for critical hits anymore, but the dungeons we crawled helped to shape the stories I tell today.

Henry Williams, sounding board and selfless giver of time.

My agent Ian Drury, to whom I am immensely grateful for placing his trust in me and sending me tumbling down the rabbit hole.

My editors Gillian Redfearn, Jessica Wade and Craig Leyenaar for their help and support in trimming and shaping this book into a leaner, punchier model.

My swordsmanship instructor David Rawlings and all those who have whacked me with sword, spear and shield over the last three years. I can reveal now that I was only letting you hit me for research purposes.

And finally, the greatest thanks must go to my mum, who from my earliest memory was instilling me with a desire to create and tell stories, and my dad, who put the first wooden sword into my threeyear-old hand. My obsession with goblins and dragons may have puzzled you at times, but I hold you both entirely responsible.